LOVE'S MAGIC

A single lamp burned in the living room. Laura glanced around, her eyes moving over the polished woods, the brass fire screens, the tall bookcases, the Vlaminck lithographs. A crumpled Players cigarette floated in a half-empty teacup. "It's just what I expected," she said, smiling. "Even the little bits of clutter. It's perfect."

"Needs a woman's touch, I expect." He took her coat and tossed it on a chair. "Would you like a drink?"

"No."

"Good." He drew Laura into his arms. He kissed her, a long, fiery kiss that made her gasp. There was a roaring in her ears, in her heart. Little lights seemed to dance before her eyes. She melted against him. Their bodies arched and swayed, locked in a white-hot blaze of passion. Time had stopped; there was nothing but this moment, this truth, this pleasure so intense it was a kind of madness. She felt as if she were soaring through air, about to fall off the edge of the world.

He turned his head and kissed her neck, just below her ear. "Do you believe in magic?" he asked.

"I didn't," she said, tightening her arms around him. "But I do now."

TURN TO PINNACLE BOOKS FOR THE BEST IN CONTEMPORARY FICTION

PAPER CASTLES (365, $4.50)
by Paula Jacobs

Maddy Granville had risen the hard way up the ladder of success: from the runways and dressing rooms of smoke-filled strip-joints to the posh boardrooms and power lunches with the Hollywood elite. Now Maddy calls the shots, tells tales and names names as the powerful publisher of *The Tattler,* Hollywood's most-read newspaper.

But now people want to destroy her, uncovering scandalous bits and pieces of Maddy's long-forgotten life and old secrets that could rob her of her brilliant career. But Maddy won't go down alone, and if they drag her off of the top, she'll bring them along for the ride!

BROKEN-HEARTED (374, $4.50)
by Nancy Weber

For years, Margo Corman has lived with the fear that her husband will die before the doctors could find a new heart for him. But at last a donor is found, and the operation is a success.

Andrea Pierce is young, beautiful, and driven nearly mad with grief when her husband John dies. When she learns that his heart was used to save Hank Corman's life, she becomes obsessed with meeting Hank, with knowing Hank, with *loving* Hank. . . .

TO TOUCH A DREAM (474, $4.95)
by Aviva Hellman

They had one wish, one desperate hope. Their hearts desired a homeland, and to gain it, they would suffer devastating loss and unspeakable tragedy. Through two world wars, the brutal persecution of the Turks, and the British Mandate, this is the story of a family who would not be shaken . . . sacrificing everything for their dream.

Tamar Danziger, Deborah Danziger, Michael Ben Hod, Gidon Danziger Hardwick: theirs is the epic struggle of love and loss, secret passions, and catastrophic tragedy—the tumultuous journey that awaits only those who have the courage TO TOUCH A DREAM.

Available wherever paperbacks are sold, or order direct from the Publisher. Send cover price plus 50¢ per copy for mailing and handling to Pinnacle Books, Dept. 17- 539, 475 Park Avenue South, New York, N.Y. 10016. Residents of New York, New Jersey and Pennsylvania must include sales tax. DO NOT SEND CASH.

KEEPSAKES

ALEXANDRA LYLE

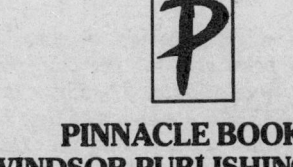

PINNACLE BOOKS
WINDSOR PUBLISHING CORP.

*To my sister Diane Harrison, with love
And to "Melrose Plant," with or without his title*

PINNACLE BOOKS

are published by

Windsor Publishing Corp.
475 Park Avenue South
New York, NY 10016

Copyright © 1991 by Barbara Harrison

All rights reserved. No part of this book may be reproduced in any form or by any means without the prior written consent of the Publisher, excepting brief quotes used in reviews.

If you purchased this book without a cover you should be aware that this book is stolen property. It was reported as "unsold and destroyed" to the publisher and neither the author nor the publisher has received any payment for this "stripped book."

First printing: July, 1991

Printed in the United States of America

Prologue

The rain started slowly, the first drops scattering like coins tossed on the pavement. Kay Bellamy glanced up at the mournful gray sky. She shivered, though not with cold.

When the traffic light changed to green, she hurried across the street. Her gloveless hands were thrust into her coat pockets; her worn black leather purse was tucked under her arm. She had forgotten her umbrella. She was always forgetting things, always being teased about her terrible memory, but nobody would tease her today; nobody would laugh. Today, she had an excuse.

Her high heels clicked sharply as she traveled past the shops and office buildings on Lexington Avenue. She tried not to notice how many of the offices were vacant, how many of the shops had gone out of business. Every month, every week, there were more of them — silent, shadowy spaces gathering dust in the hard times of the Depression. She still couldn't understand what had happened. One Friday in 1929 the stock market had crashed and the world had changed forever. Overnight, or so it had seemed, her own world had been destroyed.

Nineteen twenty-nine. Only four years ago, thought Kay; not a long time, and yet everything was so different then. Her daughters were barely into their teens, giggling girls sharing clothes and secrets. Her husband, John, was alive. He'd had a good job, rosy plans for the future, and a wide, slightly crooked smile that melted her heart. "Johnny," she murmured, as much in confusion as in pain. He had been the center of her existence. How could she forgive him for dying?

The rain grew heavier, blowing and swirling in a brisk October wind. There was a single explosion of thunder, an ominous darkening of the sky. People scurried in all directions, taking shelter beneath umbrellas or folded newspapers, ducking into doorways to wait out the storm. Kay hunched her slim shoulders and kept walking. She was soaked. Her little feathered cloche was plastered to her head, water running from the narrow brim. Her brow was matted with limp, soggy curls. Her stockings were wet, sticking to her legs. Puddles were collecting in her shoes. Her best shoes, ruined.

A taxicab whizzed by, sending up a spray of dirty water. Kay jumped back, but too late; the dull stain spread across her coat like a tide. A miserable end to a miserable day, she thought. Her gaze moved to the street sign: thirty blocks and she would be home.

She took a few steps toward Third Avenue and the el train, then changed her mind. It was almost five o'clock; the el would be crowded. It would be noisy, the old cars rattling along the overhead track, brakes screeching at each stop. She had been riding the el for years, but now she needed quiet, needed to calm her jittery nerves. Everything will be all right, she told herself, though without much conviction. She drew a breath and continued walking. Her eyes fluttered to another street sign: twenty blocks and she would be home. And what then? she wondered. What could she tell her family? How could she explain?

It wasn't her fault; old Eli Harding had said so. Of course she had known what he was going to say even before he'd said it. The moment he'd called her into his office, she'd known. She'd started talking, babbling on and on in a futile attempt to postpone the inevitable. He had humored her, but only for a little while. Finally she'd heard the words she had been dreading: "Sorry, Kay, there just isn't enough work. I'll have to let you go."

Sorry. She had two daughters in school and a destitute spinster sister-in-law to support. She had bills, responsibilities. Now she had no job. What good did *sorry* do? It certainly wouldn't pay the rent. Landlords didn't care who was sorry or why; they wanted their money and no sad stories, even in the middle of the Depression.

An angry symphony of car horns jolted Kay from her reverie. She saw that the light had turned red; quickly she retreated to the curb. Rain was slanting into her eyes; she tried to brush it away. She stared down at the streaming gutter and a frown settled on her forehead. She saw something floating past — a torn section of cardboard, part of a hand-lettered sign. She could make out only the first couple of words: "Help the Unemp . . ."

She didn't need to see the rest, she knew it by heart. There were hundreds of such signs around the city: HELP THE UNEMPLOYED. BUY TANGERINES, 2 FOR 5 CENTS. BUY APPLES, 5 CENTS. She had seen the stands, the upended packing crates neatly heaped with fruit. She had seen the men, solemn men dressed so formally in ties and suits and fedoras, they might have been bankers. They might have been, except that they were camped on street corners, selling fruit.

Fear prickled Kay's spine. She had two hundred dollars hidden in a bookcase in her bedroom, and fifty dollars severance pay pinned inside her blouse. It was all the money she had and she wondered how long it would have to last. What if she didn't get a job right away? Jobs were so scarce. What if there *weren't* any jobs? The light turned green and she splashed to the other side of the street. She looked up: eight blocks and she would be home.

She'd have to tell them the bad news, but not immediately; after supper would be soon enough. After the macaroni and cheese and the beet salad and the lemon pie. She hadn't always got along with her sister-in-law, but at least Margaret was predictable. Ever since Margaret had taken over the cooking, Fridays meant macaroni and cheese, beet salad, and lemon pie.

Cafeteria food, thought Kay as she neared Seventy-fourth street. She slowed her pace, gazing through the rain at the handsome eighteen-story apartment building that was home. Her eyes went to a row of windows on the tenth floor, scanning them until she recognized the yellow and white checked curtains in her kitchen. She used to love puttering around the kitchen, but that was before the Depression, before dreams and lives had been shattered. It was before Margaret had moved in, bringing suitcases, knickknacks, family albums, and a recipe booklet entitled *101 Budget Meals*.

Kay's gaze swept down the row of windows to her daughters' room. Eliza was at school in Connecticut, but Laura was here. For a moment, Kay couldn't help wishing it were the other way around. She wasn't sure she had the strength to cope with her younger daughter today. Laura would ask questions, probably complicated questions. Unlike Eliza, Laura would have opinions. Kay sighed; opinions often led to arguments and she was in no mood for those.

The wind gusted, flinging rain into her face. She turned and ran the last half-block, darting under the canopy and reaching her hand to the heavy glass doors. There was a face reflected in the glass, her own face, though at first she didn't recognize the pinched expression, the eyes hooded and glazed with worry. Worrying wouldn't solve anything. Hadn't she said that to John a thousand times? Hadn't she told—

"Mrs. Bellamy?"

Kay spun around to see the plump figure and commanding gaze of her eighth-floor neighbor Beatrice Wesley. "Oh, you startled me, Mrs. Wesley."

"Yes, I expect I did. You seemed quite lost in thought. No other reason to be standing out here in the rain." The older woman closed her umbrella and thumped the pointed metal tip on the sidewalk. She gave it a final shake then pushed open the door, shooing Kay into the deserted lobby. "Weren't waiting for the doorman, were you? Eugene is hopeless. *Never* around when you want him. *Never*. Irish, you know. Can't do a thing with the Irish." Her eyes locked speculatively on Kay. "Are you all right?"

"Yes, I'm fine."

"Are you?"

Kay scraped the wet hair off her brow. She shrugged. "Well, maybe a bit waterlogged."

"My dear, you're absolutely drenched! And I can't say much for your color. Have Margaret fix you a toddy. A hot bath and a toddy, that's what you need."

No, I need a job, thought Kay. She rang for the elevator.

"Old-fashioned remedies are still the best," continued Beatrice Wesley, "even for you modern women."

"Don't worry about me, Mrs. Wesley. I'm fine."

"I suppose you have to be, what with your family depending on you. No choice, eh?"

"No choice," agreed Kay, her voice almost a whisper. She wished Mrs. Wesley would stop talking, wished the elevator would come. She inched forward and pressed the button again.

"Very brave of you to take all that responsibility. I was commenting on it to my husband just the other day. 'Where would that nice Bellamy family be without *Mrs.* Bellamy?' Those were my exact words. 'Thanks to *Mrs.* Bellamy, poor Margaret has a home and the girls are getting a proper start in life.' That's what I said."

Kay said nothing. Her head had begun to ache. There was a cold, sick feeling in her stomach. She had been so anxious to get home, but now she wanted to run, to run and hide where no one would find her.

"Lovely girls they are, too," declared Beatrice Wesley, nodding her approval. "Oh, Eliza is quite beautiful," she added with a wave of her gloved hand. "Eliza will make her own luck; wait and see if she doesn't. As for Laura—I'd say Laura will need a different *sort* of luck."

The elevator door slid open. Head bent, Kay followed her neighbor into the car. She'd stopped listening because she'd stopped believing in luck. Money was what mattered. A job. Dear God, what if there weren't any jobs?

Chapter One

Laura Bellamy parted the ruffled white curtains and stared out at the rain. She smiled. As a child, the rain had soothed her, but now it stirred her imagination. It made her think of faraway places, of secret, romantic places she visited only in dreams. Absently, she fingered the gold locket clasped around her neck. Be careful of dreams, she warned herself, not for the first time. Be careful what you wish for.

Laura was seventeen, an old seventeen in the same way she had been an old child. There was a gravity about her, a quiet that was often unsettling. It was hard to know what she was thinking, harder still to change her mind once it was made up. She could be moody, withdrawing into a somber reticence. She could be funny, turning her wry humor on herself. To her mother, she had always been a puzzle.

Sighing, Laura closed the curtains and went to her dressing table. She sat dawn, switching on a little pink lamp ornamented with seashells. The sudden flare of light outlined her reflection in the mirror. She leaned forward, studying the long tawny hair, the tawny skin, the small, straight nose, the amber-flecked hazel eyes. "Maybe a new hairstyle," she murmured, then shook her head no. She'd changed her hairstyle twice in the last month and hardly anyone had noticed.

She was a pretty girl but unsure of her looks, for she

had grown up in the shadow of her sister, the beautiful Eliza. Almost from the cradle she had understood that Eliza was special, the adored child pampered and fussed over by besotted parents. The Bellamys had once lived in a crumbling flat in an ancient Yorkville brownstone, but even then money had somehow been found for Eliza. For silk hair ribbons, thought Laura, recalling those days. For dresses trimmed with lace.

She lowered her eyes to the photographs propped against the base of the mirror. The snapshot of her parents had begun to curl at the edges. She smoothed it, holding it closer to the light. A beaming John and Kay seemed to leap out at her. How happy they'd been, and how much alike — working so diligently to get ahead; spending money they didn't have but spending it anyway because better days were coming.

The Depression came instead, Laura remembered. Her father lost his job, but with his usual optimism he'd called it a blessing in disguise, an opportunity to move on to bigger things. His optimism had been his strength, though in the end the Depression took that too. It took his pride; perhaps worst of all, it took his dreams.

She closed her eyes, listening to the sound of the rain. Her father had died on a sunny spring morning, an ordinary morning until he'd clutched his chest and slumped to the floor. She remembered her mother's screams. She remembered the sirens. She'd never had a chance to say good-bye; her father had died in the ambulance on the way to the hospital.

Laura put the picture down. Next to it was a small portrait of her aunt Margaret, and next to that were several snaps of a tall, handsome young man in a Yale sweater. He was Robby Collier, the first and only boy she'd ever kissed. Her dark lashes fluttered; her smile returned. He was also the boy she expected to marry someday.

Happiness bubbled up in her when she thought about

Robby. He was, she felt, the one truly lucky thing that had happened in her life. She hadn't been born beautiful, like Eliza, or brilliant, like her friend Doris Sweeney. She hadn't inherited her mother's artistic talents, or her father's extravagant spirit. She considered herself average, unremarkable, and yet Robby had asked her to be his girl.

That was four months ago, shortly after the Colliers moved into the building. They had rented a sprawling duplex apartment and given a party for their new neighbors; an open house, Robby's mother had called it. Laura's smile widened as she remembered her first glimpse of Robby. She had turned to get a cup of punch and there he was: tall, slender, with eyes the color of jade, hair the color of polished gold. She stared at him, too dazzled to speak and he stared back, amused. Laughing, he'd bowed suddenly and kissed her hand. In that moment she lost her heart to Robert Jamison Collier.

For days afterward Laura had moped around, pondering the futility of her cause. Most of the girls in the neighborhood had set their caps for Robby, girls prettier than she, girls from better families. Compared to them, what had she to offer? Nothing, she had finally decided. Nothing at all.

But Robby had his own ideas on the subject. Much to Laura's astonishment, he appeared on her doorstep with a bouquet of purple iris and an invitation to lunch. He suggested the Palm Court; she stammered her acceptance, blushing bright red. She rushed to change into her good dress and then they went off to the Palm Court at the Plaza Hotel. Some of her shyness disappeared during that lunch; the rest of it during a long, lazy summer of boat rides and picnics and dances and walks on the beach. Robby gave her a gold locket the night before he left for Yale. He asked her to be his girl, and without the slightest hesitation she said yes.

It wasn't exactly an engagement, but it would do for

now. Yes, it would do, thought Laura, nodding at her reflection in the mirror. Robby still had nearly three years at Yale and nothing must interfere with his education. She didn't mind waiting. In the meantime, she planned to work, to build a small nest egg of her own. After she finished business school next month, she would go looking for a job.

Laura turned when she heard a knock at the door. "Come in."

The door opened. Margaret Bellamy poked her head inside. "Didn't you promise to set the table?"

"I'll be right there, Aunt Margaret. I was just . . . thinking."

"That's the problem with young girls today. Too much thinking, too much brooding. Now when *I* was a girl—"

"I wasn't brooding," interrupted Laura, trying to thwart another of her aunt's lengthy recollections. "And I'll be there in a minute."

"If you say so, dear."

Laura smiled. "I just did."

"Yes." Margaret looked doubtful. "Yes," she said again, and closed the door.

Laura glanced around the room. Two years earlier she had surrendered her own room to Margaret and moved her things in here, with Eliza. It had been fun at first, almost like the old days in the Yorkville flat, but then Eliza had gone away to school. Crossfield was one of the East's more exclusive junior colleges. It was expensive. Laura was certain the tuition had used up the last of her father's life insurance. Well, why not? Her father had always said Eliza had to have the best.

Laura turned back to the mirror. She pulled a comb through her hair, straightened the collar of her blouse, and dimmed the seashell lamp. She stood, brushing at her skirt as she walked to the door. Margaret's eagle eyes noticed *every*thing, even lint.

* * *

Margaret Bellamy had been a girl of eighteen when her fiancé ran off with the minister's wife. It had been a scandal, the worst in the history of tiny Alber Falls. For months, gossip had raged from one end of town to the other. Details were debated, embellished. Everybody had something to say, and even school children giggled behind their hands. But beyond all the talk there was sympathy. The minister's pantry had filled up with cakes and pies and covered dishes—tokens of support for the wronged husband. Margaret, secluded in her parents' modest house, had been referred to as "that poor, unfortunate girl."

In truth, Margaret had been more angry than hurt. Her fiancé, Wilbur Hobart, had seemed so meek and mild; obviously she had been deceived. She had accepted the town's sympathy as her due, but she'd had no real need of consolation. Better not to marry than to marry a wolf in sheep's clothing.

"Starchy" was the way Joseph Bellamy had described his daughter; "bossy" had been her brother's description. Despite slightly differing views, both men had seen in Margaret the makings of a spinster. Her thick, fair hair and graceful figure had attracted other suitors after Wilbur Hobart, but none had proposed marriage. By the time of her twenty-first birthday, it had been clear that her chances had slipped away.

"Wilbur ruined my life," she'd often insisted, though she'd nonetheless managed to get on with it. She'd kept herself busy—giving piano lessons, directing the church choir, organizing the annual flower show and the charity bazaar. She'd worked at the hospital during the Great War; after the Armistice, she'd formed a committee to raise funds for a veterans' memorial. With her brothers long gone from the modest house on Sycamore Street, she'd nursed her aging parents through their various illnesses, and at the last, had planned the funerals that had laid them peacefully to their rest. Alone finally in the Sycamore Street house, she'd scrubbed and painted and polished, and decided to take in boarders.

Margaret had never heard of Wall Street until the Crash of 1929, and by then it was too late. Her small inheritance had disappeared in the failure of the Alber Falls Bank. When the glass factory and the department store shut down, her boarders disappeared also. She was left with her house and the contents of her cookie jar: eight dollars in coins.

"Wall Street ruined my life," she'd written to her youngest brother. John Bellamy had had serious problems of his own, but still he'd sent his sister a postal money order and a train ticket. Days later she'd put her house up for sale, packed her bags, and boarded the southbound train to New York City. She'd had no regrets. After forty-five years in Alber Falls, a change might do her good.

Now, Margaret slid a casserole dish into the oven and turned up the heat. She wiped her hands on her apron. Supper would be ready in ten minutes. Where was Kay? And where was Laura to set the table? "They expect me to do everything around here," she grumbled, striding briskly through the door. "Spoiled, that's what they are. Just plain spoiled!"

The long hallway was in shadows. At the opposite end, the foyer light glowed. Margaret squinted, watching Kay struggle out of her coat. "You're late," she called.

"I walked home."

"In this weather?" Margaret started toward her sister-in-law, but she stopped when Laura appeared in the hall. "It's about time, missy," she said, her pale brows drawing together. "Help your mother with those wet things. And then set the table."

"You don't have to keep telling me, Aunt Margaret."

"Don't I? Well, maybe you already set the table and I didn't notice. Maybe I'm going blind in my old age," she added, marching back into the kitchen.

Laura laughed. "I'm sorry, Mama," she said, coming

up beside Kay. "But Aunt Margaret's been nagging me all afternoon."

"She nags everybody."

Laura heard the weariness in her mother's voice. She heard something else, something she couldn't quite identify. "Your coat's so wet it's sticking to you. Let me help, Mama. Hold out your arms . . . There, that's better. I'll hang it in the bathroom to dry."

"Thank you, dear."

"Your hat's probably ruined."

"My hat? Oh yes." Kay pulled the sodden mess from her head. "Yes, well, it doesn't matter. It's been out of style for years. Like me. I'm out of style too, in case you were wondering."

"What's wrong, Mama? You don't . . ." Laura's voice died away when she saw the look in Kay's eyes. It was a strange look—a little sad, a little dazed, a little frightened—but Laura knew instantly what it meant. Not again, she thought to herself; please not again. "I'll just hang this up," she said. "Are you going to change your clothes?"

Kay sneezed. "I guess I should." She glanced down at the mail waiting on the hall table. She shook her head. Bills; there were always more bills.

"Mama—"

"Not now, Laura. Whatever it is, not now. It's been the most rotten day."

Kay walked off. Laura watched her mother go. She hugged the wet coat, and a frown crossed her brow. She was very still, though her gaze shifted at the sound of a loud, impatient *"Ahem."* She saw Margaret stationed outside the kitchen door. She saw the pursed lips, the folded arms. "Coming, Aunt Margaret," she called. "Coming."

Margaret took the casserole out of the oven and set it on the counter. Deftly, she switched the potholders around and lifted the cover, inhaling the fragrant steam. Her tasting fork was nearby; she scooped out a bit of macaroni and popped it into her mouth. Delicious, even if she did say so herself.

"Here I am," said Laura, entering the kitchen. She went to the cupboard, removing three plain white china plates. She removed three smaller plates and stacked them on top. "Mama will be in as soon as she changes her clothes."

"Did you wash your hands?"

Laura nodded. "I'm ready for inspection."

"Don't be fresh," replied Margaret, though a smile flickered about her lips. She was fond of Laura, of the girl's spirit, which she felt was like her own. Laura, she often thought, could be the daughter she'd never had. "There's no harm in asking a simple question, is there? Sometimes you put off doing things. You know how you are."

Laura carried the plates to the table and laid them on the scrubbed yellow oilcloth. She made another trip to the cupboard for glasses, and another for forks and spoons and napkins. In the icebox was a large bowl of beet salad. She put that at the center of the table and sat down. "I think Mama lost her job."

Margaret's hand flew to her throat. She glanced swiftly at Laura, then turned away, staring at a spot above the stove. It was her nature to expect the worst, but it was also her nature to hope for the best. Right now she hoped Laura was mistaken. "Is that what you think, or what you know?"

"I'm guessing, but I'm pretty sure. There's a kind of look . . . Papa had it when *he* lost his job. And so did Papa's friend, Mr. Revere. It's just a kind of look, that's all." Laura picked up a fork and put it down, moving it from side to side. "There are times I pass people on the street — strangers — and I know they've lost their jobs. They have the look."

"The look! I never heard such foolish talk! I'm surprised at you, Laura Bellamy. A sensible girl like you." Margaret brought the casserole to the table. She pulled out a chair and sat across from her niece. "You're the sensible one in this family. My brother John, rest his soul, was a dreamer. Kay's no different; holding on to those fancy ideas of hers. But you've got your feet on the ground. That's smart. That's the way to be."

"Eliza isn't—"

Margaret shook her head so vigorously that a lock of graying blond hair broke loose from the coil at the back of her neck. "Never mind about Eliza. It's a cruel world, but not for girls with angel faces. Eliza can do as she pleases. *You* have to keep your feet on the ground. Take my word, missy. Take my word."

It sounded like an order, and that was typical. Margaret's opinions, her observations, were stated as fact. Whatever the subject, she knew best; to disagree was to invite an argument. She was petite, only an inch or two over five feet, but she was all sharp angles and edges, and she was frequently intimidating.

Laura alone seemed immune to Margaret's bluster. She had heard the story of Wilbur Hobart and the minister's wife. She had heard the stories of life in Alber Falls. On the whole, she felt her aunt was entitled to a few quirks. Despite the nagging, despite the odd turns of mind, she liked Margaret. She sensed that under the stern veneer, Margaret liked her too—and maybe even better than Eliza.

"You didn't have to wait for me," said Kay, walking into the kitchen. "The macaroni will be cold."

"We always wait for you," replied Margaret. She snapped open her napkin and draped it across her lap. "When did you ever know me to serve cold macaroni?"

Kay sighed. *Why* are we talking about *macaroni?* She took a pitcher of water from the icebox, and then took her usual seat at the head of the table. She had changed into an old pleated skirt, a blue Shetland sweater out at one elbow, and flat-heeled shoes. Her dark hair, still wet, was brushed off her face and tied with a blue ribbon. She looked pale. "I didn't mean anything, Margaret. You shouldn't be so sensitive."

"Sensitive! Me? What a thing to say!"

"It's not an insult, you know." Kay poured a glass of water. She felt Laura's eyes on her and she turned in her chair. The kitchen was pleasantly warm, scented with the herbs Margaret grew in little pots on the windowsill. It was a cozy room. The walls and the checked curtains were yellow. Two glass-fronted cupboards were stuffed with crockery and knickknacks: porcelain shepherd girls, stoneware cats, a Staffordshire dog. Everything was immaculate, everything in its proper place. Everything but me, she thought. "Laura, I wish you'd stop staring."

"I'm sorry." Laura pushed the macaroni around her plate, nibbling at bits of crusty cheese. "It's just that you look so sad."

"Do I?"

"Mama, I'm not a child anymore. You can tell me things."

"There's nothing to tell." Kay heard the tremor in her voice. She was quiet for a moment, staring down at her plate. "All right," she said finally, pushing the plate aside. "All right, we might as well get this over with. If I look sad, I have a good reason. I was fired today." She took a sip of water. Nervously, her eyes roamed from Laura to Margaret and back again. "Mr. Harding said there wasn't enough work. He has three other artists on staff and not enough work. I was the last to be hired, so I was the first to be fired. It's fair I suppose. That doesn't make it any easier."

"Not much call for artists, these days," commented Margaret.

"No, not much. A lot of advertising agencies are letting people go: not just Harding . . . But I'll find something else. It doesn't matter what, as long as it's a job."

Laura had been silent, sitting so straight and still she

scarcely seemed to breathe. Now she leaned forward. "Do we have any money?"

"You mustn't worry about that. I never wanted you girls to have to think about money. It's my responsibility."

"Why?" Laura's expression hadn't changed, but two spots of color flared in her cheeks. "I'm *not* a child anymore, Mama. Neither is Eliza. Why can't we help?"

Kay pressed her fingers to her throbbing temples. She hated talking about money, hated worrying about it, though she had grown up worrying about little else. Her parents, owners of a small Yorkville dry goods store, had agonized over every penny they spent. They'd argued over every penny too. How many nights had she lain in her bed, listening to their angry shouts?

"Mama?"

Kay glanced up. "You have to learn when to leave things alone. I said I'd find another job and I will. Trust me, Laura. I know what's best."

"But do we have any money?"

"Some. Enough to keep us until I find another job." It wasn't exactly a lie. If she didn't pay all the bills, she'd have enough money for a month, maybe two. She'd have a new job by then; surely she'd have a new job. "Of course we'll have to be . . . a little careful."

"And we'll start by not wasting food," said Margaret, rising to her feet. "If you two won't eat your supper, it's going into the icebox for tomorrow." No one spoke as she cleared the dishes from the table. Laura was deep in thought, considering the possibilities. Kay was staring into space. "Who wants coffee?" asked Margaret after the dishes had been scraped and the leftovers put away. "Coffee or tea, take your choice."

Kay wanted a drink but she didn't want to say so. There was a bottle of whiskey in her room. She hadn't touched it, or even thought about it, since the day of John's funeral. That terrible day; again she pressed her fingers to her temples.

"Kay, shall I put the coffee on?"

"What? Oh no, not for me. I think I'd rather have tea."

"Tea," agreed Laura. She sat back, gazing steadily at her mother. "I could talk to Robby," she suggested. "He's coming in on the noon train tomorrow. He could ask Mr. Collier—"

"*No.* You're not to talk to *any*body, Laura. I'll do this on my own. No charity. And you're not to write anything to Eliza either. Just—just stop making a fuss." Kay clasped her hands together, rubbing the wedding band she still wore. "Laura," she continued in a softer voice, "nothing's really changed. We'll go on the same way as before: Margaret looking after the house, you finishing your courses at business school, and Eliza at Crossfield. The only difference is that I'll be hunting for a job."

Surprise was sketched on Laura's face. "Do you mean Eliza's going to stay at Crossfield?"

"The tuition's paid for the year. Why shouldn't she stay?"

"But they'd return part of the money if Eliza left. She didn't want to go there in the first place. And now . . ." Laura reached her hand to Kay. "Mama, you may *need* the money."

"She's right," said Margaret. "You can't afford that fancy school. It was a nice thing you tried to do for Eliza, but facts are facts. That's a school for rich girls, not the likes of us."

Rich girls have rich brothers, thought Kay, and wasn't that the whole idea? Crossfield would give Eliza the chance to meet some of those very eligible young men, perhaps the chance to make a brilliant marriage. There wasn't any chance of that here. Here were families like the Colliers and the Forresters—well off, yes, but not *rich*. Crossfield was an investment, a risky, expensive investment in Eliza's future.

It was true that she hadn't wanted to go. She'd never been happy in school and she'd wanted to be done with it. But Kay had prevailed: Eliza had been sent to Crossfield; Laura, an excellent student who loved books and learning, had been enrolled in the Acme Business Institute. Kay preferred not to think about the fairness of her decisions. She loved both her daughters, and yet she knew that her firstborn had always had a special place in her heart. She had such hopes for Eliza. All she needed was a little more time.

Laura watched the play of emotions on Kay's face—anxiety yielding to doubt yielding to a wistful determination. "What are you thinking, Mama?"

"Eliza has to stay at Crossfield and that's all there is to it." The words came in a rush, as they often did when she expected a protest. "I know you both disagree, but it's my decision. Anyway, it's what John would have wanted."

Margaret took the kettle off the stove. "My brother John could never see things plain. I used to say he had rose-colored glasses. Oh, he thought the world was a fine place. A *good* place. He never saw the bad." She fixed their tea and brought three cups to the table. "He was a dreamer, John was."

"What's wrong with that?" asked Kay. "What's wrong with wanting something better?"

"Wanting and getting are two different things. It depends on luck, you know. Our family isn't lucky. You can go way back and you won't find one lucky Bellamy in the whole bunch."

Laura smiled. "That's what I like about you, Aunt Margaret; you're so cheerful."

"Do you know where there are lots of cheerful people? In the insane asylum, that's where!"

Kay slammed her cup down. "Oh, for heaven's sake, Margaret, what's that supposed to mean? Why must you say those awful things?"

"Sometimes the truth hurts."

"Truth!" Kay shook her head. "*Whose* truth? Certainly not mine. I haven't given up. I'd rather be dead than give up."

Laura opened her mouth to speak, but no sound came. She knew the thread of the conversation had been lost in this squabbling. Nothing would be settled; nothing ever was. She thought, We just drift from one problem to another, one crisis to another, and the only rule is that Eliza mustn't be bothered. "If you don't mind, I'm going to my room now."

"I don't mind," said Margaret. "But stop scowling like that. You'll get wrinkles."

A faint smile touched Kay's mouth. "It's a little soon for Laura to be worrying about wrinkles."

"It's never too soon. No use waiting till she's an old crone like me."

"You're not an old crone, Margaret."

"Sure I am. In just a year I'll be fifty. Fifty! When I was a girl, I thought fifty was one step away from the graveyard." Margaret finished her tea and pressed the napkin to her lips. She shrugged. "Well, we're all getting on, aren't we? If I'm not mistaken, there'll be forty candles on your next birthday cake."

Kay laughed despite herself. "Oh no, there won't! I'm going to be thirty-nine forever."

Laura saw that she had been forgotten. Quietly, she left her chair and went to the door. She paused at the threshold, glancing over her shoulder as she heard more laughter. She wondered if she would ever understand these two women. Most of the time they seemed locked in a conflict of wills and opinions, but there were other times, when they seemed to share something like friendship. She knew they were both lonely, especially her mother, and maybe that was the reason they occasionally put their differences aside. Maybe, in such hard times, they just needed to laugh.

Laura reached for the light switch and flopped down on her bed. She laced her fingers behind her head, staring up at the ceiling. The radiator clanked suddenly. She turned her head. She smiled. They hadn't had steam heat in the old flat; they hadn't had much of anything. Not until Papa's promotion, she thought to herself. She recalled his promotion to the sales department of the Royalton Textbook Company. She recalled the celebration: the cake, the crepe paper, the ginger ale that had passed for champagne in those Prohibition days. There had been another celebration a few years later, that one with genuine bootleg champagne to toast her father's promotion to sales manager.

Kay had wasted no time finding a new place to live. She found her dream apartment: six rooms in a stylish, fully staffed building just a stone's throw from Park Avenue. The rent, then and now, was sixty-five dollars a month. A lot of money, thought Laura. She started to make a mental list of all their other expenses: the gas and electricity; groceries; insurance; time payments on the furniture; payments on Dr. Weston's bill; payments on the Zenith radio set. So deep in thought was she, she didn't hear the knock at the door.

"Laura?" Kay stood in the doorway. "Laura, I was hoping we could talk."

"Certainly, Mama." She sat up, smoothing her hair, pulling her skirt over her knees. "I'm sorry if I upset you before. I didn't mean to."

"I know that." Kay sank into the chair by Laura's bedside. She folded her hands in her lap. "I'm the one who should apologize," she said quietly. "I haven't done a very good job of explaining. I mean, it must be hard for you to understand about Crossfield."

"It always was," replied Laura, more sharply than she had intended. She glanced off toward Eliza's half of the room. There was a narrow single bed covered with a pink chintz spread, a white bombé chest of drawers stenciled with roses, a matching mirror, and a small dressing table encircled by flounced white silk. Eliza hadn't added any pictures or decorations. Apart from a Bible she had been given as a child, she'd never owned a book.

Laura's furniture was identical, but her half of the room was crowded with keepsakes and curios. And with books, she thought, looking around. She still had the favorite books of her childhood: *Grimm's Fairy Tales* and *Alice in Wonderland* and *Little Women*. At thirteen, she had saved for months to buy her own copies of *Jane Eyre* and *Wuthering Heights,* and those books, cherished as they were, remained close at hand on her night table. At sixteen, she had been mesmerized by Dickens. This summer, she had discovered F. Scott Fitzgerald.

Now, Laura opened the drawer of her night table and took out her dog-eared library card. She stared at it, then put it back. "Crossfield always seemed like a waste," she said, her hazel eyes turning a deep, dark blue. "Eliza couldn't care less about school."

"I know that too. But school wasn't really the point. I didn't send Eliza to Crossfield for an education. And I didn't send her to be 'finished,' as they say. I just wanted her to meet the right people." Kay paused, clasping and unclasping her hands. She was sorry she'd started this conversation. "Laura," she said wearily, "I'm trying to look to the future. There are people in the world with so much money that nothing can hurt them. Not the stock market crash, not even the Depression. *Nothing.* Old money, it's called. Well, there's plenty of old money at Crossfield." Again she paused, her mouth tensing. "It was a struggle getting Eliza admitted. It was one problem after another. But thanks to Eli Harding—and some of his society friends—everything worked out. I'll always be grateful, because this is Eliza's chance to have the life she deserves."

Laura had grown up hearing about all the things Eliza deserved. She hadn't asked why Eliza deserved them, nor had she objected, but she'd felt more and more left out. She loved her sister yet at times she was jealous, and she blamed Kay. "What do *I* deserve, Mama?"

Kay blinked. "I don't understand."

"We're in trouble now, but all I've heard tonight is Eliza this, and Eliza that. I'm your daughter too. Can't you find anything good for me to deserve? Any little thing?"

Kay was astonished, not only by Laura's words, but by the chilly anger behind the words. It was, she thought, as if each syllable had been covered with frost. "Laura, I—I don't know what to say. I wasn't thinking. I . . ." She pulled herself from the chair and went to Laura. "I suppose I've been going on about Eliza because . . . well, because one of these days she might be able to help all of us."

"Oh, Mama, how is she going to do that? Do you expect her to marry a Rockefeller?"

"Why not?"

"Rich people marry their own kind, that's why not." But Laura couldn't stay angry. She knew her mother would never change. Hope would always flicker in those lovely violet eyes, hope mixed with worry, with fear. Laura threw up her hands. "Maybe you're right," she said, sighing. "Maybe a miracle will happen after all."

"Does that mean you're not mad at me anymore?"

Laura smiled. "I *want* to be, but I'm not." She leaned closer to Kay and kissed her cheek. "Mama, you feel warm. I think you have a fever." She touched Kay's forehead. She frowned. "Yes, I'm sure you have a fever. You probably caught cold walking home in the rain."

"I'll be fine. A good night's sleep and I'll be a new woman."

"Margaret could fix you a toddy."

"Don't drag Margaret into this. If I ask for a toddy, I'll also get a mustard plaster and a smelly cloth for my throat. Margaret doesn't do things by halves." She stood, gazing down at Laura. "What are your plans for tonight? Are you going to the movies with Doris and Jane?"

"No, I don't think so. They're going to see *King Kong*—you know, the one about the giant gorilla. I'd rather wait and see it with Robby. Besides, I ought to wash my hair."

"Don't forget to use a little vinegar in the rinse water. It brings out the shine . . . You have such pretty hair."

Laura was still, basking in the unexpected compliment. "Do I really?" she asked after a moment.

"Yes, really," answered Kay as she walked to the door. "So don't forget the vinegar. A girl has to make the most of what she has."

"Jean Harlow said the same thing in *Screen Stars* magazine."

"See? It must be good advice."

Kay departed and Laura flopped down again on the bed. She listened to her mother's footsteps fading in the hall. She heard a sneeze, and then nothing but the sound of rain beating at the window.

She tried to focus her thoughts on Robby. Tomorrow at this time she'd be with him — maybe sitting in a darkened movie theater watching *King Kong;* maybe eating subgum chow mein at Ruby Foo's; maybe drinking ale at Maxl's Brauhaus. And what would Aunt Margaret say about *that?*

Don't think about Margaret, she told herself, shifting around on the bed; don't think about anyone but Robby. She settled back against the pillows and in her mind's eye she saw Robby's handsome face. It was a clear image, almost like a photograph, though a moment later it blurred and finally it dissolved.

Laura swung her legs over the side of the bed. Once more she went to the window and stared out at the rain. For no particular reason she thought about the dining room furniture, about the eleven payments still owed on it. She thought about the breakfront, and how much her mother loved the breakfront. "Poor Mama," she whispered. Unbidden, a tear slid down her cheek.

Chapter Two

"Mama's sick," said Laura to her friend Jane Walder. It was the morning after the rainstorm, a cool, dry morning glazed with autumn sun. It was early, not quite eight o'clock, but people were already out and about — on their way to work, to the stores, to Saturday errands. "Her temperature's a hundred and one," continued Laura as they stopped at the traffic light. "And she's lost her voice."

"Laryngitis? I bet you wish *Margaret* had laryngitis instead."

Laura smiled. She glanced at the freckled, red-haired Jane who, like all the Walders, said whatever came to mind. "Well, right now I'm glad she's there to take care of Mama."

"I guess so."

The light changed and the girls crossed the street. They were both slim, of medium height. They were the same age; classmates during their last two years of high school, classmates at the Acme Business Institute. Every Saturday, as part of Acme's advanced training, they worked together in the actuarial department of an insurance company. From eight-thirty in the morning until five in the afternoon, they typed endless lists of names and numbers. For this they were paid the sum of one dollar, plus fifteen cents lunch money and ten cents carfare. Laura and Jane ate lunch at a local soda fountain, but they walked to and from work and saved the extra ten cents.

"At least I won't have to worry. About Mama needing anything, I mean."

"You know, Laura, sometimes I wonder who's the mother and who's the daughter in your house. You're *al*ways worrying. I wouldn't be surprised if your hair turned snow white."

"Oh, you're exaggerating."

"I'm not."

Laura shrugged. She lifted her head, watching a band of puffy clouds tumble across the sky. It occurred to her that Jane didn't have any worries because the Depression hadn't really touched the Walders. Jane's father worked for the city in some kind of political job. By all accounts the pay was generous, and even in these uncertain times, it was steady. "You don't understand," she said. "Nothing bad's ever happened to you. Thank God for that," she hastily added, "but you have to admit there are things you just don't understand."

"You're saying I can't put myself in your shoes."

"Well? Can you?"

Jane pondered this. She fixed her light blue eyes on the pavement and wrinkled her brow. "No," she conceded after a few moments, "I suppose not. You're right, I've been lucky." She glanced up. "But I still wish you wouldn't take everything to heart. It's not good for you, Laura."

"I'm okay. Next month I can start looking for a job. That'll solve a whole bunch of problems."

"Let's try to get jobs in the same office. Wouldn't that be fun?" She poked Laura. "Come on, say we'll try."

"It's a crazy idea. *One* job is hard enough to find, much less two."

"My gosh, you're so . . . so *practical*."

Laura laughed. "Boring, isn't it?"

The two friends fell silent, glancing into shop windows as they strode along Lexington Avenue. They wore similar, dark wool coats in the latest mid-calf length, and small-brimmed hats tilted over one eye. Beneath the coats were white blouses and tailored black skirts—outfits recommended by the Acme Business Institute. Both girls had far nicer outfits at home. Jane made many of her own clothes, using good fabrics and a lively imagination. Laura got Eliza's expensive hand-me-downs.

"What should I wear tonight?" asked Laura now. "Do you like my green dress? The one with the little gold buttons?"

"Robby likes you in pale colors."

Laura turned, surprised. "Does he? How do you know that?"

"Well, I remember Doris's birthday party. You were wearing a silky beige dress and Robby kept saying how keen you looked."

"Not to me. He didn't say anything to me."

"Well, to everybody else, then. There were a couple of other times also . . . Take my word for it: he likes you in pale colors." Jane smiled. "I think I know why. Pale colors make you look sort of slinky."

" 'Slinky!'"

"Sure, when you're all done up."

Laura shook her head. "Why didn't you tell me this before?"

"I don't know." Again, Jane lowered her thoughtful gaze to the pavement. "There's always so much to talk about. And anyway, you're so impossible when it comes to compliments. You never believe me."

"Is 'slinky' a compliment?"

" 'Slinky' is one of the *best* compliments. If you're slinky, that means you have IT. Sex appeal . . . And don't start blushing all over the place. Every woman wants to have sex appeal. Every woman who wants to get a man."

"Honestly, Jane, is that all you can think about? Getting a man?"

"You'd be thinking about it too, if you didn't already

have Robby. I'd hate to wind up an old maid."

Laura's eyes twinkled with amusement. "You an old maid? Not in a million years."

"I hope not." Jane's smile seemed to droop. She looked away. "Do you ever feel as if . . . as if . . . I don't know how to put it. As if you're waiting for your life to begin? Do you ever wake up in the morning and think, Today's the day my life begins? Only today *isn't* the day, and tomorrow isn't either." She looked back at Laura. "It's never the day."

"Oh yes, I feel that way sometimes. I just want to get on with things, but I'm not exactly sure what things I want to get on with. It's very confusing . . . I guess it's supposed to be, at our age. Growing pains."

"But we're all grown."

"Almost," replied Laura as they reached the Fidelity Insurance building. "Maybe the last part is the hardest."

"Yes, maybe."

The Fidelity building was twenty-six stories tall, austere, and gray—gray stone on the outside, gray marble within. At the front of the cavernous lobby was an information desk staffed by an elderly man wearing pince-nez. At the rear was a bank of elevators, each of four cars attended by a gloved, uniformed operator. Four other cars had been shut down in an economy measure, but there was a newsstand, and tucked away in a corner, a small shoeshine stand.

Laura waved to the shoeshine man and rang for the elevator. She glanced around at the knot of young women standing off to the side. Clerks, she guessed, though not in the actuarial department. "I've been thinking," she said to Jane, "if we can't find secretary jobs anywhere else, maybe Fidelity—"

"Oh no." Jane shook her head. "Not on your life! I want to work someplace *glamorous*. Someplace with nice furniture, and flowers on the desk. I want a handsome boss, too."

"Is that all? How about a chauffeur to drive you to

work?"

"You can laugh, but I know what I want. If you don't know what you want, you'll never get it."

Laura's tawny brows shot up. "And do you get something just because you want it?"

"Okay, okay, maybe it's not that easy. But this *is* New York, you know. If we can't find a little glamour in New York, we ought to be ashamed of ourselves."

Laura was spared a reply by the arrival of the elevator. She followed Jane into the car, waiting quietly while it filled with other passengers. "Sixteen, please," she said as the last two passengers dashed in. She drew off her gloves and flexed her fingers. She was a good typist, but the long columns of figures on the Fidelity charts made her nervous.

The elevator doors opened at the sixteenth floor. "Excuse us," said Jane, pushing forward. "Excuse us, we're getting out here."

Jane cleared the path and again Laura followed. "I hope we don't have to do more charts today," she said when they entered the corridor. "I'm terrible at charts."

"So what? This isn't a real job. It's just practice for us, not to mention cheap labor for dear old Fidelity."

"Yes, I know. Still . . ."

Jane looked at her friend and smiled. "You don't have to be perfect, not for a dollar a day."

Would she have to be perfect if the pay were higher? Laura shrugged but said nothing. She opened the door of room 1609, a deep, windowless room painted a sickly green and furnished with long, straight rows of desks and chairs. A clock, like some huge unblinking eye, stared down from the wall.

Laura took off her coat and hat. She called hello to the other clerks already gathered in the room—men and women who were regular employees of Fidelity Insurance and who earned fourteen dollars a week. The day's work wouldn't begin until exactly eight-thirty. In the meanwhile, there was the usual shuffling of papers, the scraping of chairs.

"Bad news," said Jane, opening one of the folders that had been placed on their desks. "Charts."

Laura dropped into her chair. She snatched the cover from her typewriter and stuffed it in a drawer. Only three more Saturdays here, she thought. Dear God, *please* let there be only three more.

She jumped as a dozen typewriters started clattering. She rolled a sheet of paper into her own machine, but her fingers seemed to freeze over the keys. All at once she felt trapped. She glanced about the room, glanced toward the door. She wanted to escape.

"Laura, what's the matter?"

"Nothing."

"Are you sure!

Laura nodded. "I felt strange for a moment . . . But whatever it was is gone now. I'm fine." She took a breath and picked up a folder. "We'd better get to work. It's going to be a long day."

To Kay, tossing fitfully in her bed, it seemed the day would never end. Since early this morning she had been the unwilling recipient of Margaret's ministrations — of foul-tasting herb teas, of chest rubs that reeked of garlic, of hot water bottles and plumped pillows and extra quilts. She had lost count of how many times a thermometer had been shoved under her tongue, how many times an alcohol-soaked cloth had been pressed to her forehead. She had been too weak to complain, but now Margaret was advancing toward the bed yet again. With great effort, Kay raised herself up on one elbow. "Can't you leave me alone," she pleaded, her voice a hoarse croak. "Just leave me alone."

"Is that the thanks I get for taking care of you? Or don't you think you need taking care of?" Margaret set a small plate on the night table and then leaned over the bed, straightening the quilts. "Well, never mind. I suppose you can't help being grumpy, burning up with fever the way you are."

Kay fell back against the pillows, but not before she glimpsed the plate Margaret had brought. On the plate were two square cakes of Fleischmann's yeast. "I'm not going to eat that. I refuse."

"It's good for you. It cleans out the blood."

Kay turned on her side, rolled over on her back, trying to find a comfortable position. "My blood doesn't need cleaning, thank you very much."

"Of course it does. You're sick, aren't you? There are poisons in your blood now, and yeast will wash them right out."

Yeast was the current health fad, said to clear the complexion, the head, and the bloodstream. Margaret was a firm believer in the healing properties of yeast. Kay was not. "It's disgusting," she mumbled, turning again on her side.

"It's why I never catch cold. There's nothing in *my* blood but blood."

"Lucky you." Kay threw off the quilts. "It's so hot in here. Can't you open the windows?"

"They're open at the top. A draft is the last thing you want. But don't worry," added Margaret as she replaced the quilts, "Bea's lemonade will make you feel better. It's coming any minute."

"Bea? Beatrice Wesley? Oh God, is *she* here?"

"In the kitchen. She brought a pitcher of her special lemonade, but then she thought you might want a bit more sugar in it. We like it tart, Bea and I, but she knows you have a sweet tooth."

Kay wanted to scream. She was sick, she had Margaret hovering over her, and now, as an extra punishment, there was Beatrice Wesley. "Keep her out of my room, Margaret."

"Nonsense! You should be grateful for the company. And for the lemonade too. It was nice of her." Margaret walked to the foot of the bed and smoothed the bottom

35

sheet. "Being sick," she said sternly, "is no excuse for being rude. I don't mind you snapping at me; I'm family. But if you're rude to Bea, she'll have it all over the building. You know how she is. Talk, talk, talk; that's Bea. She's my friend, but she does go on."

She's not the only one, thought Kay. "All right. Just promise she won't stay long. I have to save my strength for the want ads."

"Get better first, then you can think about want ads."

Kay started coughing. Margaret hurried over and thumped her on the back. "See what I mean? What good will you be if you're sick? And stop squirming around. You have to keep those covers on you till your fever breaks . . . Tonight after supper I'll fix a mustard plaster for your chest."

"Old-fashioned remedies are still the best," said Beatrice Wesley, sailing into the room. She carried a tray on which had been arranged a pitcher of lemonade, a glass, a napkin, and a paper drinking straw. She was smiling. "All my four sons thrived on old-fashioned remedies."

"Thrived," repeated Margaret, in case Kay hadn't heard.

"You should have taken my advice yesterday, Mrs. Bellamy. A hot bath and one of Margaret's toddys; you would have been right as rain."

"She won't eat her yeast, Bea."

"Really?"

"I'm a terrible person," said Kay, rolling her eyes. "Shoot me."

"I'll do something much more useful," replied Beatrice. She poured a glass of lemonade, crumbled a square of yeast into it, and stirred the mixture with a straw. "Drink it," she said. "Mustn't take chances with your health."

Kay took the glass and sipped the cloudy liquid, saying nothing as the two older women chatted away. Her feverish eyes prowled around the room—the room that had been her haven when she'd shared it with John. She and John had chosen everything together: the rose-sprigged wallpaper, the big brass bed, the matching slipper chairs, the antique dresser discovered in a junk shop, the pretty frames for Kay's watercolors.

There were seven watercolors in all. The largest one, hanging over the fireplace, had been copied from John and Kay's wedding photo. The others were studies of Laura and Eliza at different ages and were scattered throughout the room. The studies were Kay's best work, capturing Laura's many moods, Eliza's serene, uncomplicated beauty. In every pose, Eliza appeared to be haloed with light.

Margaret plucked the empty glass from Kay's hand. "I'll leave the pitcher here, but you should try to sleep for a while. A bad cold like that takes a lot out of you."

"What time is it?"

Beatrice looked down at the watch pinned to her ample bosom. "Nearly five." She frowned. "Didn't realize it was so late! I must be going."

"I'll see you to the door, Bea."

"No need, I'll find my way." She turned, shaking her finger at Kay. "You take care of yourself, Mrs. Bellamy. Do as Margaret says."

"Thank you for the lemonade."

"Don't mention it."

Beatrice Wesley said her good-byes and left the room. Kay burrowed deeper into the pillows. One gone, she thought; one to go. "You don't have to stay with me, Margaret. I'll be all right. I have a magazine to read."

"Sleep would be better."

Kay sneezed. "No, I want to see Laura when she comes home."

Margaret pulled a fresh handkerchief from her sleeve and gave it to Kay. "She won't be home long. Robby's coming at seven. He stopped by earlier this afternoon and said she should be ready at seven."

"I wish we hadn't had the telephone taken out. It's kind of awkward for the girls and their dates."

"Of all the things to worry about! Boys and girls managed just fine before there were telephones. We all did. If you ask me, a phone is a waste of good money."

"Yes, but Robby—"

"He lives on the sixteenth floor," said Margaret, pointing toward the ceiling. "That's not exactly on the moon. Anyhow, this is no time to be running up more bills. The phone's out; let it stay out." She leaned over Kay. "Sit up, I want to fix your pillows . . . You know," she continued, shaking and pounding the pillows into shape, "Laura has her heart set on Robby."

"Oh, I know. I'm keeping my fingers crossed." Kay believed that the Colliers had less money than most people assumed, but still she felt Robby was a wonderful choice for Laura. He had a small trust fund, he was a student at Yale, and one day he would inherit his father's business. To Kay, all these things meant security. If he wasn't rich, at least he would never be poor. "Laura could have a good life with Robby. Don't you think so?"

"He's a charmer, that boy. But I don't think he's as smart as Laura, for all his fancy schooling."

Kay thrashed impatiently under the quilts. "What difference does it make? I wish you wouldn't always look for something wrong. Who's smart and who isn't . . . has nothing to do with why people get married."

Margaret's thoughts crept back almost thirty years to Wilbur Hobart. "Is marriage all the bedroom, then?"

"No." Kay glanced up. "I don't know what marriage is," she said, coughing again. "It's so many things. You have to be lucky. John and I were lucky, right up to the end." She was fussing with the quilts—pushing them aside, pulling them back, smoothing the soft, flowered cotton. "Why are we having this conversation, Margaret? The point, the only point, is that Laura has a chance for a good life."

"You're talking about money."

"That's just part of it," replied Kay, but too quickly.

"If you say so." Margaret picked up the copy of *Vogue*

and placed it next to Kay on the bed. "Magazines like that put ideas in your head."

"Ideas?"

"Wishing won't make us the kind of people in that magazine. High life people. Rich people. You know what I mean, Kay."

"I know what you mean; I don't happen to agree."

"No, I didn't think you would." Margaret straightened the bed one more time. She felt Kay's brow, buttoned the top button of her nightgown, and stepped away. "I'd best get supper started. I'm fixing a custard for you. Some nice beef broth and a custard. That ought to keep your strength up." She switched on the lights, closed the curtains. "Try to rest," she said, walking to the door.

Kay poured another glass of lemonade and lay back on the pillows, savoring the quiet that followed Margaret's exit. She took her magazine onto her lap, thumbing through the glossy pages. After a while she put both the glass and the magazine down. Her eyes felt heavy. She drowsed.

In the netherworld between sleep and wakefulness, she saw random images of her daughters — of four-year-old Eliza, all ruffles and golden curls, blowing out the candles on her birthday cake; of nine-year-old Laura playing hopscotch, her tawny hair lifting in the breeze as she tossed a pebble on the chalked square and jumped. But why was it suddenly so dark? What were those shadows? "Laura," murmured Kay. Was Laura lost somewhere in the swirling black shadows?

"Mama," said Laura now, gently shaking Kay's shoulder. "Mama, wake up . . . Wake up, you're having a bad dream."

Her eyes opened, blinking at Laura. "Oh, you're here. I . . . I must have dozed off."

"Your throat sounds much better. How do you feel?"

"I have a bad cold; that's all it is." Kay reached up and touched Laura's cheek. "I was looking for you . . . In my dream, I mean. It was so dark."

"You still have a fever, Mama."

She smiled. "Do you think I'm delirious? Raving mad?"

"No." Laura smiled too. "But you have to expect strange dreams when you have a fever." She sat at the edge of the bed, resting her hand on Kay's. "Do you want me to stay home tonight?"

"No, of course not. You and Robby go out and have a nice time. Enjoy being young, Laura. Time goes so fast . . . We get caught up in all the day-to-day things and we forget time is passing."

She brushed the hair from Kay's warm brow. "Why are you worrying about time?"

"I don't want you ever to look back and feel you missed something."

"Is that how you feel, Mama?"

"I would, if I hadn't married your father . . . He'd have liked Robby, you know. Robby's just the kind of boy we used to wish for you." Kay moved her pillows around, sitting straighter in bed. "And that's why I hope you won't . . . burden him with problems. Everybody in the building's going to know I lost my job; Mrs. Wesley will see to that. But nobody needs to know we're a little short of money. There's no reason to talk about it, especially not with Robby."

"Mama, Robby already *knows* we're short of money. Why else would you be working?"

"Some women work because they want to, not because they need to."

Laura sighed. "Robby also knows there's a Depression on. It's not your fault there's a Depression, Mama. You're talking as if you have something to be ashamed of."

Kay's lovely violet eyes darkened a shade. "Don't you understand? Robby mustn't think he's going out with a — a *waif*. The Colliers mustn't think it. That's not what they want for their son."

"You have to stop worrying. The Colliers seem to like

me, but even if they didn't, it wouldn't help to pretend we're rolling in money."

A raspy cough shook Kay's shoulders. She drank more lemonade. "I'm not telling you to pretend anything," she said when she was able to speak. "It's just that you can't be sure of the Colliers."

"It doesn't matter," replied Laura, feeling a rare surge of confidence. "I can be sure of Robby."

Robby Collier, whistling to himself, crossed the hall and rang for the elevator. He rang again, and then glanced at his wristwatch. It was five minutes to seven; five minutes to Laura, he thought with a smile.

Smiles came easily to Robby. The only child of Mike and Eleanor Collier, he had been indulged, if not precisely spoiled. His nursery had been filled with toys and games; he had had nannies and trips and good schools. Now, at nineteen, he had a handsome monthly allowance, an account at his father's tailor, and a brand new Packard convertible, bright red.

He resembled his mother, the former Eleanor Jamison of Main Line Philadelphia. The resemblance was physical: the same green eyes, golden hair, aristocratic cheekbones. In temperament, Robby resembled his father, though without the shrewdness.

The elevator arrived. Jimmy, the young elevator operator, opened the door. "Sorry to keep you waiting, Mr. Collier. The Morgans are having a party tonight. Big crowds going upstairs."

"Oh, I understand."

"Tenth floor, Mr. Collier?"

"You know all my secrets, Jimmy." Not that Laura was a secret; Robby often felt as if the whole building knew about his dates with her. He didn't mind. She was pretty enough to make heads turn, but unlike the other girls he'd escorted around town, she had what his mother called "depth". It pleased him to think he had chosen someone with depth. "Thanks," he said now, stepping off the elevator at Laura's floor.

"Okay, Mr. Collier."

All the hallways in the building were painted dove gray and carpeted in black. Opposite the elevators on each floor was a lacquered black console table, and a mirror in a frame of frosted glass. Robby paused briefly in front of the mirror. He tossed his camel's hair coat over his arm, settled his tie, and smoothed the lapels of his double-breasted suit. Whistling again, he walked off toward the Bellamys' apartment.

Margaret answered his ring. She pulled open the door and waved him inside. "You're right on time," she said, offering a quick smile. "Laura's not ready yet. But that's part of the game, isn't it? Keep the fellow waiting and make a grand entrance?"

"Yes, ma'am, I suppose it is."

"Well, hang your coat on the rack there and we'll go into the living room."

Robby, accustomed to Margaret's directions, did as he was told. She reminded him of one of his old nannies, a woman who'd bustled about the house, issuing orders and opinions by the score. She'd been a good sport, though, and he'd liked her. He liked Margaret too; in his amiable, carefree manner, he liked almost everybody. "Is Mrs. Bellamy feeling better?" he asked when they reached the living room.

"I just brought her some honey and lemon. Of course it'll still be sitting there an hour from now. I don't know why I bother." Margaret turned on the lights, motioning Robby to a chair. "Make yourself comfortable. I'll get Laura."

"No hurry."

"I'll get her."

Robby sat back and took a pack of cigarettes from his jacket pocket. He clicked his small gold lighter and exhaled a stream of smoke. The room was quiet. It was a pleasant room, with soft peach walls, two flowered wing chairs, a bottle-green sofa, and a large radio set encased in a dark wood cabinet. On the mantel were more of Margaret's knickknacks: a porcelain trinket box and three porcelain eggs. On the walls were several of Kay's watercolors, seascapes she had painted years before.

Robby looked past the seascapes, watching a thin ribbon of smoke curl toward the ceiling. He noticed a crack in the plaster and he smiled. His mother would have called it sloppy housekeeping.

"Here I am," said Laura, hesitating in the doorway. "I always seem to be late."

Robby put out his cigarette and stood up. "Your aunt Margaret has a theory about that."

"Yes, I'm sure she has."

He went to Laura, taking her in his arms. "You look wonderful," he murmured against her upswept hair. "I stared at your picture all the way from New Haven . . . But this is better." He kissed her. "Much better," he said, smiling into her eyes.

"Did you miss me?"

"What do you think?"

In the lamplight, Robby's hair was a cap of pure gold. His face, so chiseled and perfect, could have been the face etched on an ancient coin. "I think I'm very glad you don't go to a coed school."

He laughed. "Oh, I can be trusted. I'm steady as a rock."

"And I'm still glad you don't go to a coed school."

Hand in hand, they left the living room and walked to the foyer. "While we're on the subject," he said, helping Laura with her coat, "how is the Acme Business Institute?"

"I'm up to seventy-five words a minute . . . my typing speed," she explained when he frowned. "That's pretty good, you know."

He opened the front door, stepping aside for Laura to pass. He followed her into the hallway. "I wish you wouldn't take it so seriously. Typing speed and all that.

43

What difference can it make? You won't be doing it for long."

"Long enough. I have to earn my living until . . ." Until I get married, she thought. She didn't dare say the words; Robby might feel she was pushing him. "It's hard to get jobs these days," she said instead. "But at least there's a chance if you have good skills."

Robby stared down at the black carpet. "Dad's offer is open, Laura. He'll find you a job. Something . . . appropriate."

Appropriate. She had come to hate that word. In her opinion, Robby worried much too much about what was, and wasn't, appropriate. It was the only thing she would change about him if she could. Well, maybe there were a couple of other things, *small* things, unimportant things. "It's best if I find my own job," she said quietly, squeezing Robby's hand. "I'm grateful to your father, and I thanked him the last time I saw him, but it's best this way . . . You know how Mama feels about charity. It's how I feel, too."

"Charity?"

Laura nodded, smiling. "Your father won't get me a real job. He'll just stick me away somewhere inconspicuous and I'll be paid a salary for doing nothing. That's charity. I want to *earn* my salary."

Robby was silent as they walked to the elevator. His hand reached to the down button, then pulled back. Of all the girls he knew, he thought to himself, Laura was the only one who had a mind of her own. The other girls he knew were more docile, perhaps more beautiful, but Laura was a challenge, and that was part of the excitement.

He watched Laura's eyes. A smile stole across his face. "Why are you so stubborn?" he asked, his arms closing around her. "Tell me why."

"I think I got my stubborn streak from Aunt Margaret. It's not my fault."

He kissed her again, and now his hands slipped beneath the jacket of her dress to her breasts. His explorations would go no further. He'd wanted Laura from the very first, but she was a nice girl and there were rules about nice girls. "It's your fault I'm crazy about you. God, I really am crazy about you, Laura."

Her heart was racing. Her breath caught in her throat. She wanted his kisses to go on and on, but as usually happened, she untangled his arms and broke free. "Robby," she gasped.

"Now you know how much I missed you." He dragged out his handkerchief, wiping smudges of coral lipstick off his face. "Now I know how much you missed me," he added with a mischievous grin. "I could feel your heart pounding."

Laura blushed and looked away. She pressed the elevator button. "Someone might have seen us."

"We weren't doing anything wrong. People are allowed to kiss."

"Yes, but I don't want Mama to hear gossip about us."

Robby laughed. "Your mother was young once, wasn't she? She must remember how it was."

"You make her sound old."

He draped his arm around Laura's shoulder. "Not old; no, I didn't mean that . . . But we're at the beginning of our lives and she . . . Well, it's different for her. She's already . . . Darn it, Laura, you know what I mean to say."

The elevator came and they stepped inside. "Lovely night," she said to Jimmy. "A little cool."

"Yes, miss. Cool for October."

Laura said nothing more on the way downstairs. She watched the blinking floor numbers but she thought about her mother. She believed her mother remembered very well how it was to be young, to be at the beginning. "Enjoy being young," her mother had urged. Yes, that's what she would do.

She linked her arm in Robby's when they got to the lobby. "Where are we going?"

"Where would you like to go?"

"Paris." She saw his startled expression and she laughed. "Robby, I was joking. We don't need Paris." They passed through the lobby, nodding to the doorman as they walked outside. She looked up. The sky was a pattern of stars, like diamonds strewn on black velvet. There was a moon, a picture book silver moon. "We don't need Paris," she said again, "because we have all this. New York. It's ours tonight."

Robby had grown used to Laura's flights of fancy — they were probably caused by too much reading. He thought they were harmless, and sometimes fun. "I'll give you New York for a present," he replied, getting into the spirit of things. "We'll start at one of those French restaurants in the Village and work our way back uptown. Let's see . . . Some dancing, and then the floor show at the Kit Kat Club, and then some gypsy music in Yorkville. Gypsy violins?"

"I *love* gypsy violins." And I love you, she thought. She longed to say the words, to shout them, but she knew she couldn't, not yet. "It's a wonderful idea, Robby."

He took her hand and they walked off. She gazed at his handsome profile. She smiled. Later she would write in her diary that he had offered to give her New York for a present.

Chapter Three

Kay had a diary also, a collection of speckled notebooks in which she'd set down her thoughts during the nineteen years of her marriage. Now, as Monday morning sunshine splashed the room, she sat at the edge of her bed and reread her last entry: "My darling is gone, but somehow I have to go on. The girls are all that matter. When they were born, we swore they'd have everything. We made a promise to ourselves, and somehow I have to keep that promise."

She closed the notebook and put it aside. On the night table were three or four want ads neatly scissored from the Sunday newspapers. She snatched them up just as Margaret knocked at the door. "I'm busy," she called.

"You're no such thing," declared Margaret, striding into the room. She slammed a cup of black coffee on the table and turned to face Kay. "What are you doing out of bed?"

"Does every morning have to start with an argument?"

Margaret planted her feet and fixed her hands on her hips. "It does when you won't behave yourself."

"*Behave* myself? I'm not a child, you know."

"Then stop acting like one. Get back into bed, where you belong."

Kay shook her head. "My cold is much better. You killed it, Margaret. All those disgusting things you forced me to drink. And that awful stuff you rubbed on my chest! No cold is safe when you're around."

"I'll take that as a compliment."

"Will you?"

"Look, Kay," said Margaret, trying a different tack, "you're only hurting yourself. Your fever will come back if you keep prancing around. You should be in bed."

"I'm going out."

"Out! You'll catch your death!"

Kay mopped the little puddle of spilled coffee. She picked up the cup and took a sip. "In case you've forgotten, I lost my job Friday. I have a pile of bills, and less than three hundred dollars to my name. When that money's spent . . . My God, I can't stand to think about it. If I can't get another job—"

"Now, now, it doesn't do any good to look on the dark side."

"Fine advice, coming from you. You *always* look on the dark side."

"Well, I've had my heartaches, haven't I?" Margaret bent, straightening the bedspread. "Of course I don't like to complain."

"Of course." Kay finished the coffee and went to her bureau, pulling out underclothes and a pair of carefully mended silk stockings. "Anyway, I have to start looking for a job. There were a few ads. Maybe I'll be lucky."

"We'll talk about it after breakfast."

"Talk about what, Margaret? I told you I'm going out. And I have to get dressed now, so if you don't mind . . ."

"I mind, all right. You're being very foolish."

Wearily, Kay shut the drawer. "How can I make you understand? I have to get a job. Shall I say it again? I have to get a job. I can't earn any money staying home."

"Will you hear me out? Can, you do that without biting my head off?"

"Sorry."

Margaret waved the apology away. "I know what the problems are," she said, "but remember I have some money of my own. From the house. I got close to a thousand dollars when I sold it, and there's five hundred left in the bank. If worse comes to worst—"

"No," interrupted Kay. "I appreciate it, I really do. But that's all the money you have in the world. And you haven't any way to earn more. No, it just doesn't make sense. I'm glad to have the five dollars a week you pay towards expenses, but that's all I'll take from you."

"I was a good piano teacher. That's why I wouldn't sell our old piano. It cost a pretty penny to have it shipped here from Alber Falls, let me tell you. I say we should put it to use."

"I wish we could." Kay looked at the clock on the mantel. She sighed. "Margaret, we've been through this before. In the first place, the piano needs tuning. That's a big expense. Even if you got a few students—"

"*If?*"

"Well, you didn't get any the last time you tried, did you? It's this Depression. Piano lessons are a luxury." Kay shrugged. "People who can afford lessons already have teachers. That's just the way it is." She looked once more at the clock. "I have to get dressed."

If Margaret's feelings had been hurt, she gave no sign. She merely took up the argument where it had begun. "You belong in bed, at least for another day or two. Another day or two isn't going to make a single bit of difference."

"You're like a dog digging for a bone, Margaret; you never give up."

"Not when I'm right."

"Right or wrong, I'm going out!"

Kay went out that morning and every morning for the next two weeks. She carried samples of her artwork in an immense manila envelope which seemed to grow heavier from one day to another. Also in the envelope was a letter of recommendation written by Eli Harding, the man who had fired her. It was a good letter, studded with praise, yet it didn't help.

Nothing helped. Kay scoured the want ads, to no avail. She made the rounds of advertising agencies, employment agencies, personnel departments, again to no avail. She went anywhere she might fill out an application or have an interview, anywhere she might gain a head start on the hundreds of people competing for the same small handful of jobs. Wherever she went, she was turned away by employers who wanted more experience, or different experience, or who wanted a man.

To save money, she tried to walk to all her destinations. For the same reason, she often went without lunch. She was up and out early every day, out in the cold, the rain. Her cough returned; grudgingly, she parted with a nickel for a box of Smith Brothers cough drops — a daily expense as her cough worsened.

Kay was tired and discouraged, more frightened than she had ever been. She couldn't forget, even for a moment, the terrors of the Depression. Wherever she walked, she saw humbled men selling fruit or holding out tin cups for the spare coins of passersby. She saw bread lines and soup kitchens. If she walked in the park, she saw Hoovervilles: crude shelters built of discarded packing crates and outsized cardboard cartons; shelters inhabited by desperate people who had no place else to go. She saw these things and her stomach twisted into knots.

It was no easier for her at home. She wrote lies to Eliza because she couldn't bear to write the truth. She silently endured Margaret's nagging because silence was her only defense. She hid from Laura's anxious looks because they mirrored her own anxieties. Night after night she closed her bedroom door and pored over the bills. Some were stamped SECOND NOTICE, but others were stamped FINAL NOTICE. Final notice, she would think to herself, pacing back and forth. It sounded like an obituary.

While Kay paced, Margaret sat up till all hours with a hot water bottle and the family albums. Laura, feeling the tension, found escape in the troubles of Rochester and Jane Eyre.

"I think I know that book by heart," she said to her friend Doris Sweeney. It was the last Thursday in October, a cloudy afternoon, and both girls had come from their classes — Laura from the Acme Business Institute, Doris from Barnard College, where she had a scholarship. "I sort of sink into it," Laura went on, "and then I'm off in a different world."

"Better than this world?"

"No, just different. I guess that's enough for now. I just try to distract myself."

Doris shifted her books to her other arm. When she needed to distract herself she did mathematical problems, the more complicated the better. She was small, blond, shy, and unlike her best friend Laura, a wizard in math. "What do you think's going to happen?"

"I don't know. I'm pretty sure Mama's running out of money. She won't talk about it. She won't talk about anything . . . But I'll be through with Acme in a few days. I'll be able to work. If I can *find* work. Keep your fingers crossed."

"Oh, I always do," replied Doris with an apologetic smile.

Laura smiled also. Even back in third grade, where they'd met, Doris had worn a vaguely apologetic look. She'd been the smartest pupil in the class by far, but she'd never raised her hand to answer a question, never volunteered to go to the blackboard. At recess, she'd worried that she wouldn't be chosen for games; once chosen, she'd worried about making mistakes. She'd turned scarlet whenever a boy came near. "You haven't changed a bit, you know."

"Changed? What do you mean?"

"I mean you're exactly the same as you were years ago. The world's gone upside down, but you're the same. I'm glad."

They reached their apartment building. Eugene, the doorman tipped his cap to Laura. "Afternoon, miss. Doris."

"Hello, Eugene." She was used to the easy familiarity in his voice. Her father was the building superintendent, and while Laura and Jane were respectfully called "miss," she was just plain Doris. Some of the building staff thought she was overstepping herself by going to college. She loved Barnard, but sometimes she wondered if they weren't right. "Your mother's got so much on her mind, maybe my coming over is too much."

"Oh, you're always welcome. Besides, Mama stayed home all day today; it'll be good for her to have company. Especially your company." They walked through the lobby and into the waiting elevator. "Mama likes you, as if you didn't know."

"Is she sick again?"

"Not again. Still. Her cold keeps going away and coming back." Laura didn't want to say anything that the elevator man could make into gossip, anything too personal. "It's hard to get rid of colds this time of year. The weather . . ."

"Oh yes," agreed Doris. "The weather."

They got off at the tenth floor and went to apartment G. Laura took her latchkey from her pocket. "Mama," she called, opening the door. "I'm home. And Doris is with me."

There was no response, but an instant later they heard a noise — a heavy, shuffling sound followed by the rumble of male voices. Laura and Doris looked at each other. They drew a step closer. "Mama, where are you?"

"Here."

The girls heard Kay's flat, tired voice drifting toward them from the other end of the hall. Even at a distance, they could see how pale she was; a ghostly figure, hugging her arms around her waist.

"Mama!" Laura threw her books and purse and gloves

on the table. She rushed forward, Doris trailing at her heels. "Mama, what in the world . . ."

Both girls stopped short, peering into the dining room where two burly men were wrapping large pads around the table and chairs. Doris pressed her lips together and looked down at the floor. She knew these men had been sent to repossess the furniture. It had happened to the Daleys in 4B, to the Brocks and the Allens; now it was happening here.

A moment passed before Laura grasped what was happening. When she did, her heart sank like a stone. "Mama, I'm sorry."

"I was . . . I was going to tell you the furniture had been taken out for refinishing. You wouldn't have believed it anyway . . . That's one lie I saved myself. One out of so many." All the light had gone from Kay's eyes. She watched the men emptying the breakfront and her face seemed to crumble. The breakfront was the last thing she and John had bought together. A ten-dollar down payment; it had been as easy as that. She put her hand to her head and turned away. "Margaret went to the grocery store. She doesn't know . . . about this."

"Don't worry about Aunt Margaret," said Laura, blinking back tears. She felt utterly helpless. She looked at her mother's stricken face, looked at the men moving the breakfront out of its niche. Anger swept over her in waves. "How can you be so cruel!" she shouted. "How can you come in here and just take our furniture! Can't you see what you're doing?" She started into the dining room but Doris restrained her. "Let go of my arm."

"Laura, they're doing their job." Doris's small face was pinched with worry. She too was fighting tears, but she managed to hold on to Laura. "It's their job."

"A *horrible* job! A job for bullies, for—"

"It's the Depression," said Doris very quietly. "People take any job they can get."

Kay didn't want to hear any more about the Depression. Without a word, she stuck her hands in the pockets of her robe and walked away to her bedroom.

The afternoon papers, folded open to the want ads, were scattered on the floor. Atop the bureau, untouched, were the soup and sandwich Margaret had brought earlier. "You have to keep up your strength," Margaret had said. Strength? wondered Kay. What strength?

She sat at the edge of the bed, staring into space. All the humiliations of the past two weeks combined couldn't equal the humiliation of this day. Strangers tramping through her apartment, through her life; she thought about it and her cheeks burned with shame.

She started to rise but a coughing spell sat her down again. She reached for her cough medicine: a thick, cherry-colored syrup that she'd bought at the pharmacy. She took a swallow and replaced the bottle on her night table. Her chest was so sore; she knew she ought to see Dr. Weston. No, she thought, not until I can pay something on his bill.

She heard a crash in the hallway, a shattering of glass. She got to her feet and went to the door, but she didn't open it; she didn't want to chance what she might see. She turned, her violet gaze settling on the portraits of Laura and Eliza. She'd let them down; she'd failed, and whether they blamed her or not, she blamed herself.

Tears streaked her face as she walked slowly, wearily, across the room. She stopped at the closet, rummaging through the shelves. Way in the back, behind a Macy's hatbox, was what she was looking for—a bottle of whisky, three-quarters full. The whisky had steadied her nerves on the day of John's funeral; she prayed it would help her now.

She took the toothbrush glass from the bathroom and poured a cautious drink. The first few sips burned her throat, but soon she felt a pleasant warmth spreading through her body. She felt soothed, lulled. With her second drink, she felt things might not be as hopeless as they seemed. She raised her glass to John's portrait. "I'm trying, my dearest," she murmured. "I'm trying."

Walter Goodfriend was sixty years old, and for thirty of those years he had run the Acme Business Institute. He'd inherited the school from his father, but the enthusiasm he'd brought to it was entirely his own. He was a cheerful man, almost chirpy. He had a firm belief in hard work and an unswerving devotion to his students. His proudest moments were the graduation ceremonies that sent new generations of women into the business world.

Acme had four graduating classes each year. Before the Depression the ceremonies had been festive affairs. Students' families and friends had been invited to the vast auditorium. Sandwiches and cakes and punch were served by waitresses hired for the occasion, and everyone received a keepsake—a monogrammed bookmark perhaps, or a fountain pen. But times had changed, and because he'd had no choice, Walter Goodfriend had made changes too. The ceremonies weren't as festive as they had been; still, he felt they captured the "Acme spirit."

"A spirit of diligence, cooperation, and common sense," he said now, concluding his speech to the November graduating class. "With this spirit—and the office skills you have learned here—I know you will all go far in life."

There was applause from the eighty students seated in the cafeteria. They were seated alphabetically; Laura near the front, Jane in the rear. When Laura heard her name called, she turned to smile at Jane, and then walked to the improvised stage to receive her diploma. A beaming Walter Goodfriend put the rolled up parchment in her hand. Mrs. Goodfriend kissed her cheek. "God bless you," said Mrs. Goodfriend.

Laura went back to her seat and watched the rest of the ceremonies, but every few moments she glanced down at her diploma. It wasn't the college diploma she'd once dreamed of, but it was something she had earned on her own and she was proud of herself.

Jane's diploma was the last to be awarded, ending the ceremonies. "We did it!" she cried, rushing over to where Laura stood. "We're honest-to-goodness secretaries!"

"If someone hires us, we are."

"Don't worry, we'll get great jobs. I feel it in my bones."

Laura laughed. "Your *bones* have been wrong before."

"Not this time . . . Do you want to stay for tea and cookies?"

"Doris is probably waiting for us outside. She said she was going to skip her noon class so we could celebrate."

Jane looked at her new gold wristwatch, a graduation present from her parents. "Okay, no tea and cookies. But the celebration's on me. Pop gave me five dollars."

Laura had fifty cents in her purse. She also had her pride. "I can pay my way, Jane."

"Don't be so touchy. Pop wanted to treat you and Doris. It was his idea, not mine." She stared at Laura, trying to read her expression. "Well, it was."

"He must know how broke we are."

Jane shrugged. "A lot of people are broke, but not everybody is so touchy about it. Doris isn't, and her family's *al*ways struggling. The Sweeneys are much worse off than you."

Laura knew that was meant to be comforting. She smiled. "Come on, let's start our celebration."

Doris was waiting halfway down the block. She was dressed in her Sunday best: a fashionable, bright green coat one size too large, and a matching green tam; gifts from her prosperous cousins in Ohio. She was squinting in the sunlight, clutching her books and her worn suede purse to her chest. "Over here," she called.

Jane and Laura waved. "She looks so cute in that big coat," said Jane.

"Don't tell her it's big."

"You mean she doesn't *know?*" Jane was still laughing when they came abreast of Doris. "Don't mind me," she said. "I'm giddy with all the excitement. A girl doesn't get a diploma every day!"

"I wish I'd been there to see it. Congratulations," added Doris, looking from Jane to Laura. "I envy you."

Laura was startled. "Envy *us?* Why? You go to *Barnard,* for heaven's sake!"

"Yes." They walked to the corner, pausing at the curb when the traffic light turned red. A policeman clamped his whistle between his teeth and raised his arm, waving cars and trucks and buses along Lexington Avenue. Doris seemed to be watching him, but her thoughts were elsewhere. "I *do* envy you," she said suddenly, looking around at her friends. "You've finished your classes. You can go out and get jobs. You can . . . you can start your lives. You're adults."

"You're an adult," said Jane.

Doris frowned. "People are only treated like adults when they earn their own money. Da still treats me like a little girl."

"That has nothing to do with earning your own money," said Laura as they crossed the avenue. "It's because all your brothers and sisters are gone. You're the last one left at home. The baby of the family. And a genius to boot!"

Doris risked a small smile. "You know my da; he thinks college is a waste. 'Why couldn't you get a scholarship to nursing school instead?' That's what he's always asking. He says nursing school is good training for a wife and mother, but college is a waste of time." She bent her head, shrinking into her big coat like a turtle shrinking into its shell. "Sometimes I have the feeling Da's right."

"That's so silly, Doris. Even the Bible says you

shouldn't hide your light under a bushel." Jane poked Doris's shoulder. "Your father can't argue with the Bible."

Can't he? thought Laura. Francis Sweeney was a fiery Irishman with an Irishman's love of arguments. His wife, Grace, was a sweet, quiet little mouse of a woman. Some of the Sweeney children took after Francis, but Doris was clearly her mother's daughter. "Let's not think about our problems today," said Laura as they headed uptown. "It's a special occasion. Let's just enjoy ourselves . . . Where shall we go?"

"Schrafft's," suggested Doris.

Jane sighed. "You have no imagination. You always say Schrafft's."

"Childs, then."

"Same thing. Did I tell you I was paying? Pop gave me five dollars."

"Five dollars! For lunch?"

"For whatever we want to do." They stopped at another traffic light. Jane turned, following Laura's gaze to an office building across the street. "What's so interesting?"

"That's where Mama used to work. In that building on the twelfth floor. The Harding Advertising Company."

"Didn't you say we shouldn't think about our problems today?"

Laura shrugged. "Easier said than done, I guess."

"No, you were right the first time. Wasn't she, Doris? We've earned our celebration. Let's just enjoy ourselves. The only question is where." She glanced around, as if hoping for inspiration. "There's nothing near here, nothing really nice."

The light changed and the girls walked on. "We could go to the place with the singing waiters," said Laura. "It's not far from home." A smile started at the corners of her mouth. "You know what else it's not far from?"

"What?" asked Doris and Jane in unison.

"Madame Zarela. The fortune-teller."

Doris's pretty blue eyes widened. "Fortune-teller? Oh, I don't know what Father Mahoney would say about that. The priests at St. Vincent are awfully strict about . . . the supernatural."

"It's only supernatural if you *believe* in it," insisted Jane. "Do you believe in crystal balls and tea leaves?"

"I don't know." Doris's arms tightened around her books. She looked worried again. "It depends. I mean, no, I don't believe in crystal balls and tea leaves. But the supernatural is more than that, isn't it? You're the one who mentioned the Bible."

"What of it?"

"Doris is trying to say there are supernatural things in the Bible. The Holy Ghost. The Resurrection. *Angels.*"

"Oh yes, I see." Jane was silent, holding on to her hat as the wind picked up. "There's magic, too," she said a moment later. "The parting of the Red Sea. The loaves and the fishes."

"Miracles," corrected Doris. "Call them miracles."

"Or lightning will strike us," said Laura with a smile. "Does all this religious talk mean we can't go see Madame Zarela?" She turned. "Are you going to be a stick-in-the-mud, Doris?"

"No . . . If we go just for fun, I guess it's all right. And if Da doesn't find out."

"He won't," promised Jane. "We won't tell anyone."

"Doris, if you don't want to—"

"No, I'll go. But just for fun."

"Then it's settled! Sometimes you have terrific ideas, Laura."

"Yes, sometimes."

The three friends continued walking up Lexington Avenue. It was a beautiful day, a tangy autumn day filled with sunshine and sudden cool breezes. Every few blocks there were vendors selling soft pretzels and hot roasted chestnuts. As always, there were men selling fruit, and the clear light seemed only to enhance the vivid hues of the tangerines and apples on their stands. Near Fifty-ninth street was a man selling huge yellow chrysanthemums. Laura watched a woman give a chrysanthemum and a crisp dollar bill to a panhandler. It was, she thought to herself, that kind of day.

They were approaching Sixty-fourth Street when she spied a familiar figure carrying a very large manila envelope. "There's Mama," she said, surprised.

"Where?"

"Straight ahead. She just came out of that building over there." Laura quickened her step. "Mama," she called. "Mama?"

Kay stopped in midstride. She transferred the envelope to her other arm and turned around. Laura was running toward her. She saw the luminous smile, the mane of tawny hair shimmering with sun, and it was as if she were seeing her daughter for the first time. "She's lovely," murmured Kay. "Lovely, and I never knew it."

"Hi, Mama," said Laura, coming up beside her. "I didn't expect to see you till tonight."

"Hello, dear . . . Hello, girls. I had an appointment here," she explained, glancing at the narrow gray building. "A design studio is looking for a sketch artist." It was another job she knew she wouldn't get. The owner of the studio had asked a few perfunctory questions, leafed idly through her samples, and then risen to his feet. "They . . . said they'd keep me in consideration . . . Whatever that means," she added with a tired smile.

Kay turned, and Laura saw how tired she really was. The sunlight accentuated the hollows in her cheeks, the dark patches beneath her eyes, the lines etched so deeply on her brow. She looked old, all used up. "Mama—"

"Show me your diploma. You too, Jane . . . It's a shame we couldn't have had a party."

"Nobody wanted a party, Mama. Don't worry about it."

"No, that's right," agreed Jane quickly. She hadn't seen Kay Bellamy for several weeks; she was dismayed by the change in her appearance. "It's only business school."

"Well, I'm proud of you both."

Laura gazed into her mother's eyes, eyes that burned too brightly. "Wouldn't you like a cup of tea? There's that nice tearoom two blocks from here."

"No, I . . . I have another appointment." It was a lie, but she didn't care; one more lie wouldn't make any difference. She fished her handkerchief out of her coat pocket, covering her mouth when she coughed. "I'm probably late already," she said when the cough subsided. "I'll just be on my way."

"Couldn't you make your appointment for another time?" asked Doris. She wasn't fooled by this talk of appointments. Mrs. Bellamy was trying to put a good face on things; it was a matter of pride, and her father had taught her never to hurt a person's pride. "If you could make a change, the four of us could have a little party of our own."

"You're all very sweet," said Kay, "but I'm not going to spoil your fun. Today is for the three of you. Run along and have a good time."

"Mama, if you won't come with us, you ought to go home and rest. You've been running around too much."

"I hear enough of that from Margaret." Kay shifted the envelope once again. She wished she could sit down. "Hurry along now. I'll see you later."

"All right." Laura fastened the top button of Kay's coat. "But you have to keep warm."

"I'm fine. Stop fussing."

She smelled the whisky on her mother's breath. It wasn't the first time. During the past week she'd suspected that her mother was taking a drink, and maybe two, with the morning coffee. Courage to face the day, she'd thought. She hadn't known what to say and so she'd said nothing.

Now she sensed Kay's impatience. She shrugged and turned back to her friends. "Are we off to Madame

Zarela?"

"I'm ready," declared Jane.

"So am I," sighed Doris.

They said their goodbyes to Kay and resumed their walk uptown. She watched them: three young women with their lives stretching out like gaily-colored ribbons. She had been their age and she still remembered all the tingling expectations, all the certainties of youth. But the only real certainty, she thought to herself, is that life will break your heart. What was it her father used to say? "You're born, life is a struggle, and then you die."

Kay was pondering this bit of philosophy when a coughing spell nearly doubled her over. She pressed her handkerchief to her mouth and it was several moments before she could catch her breath. She dropped her envelope, picked it up; dropped her purse, picked it up. She didn't feel well. Her chest was sore, her back ached, and despite the cool weather, she had begun to perspire. She unbuttoned her coat, fighting the dizziness that blurred the sidewalk. When she got to the corner, she braced herself against a mailbox until the dizziness passed.

The light changed and she trudged across the street. She juggled her purse and her envelope from arm to arm, counting off the blocks as she drew closer to home. She wanted to crawl into bed and disappear under the covers, disappear into sleep. She felt as if she hadn't slept in months.

Kay's face was pink with fever by the time she reached Seventy-fourth street. She stopped for a moment, looking at the handsome apartment building — the symbol of everything she and John had desired. "John," she murmured. "Why did you leave me?"

Points of blackness danced before her eyes. She swayed. She put her hand to her head, and then a big black pit opened at her feet.

"Mrs. Bellamy!" Eugene cried. Then the doorman rushed forward, bending over her prostrate body. "Mrs.

Bellamy, can you hear me?"

Curious passersby had started to gather. Eugene looked beyond them to the building's service entrance, where Francis Sweeney was polishing the brass bell. "Mr. Sweeney," he called. "Mr. Sweeney, come and help me. She's fainted dead away!"

Chapter Four

"You have a strong lifeline," said Madame Zarela, staring at Laura's palm. "This is good. It means you will live to old age. Seventy years, maybe. Eighty years. It will be old age."

Laura was silent but she could hear Jane giggling softly in the background. She turned. Jane and Doris were seated on rickety folding chairs at the side of the storefront parlor. In the window was a vase of dusty paper flowers and a paper cutout of a hand with crisscrossing palm lines drawn in different colors. Snoozing in a corner of the window was a sleek black cat, its tail curled around its paws. Laura smiled and turned again to Madame Zarela. "Sorry."

"You are a very determined person," continued the woman. Her hair was as black as the cat's, drawn off her face by a cotton scarf. Her eyes were dark also, edged with long, dark lashes. She wore gold hoop earrings that swung back and forth when she inclined her head over Laura's hand. "Yes, I see here all your determination. You have many worries, many worries . . . but they will be solved if you are determined. Others will try to lead you. They will try to . . . force their ideas. This you must not allow. No, all will be well if you are firm. If you are determined in your own ideas."

"Will I get married soon?"

"You will marry," replied Madame Zarela. Her eyes searched Laura's palm. "A man with light hair . . ."

"Golden hair."

"A man with light hair." Now her eyes moved from the right hand to the left. "This is not clear . . . There is a man with light hair. There is another man, a different man. This man, he is also a very determined person."

"But *when* will I get married?"

"Soon. This is not what you expect, but you will marry soon." Madame Zarela brought Laura's hands together. "I see two children. I see you will travel to many places . . . And here is the other man again. A man with dark hair. A man stepping out of the shadows."

"A lover!" crowed Jane. "You have all the luck! Will she be rich too?"

"It is not for you to ask the question," replied the fortune-teller.

Laura leaned forward. "Will I?"

"Money will come to you if you are true to what you believe. There is money here. I see it. I see also the people who will try to lead you. If you don't allow this, then money will come." She let go of Laura's hands. "It will be an interesting life. To see more, I must read the cards."

"Cards?"

"The tarot."

Laura rose. "Maybe another time. Thank you, Madame Zarela."

Doris and Jane pushed their chairs back. They stood. They had already had their readings: tea leaves for Jane and the crystal ball for Doris. The three readings cost a total of eighty cents, which Jane deposited in Madame Zarela's small drawstring purse. "Are you here on Saturdays?" she asked.

"I am here always."

"I'll remember that."

A bell tinkled above the door as the girls walked outside. Laura took a last glance at the cat, who raised its head, flicked its tail, and went promptly back to sleep in the cozy corner. "Not a bad life," she said, smiling.

"For a cat."

"Are you really going to have another reading, Jane?" asked Doris.

"Maybe a palm reading. Madame Zarela is good at that . . . Laura got the best fortune."

"I did not." She looked up at the sky. The sun was lower now, paler. Clouds scudded past, feathery brushstrokes of white. "We all got the same fortune. We're all going to marry and have children and take trips. Pretty safe predictions, it seems to me. Trips . . . Trips could mean anything: a subway ride to Brooklyn, a bus to Chinatown."

Jane shook her head and a lock of red hair flopped onto her brow. "But you got something *extra*," she insisted. "You did. You're going to be rich and have a lover."

Laughter spilled from Laura. "Am I? That isn't what *I* heard in there . . . And besides, it's all just silliness. Our Madame Zarela makes things up as she goes along."

"How do you know?"

"Jane, you're impossible! It was fun, lots of fun, but let's leave it at that."

"For Father Mahoney's sake," added Doris.

"Well, I can't help it if Laura got the best fortune."

They argued the point all the way home, but Jane wasn't persuaded. She called on Doris's excellent memory to point out the differences in the fortune-teller's predictions. Almost triumphantly, she seized on every word. "So there you are! Doris and I are going to be boring old housewives, while *you* have some mysterious man stepping out of the shadows."

"Probably a bill collector," replied Laura.

"Come on, be serious."

"I can't. It's too silly."

They turned into their street. They were approaching the apartment building when Eugene hurried up to them. "Miss Bellamy, your aunt's been looking for you. She said you're to come straight home."

The smile left Laura's face, replaced by a frown. "Is something wrong?"

"Well, miss, it's your mother. She collapsed a few hours ago. Right here, it was. Or just a few yards away, anyhow."

"Collapsed!"

Doris and Jane saw the color drain from their friend's face. "Laura . . ."

"I have to go."

She rushed off, dashing into the lobby. Dear God, please let it be all right, she silently prayed. Dear God, *please*.

"It's pneumonia," said Margaret, meeting Laura's anxious gaze. "The doctor's come and gone." Her hand went to her throat. She sighed. "Your mother's been running herself ragged. That cough getting worse by the day. The fevers . . . But she wouldn't listen to me. And then today she just collapsed in the street. Poor woman, she was burning up with fever."

Laura dropped her things on the hall table. "How's Mama now? I want to see her."

"I won't stop you from going in, but she's asleep. Dr. Weston gave her some kind of sedative . . . He's coming back at the end of the day. He said he might have to arrange for oxygen."

Laura looked up. "This is really bad, isn't it?"

Margaret shrugged. "It's pneumonia."

"But Mama's going to get well? I—I know she's really sick now, but she's going to get well. That's right, isn't it?"

"We have to build up her strength. Ever since she lost her job she's—"

"But what did the doctor *say?*"

"Doctors! They all talk in riddles."

"Is that all you're going to tell me, Aunt Margaret?"

"That's all there is to tell."

Laura went to her mother's room. She hesitated at the door, taking a deep breath as if to steel herself. Quietly, without knocking, she tiptoed inside.

The room was very warm, the radiator hissing steam. Kay slept soundly, her head propped on three pillows, the covers drawn to her chin. On the night table were the medicines Dr. Weston had brought: a vial of small white pills, a bottle of greenish liquid, and another bottle filled with a thicker, darker mixture. There was a bottle of rubbing alcohol, a clean cloth, and a thermometer. Laura looked at the crowded table and sadly shook her head.

She pulled a chair next to the bed. She sat down, her eyes riveted on Kay. Her mother's breathing didn't seem labored, but with every breath there came a dry, tinny wheeze. The sound frightened Laura. For the second time in a week, she felt utterly helpless. Pneumonia; even the word filled her with dread.

The room grew darker and Laura switched on the lamps. Kay began to stir, turning from side to side, thrashing her legs under the covers. Laura stroked her forehead until she slipped back into a deep sleep. The radiator hissed. The mantel clock ticked the minutes away. Soon it would be night.

Laura had lost track of time. She sat like a sentry at her mother's bed and tried to make sense of her jumbled thoughts. There were things she should be doing, but she wasn't sure what. Should she send for Eliza? Should she go through the unpaid bills? Should she telephone Robby at Yale? "Robby," she whispered. She wished he were with her right now.

"Laura," said Margaret, opening the door, "here's Dr. Weston."

She glanced up, getting hastily to her feet. "Mama's been sleeping," she explained.

"Best thing for her. She's exhausted; her mind as well as her body. Women weren't meant to carry the weight of the world on their shoulders." Dr. Charles Weston was a tall, gray-haired man in his fifties. He had a direct, decisive manner, a friendly smile, and a fondness for bow ties. He was a good doctor, very thorough. His patients trusted him. "Why don't you two wait outside," he said now. "Let me do my examination in peace . . . Better still, why don't you put on a pot of coffee."

Laura was reluctant to leave. She gazed down at Kay and gently touched her cheek. "Maybe I should stay."

"There's nothing for you to do here. At this particular moment, you'll be much more useful in the kitchen. Go on now, both of you."

"Laura, come with me," said Margaret. She ushered her niece into the hall and closed the door. "Don't look like that. Dr. Weston knows what he's doing."

"I'm worried, Aunt Margaret."

"Well, of course you're worried. I'm worried too. But Kay's in good hands; that's the important thing."

They went into the kitchen. Margaret spooned coffee into the coffee pot while Laura put cups and saucers on the table. "I've been thinking I ought to call Eliza. She should be here."

"She should have been here all along," said Margaret.

Laura shrugged. "It's not her fault. Crossfield was never her idea. You know it was what Mama wanted."

"And your mother got her wish, at least for a while.

But now it's time to be sensible." Margaret set the coffee pot atop the stove and turned on the gas. "It's up to you, Laura. Your mother's in no condition to be making decisions. It's up to you."

"What's up to me?"

"Someone has to be the head of the house, missy. Someone has to be boss."

"But you—"

"No," said Margaret with a firm shake of her head. "I've been doing some thinking also. And it's not my place to decide for you and Eliza. Oh, I have my opinions on things. I'm not shy about telling them, either. But opinions aren't the same as decisions. You're the one who'll be earning the money now. You have the right to say how it'll be spent. That's fair. Even if Eliza doesn't think so."

"She won't care."

"Don't be too sure. Your mother has a drawer full of bills just for Eliza's clothes. Bills from Saks and B. Altman, fancy stores like that. It's what Eliza's used to. Well, you'll have to change all that. Lay down the law; that's what you'll have to do. Believe me, you won't get any thanks for your trouble."

Laura sat at the table and put her head in her hands. Lay down the law to Eliza? How could she? It was true that these extravagances had to stop, but why did *she* have to stop them? "No, I can't, Aunt Margaret."

"Can't what?"

"If I try to tell Eliza what to do, she'll laugh in my face. And I wouldn't blame her."

"Let her laugh. Let her dance a jig if she wants. Anything, as long as you make her understand there's no money. Because that happens to be the truth, Laura. There's no money. I've been through all Kay's hiding places. I found a hundred dollars and another three dollars in coins. That's all there is."

Laura's hands fell away. She turned her head slowly to Margaret. "That can't be right. There must be more than a hundred dollars. There must!"

"She paid the rent, the gas and electric, the insurance policies, and the grocer. I think there was also a payment to Schultz the butcher, and maybe a small payment on the radio set. Everybody else is threatening to sue us. Or to repossess the rest of the furniture. The living room's not paid for, you know."

Laura stared at Margaret. Her mouth seemed to tighten, but otherwise her expression was unchanged. "I don't want to hear any more."

"You have to know these things. Your mother could be bedridden for weeks, months. Even when she's well again, there's no guarantee she'll find work. Who needs artists in the middle of the Depression?"

"Mama won't have to worry about work. I'll get a job; I swear I will. I don't care what I have to do. One way or another, there'll be money coming into this house."

It was the reaction Margaret would have expected. Eliza was passive about most things, Kay too slow to face facts, but Laura was different. Beneath the girlish insecurities and the romantic dreams, there was a resolute spirit. A sturdy spirit, thought Margaret, sturdy enough to withstand life's tricks. "You'd better have a look at the bills. I'll show you where they're hidden."

"You've been going through Mama's papers?"

"Of course I have! We have to know where we are, don't we? I have five hundred dollars in the bank. That's what's left from selling my house. I've been paying my own expenses, and giving Kay five dollars a week toward rent. That's the situation . . . I offered to use the five hundred to tide us over, but your mother said no. The offer's still open. The way I see it, we're in the same boat. If one of us sinks, we all sink."

Laura tried to imagine the kind of boat they'd all be

in: small, faded, slow, and full of holes. "I'll look at the bills later, Aunt Margaret. I can't think straight right now." She jumped to her feet when Dr. Weston appeared in the doorway. "How's Mama?"

"She's a sick woman, Laura. She'll need a lot of care, a lot of rest. I'd put her in the hospital but I'm afraid it would be too stressful. I know your mother; she'd spend every moment worrying about the expense. We want to *ease* her mind, not give her more worries."

"Yes, Doctor, I understand."

Margaret lifted the coffee pot off the stove and carried it to the table. "I can take care of Kay. Maybe I don't have a little white cap, but I can do as well as any hospital nurse. Lord knows I have the experience."

Dr. Weston sat down. "What experience is that, Margaret?"

Don't get her started, thought Laura, but the flood of words had already begun.

"Family experience," Margaret was saying. "When I was a girl, I nursed my brothers through their chicken pox and measles and mumps. Scarlet fever, too. It was John who had the scarlet fever. That was back in . . ." She frowned, tugging at her ear. "Let's see . . . That was back in '06. Maybe '05. It was winter, because I remember the snow. And then—"

"Excuse me, Aunt Margaret, but could we get back to Mama?" Margaret shrugged and poured the coffee. Laura turned to Dr. Weston. "I heard something about oxygen. Does Mama need oxygen?"

"Not at present. I intend to keep a close eye on her, Laura. If oxygen becomes necessary, I'll make the arrangements." He sipped his coffee. "Her breathing is fairly clear, all things considered. Her fever's down a bit . . . You may go in to see her, but I wouldn't stay too long."

"She'll be all right, won't she?"

"As I said: a lot of care, a lot of rest."

Laura had noticed the split-second hesitation. "But Mama will be all right?"

Dr. Weston put his cup down. He leaned away from the table, pressing his fingertips together. "Sometimes people must *want* to get well," he replied. "And sometimes they must fight. Your mother . . . is tired. Mind and body, body and soul. Tired . . . At your age, that's hard to understand."

"No, it isn't, Doctor. No, it's not hard at all."

"You gave us a scare," said Laura, perching at the side of Kay's bed. "I guess you gave yourself a scare too."

"I forgot to eat lunch. That's all it was."

She clasped her mother's hand. "Dr. Weston says it's pneumonia."

"I know. That's what they say when they can't think of anything else . . . I'm sorry I ruined your day. Margaret was going to bake a special chocolate cake . . . in honor of the occasion. Double chocolate . . . Double chocolate mocha."

"Does it hurt you to talk, Mama?"

"No. My chest is a little sore . . . It's nothing."

Laura didn't believe that. She heard the wheezing sound in the pauses between Kay's words. She saw the hollow cheeks, the empty expression. "Try to sleep, Mama. I'll come back later."

"No, wait. You have to promise . . . not to call Eliza."

"Don't worry about it."

"Promise."

Laura took a breath. "I can't. I just can't. I don't want to upset you, Mama, but it's time for Eliza to come home." Kay pulled her hand away. Laura took another breath and went on. "I'm going to get a job. Everything will be fine. For now, though, Eliza belongs here."

Tears welled in Kay's eyes. "Don't ruin things for her . . . There's no reason. The . . . tuition is paid."

Don't ruin things for Eliza. It seemed to Laura that she'd been hearing those words all her life. Like an unexpected, undeserved slap, the words hurt. She clasped her hands tightly in her lap and thrust out her chin. "I don't want to ruin anything for anybody, Mama. Especially not Eliza. But we're . . . we're in trouble. We can't keep pretending. Look what it's done to you."

"You don't understand." Kay tried to raise herself on her elbows, but after a brief struggle she gave up. What was the use? "It's all been for nothing," she murmured.

"Listen to me," said Laura, drying her mother's eyes. "Everything's going to be fine. That I *do* promise you. But for now, for a little while, there have to be changes. We have to—get caught up with ourselves. And that means Eliza has to come home."

"But what will happen to her?"

Laura's eyes widened. "To Eliza? Oh, Mama, she'll never have to worry about anything. My goodness, not Eliza."

The shadow of a smile flickered at Kay's mouth. "You sound so sure."

"I am. Eliza will marry a rich man and live happily ever after. Just like a fairy tale."

"I hope God is listening," replied Kay. She began to cough. Obediently, she swallowed the medicine Laura held out. "I want both my girls to live happily ever after."

"I'm going to try, Mama."

Laura started to rise but Kay grabbed her arm. "Wait, there's something else. Something I wanted to tell you . . . It seems like such a long time ago . . . But it was only this afternoon."

"What was?"

Kay settled her head on the pillows. "When I saw you outside. It was so sunny; the sun was in your hair . . . I saw—I realized how lovely you are . . . You're a lovely young woman and I . . . I don't think I realized it until today."

For an instant Laura wondered if her mother was teasing. "Do you mean that?" she asked in a wary voice. "I didn't look any different today."

"That's just the point. You looked like you . . . And you're lovely." She reached to the night table and took a sip of water. "Open a window, will you, Laura? It's hot in here."

"It's the fever. Do you want a cold cloth? Or I can soak a cloth in alcohol."

"No, there'll be enough of that when Margaret—" Kay couldn't finish. She was hunched over, coughing and gasping for breath. When the coughing spell passed, she slumped back against the pillows. Her chest was burning. She winced with pain. "Water, Laura."

Laura refilled the glass and put it in her mother's hand. "I'll get Dr. Weston."

Kay turned her head. "Is he still here?"

"Yes. I'll get him. Try to rest."

Laura went quietly from the room. She was frightened for her mother, for herself, but she held off her fears with thoughts of the many things that had to be done. She had to telephone Eliza, and after that, Crossfield's dean of students; maybe she could get some of the tuition money refunded. She had to go through all the bills and talk to all the creditors; maybe she could arrange more time. She had to telephone Robby and tell him what was happening. She had to find a job. "Dear God and President Roosevelt," she whispered, "please let me find a job."

* * *

"I have to find something right away," said Laura the next morning. It was only a day after her graduation but she was back at the Acme Business Institute, sitting in Walter Goodfriend's spacious, cheerful office. The walls were covered with plaques and awards and framed photographs of earlier graduating classes. Classroom manuals bound in bright yellow and red were stacked upon the desk. One of the first Underwood typewriters ever made had pride of place atop a large, square table near the window. "That's the problem," she continued. "Finding something *right away*. My mother is sick, you see. We have bills to pay and . . ." She blushed, ducking her head. "I didn't come here to tell you my troubles. It's just that I was hoping you might know somebody looking for a secretary. Somebody who wouldn't insist on experience . . . I went to an employment agency before I came here, and the man said experience was required. He said employers could afford to be very choosy these days. I thought—I mean I hoped you might have some suggestions." She gazed across the desk at Walter Goodfriend. "I'm sorry for going on and on. I probably shouldn't even have come, but I didn't know what else to do."

"Why, you did exactly the right thing. I'm pleased to assist our former students whenever I can. And I do indeed hear of things from time to time." He adjusted his steel-rimmed spectacles, reaching for a file folder. "You were one of our best students, Miss Bellamy," he said, scanning her records. "Yes, you're well qualified. I'll certainly be glad to recommend you."

"Do you know of any jobs, then?"

He smiled happily. "As luck would have it, there's a secretarial position open at Crawford & Jones. That's a costume company on the West Side. They're willing to accept a beginner. Between you and me, I think they'd prefer it. A matter of lower wages."

Laura's heart was pounding. She inched forward in her chair. "Do you think they'd hire me, Mr. Goodfriend?"

"There's one drawback; the job is part-time. Three days a week: Friday, Saturday, and Monday. You would be paid twelve dollars each Monday."

It wasn't enough, but it was a start. "If I got this job," she said, thinking out loud, "then maybe I could get *another* part-time job for Tuesday, Wednesday, Thursday. That would be all right, wouldn't it?"

"I'm certain it would. Shall I try to arrange an appointment for you?"

"Oh yes, please. I could go over there right now."

"Very well," said Mr. Goodfriend, reaching his hand to the telephone. "If you will wait outside, I'll see what I can do."

Laura was across the room in a flash. She opened the door, closing it softly behind her. Smiling, she held up two twined fingers. "There may be a job. Wouldn't that be wonderful?"

"Wonderful," agreed Mrs. Goodfriend. "Come and sit down," she said, gesturing to the chair beside her desk. "We'll wait together. Is it Crawford & Jones?"

"Yes." Laura took the chair she had been offered. "A costume company, I think. It doesn't matter. I really don't care where I work." She glanced around the office. Like the other, it was crammed with plaques and photographs. "As long as there's a pay day, I don't care."

"You were a clever girl to come to us. Too many of our students forget us the moment they have their diplomas. I don't know why. We're here to help." Eunice Goodfriend, a trim woman with wavy gray hair and a motherly smile, winked at Laura. "We do have our resources, after all. Years of satisfied employers. Years and years. We have a splendid reputation."

"Yes, I know."

They both looked up as the office door opened. "The wheels are in motion," announced Mr. Goodfriend. "I've made an appointment for you at Crawford & Jones. You're expected in half an hour. The person to see is the manager, Sam Roth."

Laura had vaulted out of her chair. Her face was flushed with excitement. "I'm so grateful," she said. "I don't know how to thank you."

"No guarantees, you understand," he replied. "But the situation looks promising."

"And this," added Mrs. Goodfriend, writing an address on a slip of paper, "is where you go. It's a very large building. You can't miss it."

Laura took the paper. "I'll go right now." She glanced from one beaming face to the other. "Thank you. Thank you so much."

"Good luck," said Walter Goodfriend.

"God bless you," said his wife.

Laura rode the subway to Times Square. By day, without benefit of the huge electric signs, the area was almost drab, a collection of movie theaters, burlesque houses, restaurants, dance halls, cut-rate clothing stores, novelty shops, lunch counters, and fruit juice stands garlanded with fake palm leaves. She saw a Salvation Army mission. She saw a man selling "genuine gold watches" for one dollar. She saw a tattoo parlor and, grimacing, she walked quickly on her way. Tonight, when the lights blazed, Times Square would be the Great White Way, a magic place; but now, to Laura's eyes, it was just a little bit shabby, a little bit strange.

She walked to Eighth Avenue and turned north. At Forty-fifth street she saw a block-long building and a sign: Crawford & Jones. She was early, but that, she decided, was better than being late. She went to the front entrance, pushing open the heavy metal door. A blast of cold air startled her. She looked around, blinking in the dim light. "Hello?" she called. "Is anybody here?"

The lobby — a deep, wide, unbroken space — was deserted. To the right were three double-sized elevators; freight elevators, she thought. To the left was a long wooden counter with a printed sign that read OFFICE, 2ND FLOOR. ALL INQUIRIES, 2ND FLOOR. She didn't see a staircase. Gingerly, she stepped into one of the big elevators and pulled the gate closed.

She felt the car shake as it began its ascent. There was a noise like the scraping of chains, and then an abrupt thump when the elevator came to a stop. She opened the gate, stepping into the brighter light of the second floor. "Hello?" she called again. "Mr. Roth?"

There was no one at the front desk. Craning her neck, she saw there was no one in the large, untidy office. Beyond the office was a row of closed doors leading to a corridor. She saw another sign, this one marked with an arrow and the words DRESSING ROOMS. She shrugged. "Mr. Roth, are you here?"

A door slammed. "On my way," called a muffled voice.

Laura spun around. She laughed, for the voice appeared to be coming from a six-foot-tall white rabbit. "Mr. Roth?" she asked as the rabbit drew near.

"Can I help you?"

"I'm Laura Bellamy. From the Acme Business Institute. I was—"

"Oh yes, you're here about the job. This is part of it," he explained, pulling off the rabbit head. "Trying out the new costumes to be sure they're all right."

"Looks like fun."

"You get used to it," said Sam Roth. He was tall and sturdy, with dark eyes and dark hair starting to thin on top. He was a younger man than Laura had expected, perhaps thirty or so. "After a while it's just business," he added, shrugging. "Let's go into the office."

She hid her smile behind her hand as his big rabbit feet clomped across the floor. She followed, thinking how she would describe the scene to Doris and Jane.

"Sit down . . . Laura, is it?"

"Yes, Laura Bellamy." She sat in a cracked leather chair, the only chair not littered with papers and yellow folders. The desk was littered also, as was a long table pushed up against the wall. Soot streaked two wide, uncurtained windows. The file cabinets were oak and brass, relics of another time. "Is this your office, Mr. Roth?"

"I like a lot of clutter," he replied. "And call me Sam; everybody does."

"Sam, then."

He swept some papers off his desk chair and sat down, bouncing around for a moment. "I have to be sure the costumes are comfortable, too."

"Are they?"

"Some are. Not the ones with tails, not for sitting anyway." Sam moved several folders from one side of his desk to the other. "The fingers work," he said, holding out two fuzzy pink thumbs. "But I suppose you want to know about the job. It's part-time; did Mr. Goodfriend tell you that?"

"Yes." Laura nodded. "Three days a week, he said."

"That's right. We get very busy around here. From the looks of the place now, you wouldn't think so, but it's true. I need someone to help Irene, the regular secretary. Typing, filing, invoices; the usual things." He smiled. "And some *un*usual things. You might have to help Burt with the costumes, trying them out or showing them to clients."

"Oh, I'd like that."

"We have a small prop department too," continued Sam. "Stage props. So you might have to do inventories. It all depends on how busy the regular staff is. I'm the manager, by the way. We don't see much of the owners."

Laura wasn't sure what to say. At Acme she had been prepared for formal job interviews, but it was hard to keep a formal tone with a man wearing a rabbit costume. "Is—is there anything you want to know about me? Is there a typing test?"

"We've used Acme girls before. They're always fine. And since you have a recommendation from Goodfriend himself, you're hired."

You're hired. Was it really that simple? Laura's heart skipped a beat. "Do . . . do you mean I can have the job?"

"That's what I mean." He saw the relief in her eyes. He understood it very well. He'd been a young accountant only a couple of years out of school when the stock market crash wiped out his job. For long months afterward, he'd had nothing but occasional day labor to support his wife and infant son. He couldn't forget those desperate times any more than he could forget that Crawford & Jones had saved his family. Now, looking at Laura, he sensed that she also had a family in need of saving. "When would you like to start? Your days would be Friday, Saturday, and Monday."

Laura shifted uneasily in her chair. "Well, you see, my sister's been away and she's coming home this Friday. Would it be all right if I started work on Saturday instead?"

"Sure; one more day won't make a difference. The hours here are eleven to seven. Most of our business is theatrical rentals; theater people prefer the later hours."

"I understand."

"You might come a little early on Saturday so Irene can explain how we do things."

"Oh, I will. I—I want to thank you, Sam. This job

means a lot to me."

He stood, tucking the rabbit head under his arm. "C'mon, I'll show you around. There's time for a tour before we open."

Laura gathered her purse and gloves and followed Sam out. With him she toured the dressing rooms, the fitting rooms, the pressing rooms, and finally the vast, cold rooms where the costumes were stored.

It was an extraordinary collection. Here on display were dragons and dinosaurs; Elizabethan minstrels and King Arthur's knights; witches and wizards and Indian chiefs. Here were military uniforms, ball gowns, wedding gowns, judges' robes, and jockeys' silks. Here was a life-size Humpty Dumpty, before the great fall.

"My sister and I used to play dress-up," said Laura, her eyes wide, "but it was nothing like this. This is wonderful."

Sam peeled off his fuzzy rabbit hands. "After a while, it's all in a day's work."

She turned. In the corner was a mannequin costumed as a stage version of a gypsy woman. She thought about Madame Zarela. Was Sam the man Madame Zarela had "seen"? The dark-haired man stepping out of the shadows? Was her twelve-dollar salary the money Madame Zarela had predicted?

Laura turned away, smiling. Predictions or not, things were starting to look up. She had a job. Her mother seemed a little better. And Eliza was coming home at last. Yes, things were looking up.

"Laura? What are you staring at?"

Her long lashes fluttered. "Oh, I'm sorry. I was daydreaming. I was thinking how pretty my sister would be in that butterfly costume."

"That one? It's very expensive. Pure silk."

She nodded. Only the best for Eliza.

Chapter Five

Heads snapped up as Eliza Bellamy glided through the arched marble hall of Grand Central Terminal. It was rush hour and the terminal was crowded, but paths magically cleared for Eliza and the smiling redcap who followed in her wake. She didn't appear to notice the admiring glances; the men, young and old, who tipped their hats. She kept her eyes focused on the exit signs and never missed a step.

Eliza was every bit as beautiful as she was said to be. From her paternal grandmother she had inherited the rosebud mouth and delicate features of a bisque doll; from her great-grandmother, a mass of silken curls that shimmered like spun gold. From her mother's side of the family had come large violet eyes and flawless skin so fair it was almost translucent. Her smile was her own—a cool, enigmatic smile that quickened men's imaginations.

Eliza made no pretense of modesty. She knew she was beautiful, knew that her beauty had brought her many privileges. She was spoiled, but for that she blamed her parents. They had given her more than they could afford to give, and in return they had expected more than they had a right to expect. A bad bargain, she had always thought.

"This way, please," she said now to the redcap carrying her bags. She turned toward the Lexington Avenue exit. A middle-aged businessman held the door open and she sailed through it. The tiniest frown crossed her brow. Laura had promised to meet the train. Where was Laura? "I suppose you'd better get me a taxi," she said after a moment.

"Yes, miss. Quick as I can."

He left the bags and hurried to the curb. She drew on her gloves, gazing out at the busy street. So many people; so many cars. The terrible noise. She didn't like New York, but still she was glad to be back. *Any*place was better than Crossfield.

"Eliza?"

She heard her name and she looked around. Laura was racing in her direction, one hand holding on to a faded green hat, the other clutching a small black purse. Eliza smiled. As much as she could love anyone, she loved her sister. The two had been close when they were children, allies in a mystifying world of adults. With only eleven months separating them, they had enjoyed the same toys, the same pranks, the same silly, made-up games. It hadn't really been that long ago, yet it seemed like a lifetime.

Now Laura came huffing and puffing up to Eliza. "Sorry I'm late. You probably don't want to hear my excuse."

"Is Mama all right?"

"Oh, she can't wait to see you. She's *so* excited."

"Excuse me, miss," called the redcap, bending over Eliza's luggage. "Taxi's waiting."

"A taxi?" asked Laura. "I thought we could take the bus."

"I don't see how. I have heavy suitcases."

"Well, if we each took one bag—"

"Don't be foolish. The taxi's right here. Come along."

Again, a path cleared for Eliza. She gave the redcap a quarter, and then slipped gracefully into the cab.

Laura climbed in after her. Twenty-five cents, she thought, and we haven't even left the curb.

There was a metallic thud as the driver slammed the trunk shut. He came around the side of the cab and slid behind the wheel. "Where to?"

Laura told him the address. He threw the flag, registering 20¢ on the meter. She frowned. The ride home would cost twice that amount, and then there would have to be a tip.

"I know what you're thinking," said Eliza "But you can stop worrying. I have money."

"You do?"

She nodded, settling back. "I have a few dollars from last month's allowance . . . Just how bad are things at home?"

"Do you mean Mama?"

"I mean money. Do we have any? You didn't say very much in your phone call."

"I was using the Walders' telephone," explained Laura. "Besides, I don't like to talk about personal things on the phone."

"How about in taxicabs?"

She took off her gloves, dropping them in her lap. She glanced at the driver, but his attention was fixed on the snarled traffic. "The truth is things are awful," she said, getting the words out quickly, as if to be rid of them. "There are stacks of bills and no money to pay them."

"*No* money?"

"None. Well, about a hundred dollars, more or less. That's all the cash we have . . . I've got a job, though. I start tomorrow. It's only part-time, but this morning I heard about another part-time job. If I can get that . . . I mean, two part-time jobs put together is like having one, full-time job. Don't you think so?"

Eliza opened her lizard purse and removed a package of cigarettes. She offered the pack to Laura. "Don't look so shocked. Haven't you ever seen cigarettes before?"

"When did you start smoking?"

"Practically the moment I arrived at Crossfield. All the girls there smoke, and at first I wanted to fit in."

"Mama won't like it, you know. Aunt Margaret will have a *fit*."

Eliza struck a match and held it to her cigarette. "Aunt Margaret is a fine one to complain. Is she still eating yeast?"

"She has her little quirks. They're harmless."

"Yes, I suppose they are." Eliza blew a perfect smoke ring. She watched it drift toward the window and break apart into tiny bluish wisps. The taxi lurched suddenly, shooting across the street just as the light changed. "You weren't exaggerating, were you, Laura? About the money situation?"

"No, I'm afraid not . . . But we may be getting some money back from your school. I couldn't get through to the Dean, but I spoke to the registrar's office. We can't get any of the fees back; that's definite. We may get as much as half the tuition back. Or at least the tuition for the spring semester."

Eliza considered this for a moment. "That money would actually be mine, then, wouldn't it?"

"Yours?"

"Well, it's my tuition money, so it would be mine."

Laura wasn't entirely surprised by her sister's remark but she was angered by it. She reminded herself that Eliza couldn't help seeing things from only one point of view. Granted, it was a selfish point of view, but what else could it be after eighteen years of pampering? "The money belongs to all of us," she said, staring straight ahead. "To the family. That's the way we have to think about any money that comes into the house. We're in this together, Eliza."

"In what?"

"The Depression. I guess the girls at Crossfield don't have to worry about a little thing like the Depression."

Eliza brushed a speck of cigarette ash from the sleeve of her lavender wool coat. "Now you're upset."

"There are a lot of problems. I don't know if you can understand. I *hope* you can, because everything's changed. Everything. It's going to be hard for you." She cranked down her window and took a gulp of cold November air. She continued, "There won't be any more charge accounts, Eliza, any more new clothes. You won't have an allowance . . . It's going to be very hard."

"I see."

Laura's brow wrinkled. "Is that all you have to say?"

"What do you want me to say?"

She shrugged. "I don't know. Something."

"Have we lost our apartment?"

"No, the rent's paid up, thank heavens. But we've lost some of our furniture. The repossessors came for the dining room set. It broke Mama's heart."

Eliza stubbed out her cigarette. "We must be the talk of the building."

"There are other people in the same boat. It's not just us. Some people are much worse off than we are."

"And some people are managing quite well."

Laura sighed. "I guess it has to do with luck. Aunt Margaret says there's never been a lucky Bellamy."

"Do you believe her?"

"I . . . believe hard times can't last forever. Things will get better, but until that happens . . . We'll just have to live like misers, watching every penny."

Eliza looked faintly amused. "Is that what you've decided?"

The taxi seemed to be getting smaller. For a moment Laura felt as if she couldn't breathe. She bent her head to the window and took another gulp of cold air. "You're making fun of me," she said in a quiet voice.

"You think I'm sticking my nose in where it doesn't belong."

"No, but this is a new side of you. Setting rules, saying what we can and can't do; that's a whole new side. Frankly, I couldn't care less."

Laura stared at her sister's exquisite profile. "What do you mean?"

"I'm not good at dealing with problems. Obviously, you are. That's fine. All I want is to be left alone."

"You're part of the family, Eliza."

"Like it or not."

"Is that supposed to be funny?"

"It's not supposed to be anything Laura. Just an offhand remark. Why are you in such a grumpy mood today? I thought you'd be glad to see me."

"I am." She gazed out the window, remembering how she had looked forward to Eliza's homecoming. She *was* glad to see her, and yet she felt a nagging resentment. Had she expected more sympathy? More concern? She sighed again. Sympathy and concern weren't things anyone ought to expect from Eliza. "You're right," she said. "I'm in a grumpy mood today."

The taxi came to a smooth stop in front of the apartment building. The meter clicked off. Eliza fished three quarters out of a tiny lizard coin purse and gave them to the driver. "Keep the change," she said with a graceful wave of her hand.

Keep the change? Laura could only shake her head in wonder. We live in two different worlds, she thought. In my world, we walk or take the bus. In Eliza's world, we take a taxicab and the driver keeps the change.

She opened the door and stepped onto the sidewalk. "I'll go in and ring for the elevator while you get your bags . . . Here comes Eugene; he'll carry them up."

"Yes, that's fine."

"Eliza . . . be nice to Mama."

"Aren't you silly! Of course I'll be nice to Mama. I even brought her a present."

"A present?"

"It's darling. It isn't anything much, but it's darling."

It was an old-fashioned sachet made of lace and long satin ribbons. Kay loved it, as she would any present given to her by her firstborn. "It's beautiful," she said, smiling at Eliza. "So delicate. I'll keep it close beside me on the night table."

"How are you feeling, Mama?"

"Oh, I'm much better." Kay, was sitting up in bed, three feather pillows stuffed behind her back, the blankets drawn to her waist. The room was comfortably warm; bowls of water nestled atop the hissing radiator, adding moisture to the air. It was early evening, almost time for her medicine. "Dr. Weston is still fussing, but I'm better."

Eliza wondered about that. She thought her mother looked horrible—white and thin and frail. She saw the unnatural brightness in her mother's eyes; a feverish brightness, she was sure. "Are you doing what the doctor says? Following his orders and all that?"

"With Margaret around, I don't have any choice. She's in here a hundred times a day . . . But this is a boring subject. I'm so tired of sickness and . . ." Kay's voice trailed away as she felt a sharp pain between her ribs. It was the same pain she'd felt just a few hours ago, though she hadn't dared tell Dr. Weston. He'd warned her not to exert herself, but in her weakened condition *everything* was an exertion: walking across the room, brushing her hair, talking with Eliza. "Could you . . . pour me some water?"

"Are you all right?"

"I'd like some water."

Eliza rose. She took the pitcher from the night table and filled her mother's glass. "What about all this medicine?" she asked, peering at the array of vials and bottles. "Shouldn't you be taking your medicine?"

"Not now. Margaret knows when it's time." Kay swallowed the water, then eased back against the pillows. "She has me on a strict schedule."

Eliza returned the glass to the night table. "Yes, she told me not to stay too long. You should be resting."

"Don't go yet. We have things to talk about. Crossfield . . . I'm so sorry you had to leave Crossfield."

"I'm not. I wasn't happy there, Mama."

"But you were meeting the right people."

Eliza blinked her eyes slowly, like a cat. It was true that Crossfield abounded with "the right people"; it was also true that she'd never been accepted as one of them. She'd been an outsider, distrusted by some because of her beauty, excluded by others because she didn't ride or play tennis, shunned by a few because her family were "nobodies." She'd had no friends, only a couple of casual acquaintances who were always borrowing her clothes. She hadn't had a single invitation.

Now, glimpsing her reflection in Kay's mirror, she smoothed a stray curl. "New York is filled with the right people, Mama."

"But how will you meet them? We don't travel in those circles."

"Things will work out. They usually do."

That languid reply was typical of Eliza, but it did nothing to lessen Kay's anxieties. All her plans for Eliza had been ruined, and she had only herself to blame. "I've made a mess of everything . . . I wanted you to have your chance. I tried . . . but I wasn't strong enough."

"I don't think it's your fault," said Eliza in her light, nearly uninflected voice. "Papa shouldn't have died."

Papa shouldn't have died. There was silence as Kay digested the words. Was Eliza blaming her father for dying? "Eliza," she began, but she felt too tired to go on. Suddenly she felt exhausted.

"Anyway, it's all in the past."

"You shouldn't dwell on the past," said Margaret, carrying a supper tray into the room. She set it atop the dresser and walked to Kay's bedside. "Your fever's up again," she declared, feeling Kay's brow. "What have you been doing?"

"Nothing."

"We were just talking, Aunt Margaret."

"Well, there's been enough talk for now. Save some for later." She looked at Kay, looked at Eliza. "I have things to do here. Go help your sister in the kitchen."

"The kitchen?"

Margaret sighed. "It's at the end of the hall. The room with the icebox and the stove."

If Eliza noticed the sarcasm, she gave no sign. "I'm not good at kitchen things, but I'll set the table."

"It's her first night home, Margaret," said Kay. "Why do you have her doing chores?"

"Chores! Is setting a table what you call *chores?* Why, when *I* was a girl, I was busy morning 'til night."

"It's not the same," insisted Kay. The rest of her argument was lost to a coughing spell that hunched her shoulders and brought tears to her eyes. She was wheezing, gasping for breath. Margaret was pounding on her back. "All right," she said when the cough stopped. "I'm all right now."

"I'll be the judge of that," replied Margaret, her mouth tight with worry. "First comes your medicine, then your supper, then a sponge bath, and then I'll see about calling the doctor. And don't tell me you don't need the doctor. I'll decide what you need." She glanced up. Eliza was standing near the door, examining a fingernail. "You can stay and help, missy, or you can go make yourself useful in the kitchen."

91

"I was just waiting to see if you'd changed your mind."

"Changed my mind? Why would I?"

"I don't know," said Eliza, drifting out of the room. "People do."

Margaret's voice followed her into the hall but she paid no attention. Talk, talk, talk; that was Margaret. And who could take Margaret seriously? Who cared about a cranky, silly old maid?

Laura turned as Eliza entered the kitchen. "Why aren't you with Mama?"

"Aunt Margaret's with her now. I'm supposed to set the table . . . But I see it's already set." She pulled out a chair and sat down. "Same boring place. I feel as if I've never been away."

Laura frowned. "It's hardly the same. All these awful things have been happening. Mama losing her job and getting sick . . . How does Mama look to you?"

"Very sick. Shouldn't she be in the hospital?"

"Dr. Weston's tried, but Mama refuses to go." Laura took the beet salad from the icebox and carried it to the table. "Aren't you worried, Eliza?"

"Worried?"

"About *Mama*."

"I love Mama too, Laura. I just don't feel as close to her as you do. I never did, not even when we were children."

"You've always been her pride and joy."

Eliza folded her hands in her silken lap. "I can't help that, can I? I didn't ask to be *any*one's pride and joy. I meant what I said to you before; I just want to be left alone."

Laura brought the macaroni and cheese to the table. She saw Eliza's nose wrinkle and she laughed. "We're having the regular Friday menu," she acknowledged, taking the chair opposite her sister. "Sorry."

"I'd forgotten about Aunt Margaret's menus."

"They haven't changed."

"So I see." Eliza felt Laura's eyes on her. She looked up. "You're staring."

"I was thinking I don't believe what you said before. You may not want people bothering you, but you don't really want to be left alone. I mean, you don't want to be a hermit, for goodness' sake. You don't want to spend your life shut away from the world."

"No."

"No. I didn't think so."

"I want to spend my life with a husband who'll take care of me." It was a simple statement of fact. Eliza worried about very few things, but certainly she had worried about ending up like her mother—scared and broken and poor. That could happen if a girl married for love. It was wiser to marry for security, she'd decided; love could come later. "I do need someone to take care of me, Laura. I wouldn't know how to earn my living, and I wouldn't want to."

"You'd make a wonderful model. You could be the Woodbury soap girl; the girl with 'the skin you love to touch.' "

Eliza's violet eyes darkened. "No, I'd hate that. I'd be miserable all the time. I'd be miserable doing any sort of work, but especially that sort . . . Marriage is the answer for me, and soon."

Laura smiled. "Have you anybody in mind? How about the Prince of Wales? You're much prettier than his friend Mrs. Simpson. Much younger, too."

"Now who's making fun?"

"Sorry."

"I don't want a prince, Laura. I don't want anybody special. Just a man who'll fix things so I have no worries . . . He doesn't even have to be rich."

Laughter flowed from Laura. "Being rich *is* the only way to have no worries."

"It's Mama who dreams about Vanderbilts and

Rockefellers. I can have the life I want on a lot less." She sat back, twirling a golden curl around her finger. "I know exactly what I want, you see. Most people don't."

"As Aunt Margaret says, wanting and getting are two different things . . . But in your case, I think you'll get whatever you want with no trouble at all. I guess you just have to find a place to start."

"I know where to start. Do you remember Amy Remington?"

Laura nodded. Amy Remington was Eliza's closest friend, and considering all the girls who were jealous of Eliza, Amy was perhaps her only genuine friend. "She's very nice."

"She's engaged now. And every Sunday her fiancé has a cocktail party at his flat in Gramercy Park. Amy says there are loads of eligible men. I'll see for myself this Sunday . . . Maybe you should come along."

"Oh no, I've found the man I want. Robby's the one for me. Now that you're home, I hope you'll get to know him better. He's wonderful!"

"Isn't he at Yale?" asked Eliza, stifling a yawn. "Or is it Princeton?"

"Yale, but he comes home some weekends. Oh, that reminds me. I'm supposed to go out with Robby tonight. We made the date before I knew you'd be here. I don't know what to do."

"Keep your date. That's what I'd do."

"I start my job tomorrow, so if I don't see Robby tonight, I might not see him at all."

"You needn't go on about it, Laura. I don't care one way or the other."

"I just thought, since it's your first night home . . ."

Eliza smiled. "You're so sentimental. First night, last night; what does it matter? Besides, I have to unpack tonight. The clothes I brought with me are the only clothes I'll have until my trunks are delivered."

"Well, I guess that puts me in my place."

"You're upset again. You're angry."

"I'm not upset." Laura looked into her sister's wide, untroubled eyes. The eyes of a child, she thought, shaking her head. "And I'm not angry." Who could stay angry at Eliza?

"She didn't even ask about my job," said Laura to Robby, "but that's the way she is. I really shouldn't let it bother me. Eliza is Eliza. She's not going to change."

He took her arm as they crossed the street. "Forget about Eliza. The more *I* hear about your job, the more I don't like it. Why must you work on weekends?"

"Not the whole weekend. Not Sunday."

"That doesn't help any. From now on, I'll be spending Sundays in New Haven. I have to, with exams coming up. Dad doesn't expect much, but he ought to get something for his money. If I crack the books, I think I can pull out a C."

"A gentlemen's C," said Laura, smiling.

"Dad would be happy with that. He never went to college, you know. He gets a kick out of my being at Yale." Robby admired his father. Mike Collier was self-made, a shrewd businessman who'd parlayed one battered delivery truck into a thriving trucking company, and who'd then sold it all to buy four radio stations. Two of the stations had been lost in the early days of the Depression, but two remained: one in New York, the other in Philadelphia. "And it's the least I can do for him," continued Robby. "So there go my Sundays. My Sundays and your Saturdays; that doesn't leave us any time."

"It's only temporary . . . No matter what, we'll have Friday nights."

They stopped at another traffic light. Robby turned Laura to him and took her into his arms. "If you worked for my father—"

"No, Robby, I have to do this on my own . . . It won't be so bad," she added, "exams don't last forever. I won't have this job forever . . . Robby, I just need some time to start getting things straightened out at home."

"Why does it have to be you?"

Laura smiled up at him. "Who else is there? Mama's sick. Nobody's going to give Aunt Margaret a job. And Eliza—well, Eliza's gorgeous but not very useful."

"A girl after my own heart."

Laura chuckled, playfully poking Robby's chest. "What's that supposed to mean?"

"I wish *you* weren't so useful. Darn it, Laura, a fellow doesn't like his girl to be too clever."

"Oh, you have no worries on that account. I'm an ordinary kind of girl. Not too clever, not too dumb. Ordinary."

The light changed but Robby didn't move. He gazed at Laura, thinking she wasn't ordinary by any means. She had a spark, a strength that was missing from the other girls he knew. She challenged him, yes, and that was exciting. She was smart, and that enlarged his image of himself. She was pretty; there were certain times, certain moods, when he thought she was beautiful.

His parents liked her. His father might have wished that the Bellamys had some money, and his mother might have wished that Laura's blood were the proper shade of blue, but all in all his parents liked her. Everything was right, and yet he was uneasy. At first he had been amused by Laura's independent streak; lately, he had begun to feel she carried independence too far. He wished she had come to him with her problems. That's the way it should be, he told himself: a fellow taking care of things for his girl.

"You're a million miles away," said Laura now.

"What are you thinking?"

He kissed her. "Does that answer your question?"

"You make me so happy, Robby." Tears misted her eyes as she snuggled her chin on his shoulder. She wanted to remember this moment, this perfect moment with cars speeding past and lights twinkling in windows and just a sliver of moon in the sky. She closed her eyes. When she opened them, she saw the indulgent smiles of an older couple who were waiting to cross the street. "We're putting on quite a show," she murmured.

"I know." His arms dropped away but he caught her hand and held it tightly. "You won't change your mind about your job?"

"I can't. Please try to understand."

Robby sighed. "Then I'm left with two matinee tickets for tomorrow. I told you I was going to get tickets for that new musical, *Boy and Girl*."

"I had an idea," replied Laura as they continued on their away. "I thought maybe you could take Eliza."

"Eliza! Why would I want to do that?"

"Why not? You won't go alone, and it's silly to waste the tickets. *And* I don't want you asking any of the girls who've set their caps for you. That's probably half the girls in New York."

"Would you be jealous?"

"*Yes*," she cried, squeezing his hand. "I'd be pea green. There's no telling what I'd do. Go after the girl with a hatchet, maybe. Oh, it wouldn't be nice to see."

They were both laughing. Now that the tension had gone, they were both having a fine time. "You're a little crazy," said Robby, steering Laura around a corner. "Do you know that?

She smiled. Girls in love were supposed to be a little crazy. "If I am," she said, "you'd better humor me. Take Eliza to the matinee."

"Why?"

"I want the two of you to be friends, Robby. This is a nice way to start. It's hard to get Eliza to do things, but she likes going to the theater, especially to musicals. This is perfect."

"It doesn't sound so perfect."

"Oh, you'll have a wonderful time. Even if you don't, you'll still be out with a *gorgeous* girl."

Robby laughed. "Okay, okay, I give up. I'll take Eliza to the show. Think of us while you're slaving away at your costume company."

"Poor me."

"Well, you know what they say: God pity the poor working girl."

A steady rain was falling as Laura went off to work the next morning. Beneath her dark coat was the latest of Eliza's hand-me-downs: a long-sleeved black wool dress with a scalloped white collar and cuffs. She wore Robby's locket, and Kay's tiny pearl earrings "for luck." Resting uncertainly in her stomach was the huge breakfast Margaret had insisted she eat "for strength."

She was very nervous. She walked right by her subway station and had to go back. She dropped her nickel near the turnstile and had to chase after it. When the No. 6 train finally rumbled along the platform, she sprinted toward it, bumping her head as she darted through the door. It was a relief to find a seat and sit down.

Laura chose to sit at the empty end of the subway car. Using her lap for a keyboard, she practiced her typing exercises all the way to Grand Central, where she changed trains. From Grand Central to Times Square, she practiced her shorthand symbols. By the time she walked into the cold, drafty lobby of Crawford & Jones, she felt ready to begin.

Irene Golding was Laura's guide to office files and

office procedures. She was a thin, fast-talking woman of thirty; the first peroxide blonde and the first divorcee Laura had ever met. "You catch on pretty quick," Irene assured her eager charge before the morning was over. "You'll do fine, kid."

Burt Rigby was Laura's guide to costumes and props. Short, stocky, a tape measure dangling around his neck and a frown etched into his brow, he took pleasure calling himself an old-timer. "I got some great Broadway stories," he declared to his captive audience of one. "Stories from way back, you know? People keep telling me I should write a book. What do you think about that, girlie?"

But Laura scarcely had time to think during her first day at work. As Sam had warned, Crawford & Jones was a busy place. Telephones never seemed to stop ringing. Messengers came and went in a constant stream. Clients crowded around the front desk, waiting for help. They were a varied group: stylists from photographer's studios, theatrical producers, artists, society women planning a costume ball, and even a private school headmaster in search of costumes for the Thanksgiving pageant.

It was three o'clock before Laura was able to stop for lunch — a cheese and pickle sandwich she'd brought from home and a cup of Irene's strong black coffee. Ten minutes later she was back at work. She typed invoices, checked inventory sheets, filed two weeks' worth of correspondence, and helped out at the front desk. Late in the afternoon she typed dozens of packing labels, entering their numbers in the logbook. At closing time, she helped Burt drape the mannequins and the wide metal racks.

She was the last to leave, crossing paths with the incoming night watchman. She was tired and yet she felt oddly exhilarated, the way she'd felt at school whenever she'd passed a test. But this was better than school, she thought, walking to the subway station; this was real life. She was a wage earner now, a grown-up. Strange, what a difference a day could make.

Laura thought about her day during the ride home. Work wasn't supposed to be fun, but she had enjoyed herself. She liked Irene and Burt and the others. She liked the parade of costumes to the fitting rooms. Most of all, she decided, she liked the feeling of accomplishment. She had done a day's work and she would get a day's pay; it was a good feeling. Would Robby understand? No, probably not.

Her thoughts settled on Robby as she climbed the subway stairs to the street. The matinee would have ended two hours ago or more. She hoped she hadn't been wrong in asking Robby to take Eliza. She wanted them to be friends, wanted some sense of family among the people she loved, but now she wondered if she were expecting too much. Eliza could be so distant. Robby could be so glib. What if they'd had a terrible time?

Rain had started falling again. Laura opened her umbrella and quickened her step. She turned the corner, struggling against a sudden gust of wind. Her hat lifted off her head. She squashed it down, shut her umbrella, and ran the rest of the way home.

"Good evening, miss," said Eugene, holding the door open. "Nasty weather we're having."

Laura agreed. Water was dripping from her hat, from her sleeves. She crossed into the lobby and shook herself like a dog. "Oh, hello, Mrs. Austin," she said to her upstairs neighbor. "I'm sorry, I didn't mean to splash you."

Mrs. Austin, a white-haired widow round as a dumpling, twinkled at Laura. "No harm done. Don't give it a thought." She rang for the elevator, pressing the button twice to make sure. "How is your dear mother?"

"Getting better, thank you. It was pneumonia."

"Yes." Mrs. Austin's smile wavered. "I was so sorry to hear about it. I'm afraid I haven't been a very good neighbor. Perhaps I can atone with some of my chocolate pie. Does your mother care for chocolate pie?"

"Mama loves anything chocolate." The elevator came and Laura followed her neighbor into the car. "Hello, Jimmy. Do you know if my sister's home?"

"I saw her about an hour ago."

"Is Eliza home from school?" asked Mrs. Austin.

"Yes. She'll be here for a while."

"How nice for you."

I hope so, thought Laura. The elevator stopped at the tenth floor. " 'Bye, Mrs. Austin. I'll tell Mama you said hello."

She passed through the hall, digging in her purse for her latchkey. She unlocked the door and went inside. The foyer light was on, but the apartment felt strangely empty. She started to call out, then changed her mind. She dropped her umbrella in the brass stand, hung her wet things on the hook, and walked off to her mother's room.

Kay was asleep, her dark hair strewn across the pillow. Her hand was pressed to her cheek. Her chest moved up and down in raspy but even breaths. Laura listened for a moment before softly closing the door. She took a few steps and stopped. There were muffled voices coming from the living room. No, not voices, she thought; the radio. She turned, following the sound.

Eliza was curled on the sofa, her head bent over the latest issue of *Vogue*. The radio was playing; a comedy program, judging by the bursts of laughter from the audience.

"Here you are," said Laura, plopping into the flowered wing chair. "I was beginning to wonder where everyone was."

"Aunt Margaret went to the Wesleys for mah-jongg. She left a plate for you in the icebox—that terrible hash she makes on Saturdays."

Laura smiled. "It's a hash of all the week's leftovers."

"Dreadful, whatever it is."

Laura kicked off her shoes and tucked her legs beneath her. "Well? Aren't you going to tell me? I'm *dying* of curiosity."

There was a faint shrug, just a whisper of silk. "Do you mean about today?"

"Yes, of course! Did you have a good time? Did you and Robby get along?"

"The play wasn't much."

"Never mind the play," said Laura with an expectant smile. "You and Robby finally had some time together. Tell me what you think about *Robby*."

Eliza put the magazine aside. She looked at Laura and a shadow seemed to brush her face. "He's all right. He has lovely manners, hasn't he?"

"But what do you think of *him?*"

"I've already told you: I think he's all right. He's fine . . . But if you really want to know, I don't think he's for you."

The only sound in the room was the laughter coming from the radio. Laura rose abruptly and shut it off. Her face had lost the look of expectation, of pleasure. "Why would you say a thing like that? Anyway, you're wrong."

Eliza picked up her magazine, idly turning the pages. "Today was your idea, not mine."

"Why would you say that about Robby and me? I love him, you know."

She turned another page. "Love is a foolish reason to do anything."

"Oh, Eliza, you're impossible! Where do you get these notions of yours?" She wheeled around. "My goodness, you didn't tell Robby what you think?" she asked, alarmed.

"No. After the theater we stopped for hot chocolate, and mostly he talked about Yale."

"And then what?"

"Then he dropped me off downstairs and took the cab to Grand Central. I'm sure he's back in New Haven by now."

"Thank heaven for that!"

Eliza looked up. "I've been home two days and you've done nothing but snap at me."

"That's not . . ." Laura sighed, turning away. "Yes, you're right," she quietly agreed. She turned to the window and stared out at the rain. Something was wrong but she didn't know what. It was something she felt, or sensed, like an undercurrent. She'd been short tempered the last two days, pouncing on Eliza's every word, but she didn't know why. Eliza hasn't changed, she thought to herself, so it must be me. "I'm sorry," she said, sitting down again. "I guess it's all the worries. There's so much on my mind."

Laura paused. A moment passed in silence. "Maybe," she wearily continued, "I've been hoping you'd offer to help."

"Help?" Eliza's long lashes fluttered. "Don't be silly. How could I possibly help? You're the one who knows how to do things, Laura. You went out and got a job, didn't you?"

"Yes."

"Well, there you are."

Where? wondered Laura, though she couldn't help smiling. "I wish I were like you, Eliza . . . You never worry, do you?"

"Life goes on."

Laura was about to reply when the sudden sharp ring of an alarm clock made her jump. "What's that?"

"Aunt Margaret didn't trust me to remember Mama's medicine. She set the clock. But since you're here now—"

"Oh no," said Laura, smiling slightly and shaking her head. "Mama's medicine is the least you can do . . . So go do it!"

"All right." Eliza closed her magazine. In one fluid motion she uncurled herself and rose from the sofa. There was a rustle of silk as she glided to the door. "Are you over your bad mood now?"

"No more bad moods," said Laura, lifting her eyes to her sister. "I swear."

Chapter Six

Laura was too busy to ponder her moods—bad or good—in the weeks that followed. She found a second job at the New Look Upholstery Company, and a third job taking tickets at the neighborhood movie theater. As Thanksgiving approached, she was working seven days out of seven, earning a total of twenty-eight dollars a week.

She hoarded the money like a miser, putting it into little envelopes marked for rent, groceries, electricity, medicine, insurance, doctor, debts, and miscellaneous. She allowed herself two dollars a week, but she rarely spent that much. She allowed Eliza the same amount, but it was never enough.

There were some days when money was all Laura could think about, days when she looked at her little envelopes, looked at the unpaid bills, and felt panic grab her by the throat. The money her mother had hidden away was gone now. The three-hundred-dollar refund from Crossfield was gone also, used to pay the repossessors when they'd come for the living room furniture. She still wondered if that had been the right thing to do. On her worst days, she thought she should have kept the money and let them take the furniture. Who needed furniture when the sky was falling in?

There were too many decisions, and too often she

felt she had nowhere to turn. In the past, she'd shared her worries with Jane and Doris, but lately, running from job to job, she'd had scant time for her friends. They were busy as well: Doris studying for exams, Jane starting work at a cosmetics company. Laura remembered a time when they'd called themselves the Three Musketeers. It was a time she had already begun to think of as the good old days.

If she hadn't seen much of her friends, she'd seen even less of Robby. He'd been spending his weekends in New Haven, preparing for exams—or at least that was the reason he'd given her. She believed it was the truth, but only part of the truth; the other part was his displeasure with all her jobs. "I wish you'd let Dad take care of things," he'd written in one of his letters. But she couldn't, and he couldn't understand why.

Kay understood. She'd raised her girls the way she had been raised: never to accept charity. Gifts were all right in certain circumstances, and it was all right for family members to help each other, but charity was never all right. She was glad Laura had rejected Robby's offer. It was a sign of character.

Not that she doubted Laura's character. During Kay's long recuperation, she'd had nothing to do but observe her family. Perhaps for the first time, she'd seen them as they actually were; warts and all, as Margaret would have said. She had been surprised by the depth of Laura's determination, and a little troubled by it too. There was strength in Laura's character, but where was the joy?

Kay had been far more troubled by Eliza. In her elder daughter she'd seen grace, beauty, and an almost stunning selfishness. Kay had tried to pretend it didn't matter, but of course she knew it mattered quite a lot. Worse, she knew it was her fault. She'd indulged Eliza for eighteen years, and always at

Laura's expense. She wanted to apologize to Laura, to somehow put things right, but she couldn't. She couldn't bring herself to criticize Eliza, even indirectly. Laura was the willing and devoted daughter any mother might have wished for, but Eliza was still the daughter of her heart.

There was no apology, no soul-searching conversation between Kay and Laura. Days rushed by and life in the Bellamy household continued as before: Eliza went to parties with her friend Amy Remington; Laura went to work.

Now, rising early on Thanksgiving morning, Laura smiled at the thought of three whole days off. Three days without typewriters and jangling telephones and subway trains; it was like a gift. She put on her robe, slid her feet into her slippers. She glanced at Eliza, asleep in the other bed, and then walked quietly to the window.

It was a fine morning—bright and breezy, with just a hint of winter in the air. Traffic on Lexington Avenue was sparse, and only a handful of people were about. Laura saw a man buying a paper at the newsstand, a woman trying to hail a taxi, another woman carrying a yellow chrysanthemum plant, and two young boys romping with a very large, very shaggy black dog.

"What time is it?"

The sleepy voice belonged to Eliza. Laura turned. "Nearly seven . . . Where do you suppose a woman would get a chrysanthemum plant at seven o'clock in the morning?"

"This is New York," replied Eliza. She rolled over on her stomach, straightened the pillow, and went back to sleep.

Laura smiled. Her gaze moved again to the boys and their dog, but after a moment she left the window. She left the room, softly closing the door. In the hall was the wonderful aroma of freshly brewed coffee. She followed her nose to the kitchen.

Margaret, wearing a clean white apron over her green print "holiday" dress, greeted Laura with a smile. "Happy Thanksgiving. I thought you'd sleep in this morning. You've earned it."

"I don't want to waste my holiday sleeping."

"Big plans, eh?"

"Oh yes," said Laura, sitting down at the table. "First I'm going to the parade with Doris and Jane. Then I'm coming back here for turkey dinner . . . And then tonight, I'm going to see Robby."

Margaret poured two cups of coffee. "Your eyes sparkle when you say his name. Did you know that?"

"It's love."

"Is it? Well, maybe it is." Margaret brought the cups to the table. She pulled out a chair. "Maybe it is. For what it's worth."

"Aunt Margaret, you're terrible!" cried Laura, pursing her lips in a smile. "What's worth more than love?"

"I wonder if you'll ask me that question ten years from now."

"You're a cynic."

"If I am, I have my reasons. Wilbur Hobart, for one." Margaret spooned sugar into her coffee. "It's not good to go around with your head in the clouds, Laura. If that makes me a cynic, so be it. There are worse things."

"Can't we just relax and enjoy Thanksgiving? I'm feeling kind of thankful, even if you're not. There's money coming into the house now. And Mama's so much better." Laura saw her aunt's quick frown. "Mama *is* better."

"I didn't say otherwise."

"No, you didn't *say*, Aunt Margaret, but you don't look convinced."

108

Margaret sipped her coffee, staring at Laura over the rim of the cup. "Maybe somebody could tell me why Kay still has that bad cough."

"Dr. Weston explained—"

"Doctors are all the same. They talk and talk and they don't say anything. It's no secret Kay still has a touch of pneumonia. The question is *why*. But all I hear from Dr. Weston is more talk about how hard pneumonia is to treat, how long it takes."

"It's the truth."

"It's doctor talk."

Laura shook her head. "The important thing is that Mama's getting better. Her breathing is clearer. She has her appetite back. She *looks* so much better."

"Well, I can't argue with that. Kay's starting to look like herself again . . . If only she could get rid of her cough."

"Those potions of yours are bound to work sooner or later."

"Laugh if you want, but people have been using herbs since the world began."

Laura finished her coffee. "I wasn't laughing, Aunt Margaret. It's just that I feel so good today. So happy. Don't spoil it for me. Please?"

"What a thing to say! When did I ever spoil anything for you? Tell me when."

"Oh, Aunt Margaret, you know what I mean. Let's try to go just one day without talking about our problems."

"That won't leave us much to talk about, then," replied Margaret, smiling at her little joke. She stood, rolling back her sleeves. "What do you want for breakfast? There's oatmeal and there's Post Toasties. You can't have eggs. I have only two left and I'll need them for my maple cake. It wouldn't be Thanksgiving dinner without maple cake."

Laura stretched her arms lazily above her head.

"I'll just have toast. Is there any jam?"

"I'm not buying any more jam. It's too expensive."

"Toast and butter, then. But first I'll bring Mama some coffee. She's probably up by now."

Margaret took the coffee pot from the stove and filled another cup. "Don't spill it. And don't be long. You can help me get the turkey into the oven. It's sixteen pounds, you know."

"Sixteen pounds! Why in the world would you buy a sixteen-pound turkey?"

"For the leftovers of course. Besides, it was a bargain price. Twenty cents a pound at Schultz's butcher shop."

"We'll be eating turkey till Christmas."

"At least we'll be eating. Count your blessings, missy. Count your blessings."

Laura smiled. "We'll, this is the right day for it."

"Don't be smart. And don't sit there like a lump. Take the coffee in to Kay while it's still fit to drink. Go on now. It's time to start the morning!"

Laura knocked at Kay's door and went inside. "Mama, are you awake? Aunt Margaret says it's time to . . ." Her voice faded, and her smile. For a moment she stood frozen in place, staring at the tousled figure in the bed. Something was wrong here; she knew something was wrong. "Mama?" Coffee sloshed over the side of the cup as she slammed it down on the night table. "Mama!"

The blankets lay tangled at the foot of the bed. Kay was soaked with perspiration, her flannel nightgown clinging to her wet skin, her hair drooping on her brow. Her chest rose and fell in short, shuddering fits. Her lungs strained for breath, and from them came a raspy sound that ended in a thin, high-pitched whistle.

Laura couldn't wake her. "Mama," she cried, shaking Kay's shoulders. "Mama, open your eyes . . . Mama . . . Mama, open your eyes!" But Kay didn't respond. Frantically, Laura slapped her wrists, her face. *"Mama,"* she shouted again and again. "Wake up, Mama! Wake up now! . . . *Mama!"*

Her shouts were loud enough to bring Margaret—and even Eliza—into the room. Eliza hung back, but Margaret rushed past her. "Have you gone crazy, Laura Bellamy? Screaming like a banshee? What's—"

"Mama won't wake up."

Margaret's hand went to her throat. She'd heard the plea in Laura's voice, the fear. Frowning, she pushed her niece aside and bent over Kay. "Are you playing games?" But one look told her this was no game. "You'd better telephone for an ambulance, Laura. And be quick about it."

An ambulance? Papa died in an ambulance. "No, I'll get the doctor."

"I don't know where you'd find Dr. Weston on Thanksgiving. Call the ambulance."

"No, not Dr. Weston," said Laura, rushing out of the room. "I'll get Dr. Cobb upstairs."

"Upstairs?" Margaret shook her head. "You can't go upstairs like that," she called after Laura. "Put some clothes on . . . Do you hear me?"

Laura heard, but she was already racing toward the front door. She flung it open and flung herself into the hall. Across the way, her middle-aged neighbor Mr. Snyder, also in his bathrobe, was just leaning down to collect the newspaper from the mat. "Good morning," she said, streaking past him to the service stairs.

She hitched up her robe and took the stairs two at a time. When she reached the twelfth floor, she had to stop at each apartment to read the engraved nameplate affixed below the bell. R. A. Cobb was at the end of the hall.

She drew a breath, swiping at her uncombed hair. She drew another breath and rang the bell. No one answered. Finally she pressed her finger to the bell and kept it there.

"Yes?" The voice was female, coated with the impatience of early morning. "Yes, who is it?"

"Laura Bellamy, Mrs. Cobb. I'm your neighbor from the tenth floor. I—I need Dr. Cobb. My mother's very sick."

A chain slid back. The door opened a half inch. "Who did you say you were?"

"Laura Bellamy. From the tenth floor? My mother's very sick, Mrs. Cobb. I'm sorry; I know it's a holiday . . . But I need the doctor. It's an emergency."

"Well . . ."

"It really *is* an emergency, Mrs. Cobb. Please."

There was a sigh, a flash of curly brown hair. "Well, all right. Wait there a moment, will you? I'll go see."

"Yes, I'll wait right here. Thank you. Thank you, Mrs. Cobb."

The door closed. To Laura it seemed an eternity before it opened again. When it did, she saw the lanky frame and aristocratic features of Robert Arthur Cobb. He was about forty, an internist with a practice inherited from his uncle. "I'm sorry," she said, "but it's an emergency."

"So I understand. Laura, is it?" he asked with a soothing smile. "Would you care to elaborate, Laura?"

The words spilled out. "It's my mother. She had pneumonia, you see. She was getting better. She was *much* better—breathing all right, eating all right. She just had this cough lingering on, but otherwise she was getting better. And then this morning when I took her coffee in—that's when I knew something had happened. Mama was perspiring, burning with fever. And there were those sounds in her chest again. And then, the worst part . . ."

Dr. Cobb saw the tears start in Laura's eyes. "Yes?" he said gently. "The worst part?"

"She wouldn't wake up. I tried. I shook her; I tried everything I could think of. But it was no good."

"I see. Who is your family doctor?"

"Dr. Weston," replied Laura. "But I wouldn't know how to reach him today. I mean, it's a holiday."

"Charley Weston?"

She wiped her eyes. "I don't know."

"Never mind, we'll sort it out later. Just let me get my bag." He looked down at the striped pajamas peeking from beneath his robe. "And my trousers," he added, walking off.

Laura looked down at her own legs. They were bare, and there was a hole in one of her slippers. She pulled her foot back, as if trying to hide it. She knew she was quite a sight—half dressed, hair flying in all directions—but she couldn't think about that now. She couldn't think about anything but her mother. Please don't let Mama die, she silently prayed. *Help* her. Dear God, help her.

"I don't understand," said Eliza, glancing first at her sister and then at her aunt. "I thought Mama was getting better. That's what everybody said."

"Everybody was wrong," snapped Margaret.

They were in the kitchen, waiting for Dr. Cobb to finish his examination. Eliza was wearing a gray skirt and a pink cashmere pullover, but Laura was still wearing her robe. Now, Laura pushed herself away from the table and stood up. Hands clasped behind her back, she paced a straight line across the room.

113

"What's taking so long?" she asked. "He's been in there forever."

"It hasn't even been five minutes."

"It's been longer than that."

"No, it only seems longer. You have to give the man a chance to do his job, Laura. He's never seen Kay before. Give him a chance to see what's the matter with her."

"I wish he'd hurry."

"Mama ought to be in the hospital," said Eliza. She took a sip of coffee, put the cup down, and daintily touched her napkin to her mouth. "It would be much easier."

Easier? Laura was about to ask what that meant but she decided she didn't want to know. Eliza's answer would annoy her and she didn't want to be at odds with Eliza this morning. She stuffed her hands in her pockets, turning just as Dr. Cobb appeared in the doorway. "Doctor, how is she?"

"Very ill, I'm sorry to say. Your mother has had a relapse, which is often worse than the original condition. There may even be an abscess starting in the lung; I can't be sure. I want ice packs, as many as you can fix. And I need to use your telephone."

"We don't have a telephone," said Margaret. "Are you going to call an ambulance?"

Dr. Cobb hesitated briefly, his gaze moving from Margaret to Eliza to Laura, and then back again. "I doubt Mrs. Bellamy would survive a trip to the hospital," he replied. "But I'm going to call the hospital for oxygen and a few other supplies . . . I'll make the call upstairs. Meanwhile, get started on those ice packs. We must try to bring the fever down."

"Dr. Cobb," said Laura, "Mama's going to be all right, isn't she?"

He'd heard that question—or variations of it—a thousand times before. As a young intern, he'd found ways to soften bad news, but as years passed, he'd realized that merely prolonged the pain. "Your mother is very ill," he said again. "There are some things we can do, but I can't promise they'll be enough. The next few hours will tell the story. If your mother can hold on, if she fights . . . then there's a fair chance. Just remember that your mother is also very weak. She may not have the strength to fight."

Laura steadied herself against the back of a chair. "You're saying Mama's going to die. You're wrong, you know. Wrong as you can be."

"I hope I am," sighed Dr. Cobb. "I'll go and make my call now."

"Laura, come help me with the ice," said Margaret when the doctor had gone. "Eliza, you bring me all the towels from the hall closet. Bath towels, dish towels; every towel you can find. And don't dawdle."

Eliza rose. She started toward the door, but halfway there she stopped and turned around. She looked confused. "Is Mama really that sick?" she asked, her hands fluttering like tiny birds. "How can that be?"

"Doctors always think the worst," said Laura.

"But you believe him. You do; I can tell."

"Get the towels," said Margaret, opening the icebox. "You can talk later . . . Go on, Eliza, I'm waiting." She picked up the ice pick and began chipping at the large block of ice. "Laura, get me some bowls from the cupboard . . . Well? Do I have to say everything twice?"

Laura did as she was told, taking bowls from the shelves and putting them on the counter. "That's all there is," she said, closing the cupboard. Her hands were shaking. She went to the sink, turned on the faucet, and splashed her face with cold water. "He's probably not a good doctor," she said, looking at

Margaret out of the corner of her eye. "He's probably what they call a quack."

"You know that's not true."

"I don't. I don't know anything about him. Did you hear what he said? He's wrong . . . Mama was fine yesterday. Well, maybe not fine, but anybody could see she was better."

"Her cough wasn't better."

"Why do you have to keep talking about that?" Laura bent her head. Tears stung her eyes but she didn't let them fall. "Mama had the new medicine for her cough."

Was it the third new medicine? The fourth? In Margaret's opinion, none of them had helped. Several times Kay had seemed better, but each of those times had ended in a sudden, inexplicable turn for the worse. Margaret's jaw tensed. "This family's never had any luck. Never! And without luck . . ."

"I couldn't stand it if Mama died."

"You'd be surprised what you can stand," said Margaret, though her hand tightened around the ice pick. With almost savage force she smashed it into the block of ice. The block splintered, cracked, but still she pounded at it, slashing away with all her might. "You'd be surprised."

It was a few minutes past eleven. Laura had changed into a skirt and blouse, and now she sat at the edge of the living room sofa. "This waiting is awful," she said to Jane, who sat beside her. "You don't have to stay."

"I want to. Don't worry about me." Jane had been at the Bellamys since nine o'clock, when she'd come to meet Laura for the parade. She'd sensed the tension in the apartment the moment she'd walked through the door. She'd seen the strained, anxious faces and she'd thought immediately of Kay. There had been nothing to do but wait. "Anyway, we're bound to hear something soon. I'm betting it's good news."

"Are you?" Laura's eyes flickered, but her expression didn't change. She looked up, watching as Eliza held a match to another cigarette. "Does that help?"

Eliza had been very quiet, listening to the conversation, but adding no comment of her own. Now she tilted her head to one side and shrugged. "Help what?"

"Nerves."

Eliza smiled slightly. "No, I don't think so. I don't think it has anything to do with nerves."

"Too bad."

"Maybe I should take up smoking," said Jane. She held out her hand, arranging her fingers as if she were holding a cigarette. "How do I look?"

"Silly."

"Thanks. I guess I'm not the sophisticated type."

They all turned at the sound of footsteps in the hall. Laura started to rise, but she sat down again when she saw that the footsteps belonged to Doris. "I thought you were the doctor."

Doris stared down at the tray she was carrying. "I brought fresh coffee. Unless anybody would like tea?" She put the tray on the table. "Should I make tea?"

"It's all right, Doris, don't fuss. Where's Aunt Margaret?"

"She decided to cook the turkey after all. She said there wasn't any other food in the house and people had to eat. I offered to help, but she sent me out with the coffee."

"And a sharp word?" asked Eliza. She watched loops of gray smoke floating in the air. Idly, she reached out a hand and brushed them away. "Aunt Margaret is so gracious."

117

"I'm used to, it. She's a lot like Da . . . That's a beautiful sweater, Eliza."

"This?"

Jane threw back her head and laughed. "Go on, say it — *What, this old thing?* You're a pip, you really are! That sweater is two weeks' salary."

"I wouldn't know."

"Of course not. What would you know about earning money? *Spending* it, yes. When it comes to spending, I bet you're the champ."

"Jealous?"

"Absolutely!" cried Jane, hooting with laughter. "Want to trade lives?"

"Who wants coffee?" asked Doris.

Laura rose and wandered across the room. She gazed up at Kay's seascapes, at the rocky coastlines and long white beaches her mother had never seen but had imagined. It occurred to Laura that her mother had never had a proper vacation: a one-week honeymoon in Atlantic City, summer Sundays at Coney Island; that was the extent of her mother's travels. She could only wonder if Kay had dreamed of faraway lands. Didn't all artists dream of going to Paris?

Laura wandered to the fireplace. She lifted one of the brass pokers, then put it down. She started to rearrange the knickknacks on the mantel, then put them back where they had been. She looked at the clock and thought that this terrible morning would never end.

"I've done all I can," said Dr. Cobb an hour later. His expression was somber as he gazed at the anxious faces turned in his direction. He looked weary. "I'm afraid she hasn't much time."

The silence was broken by Laura's strangled cry.

She was ashen, gripping the back of the sofa for support. Tears burned in her throat. "There must be something else you can do," she said when she was able to speak.

"No." Dr. Cobb shook his head. "I'm very sorry."

"We'll go see her now," said Margaret, rising slowly to her feet. "Will she know we're there?"

"I can't be sure."

Eliza rose also. Her golden brows drew together as she glanced at aunt, at her sister. They were her family, and perhaps the last of her family, but she couldn't feel anything for them. She kept thinking that soon she would be an orphan, unprotected and alone in the world. It was all she could think about, all she could feel. For the first time in her life, she was frightened.

Doris went to where Laura stood, draping an arm around her shoulder. "I'll go in with you, if you want. Jane too."

"No, that's all right."

"Is there anything I can do, then? Do you want me to get Robby?"

"He's not home. He and his parents are with friends in Beekman Place. He won't be home for hours."

"Laura?" Margaret stood in the arched doorway. Her back was ramrod straight, but her fingers plucked nervously at her handkerchief. "Are you coming?"

Laura joined the sad procession to Kay's bedroom. No one spoke; no one knew what to say. In their eyes was the stricken look so familiar to Dr. Cobb. He felt sorry for the Bellamys; two young women—girls, really—and only a maiden aunt to guide them. It won't be easy, he thought, not for the girls, and not for the aunt.

He opened Kay's door, ushering the family inside.

"She isn't in any pain," he said. "I hope that's some small consolation."

"Very small," sighed Margaret.

"Yes. I'm sorry I can't offer anything more."

She looked at him. "At least you're honest. There's no use stirring up false hopes, is there?" She turned her head, glancing at her nieces. "It would have been much harder on them. Especially Laura. Poor thing, she's always getting her hopes up."

From the beginning, Laura had believed her mother would recover. Now, seeing the nurse Dr. Cobb had summoned, seeing the oxygen equipment, the inhalers, the trays of tubes and syringes, she knew she had to accept the truth. *Mama,* she silently cried, walking to the bed.

The clear, stiff fabric of the oxygen tent seemed to blur Kay's features, but Laura could see that her eyes were closed, her lips bluish and slightly parted. Her chest quivered with every breath. The raspy sound was worse, harsher and more intense.

Tears streaked Laura's face as she leaned over the bed. "Mama, can you hear me?" she said softly. "Mama?" Kay thrashed about for moment but she didn't wake. Laura looked to the foot of the bed. "Eliza, come talk to Mama. Come around the side."

"This way, Miss Bellamy," said the nurse, stepping back.

"No, I don't want to. I don't want to remember her in . . . in that thing. It's horrible."

"Eliza—"

"I said I don't want to . . . Why should I? It's not as if she'll hear what I say."

"She might. *Try,*" urged Laura.

Eliza took one step around the side of the bed, one step only. "Mama?" she called, fixing her eyes on the night table. Amid a jumble of medicine bottles and wet cloths, she saw the lacy sachet she'd given to her mother when she'd returned from Crossfield. She swallowed, for suddenly there was a lump in her throat. "Mama? It's Eliza. Can you wake up now?"

Again, Kay started to thrash about. The nurse adjusted the gauge on the oxygen tank. She nodded at Dr. Cobb and he came forward, raising his stethoscope to his ears. "Keep talking to her," he said. "She may be coming out of it."

Kay thought she must be dreaming. She heard voices, but they were garbled—snatches of sound echoing toward her and then sliding away. She saw shafts of light illuminating a dark, unknown place. A tunnel, or maybe a cave? No, it wasn't either of those. It was a place without walls, without a roof; as the light grew stronger, chasing the darkness, she saw that it was a kind of meadow. In the distance were swirling white mists, and from them emerged the figure of a man. His hands were outstretched. He was calling to her.

The distance seemed to narrow: Kay wasn't sure where she was, but all at once she felt as if she were floating on air, floating closer, blissfully closer to the man she couldn't quite see. The light was brilliant now, a blaze of gold. Kay felt her heart pounding, and suddenly she knew the man was John. She reached her hand to his. Their fingers almost touched.

"Mama," said Laura, bending down, "we're all here. Eliza and Aunt Margaret and I. We're waiting for you to wake up. Can you hear me, Mama? Open your eyes. Open your eyes and talk to us. We're waiting for you . . . Can you hear me, Mama?"

Kay heard the garbled voices again. She tried to make sense of them, but she couldn't. John would help her; he'd always helped her. She floated back to him, smiling radiantly as once more her hand reached to his.

"She's smiling! Mama's smiling!" Laura looked at Dr. Cobb. "What does that mean?"

"I'm sorry, but I don't know. It's impossible to know what's going on in her mind. Just keep talking."

"Mama? *Mama*, we're all waiting for you. We're here. Open your eyes. You can do . . . Mama?"

All the mists had lifted. Kay gazed at her darling Johnny and her heart leapt with joy. She would stay here in this place of golden light. Here, she and Johnny would be together as if they'd never been apart, as if they were young again—just a boy and a girl in love.

The voices were so faint now, so far off. Kay knew she wouldn't have to worry about them anymore. She reached out to Johnny. Their hands touched, clasped. With her last breath she spoke his name. She was home.

"Mama," cried Laura. *"Mama, no."*

"I'm sorry," said Dr. Cobb. "She's gone."

"No."

Margaret pressed her wadded handkerchief to her mouth. "Poor thing," she murmured. "Poor thing."

Eliza backed away from the bed. She felt the lump in her throat again, felt it choking her. She turned and ran from the room.

Laura didn't move. The doctor was speaking to her, but she didn't hear. Mama's dead, she thought. Dear God, Mama's dead. She leaned her head against the bedpost and wept.

Chapter Seven

Laura flew into Robby's arms. Robby was here now and she would be all right; she would be safe.

"I'm very sorry about your mother," he said, stroking her tawny hair. "I'm sorry I wasn't with you. If I'd known—"

"You couldn't have known. We all thought Mama was getting better. We never expected . . ." Laura buried her head on Robby's shoulder. "Dr. Cobb said she had a relapse. He said there wasn't anything anyone could have done."

Robby led her to the sofa and sat her down. It was early evening. Margaret was in the kitchen with Beatrice Wesley; the two of them making lists for the funeral. Eliza was in the bedroom, making a list of her own. Somewhere in the apartment a pipe was clanging, and the rhythmic sound had begun to grate on Robby's nerves. "You ought to talk to Sweeney about the plumbing."

Laura glanced up. "What?"

"Nothing." He took his handkerchief from his pocket and gave it to her. "It's just that I wish I could help. I'm not awfully good in situations like this . . . Nothing like this has happened to me yet, so it's hard to know the right thing to say. Or do."

She dried her red-rimmed eyes. "Being here with me is the right thing."

"Are you sure you wouldn't rather have Doris? Or Jane?"

"Don't you want to stay?"

"Well yes, sure I do. I just thought maybe girlfriends would be more . . . Well, sometimes people want to be with their own kind. You know how it is."

She didn't, but she knew he was uncomfortable around tears, around strong or complicated feelings. Robby was happiest with life when it proceeded in a straight line. For the Colliers it often did exactly that, but not for the Bellamys. "I wouldn't blame you if you were getting tired of all my problems," she sniffled. "So many bad things have happened. This is the worst of all."

"I'm sorry, Laura."

"I wanted to tell Mama I loved her. It's funny but I—I couldn't remember if I'd ever told her before. I stood there beside her bed, wondering. But she never woke up . . . She smiled, you know."

"Smiled?"

Laura nodded. "Toward the end. She was probably dreaming. And I mean, if it had to happen at all . . . She smiled, and then the next minute she was gone."

"Try not to think about it."

"Not think about it?"

Robby shook a cigarette from a pack of Lucky Strike. His small gold lighter twinkled in the lamplight. "You shouldn't dwell on all the little details, Laura. They'll get stuck in your mind and you'll never get rid of them." He heard the rebuke in his voice. He sighed. "Forgive me," he said. "Here I am lecturing you when I ought to be consoling you. That's what I meant: I'm not good at this. I'm not helping."

"You're here; that's all that matters." And to Laura it was. It was hard for her to criticize him, to think badly of him. There were times when he disappointed her, but it was simply easier to blame herself. She told herself that she expected too much of him, or expected the wrong things. He didn't always understand her feelings, he didn't always try, but she didn't care. He was the boy she loved and that was enough; it was everything. "Your being here," she continued now, "makes me feel better. It's as if you give me strength."

"You don't look better."

Laura offered a brief, wan smile. "It's the shock . . . I was thinking it was just like with Papa. So sudden, I mean. I didn't even have a chance to say good-bye."

The pipe was still clanging. Robby crushed his cigarette in the ashtray. He stood. "Why don't we go out and get some air?"

"I can't."

"Why not? You haven't been out all day."

"Mr. Flynn from the funeral home will be here soon. There are . . . arrangements." She bowed her head and her lashes cast spidery shadows on her cheeks. Mr. Flynn's men had already been here—to 'remove the deceased,' as one of them had said. "I have to stay."

"Can't Margaret see to the arrangements?"

"I suppose, but it's something I should do myself. It's the last thing I'll ever be able to do for Mama."

"Well, if that's what you want."

Laura shifted around on the sofa, lacing and unlacing her fingers. "Don't be upset, Robby. Please don't."

"I'm not upset. I worry about you, though. I think you try to do too much." He shrugged, resting his arm on the mantel. "But that's the way you are."

"I can't help it."

"I know." He smiled, nodding his golden head. "I'm

not trying to change you, Laura. It wouldn't do any good if I were. I know what it means when you stick out your chin like that."

She frowned. "Do I stick out my chin?"

"Only when you're being stubborn. Which is about half the time."

She knew he was teasing, but still she was taken aback by his remark. A lot could be read into it, she thought. Maybe he was teasing, but maybe he was serious, too. Hadn't she heard a ripple of impatience beneath his light, humorous tone? Her question went unanswered, even in her own mind, because Eliza had glided into the room.

Clad in black, with just a bare hint of pink lipstick on her rosebud mouth, Eliza sank gracefully into one of the wing chairs and crossed her ankles. "Hello, Robby. I didn't know you were here."

"I'm sorry about your mother," he said. "Please accept my condolences," he added more formally. "If there's anything I can do . . ."

"Thank you."

Eliza lowered her eyes, bending her head over her folded hands. At that moment she looked as vulnerable as a child, a child mourning for its lost mother. She looked the very picture of grief.

Laura, watching her sister, was surprised. She had expected Eliza to be sad and perhaps more distant than usual, but she hadn't expected grief. For a split second she wondered if it was an act; no, she quickly decided, chasing the suspicion away. No, of course not.

She started when she heard the doorbell. Eliza glanced up. Robby turned. "Shall I get that?"

"Yes please," said Laura, She knew who it was. She felt her throat go dry. Her stomach started to churn. Maybe Robby was right, she thought to herself; maybe I should leave the arrangements to Aunt Margaret. "That will be Mr. Flynn," she explained to Eliza.

"Oh?"

"From the funeral home."

"Oh, I see."

Laura looked toward the doorway as she heard voices coming nearer. Everybody seemed to walk in at once: Margaret, Beatrice Wesley, Jane, Robby, and last of all, Raymond Flynn.

Jane broke away from the others and went to Laura, who had risen unsteadily. "Moral support," said Jane. "I ran into Mr. Flynn downstairs and I thought I'd better come back. Do you mind?"

"Mind? I'm grateful."

Raymond Flynn, silver-haired and pink-cheeked, held out his hand to Laura. "May I offer my deepest sympathy, Miss Bellamy. Your dear mother was so young. It's a terrible loss, terrible . . . But she's gone to a happier place now, hasn't she?"

Tears gathered in Laura's eyes. She remembered her mother's sudden, radiant smile. A happier place? She hoped so. "I . . . don't think you've met my sister, Eliza," she sniffled.

"May I offer my deepest sympathies to you as well, Miss Bellamy," said Mr. Flynn, holding out his hand again. He had been consoling people for most of his adult life and the words, repeated thousands of times, had become automatic. It had been many years since he had been moved by pain or grief, but now, observing the beautiful Eliza, the sorrowful Eliza, his heart went out to her. "My poor child, he murmured. "I know it's hard, but you must be brave."

Her head bobbed up and down. Her golden curls spilled across her brow. She said nothing.

For a moment or two, all eyes locked on Eliza. She was the center of attention, as if the tragedy of Kay's death had happened to her alone.

Jane, thinking about this, snorted. "How about a cup of tea, Mr. Flynn?" she asked, shattering the hypnotic silence. "Wouldn't you like a nice cup of tea?"

The spell had been broken. Raymond Flynn acknowledged that he would indeed enjoy a cup of tea, if it wasn't any trouble. Mrs. Wesley, declaring that tea was "just the thing", marched off to the kitchen.

Margaret planted her hands on her hips. "I'm glad we settled the refreshments," she said with a scowl that was anything but glad. "Now maybe we can get started. The sooner we start, the sooner we'll finish."

"Let's . . . let's all sit down," suggested Laura, though she continued to stand. "Robby?" Her eyes darted about the room. She saw him leaning against the window seat and a smile touched her mouth. "Oh, there you are."

"Laura," said Margaret, "we have things to do."

"Yes, all right." She took a long, thick envelope off the table and gave it to Mr. Flynn. "That's Mama's insurance policy."

"May I?" Laura nodded and he opened the envelope. He glanced at the policy, his practiced eye picking out the amount: five hundred dollars. "Flynn's can provide a superior five-hundred-dollar funeral. Two cars, a mahogany casket—"

"I don't want to listen to this," interrupted Eliza, rising to her feet. "It's morbid."

"I'm afraid it's necessary," replied Mr. Flynn, smiling kindly. "A funeral is a way of paying our last respects to our loved ones."

"Yes, but talking about it is morbid." She turned to Laura. "You don't need me here. I'm going for a walk."

"A walk where?" asked Margaret. "It's dark out."

"It's been a horrible day and I've been cooped up in this apartment and now I need a breath of air. I'll be perfectly fine, Aunt Margaret. Don't worry, I won't be long."

Margaret shook her head. "Long or not, I don't like the idea of you wandering around by yourself." Her gaze jumped to the other side of the room. "Robby, you go with Eliza. Go on, make yourself useful."

He straightened up. "Me?"

"Is there another Robby here?"

"No, but . . . I promised Laura I'd stay."

Margaret sighed. "She can manage without you for a while."

And I can speak for myself, thought Laura. She wanted Robby to stay, but deep down she knew he didn't want to be here. Like Eliza, he would find Mr. Flynn's presence and conversation "morbid." She lifted her head, staring at him. "A walk will do you both good," she said quietly.

"If you're sure . . ." He didn't finish. Laura was still staring at him, and while he couldn't always tell what she was thinking, her thoughts seemed clear enough now. He'd disappointed her; he could see that in her eyes. Because he hadn't *insisted* on staying, he'd disappointed her. A noble gesture, that's what she had expected. Well, he'd never claimed to be noble. He looked away, fiddling with his tie as he walked over to Eliza. "I guess we're the deserters," he said, though his jaunty tone was betrayed by a nervous laugh.

"We're the fifth wheel," replied Eliza. "Laura doesn't need us."

Laura said nothing to this. She watched them go, sitting herself down on the sofa next to Jane. "You have to admit they look good together."

"Why shouldn't they? They're a matched set!"

Slowly, Laura returned her attention to Raymond Flynn. There were no more distractions, no more excuses. Now she would have to talk about the funeral. She took a breath. "We want a simple funeral, Mr. Flynn. At least that's what Mama would have wanted."

"Simple and dignified."

"Yes, that's right."

He drew a small leather notebook from his pocket. "As I started to say, Flynn's can provide a superior five-hundred-dollar funeral. Two cars, mahogany casket, a spray of carnations, and of course the pallbearers."

Five hundred dollars. Laura remembered her mother putting aside the insurance money every month. It had come right after rent and food because, since childhood, Kay had been haunted by the thought of the unmarked graves in the pauper's cemetery at Potter's Field. John had had a two-thousand-dollar policy, but five hundred was all Kay had been able to afford for herself and Margaret and the girls. Burial policies, she'd called them. She had once joked that the Bellamys couldn't afford to go to the hospital, but they could afford to die.

Laura blinked, fighting the tears that had rushed again to her eyes. "I—I don't want to haggle over money at a time like this, Mr. Flynn. The problem is I don't know if I should spend all the five hundred dollars. We have bills . . . We're not rich people."

"Times are hard."

Margaret hurled a dark look in Mr. Flynn's direction. "Not for you, I'll wager. No hard times in the funeral business."

"Aunt Margaret, please." Laura held Robby's crumpled handkerchief to her eyes. "I want to have this done with, Mr. Flynn. And I want to do what's right. But I don't *know* what's right. Can you understand?"

He could. In his business he had learned a great

deal about people and the conflicts they suffered when faced with these decisions. He'd learned how to resolve the conflicts to benefit Flynn's Funeral Home, how to sell a grieving family just a little more than they'd planned to buy. It was all a matter of salesman's tricks; sometimes he used them and sometimes he didn't. This was one time when he knew he wouldn't. Perhaps it was because of that beautiful young girl, Eliza. Or perhaps it was because of Laura—so pretty, so earnest, so sad.

He put his notebook back in his pocket. "We can provide quite a fine funeral at a lower price. Say, three hundred dollars?"

"You're an honest man," said Margaret, revising her opinion of Raymond Flynn.

"Yes," agreed Laura. "I'm grateful to you, Mr. Flynn." She hesitated, a frown creeping across her brow. "It will be a nice funeral, won't it? I want it to be nice for Mama."

"You have my word, Miss Bellamy. Everything will be first class."

"First class," murmured Laura, brushing at her eyes. "Thank you, Mr. Flynn . . . Mama would like that."

Kay was buried beside John in a beautiful old cemetery fifty miles north of the city. It was a rainy morning and the freshly turned earth had a sweet, clean scent that reminded Laura of spring. But Mama won't see another spring, she thought, lifting her head to the pewter clouds. Never another spring.

Laura's eyes were dry; she had no more tears. She hadn't cried at all during the funeral service at St. James Methodist Church. Sitting between Margaret and Eliza, she'd stared at the dark wood casket, her hands clenched so tightly that the knuckles sprang out beneath the skin. Eliza had sniffled and Margaret had heaved many sighs, but Laura hadn't uttered a sound.

Now she lowered her gaze to the spray of gardenias that adorned the casket. There were other flowers: a wreath of lilies from the Harding Advertising Company, a wreath of yellow and white chrysanthemums from the Walders; a spray of yellow roses from the Wesleys, and a large basket of white roses from the Colliers. Almost lost among these displays was a modest bouquet of carnations—the offering of a distant cousin, Paul Brent. Laura glanced around. Yes, there he was—the sandy-haired man standing next to Doris. She'd hardly noticed him during the ride here. Had he been in the same car? She couldn't remember.

"Earth to earth, ashes to ashes, dust to dust," intoned Reverend Fletcher, concluding the service.

Margaret took a few steps forward and placed a single red rose on the casket. Eliza followed, her downcast eyes carefully avoiding the black chasm that would soon be Kay's grave. Laura followed last. "Good-bye, Mama," she whispered, laying a third rose beside the others. "Good-bye."

It was Paul Brent who grasped Laura's arm and steered her along the gravel path to Mr. Flynn's waiting limousine. "The worst is over now," he said, helping her into the car. "Don't worry, you'll be home before you know it." He turned, holding out his hand to Eliza. "In you go . . . And you, Aunt Margaret . . . Watch your head."

"Never mind my head. Hurry up and get in. The rain's starting to blow."

Paul ducked inside, folding his tall, reedy frame into the jump seat. The driver closed the umbrella, closed the door, and got behind the wheel. There was a crunch of gravel as the car pulled away.

Laura turned her head, staring out the back window. The other limousine was just leaving; trailing after it was Robby's bright red Packard. "I wish Robby had come with us," she said to no one in particular. "He didn't have to bring his car."

"*This* car is for family," said Margaret. "Robby's not family."

Not yet, thought Laura, craning her neck as the driver increased speed. Not yet.

Eliza reached into her purse for a cigarette. "Thank you," she murmured when Paul struck a match. She drew on the cigarette, exhaling a stream of wispy blue smoke. "You're forgetting about Robby's mother. I'm sure Mrs. Collier didn't want to be squeezed in with us. The two of them are quite comfortable in his car."

"The three of them," corrected Margaret. "*You're* forgetting Reverend Fletcher."

Paul smiled. "The old guy really lit up when he saw that car. Did you notice?"

"Don't be disrespectful," scolded Margaret. "That's no way to talk about a minister."

"It's true, though," replied Paul, his smile widening. "I'll bet he doesn't get too many chances at a shiny red Packard. Not these days."

The shiny red Packard disappeared from view. Laura shifted around in her seat again. She unbuttoned her coat, pulled off her gloves. Through a haze of smoke, she looked at Paul Brent.

He was almost twenty-two, an unassuming young man with a gentle smile and a dimpled chin. His eyes were a pale, clear blue, slightly crinkled at the corners. Little reddish highlights flickered in his hair. He wasn't handsome, but his boyish good looks were as appealing as his personality.

Laura hadn't seen him since her father's funeral. He'd been a student at New York University then, but not long afterward he'd had to leave school to get a job. He'd gone back home to the small upstate town of Greenville, and there (according to Margaret) he'd worked in a hardware store.

"It was Dad's hardware store," Paul was saying now. "He had a good business, until the Depression hit. The glass factory closed, and then the brickyard. That was the end for most of the stores on Main Street. It was for us."

Margaret nodded. "The last time Harry wrote, he said he was hoping to find work at the plant nursery."

"The nursery closed too. Dad's working part-time at the department store in Loganport. That's the next town over. It's not much of a job, but it helps. Things were pretty bad there for a while."

"Not so bad," snapped Laura. "At least your parents are still alive."

"You mind your tongue!" said Margaret, looking sternly at her niece. "We're all family here."

"I don't care." Laura's gaze moved to the window. She wanted to cry but she couldn't. She could only stare at the blur of road and cars and traffic signs. The rain had stopped. The sun peeked out for a moment before rushing back behind the clouds. "I don't want to listen to anybody's sad stories today," she said, as if to herself. "I have my own sad stories. That's enough."

"Laura!"

"It's all right, Aunt Margaret," Paul patted her hand. "It's all right."

He smiled. Anything Laura said or did would have been all right with him. He loved her; he'd loved her ever since his twelfth birthday, when she'd given him a real Central Park frog. The frog hadn't lasted very long, but the love had. It was nearly ten years now. It was his secret.

* * *

An informal lunch of sandwiches and cookies had been planned. A neighbor, Mrs. Austin, had volunteered to have everything ready when the family returned from the funeral. Bustling about in a frilly white apron, she fixed two large platters of finger sandwiches and arranged three dozen of her homemade chocolate cookies on dainty paper doilies. She'd bought her sherry glasses, and these she set out on a round silver tray. Sherry was such a good idea, she thought. So soothing at a time like this.

Now, sherry glasses in hand, the lunch guests milled around the living room. In the room were family, neighbors, Laura's friends, and a few old friends of Kay's. There was some mingling, but after a while, people drifted into somber little groups of their own—neighbors with neighbors, old friends with old friends. Margaret went from group to group, sharing their reminiscences. Eliza stood off to the side and let everyone come to her.

Laura tried to keep busy. She refilled glasses, offered sandwiches, emptied ashtrays. She didn't want to talk. She didn't want to hear any more polite, empty phrases. She wished everybody would go home.

"You can't hide, you know," said Paul, coming upon Laura in the kitchen. "If that's what you're trying to do."

"It's not."

"I think it is." He leaned against the counter, crossing his arms over his chest. "I've been watching you. You tried to make yourself invisible out there, and when that didn't work, you sneaked in here."

"I didn't *sneak*, Paul. I just don't see much point in all this. Mama's gone. Serving sherry and cookies won't bring her back."

"Being with people is supposed to be a comfort."

"Well, it's not." She opened the icebox and peered inside. She'd never seen it so stuffed before. The shelves practically sagged under tureens and bowls and casserole dishes—all brought by various neighbors. "Everyone's been very kind," she said, closing the door. "But that doesn't change anything. It doesn't change how I feel. I don't feel like smiling and making small talk today."

"I understand."

"It's different for Eliza. I mean, she's always been able to block out anything upsetting. She's there but she's not there, if that doesn't sound too crazy. She's in the living room right now, but she's not *really* in the living room. She's off in some world of her own . . . She can escape. I can't."

"I know."

"How do you know?"

Paul shrugged, his pale blue eyes smiling at Laura. "Maybe I sense things. We're related, after all."

"Distantly."

"True. A great-great-grandfather doesn't count for a lot. Poor old Horace."

She glanced up. "Horace? Was that his name?"

"Horace Bellamy. He was the first Bellamy to come to America, and he's the ancestor we have in common. Don't you know your family history?"

Laura shook her head. "That's Aunt Margaret's department. Although to hear her tell it, most of our family are dead."

"What about your mother's family?"

"Her parents died years ago. I can scarcely remember them. Mama never had any brothers or sisters."

"Then it's just the three of you now."

"Not for long." Laura went to the sink and filled a glass with water. She drank half and spilled out the rest. "I expect Eliza will marry soon."

"What about you?"

She had no answer. Robby had almost three years left at Yale; that was the only certainty. Beyond that there were no plans, no promises. He had asked her to be his girl, but he hadn't yet asked her to be anything else. "I have a stack of bills up to the sky," she said after a moment. "And I have to take care of Aunt Margaret. I guess I'll be busy working."

"A career girl."

No, thought Laura, just a girl with a bunch of jobs. She saw the sudden burst of sunlight at the window. It was going to be a nice day.

"Here you are," sighed Margaret, stamping into the kitchen. "A poor excuse for a hostess!"

"There aren't any more sandwiches. I looked."

"Of course there aren't any more. This isn't a restaurant, is it? We can't be serving food all morning long. If anyone's still hungry, there are plenty of cookies. Anyway, it's the sherry people really want. You'd know that, if you were in the living room with your guests."

"Blame me," said Paul. "I kept Laura talking."

"No, that's not true. I just didn't want to be in there, Aunt Margaret."

"Your guests are in there."

"My guests? I didn't invite these people here; you did."

Margaret's eyes, the same pale blue as Paul's, seemed to darken. "Now you listen to me, missy. There are certain things we have to do whether we want to or not. There are rules, even for funerals. So get yourself back inside and make an effort. Make your mother proud."

"Leave Mama out of this."

"I don't see how I can. You know how she was. Tell me if she'd want you to forget your manners this way. You're letting her down and that's a fact."

"All right, all right!" Laura threw her hands in the air and started toward the door. "There's no one like you for building mountains out of molehills, but all right!"

Laura paused at the edge of the living room, her gaze sweeping over the small crowd. Voices were louder now; faces not quite so sad. Someone had opened a second bottle of sherry.

Beatrice Wesley was holding forth at the other end of the room. Her finger wagged; her head bobbed up and down; her mouth never stopped moving. In the midst of one of her famous — or infamous — monologues, she hardly seemed to stop for breath.

Laura watched. She saw Robby slip away from the group and a smile brushed her lips. "I was afraid Mrs. Wesley had you trapped," she said as he came up to her.

"Where the devil have you been, Laura?"

"I was in the kitchen. I wanted to be by myself, but then Paul came in. We started talking."

"Well, that's just fine," said an unsmiling Robby. "I stayed an extra day because I thought you'd want me here. If I'd known you were going to disappear with your cousin—"

"It had nothing to do with Paul. It's my fault. The room seemed to be getting smaller and smaller. All these people . . . I needed a few minutes alone. I'm sorry, Robby."

"I thought you'd forgtten about me."

"Never," she earnestly insisted. " 'Never in this world."

His face softened; the sulky line of his mouth relaxed. "You need to get out for a while. I'm catching the early train to New Haven. Ride with me to the station."

"Now?"

"I'll send you back in a taxi."

"No, it's not that." Laura glanced anxiously around the room. She could almost hear Margaret's voice. *Make an effort. Make your mother proud.* "I—I can't leave now. I haven't even spoken to anybody yet. It would be wrong." She saw the flash of impatience in the green depths of his eyes. "Robby, try to understand. Put yourself in my place."

"I could ask you to do the same thing. You don't have any time for me anymore. What am I supposed to think?"

"You're supposed to think that my mother just died and I'm very upset. We're all very upset. We're not ourselves . . . Those are the things you should think, because they're true." She had spoken sharply, and now color flared in her cheeks. She dropped her gaze to the floor, a moment later looking up at Robby through her dark lashes. "I guess I spoke out of turn. That's what I meant about not being ourselves."

"You were calling me selfish, weren't you?"

"No." Laura shook her head. "No, I was asking you to understand. To be patient."

There was silence. He stared at her and a muscle tensed in his jaw. "Well, the train won't be patient," he said finally. "I've got to go." He bent, his lips barely grazing Laura's cheek. "Make my excuses to Margaret."

"When will I see you?"

"Exams are coming up."

"I know," she replied quietly. "But that's not an answer."

Robby glanced at his watch. "I'll miss my train . . . Sure you won't ride along? Last chance."

Again she shook her head. "I can't." She jumped when she felt a hand on her shoulder. She looked around. "Yes, Paul?"

"Jane sent me," he explained with a sheepish smile. "She said you should come rescue her."

Laura looked past him to a group of people in the corner. She sighed. Beatrice Wesley and Polly Austin appeared to be having a disagreement; standing between them was Jane. "Yes, I see what she means." Laura turned back to say good-bye to Robby, but he had gone. "Oh, Robby," she murmured.

"Is he your boyfriend?"

"Yes."

She walked off with Paul, stopping every few steps to talk to people, to thank them for coming. She was halfway across the room when she thought she heard Robby's voice. She looked over her shoulder to see Robby leaving the room with Eliza. She saw them walk into the hallway together, saw Robby take Eliza's arm. An instant later she heard the scraping of hangers on the coat rack, and then the click of the front door.

"Something wrong?" asked Paul.

She wasn't sure. She knew Robby was annoyed with her, and she assumed he'd asked Eliza to ride to the station, but she wasn't sure what that meant. Probably nothing, she thought, yet there was a funny feeling in the pit of her stomach.

"Laura? What's the matter?"

"Nothing," she said. Or everything, she silently added.

Chapter Eight

"Well, Laura wanted them to be friends," sighed Doris, sinking deeper into her big coat. "She wanted Robby and Eliza to like each other. I guess she got her wish."

"Yes," agreed Jane. "She wants everybody to be one big happy family. Only it never works out that way."

Doris glanced up at the sky; a bleak, almost colorless sky hovering over the wintry December afternoon. She hoped there wouldn't be snow. "Did you know they had lunch together? Robby and Eliza? The weekend after the funeral, it was. Laura was working. Robby was in the city for the day and he took Eliza to lunch. Pretty fancy, too. He took her to that place where the celebrities go: "21." They were there for hours."

"I heard."

The girls crossed the street and turned a corner, toward First Avenue. "You haven't said what you think, Jane."

"Oh, I'm the suspicious type. I had the feeling Laura was a little suspicious herself, at first."

Doris nodded. "She was. But then she talked to Eliza, and Eliza said just what I did—that Laura *wanted* them to be friends and now they were. It's kind of hard to argue with that. And besides, Eliza has all those other boys chasing after her."

"That's the most important thing," declared Jane. "Because each one of those boys is richer than the next. *And* richer than the Colliers. So why should she want Robby?"

"Then you think it's all right?"

"I'm *al*ways suspicious of Eliza, but this time I suppose there's no harm done. God knows Robby's a catch, but Eliza's out for bigger fish."

"Do you think so, Jane?"

"Sure. Laura thinks so, too. That's why she wasn't really worried about Eliza. She *was* worried about Robby. Look how he behaved the day of the funeral. Getting huffy the way he did. Expecting Laura to turn her back on everyone and ride to the station with him . . . He's spoiled. He wants what he wants and that's all there is to it. If he couldn't get Laura to ride with him, he'd get Eliza instead. He's spoiled all right."

A worried frown pinched Doris's brow. "I like Robby."

"Oh, everybody likes Robby. And Robby likes everybody. But he's used to having people kowtow to him, especially girls."

"Laura doesn't do that."

"No," answered Jane, turning up the collar of her coat. "She does a lot of apologizing, though. Haven't you noticed? Robby should have apologized for the way he behaved. But in the end it was Laura who said she was sorry."

"Anything to keep peace."

"What?"

Doris shrugged. "I see my mother do the same thing when Da's in one of his moods. She'll apologize, take the blame on herself. It keeps the peace, she says."

"Well, your father's an Irishman. In Ireland the

man's the boss, isn't he?"

"Not only in Ireland." Doris offered a wary smile. "They say it's a man's world, you know."

"Oh, I don't believe that. Not at all."

Doris and Jane held fast to their hats as they turned the blustery corner. They walked north on First Avenue, their rapid strides taking them closer to the heart of the Yorkville neighborhood. It was Sunday. Shops were closed, traffic was light, and children were everywhere; little boys bundled in heavy jackets or several layers of sweaters, knitted caps pulled down around their ears; little girls wearing long woolen stockings and shabby coats too small.

Doris saw the hopscotch squares chalked on the pavement and she smiled. "Laura used to be the best one on the block at hopscotch. You should have seen her."

"What were you best at? Besides math?"

"I wasn't good at games. Mostly I just watched."

"And did long division in your head. Quick—what's 34,869 divided by 184?"

"You're always teasing," replied Doris, her chin burrowing into her coat collar. "I can't help it if I'm good at math."

"Help it? For goodness' sake, Doris, you should be proud. *I* would be. I'd probably be impossible."

"You'd get tired of—of being different."

"Oh no, I wouldn't. I'd love it!"

They continued walking. Doris glanced at a clock in the window of a jewelry store. "It's quarter past one," she said to Jane. "Laura will be waiting."

"No, I told her one-thirty. She had that errand to run for Sam Roth, and I wasn't sure which Mass you were going to, so I told her one-thirty."

"With her busy schedule, I was afraid we wouldn't be able to meet today."

"Laura would have made time, no matter what.

We always do our Christmas shopping together. It's a tradition."

The tradition had begun when Laura and Doris were ten years old; old enough, they'd decided, to choose their own presents for their families. They'd investigated all the little shops in the neighborhood, but finally they'd taken their precious dimes and nickels to Woolworth's. Woolworth's remained their store through four Christmasses—until the Depression brought pushcarts back to Yorkville.

Laura had stared at the sprawling pushcart market and called it a bazaar; Doris remembered that. She remembered also that that was the year Jane had become part of their Christmas tradition. "Time goes so quickly," she murmured. "I can't believe it's almost Christmas again. Can you?"

"I'll be glad when it's New Year's. I'll be glad when *this* year is over."

"Yes . . . You know, I thought you might want to shop at a real department store this year. Now that you're working, I mean."

Jane shook her head and wisps of red hair flew up around her hat. "No, we all shop in the same place. The Three Musketeers, that's us! One for all and all for one."

The traffic light blinked. The girls crossed the street. "There are the pushcarts," said Doris, gazing into the near distance. "There's the start . . . Oh, and there's Laura." She waved her mittened hand in the air. "Laura," she called, waving her hand back and forth. "Here we are!"

Laura turned. She saw her friends and suddenly the streets seemed to come alive. She noticed the bright colors of the carts, the excited voices of the peddlers, the wonderful scents of cinnamon and ginger and pine. A smile leapt across her face. She knew there would be Christmas after all.

She hadn't wanted to think about Christmas. Her mother had been dead only a few weeks and the hurt was still too fresh. How could she think about Christmas when sorrow still dragged at her heart?

She'd tried to ignore the festive decorations in store windows, the sidewalk Santas ringing large, silvery bells. Whenever Christmas carols started playing on the radio, she'd switched it off. We'll have Christmas *next* year, she'd told herself. Next year will be time enough.

But now, watching her friends hurrying toward her, watching their expectant faces, she realized that she needed this particular Christmas, needed to feel happy again, even if just for a little while. The shock of Kay's death weighed heavily, and Robby had given her a bad scare. Maybe Christmas was a way to put the worst behind her.

"We kept you waiting," said Doris, ready to apologize.

"No, I got here only a couple of minutes ago."

"Did you bring your shopping list?" asked Jane.

Laura smiled slightly. "It's not a very long list. Not like yours. Not pages and pages."

"Well, I don't like to forget anybody."

"No chance of that. Come on, let's look around. I think there are more pushcarts this year."

The carts lined both sides of the avenue for five or six blocks. Each cart sold something different: toys or dolls or inexpensive games, scarves or gloves or lacy camisoles; bottles of cologne or hand lotion or bath oil. Food carts offered everything from tinned fruit cakes to sacks of cinnamon sticks. Jumble carts offered odds and ends: a set of tortoiseshell combs, a length of red flannel, a toast rack, a pincushion, a garnet brooch that might be antique. No one knew what small treasure might turn up in the jumble carts.

The girls decided to save "the jumbles" for last. They browsed leisurely among the other carts, glancing at prices while they checked their lists. Jane had the most money to spend and she spent it with great glee. This was in contrast to Doris and Laura, who doled out their coins with a wariness that would have pleased Scrooge. Everyone of their purchases required a discussion, a curbside conference: Was 98¢ too much to spend on a pair of men's pajamas? Were those handkerchiefs real linen? Was a one-pound box of peppermints too extravagant? And on and on.

Jane watched, amused. "You're like two little old ladies," she said, dropping another package into her shopping bag. "Like those two old crows who are always haggling with Schultz the butcher."

"Were not haggling," said Laura. "Were just being careful." She smiled. "As Aunt Margaret would say: waste not, want not."

"I think I saw that embroidered on a pillow in that cart over there . . . I'm serious," she added when Laura rolled her eyes. "I'm sure I saw it. Should I buy it for Margaret?"

"Listen to Diamond Jane," teased Laura.

"Well, it's Christmas."

"Save your money. Aunt Margaret embroiders her own pillows."

"Yes, she would."

Laura looked into her shopping bag "Are we ready for the jumble carts yet? I hope they're good this year. I need to find something for Eliza. And something special for Robby."

"What's he going to get you? asked Doris as they resumed their walk along the avenue. "Has he hinted around?"

"There hasn't been any time for hinting. I've only

seen him once since . . . since the funeral. That was the night we went to the Music Hall." And that was the night he'd invited her to go to a weekend house party in Greenwich. He'd said there would be sleigh rides and ice skating, said he wanted her to meet some of his Yale friends. He hadn't seemed surprised when she'd told him she couldn't go. He'd mumbled something about "all your jobs," and then changed the subject. "We didn't talk about Christmas."

"But he writes to you."

"Yes." Not a week passed without one or two of Robby's scribbled notes. They were breezy and funny and nice and she was glad to have them, but they weren't love letters. In her secret heart she yearned for love letters. "He writes about what he's doing at Yale," she said. "And about sports and his car and things like that. He hasn't mentioned Christmas."

"Then *you* mention it," said Jane. "What's the best present you can imagine?"

"From Robby? I don't know . . . something romantic. My locket was a romantic present." Laura shifted her shopping bag to her other arm. She looked up, staring at the ashen sky. "I know the best present I could give Robby—more time. If I could just stop working all these different hours. If I could have one regular job instead of three."

"I've been keeping my eyes open at Jobina Cosmetics," said Jane. "But things are tight. I wouldn't have a job there myself if Pop hadn't done some business with one of the company's suppliers. You could say he pulled some strings."

Laura smiled. "At least you got the glamorous job you wanted."

"Hah! I *thought* it would be glamorous. And I suppose it is, for Jobina Grant. Not for me, though."

"Don't you like your job?" asked Doris.

"It's all right. I get to try out all the cosmetics and

that's fun. It's just not what I thought it would be."

Laura shrugged. "It's still better than running from one job to another . . . Take today, for example. It's Sunday, but I have to be at the movie theater at four o'clock. I won't get home till midnight, and then tomorrow morning, it's back to Crawford & Jones. I can see why Robby gets upset."

Jane and Doris glanced at each other. "What can you do about it?" asked Jane.

"Well, I've been watching the ads in the newspapers. I have a little experience now; that should help . . . The only problem is I'd feel so guilty if I ever left Crawford & Jones. Sam's been very kind to me. And it was Mr. Goodfriend who helped me get the job in the first place. I think about leaving, and I feel as if I'm letting them down."

"That's crazy."

"It's how I feel."

"Here are the jumbles," said Doris, taking Laura's arm. "You can have first choice because of Eliza and Robby. Because they're both so fussy, I mean. We'll help you look, won't we, Jane?"

"Sure, but what exactly are we looking for?" She squeezed past several other browsers and peered into the cart. A dainty enameled trinket box caught her eye. She picked it up, studied it, put it down. "I see a couple of things that would be okay for Eliza," she said, digging around in a basket of mismatched hair clips, "but I don't know what you'll find for Robby."

Time, thought Laura. Somehow I have to find time.

"I think I hear Laura now," said Margaret, rising from the kitchen table. "We'll see what she has to say about all this."

It was after midnight. Eliza stifled a yawn. "It

doesn't matter what she has to say. I can make my own decisions."

"Laura pays the bills around here. *Your* bills too, in case you need reminding. That gives her some rights."

"But not the right to tell me what to do, Aunt Margaret. Laura's only my sister. My younger sister at that."

"You're taking advantage. You're taking advantage and you know it." Margaret stepped into the hall. She blinked, adjusting her eyes to the dim light. At the far end of the hall, she saw her niece. "Laura, come in here," she called. "There's something we have to talk about."

"It's late. What are you doing up?"

"Never mind that. Just come in here."

Laura pulled off her gloves. She removed her coat and hat, and unwound her muffler. She was tired; she didn't even want to guess what this latest problem might be.

She drew a breath and went to the kitchen. She was surprised to see Eliza sitting there. She hadn't seen her sister since Thursday night, when Eliza had been packing for a weekend in Long Island with Amy Remington. "I thought you were coming back tomorrow. What happened?"

"Some people were driving back tonight and they offered me a ride. It's a much nicer way to travel than that drafty old train."

"Did you just get home?"

"About an hour ago. I wanted to go straight to bed, but Aunt Margaret had other ideas."

"Tell her why."

"Yes," said Laura, sitting down at the table, "tell me why."

Eliza's violet eyes were calm, faintly amused. "All right, I will. The Remingtons invited me to spend

149

Christmas in Oyster Bay. I accepted. Aunt Margaret wasn't happy to hear that."

"Was I supposed to be happy? Imagine deserting your family on Christmas! And with your poor mother hardly cold in her grave!"

Laura winced. "Aunt Margaret, *please.*"

"I'm not saying anything you're not thinking, missy. It's wrong to be going off to parties so soon after Kay's death. It's just plain wrong! In *my* day, people had respect. In *my* day—"

"It isn't your day anymore," interrupted Eliza. "It's mine, and I plan to make the most of it . . . A girl has to think of her future. I expect this Christmas will mean a lot to my future. It could mean everything."

Margaret didn't know what to say. She opened her mouth, closed it, and then looked at Laura.

Laura was staring at Eliza. "Have you met someone? Who is he?"

"I'm not going to say anything else until I'm sure."

"But are you serious about him, Eliza? Are you in love?" She leaned across the table, her face almost shining with expectation. "Tell me if you're in love. Just tell me that much."

There was a silence. Eliza lowered her eyes to the table and for a moment her brow seemed to cloud. "I think you read too many silly books, Laura."

"I don't understand."

"That's right, you don't." She glanced up, meeting her sister's bewildered gaze. "I'm not in love," she said. "Love has nothing to do with it. I've met someone . . . who'll take care of me. Someone who's *like* me in certain ways. There won't be any surprises and that's fine. That gives me the upper hand."

"The upper hand, is it?" Margaret glared at her niece. "Is that the way girls think about marriage these days?"

"If they're smart. If they think at all. If love doesn't confuse everything."

"Is that what you learned at your fancy Crossfield?"

"That's what I learned at home."

Laura's smile had long since faded; her head had begun to throb. She'd heard Eliza say many of these same things before. She'd thought it was a pose, but now she wondered. "*What* did you learn at home?" she asked.

"What you should have learned yourself: that love isn't an answer to anything." Eliza smoothed a tiny wrinkle in the sleeve of her silk blouse. She rested her arm lightly on the table and looked up at Margaret. "You loved Wilbur Hobart. Where did it get you?"

"Eliza!"

"It's true. Think about Aunt Margaret and Wilbur Hobart. Think about Mama and Papa. They loved each other too, and where did it get them?"

Laura smiled. "It made them happy."

"Did it?"

"Of course it did," said Margaret. "You take the prize for queer ideas and that's a fact. I hope this *someone* of yours knows what he's in for. Poor boy, my heart goes out to him."

"That's not very nice."

"It's not very nice of you to spend Christmas away from your family. Future or no future, your place is here with your sister and your aunt . . . If the boy means so much to you, ask him to have Christmas dinner with us."

"No, that wouldn't work."

"Why not? Are you ashamed of us?" Margaret's stern gaze moved to Laura. "You haven't said anything about all this."

"I've been listening."

"And?"

She sighed. She didn't want to be put in the middle of this argument. She knew family always came first to Margaret, knew family didn't really matter to Eliza. She rubbed her tired eyes, wondering if *anything* really mattered to Eliza. "I guess I thought we'd be together on Christmas," she admitted. "I'm going to see Robby on Christmas Eve, but I thought we'd all be together Christmas day."

"There!" cried Margaret "Laura agrees with me!"

Eliza looked at her sister, then slowly shook her head from side to side. "I'm sorry, my plans are already made. It's no use, Aunt Margaret. You can keep me here all night and it still won't be any use."

"Laura?"

"What do you want me to say? Eliza's not going to change her plans . . . Maybe I wouldn't either, if I were in her shoes. I mean we don't have much to offer here, do we? Not compared to Oyster Bay. And now that Mama's gone . . ."

Margaret turned her back, rattling some pans on the stove. "All right. All right, if that's how you both feel. Well say no more about it. From now on, Christmas is just another day of the week. Nothing special; no reason to fuss."

"Aunt Margaret—"

"Just another day of the week."

"Now we can go to bed," said Elisa, rising. "I'm exhausted."

"Yes, well, there *is* one thing," said Laura. "We don't have any money for new clothes, not even for Oyster Bay. Do you understand?"

"I don't need any clothes right now. All I'll need is the train fare . . . Oh, and a few dollars to tip the servants."

A few dollars to tip the servants. Laura started laughing. Great whoops of laughter burst from her, grow-

152

ing louder and louder until her shoulders shook and tears welled in her eyes. "Do . . . do you know what my night was like?" she asked, wiping her eyes with the back of her hand. "I'll tell you what it was like . . . I was on my feet for six hours, taking tickets at the Royal . . . And when I wasn't taking tickets, I was taking inventory at the candy counter. And when I wasn't doing that . . . I was sweeping the lobby." She paused, wiping her eyes again. "And now," she continued, breaking into new gales of laughter, "now my amazing sister wants my hard-earned money . . . to tip the servants. The servants! Dear God, that's the funniest thing I've ever heard!"

She rose, her gaze skipping from Margaret's astonished face to Eliza's bowed head. "The servants," she said in perfect imitation of Eliza's voice. Her mouth twitched with laughter as she went to the door. "My, my, my, the servants!"

"My sister's away," said Laura, glancing across the desk at Sam Roth. It was Christmas Eve. The last Santa Claus costume had been rented, the last elf suit, the last pair of gilded antlers. For a while, people had been three-deep at the counter, but now all the people were gone and it was time to go home. "My aunt and I are planning a quiet holiday. This year we're treating Christmas like any other day."

"I'm sorry."

She closed a file folder and put it aside. "At least this awful year is coming to an end. I'll be glad to get rid of it."

"Yes, I know what you mean." He ran his hand through his dark hair, absently patting the bald spot at the back of his head. "Look, I brought my car today. I'll give you a ride home."

"Isn't it out of your way?"

"It's *on* the way. I'm meeting my wife at her mother's. That's between First and Second Avenue."

Laura smiled. "Perfect. Thanks, Sam, I'd love a ride."

He stood, reaching for his jacket. "We might as well leave now. I'll go lock up . . . Here are the invoices; they'll keep till next week."

She took the invoices and collected the files from the desk. Bit by bit, she'd managed to reduce the clutter in the office, but she hadn't been able to do anything about Sam's desk. He'd warned her that he liked clutter, and he was always adding to it — little scraps of paper, magazine clippings, check stubs, old manila envelopes stained with coffee and ink. Even the ashtrays overflowed.

Laura glanced at the mess but left it as it was. She slid the files into the oak cabinets, closed the windows, and pulled down the shades. "All set," she said when Sam returned to the office.

"Then let's get out of here."

They gathered their coats and hats and went to the elevator. "I'm so glad I won't have to take the subway tonight," she commented as the car made its bumpy descent. "There are bound to be crowds. Last-minute Christmas shopping, you know."

"Did you finish your own shopping?"

"There wasn't much of it." She thought about the scrawny Christmas tree Margaret had dragged home. It had cost only a quarter and that was all it was worth. The runt of the litter, she thought, smiling to herself. "We didn't do any splurging this year."

"Maybe next year will be better for you."

"It couldn't be any worse." She shook her head. "No, I shouldn't have said that. I take it back. No matter how bad things are, they can always be worse."

The elevator clanked to a stop. Sam opened the

gate and followed Laura into the cold, drafty lobby. "You can leave the lights on," he said. "The night watchman will be here soon . . . I'll get the door."

A blast of icy air greeted them as they stepped outside. Laura bent her head against the wind and held on to her hat. "Do we have far to go?"

"The car's right there," replied Sam, pointing proudly to the dark blue Ford parked at the curb. "There she is."

Laura heard the sudden warmth in his voice, the affection. Obviously, he doted on this car "It's . . . she's very nice."

"A beauty," he declared, opening the passenger door. "I got her for sixty dollars, secondhand. The best sixty dollars I ever spent!" He closed the door, listening for the gentle click, and then went around to the other side. "Wait'll you hear the engine," he said, turning the ignition key. "Purrs like a kitten."

"Yes, very nice."

"You don't drive, do you?"

"No, we never had a car. Robby . . . My friend Robby Collier has a Packard, but he wouldn't let me drive it even if I knew how."

"Is that your boyfriend?"

Laura smiled shyly. "Yes. He's at Yale. Well, he's not at Yale now; it's the Christmas break. He's been away, but he'll be home tonight. We wanted to be together for Christmas Eve."

Sam kept his eyes on the tangled traffic, glancing every few moments in the rear-view mirror. "Are you going to marry him?"

"He hasn't asked me yet."

"But he will?"

Laura blushed, smiling again. "Someday," she said, her smile widening. "Robby has to finish school first. And I have all my jobs."

"Too many jobs. They'll wear you out. If you don't

marry this guy soon, you ought to find yourself one good job and stick to it."

She looked up. "You're not trying to tell me something, are you? I mean, you're not getting ready to fire me?"

"No, it's just advice. You're the best girl we've had, but I know you're not going to stay very long. None of the part-time girls do." He turned the car into an intersection, cursing under his breath as another car passed too close to the Ford. "So when you leave us, make sure it's for a good full-time job."

"They're hard to find, Sam."

"I know. This damn Depression . . ." He turned the wheel and the car turned the corner. "I'm counting on Roosevelt," he said. "Things will start to get better."

"What if they don't?"

"At least you've got your Yalie waiting in the wings."

"Yes," agreed Laura, her face lighting up. "Yes, I've got Robby."

"I'm home," called Laura, hanging up her coat and hat. "Aunt Margaret, where are you?"

"In here."

She went to the living room. It was early evening, and in the amber lamplight she saw Margaret seated on the sofa. She was surprised to see Robby's father. "Oh, Mr. Collier, I . . . Merry Christmas."

He stood. "Merry Christmas to you, Laura." Mike Collier was tall and attractive; any defects in his middle-aged figure were concealed by expensive tailoring. His dark hair was sprinkled with gray. His eyes were brown and very shrewd. He had an easy, amiable smile. "I've brought a message from Robby."

"A message?"

"I'll get straight to the point, Laura. Robby's not coming home tonight. He's decided to spend the rest of his holiday in Greenwich. He would have telephoned you to explain but—"

"But we don't have a telephone," she said, shrugging.

"I'm not making excuses for my son. It was wrong of him to change his plans at the last minute and I told him so. But they've got a big house party going—a lot of his college pals and ice hockey on the pond and all that kind of stuff. He's sorry—he asked me to tell you he was sorry—but he's not coming home and that's the end of it."

Laura sank down next to Margaret. "I understand. He—he must be having a wonderful time."

Mike shoved his hands in his trouser pockets. "You have a right to be mad, Laura," he said jingling some coins. "I hope this doesn't ruin your Christmas."

She lowered her head, trying to hide the tears that glistened in her eyes. She wasn't angry but she was hurt. She felt as if she had been abandoned and she wondered if there was more to it than college pals and ice hockey on the pond.

"Robby said he'd write to you," continued Mike. "In the meantime, he wanted you to have your Christmas present." From his jacket pocket he took a small blue Tiffany box. He went to Laura and put the box in her hand. "There's supposed to be a card. Robby said there was a card, but I couldn't find it."

"That's all right. It doesn't matter."

He watched Laura, wishing there were something else he could say. He shook his head. Nothing he might say could change the truth, and the truth was that Robby had chosen to be elsewhere. Like Laura, he suspected there was more to it than Robby had admitted. "I didn't realize it was so late," he said now, glancing at his gold wristwatch. "I'd better be going."

157

"How about some eggnog?" asked Margaret. "It's my best yet, even if I do say so myself."

"Thank you, but Eleanor's waiting for me."

"I'll see you out, then."

"Good-bye, Laura."

"Good-bye, Mr. Collier." She looked up, forcing a smile. "Tell Mrs. Collier I said Merry Christmas."

"I will. I certainly will."

He left the room with Margaret. Laura heard their footsteps in the hall. She heard voices, but she couldn't make out what they were saying. She gazed down at the Tiffany box and set it on the table. Gently, she touched her locket. It had been Robby's first present and it, too, had come from Tiffany. She remembered how happy she'd been and her hand fell away from the locket. What good did it do to remember?

After a moment she reached for the Tiffany box and untied the white ribbon. "Robby," she murmured, lifting out a delicate bracelet of opals and filigreed silver links. She fastened the bracelet on her wrist, brushing her fingers over the milky stones. "Oh, Robby."

The front door closed. Mike Collier had gone but there were other voices, other footsteps moving toward the living room. Frowning, Laura glanced up. "Paul," she exclaimed as Paul Brent walked in. "I didn't know you were coming tonight."

"Aunt Margaret said you were running low on family," he explained with a grin. "So here I am."

"My goodness, did you come all the way from—where is it—Loganville?"

"Logan*port* is the next town over. *Green*ville is where we live. Or at least my folks live there. I live here now."

"Here? In New York? Really?"

"Sure." Paul sat down in the chair opposite Laura.

He leaned back, his blue eyes crinkling in a smile. "I came to New York to seek my fortune."

"But you didn't say anything. About living here, I mean."

"I wanted to wait."

Laura's frown deepened. "Why?"

"Well, it's silly, I guess. I wanted to ask you to dinner, but I thought I'd wait till I could afford to buy a better suit. This is the best I have," he added, looking down at the slightly shabby, slightly baggy, dark blue wool. "I thought *everything* ought to wait till I could afford better . . . But that may take a while. Years, maybe. I haven't found any gold in the streets of New York."

"You don't look worried."

Paul shrugged, crossing his ankle over his knee. "Some things are worth worrying about, but not money."

"I worry about money all the time," sighed Laura. "All the time."

"Even on Christmas Eve?"

She glanced quickly at her new bracelet. What was Robby doing now? she wondered. Was he with his college pals? Or was he with a girl? "It isn't much of a Christmas this year."

"It's as much of a Christmas as we make it," said Margaret, carrying a tray of eggnog into the room. "You'll see I'm right once we start trimming the tree. Paul can do the top branches. He's nice and tall."

Laura looked at the tree, at the pinched, skimpy branches and the bare spots where there were no branches at all. Only Margaret would have bought such a tree, but Laura was suddenly glad she had. If not for Margaret, the tree would have been thrown on some trash heap; an orphan left to shiver in the cold. "Where are the ornaments? Do you have Mama's star?"

"Of course," said Margaret. "Everything's in a big box in the closet. On the top shelf, out of harm's way. Paul will get it down. But first I think we should drink a toast." She ladled the eggnog into three fluted glass cups. "I warn you, it has a kick to it. I traded Bea a bottle of sherry for a bottle of brandy, and I used more than half."

"Delicious," declared Paul, tasting the creamy liquid. "Good thing I'm not driving."

"Do you have a car?" asked Laura.

"Well, I have a car I can borrow when I need to."

"Nobody needs a car in New York," said Margaret. She lifted her cup. "Now let's have our toast . . . To our loved ones; they'll always be in our hearts."

Laura thought about her loved ones, about her father and mother, gone and never coming back; about Eliza, off with friends in Long Island; about Robby, off with friends in Connecticut. She stared into her eggnog and said nothing.

Paul touched her arm. "What's wrong?"

"Sorry. I was thinking this hasn't been a very good year for loved ones."

He smiled. "Then let's drink to the *new* year."

"A week early?"

"Why not? I'll start . . . Happy New Year, Laura Bellamy. Happy New Year and all the best!"

Chapter Nine

Snow had been predicted for New Year's Eve and now Laura watched the first lacy flakes whirl past her window. It was five o'clock, already dark outside. Church bells were ringing somewhere in the distance. "It's just practice," she said, and that was true. At midnight there would be a great chorus of bells.

Doris tilted her head like a bird. "I love the sound, don't you?"

Laura nodded, watching the streams of people hurrying along the avenue. She would have been one of them, but Sam had closed Crawford & Jones for the New Year's weekend. "Everybody loves church bells."

"Especially on holidays."

Laura drew the curtains. She turned from the window, smiling at Doris. The two friends had spent the afternoon together and they both wore thick, greasy white cream on their faces and curlers in their hair. Laura wore her old bathrobe and her slippers with the hole in the toe. Doris wore a pleated skirt and a sweater (someone's castoff) that was several sizes too big.

"We're a pretty sight!" said Laura. She sat down at the dressing table and peered into the mirror. The face cream had cost her twenty cents — a foolish expense, she thought, except that she had a date with Robby tonight and she wanted to look her best. She hadn't seen him for weeks. She hadn't heard from him until yesterday, until his telegram: ARRIVING TOMORROW 8PM. MUST SEE YOU. The urgency had made her heart flutter; he'd said *must,* and surely that was a good sign. "Do you think the cream's been on long enough?"

"It's supposed to seep in. That's what Jane said."

"Well, I think it's seeped long enough." She picked up a cloth and started wiping her face. "I don't see much difference," she said after a few moments. "Take a look."

Doris went to the dressing table. She bent, staring at Laura's reflection. "Oh, I see a difference. There's . . . sort of a glow. Yes, I'm almost sure there is."

They were still studying her reflection when they heard a knock at the door. "Come in," called Laura. She turned. "Yes, Aunt Margaret?"

"You'd better come with me."

"I'll set the table as soon as—"

"Never mind the table. Just do as I say for once."

Laura noticed how pale Margaret was, how stiffly she held herself. Something was wrong. Dear God, what now? "You have such a strange expression, Aunt Margaret. You're scaring me . . . Has something happened?"

"You could put it that way, yes. Robby's here."

"Robby? So early?"

Margaret's mouth tightened. "He took an early train. He's in the living room, waiting for you. You'd better come now."

Fear, cold and quick, raced along Laura's spine. Something was wrong and it had to do with Robby. Dear God, not Robby. She wiped the last traces of cream from her face and pulled the curlers out of her hair. "I'm—I'm not dressed."

"It doesn't matter."

"It doesn't?" Laura and Doris glanced at each other. "I'll stay here," said Doris. "In case you need

162

me."

Laura rose. "All right, Aunt Margaret," she said, her hands jumping nervously at her sides. "Whatever this is, let's get it over with."

Margaret opened the door. "Eliza's here too."

"Eliza?"

"Yes. Eliza."

Eliza blew a perfect smoke ring and watched it drift away. Her face was utterly serene, her free hand resting lightly on the sofa cushion. Behind her stood Robby. He looked bemused, as if he weren't quite certain where he was, or how he happened to be in this place. He kept glancing toward the door; he kept frowning. He started to reach in his pocket for his cigarettes, then changed his mind.

Eliza saw Laura first. Her composure seemed to slip, but only for an instant. "Come in and sit down," she said quietly. "There are things . . . to talk about."

Laura didn't move. She had wanted to run to Robby, to throw herself in his arms, but something had stopped her. Something in his manner, perhaps. Something in the way he stood so close to Eliza. Something in the way he and Eliza looked together. *They're a matched set.* Where had she heard that? From Jane, and Jane had been right.

Laura stood rooted in the doorway, clutching her robe and staring at the golden couple. A terrible suspicion had crept into her thoughts. She tried to push it away but she couldn't. "You . . . were together this week, weren't you? The two of you . . . You were together."

"We stayed with friends in Greenwich," replied Eliza.

Laura felt sick. Again and again she shook her head. "My God," she said when she could speak. "My God."

Eliza shrugged. "But that's not important."

"Not important!"

"Laura, I wish you'd sit down."

"I don't care what you wish. I don't care." Her anguished gaze moved to Robby. He hadn't said a word; he hadn't even looked at her. Now he turned and slowly raised his eyes. "Robby, why?" she asked. "I don't understand."

"I'm sorry. I . . . I should have . . . This is very difficult, Laura."

"For heaven's sake, Robby," said Eliza, "tell her."

Laura had taken a few steps into the room. She took a few more, stopping only inches from him. "Tell me what?"

He looked into her eyes, watched them flicker from brown to a dark, intense blue. "Everything happened so fast," he said. Too fast, he thought. It was as if he were waking from some strange dream, parts of which he couldn't remember. It was as if his whole life had spun suddenly out of control. "I don't know where to begin."

"Tell me what?"

Eliza put out her cigarette. "Laura, Robby and I were married this morning. We were married by a Justice of the Peace in Maryland."

The room seemed to dim, to sway. Laura grabbed the back of the sofa and held on. "Are you trying to be funny, Eliza? That's not a very funny joke."

"I couldn't be more serious. Robby and I were married this morning."

"No, I don't believe you."

"It's true," said Robby. "I had my car and we drove to Maryland. We drove most of the night. Whit Palmer came along. He was our witness . . . It's true, Laura."

"No."

"It's true."

She slapped him so hard that the imprint of her hand flamed his cheek. "Get out!" she cried. "Get out of here right now!"

Robby was too stunned to move. He stared at Laura and she slapped him again. "If you'll just let me—"

"Get out of here, I said. Get out!"

Eliza glanced across the room. "Why are you just standing there, Aunt Margaret? Can't you help?"

"Is it help you want? Since when? You didn't have any trouble helping yourself to your sister's boyfriend."

Eliza looked at her sister. She saw anger and hurt and tears. She looked at her new husband and she saw him backing away. "Robby, you'd better go . . . Go on, it's all right. I'll get my things and meet you upstairs."

"Yes, go on," said Margaret. "Do as she tells you and get used to it. There's no doubt who'll call the tune in this wonderful marriage of yours."

"Really, Aunt Margaret," sighed Eliza, "you're only making things worse."

"If I am, it's what you deserve. You ought to be ashamed of yourself."

Robby didn't want to hear any more. He touched Eliza's shoulder and then walked quickly to the doorway. He was almost in the hall when he stopped and looked back at Laura. "I'm sorry," he said. "I'm sorry I hurt you."

She had a last glimpse of his handsome profile, his golden hair. A moment later he was gone. The front door clicked open, slammed shut. She dropped onto the arm of the sofa and stared blindly into space.

"I'll get my things," said Eliza, rising.

She left, and for a little while there was silence. The smell of cigarette smoke lingered in the room. Margaret wrinkled her nose and opened a window. "We can use some fresh air," she muttered.

Laura glanced around. "Where's Eliza?"

"She went to gather her things. Didn't you see—"

"Her things?" Laura sprang up. "No. No, she's not taking *anything* out of this apartment. Not even a hairpin!"

"Where are you going?"

"To have a few words with Eliza . . . And then I never want to see her again!"

The closet doors were open, and the drawers of the bureau. A large suitcase lay open on Eliza's bed. "I wonder," she murmured. "I wonder how much I should take with me tonight. I have to come back next week to pack a trunk . . . In the circumstances, I don't suppose I could ask Laura to pack for me."

"I don't understand you, Eliza," said Doris in a small, worried voice. She edged deeper into the corner, shaking her curly head. "How could you do this to your own sister?"

"Robby and Laura weren't engaged, you know. He was fair game. Besides, it never would have worked out for them. They would have been miserable together."

"You don't say." Laura had come into the room and now she was walking around, closing closets and drawers. She closed Eliza's suitcase and sat on it. "You don't live here anymore, Eliza. I want you to go."

"I will, as soon as I decide what to take with me."

"Oh, that's simple. You're not taking anything. The clothes on your back; that's all you're leaving with . . . And this," she added, tearing Robby's opal bracelet from her wrist and hurling it at Eliza.

Eliza blinked. "Have you gone crazy?"

"I wouldn't be surprised."

"This is ridiculous, Laura. Get out of my way and let me get my things."

"I'll throw them out the window; I'll set fire to them before I'll let you have any of these things. I mean it. You're walking out of here with the clothes on your back and that's all." Laura's eyes flashed. "You've taken enough from us already,"

"*Us?*"

"Papa and Mama killed themselves trying to give you a fancy life. I've been working at three jobs trying to pay off the bills. Your bills, Eliza. And while I was busy working, you were busy taking my boyfriend. Stealing him. Well, you're not stealing anything else."

"But . . . But don't you see? These are *my* things."

"No, they're not. Not anymore."

Eliza saw the resolute set of Laura's chin. She shrugged. "You can sit there all night if you want. I'll just get my other suitcase."

"No, you won't." Laura was across the room in an instant. She stood in front of the closet, blocking the door. "The suitcases will bring a nice price at Mr. Goldberg's pawnshop," she said.

Doris came to stand with her. "You ought to leave, Eliza."

"This isn't any of your business. You're both behaving like children."

"And how have you been behaving?" asked Laura. "I'll never forgive you. Never."

"Never is a long time. We're still sisters."

Yes, we're sisters, thought Laura as tears burned her eyes; that's why it hurts so much. "Robby was the one good thing in my life. The only good thing. But you had to take him from me . . . Dear God, it's so unfair. You could have had anybody. You could have had your pick. A society boy—"

"No," said Eliza. "What I learned at Crossfield is that you can't get along in Society unless the women like you. Women don't like me. Except Amy, and even she started watching her fiancé when I was around . . . Then there's the problem of not having any money. Of everybody thinking I was a gold digger. They close ranks against gold diggers, you know."

"Poor Eliza."

"Step aside and let me get my suitcase."

Laura moved closer to the door. "You don't love Robby. I know you don't."

"I understand him, and that's more important. Robby and I are alike. I knew that from the beginning. It's how I knew he was wrong for you . . . In a way, I did you a favor."

"Are you expecting thanks?"

Eliza wasn't sure what she had expected. That Laura would be upset; that Margaret would be angry; that there would be a few awkward moments. "I expected a fuss, I suppose, but you're carrying it too far. Stop being silly, Laura, and let me get my things."

"I want you to leave now. You don't belong here."

"But—"

"Get out, Eliza."

For a split second she thought Laura was going to hit her. She stepped back, and sighing, turned away. "I can see it's no use. I'll just have to leave everything here until you've calmed down."

Laura saw Eliza's purse sitting atop the bureau. She reached for it.

"What are you doing?"

"Taking your keys. You won't need them . . . You might try to sneak in while I'm at work." Laura slipped the keys into her pocket and handed the purse to her sister. "Good-bye, Eliza."

"Good-bye, Laura." She went to the door, brushing past Margaret. "You could have made this easier for me," she said to her aunt. "At least you might have tried."

"Don't look for sympathy, not after what you did. Not after stabbing your sister in the back."

"You don't understand."

"Oh, I understand all right." Margaret's eyes clouded with memory, with old resentments. "Why

168

wouldn't I understand? This is Wilbur Hobart all over again!"

Laura was alone in her room when a clamor of horns and bells and whistles announced the new year of 1934. She lay on her bed, listening to the sounds, trying not to think. Beside her on the night table was her keepsake box—a small, old-fashioned hatbox she had covered with silk and trimmed with bits of lace. She glanced at it. After a moment she sat up and took the box in her lap.

Gently, she lifted the lid. Nestled among curls of tissue paper were souvenirs of her life: a medal she'd won in a grade school essay contest; little pink sea shells from Coney Island; a snapshot of Doris and Jane; an empty perfume vial; dried flowers wrapped in a handkerchief; Gloria Swanson's autograph; a lace fan. Hidden under the tissue paper were all of Robby's letters and notes. She wanted to destroy them but she couldn't; it was too soon. She hid them again. She unclasped her gold locket and hid that also.

Laura closed the box and returned it to her closet shelf. The horns and bells and whistles had stopped now. She noticed the sudden quiet, the stillness broken only by the ticking of the clock. She thought about the minutes ticking away; the minutes, the hours, the days, the weeks. In three weeks she would be eighteen.

And then what? she wondered, flopping down on the bed. She had no boyfriend, no money, practically no family, and no prospects beyond her three stopgap jobs. She could see the dreary, empty days stretching ahead. She could see herself turning into Margaret. *This is Wilbur Hobart all over again.*

To Laura, it was worse. She had been betrayed by her own sister, and that was something she could neither forgive nor forget. She blamed Robby too, though not nearly as much as she blamed Eliza. Just the thought of Eliza stirred deep wells of hurt and anger. The hurt would be with her always, but the anger she would use as a spur. Somehow she would make a life for herself and it would be a good life. She would have the things she wanted, and like Eliza, she would set the terms.

Anger got Laura through the night, through the weekend. When she went off to her job on Monday morning, she seemed unchanged; a little paler, perhaps a little thinner, but otherwise unchanged. She rode the subways, she did her work, she joked with Irene, she helped Margaret tidy the kitchen after supper, and she did all these perfectly ordinary things in a perfectly straightforward way. There were no undercurrents, no dark shadings. She refused to discuss "the Colliers," as she now referred to Robby and Eliza, but apart from that, she was herself.

"Or so she wants us to think," said Margaret with a terse laugh. "But I know better."

"Yes," said Jane, "you're probably right." It was two weeks into the new year, two weeks during which she'd seen almost nothing of Laura. Work had been the excuse and she'd accepted it, but she'd also accepted Margaret's invitation to supper. "Will she talk about Robby and Eliza yet? Does she know they've moved to Philadelphia?"

"I tried to tell her last night. She said she wasn't interested. But I have a hunch she'd already heard the news from Eugene. What a big mouth he has! Thanks to Eugene, there are no secrets in this building." Margaret leaned forward, resting her bony elbows on the kitchen table. "It doesn't matter, though," she continued. "The important thing is they're gone. *The Colliers* are gone. Good riddance to bad rubbish!"

Jane smiled. "I happen to know exactly how it happened. Pop had drinks with Mr. Collier. He got the whole story. Oh, Mr. Collier's so mad. Boiling mad,

170

Pop said."

"And since when are they such friends?"

"They're not friends, not really. Sort of like cronies. It's something to do with politics and Mayor LaGuardia . . . But Mr. Collier must trust Pop. He told him everything . . . Do you want to hear?" asked Jane, her eyes twinkling. "Or will you accuse me of being a big mouth?"

"It's different circumstances. You have a right to talk; you're Laura's friend. And I have a right to listen."

"Okay then, I'll start from the beginning . . . Now you really have to picture this. I mean, you really have to see it in your mind . . . 'Cause if you do, you can understand how it happened. Well, more or less."

"Laura will be home soon. You'd better do your telling now, or else forget about it."

"Okay. This is how Robby told it to Mr. Collier, and how Pop told it to me . . . Remember, you have to picture it in your mind."

Margaret looked up at the clock. "Laura will be home in fifteen minutes."

"All right, all right; just let me explain the setting . . . Robby and Eliza were at this beautiful country house in Greenwich. There was a fire going in the big stone fireplace. It was snowing and they could see the snow through the French doors . . . It was a cold night. They were drinking brandy and buttered rum and things like that. Anyway, Eliza is sitting on cushions near the fireplace. And Robby is sitting near her, watching the firelight glisten in her hair . . . It's sort of late, and he's been drinking. He's feeling a bit—well, kind of mellow. And then Eliza gazes up at him through her long, fluttery eyelashes. She says . . ."

". . . I feel so safe here, Robby. Sitting here with you, I feel as if nothing bad will ever happen to me."

He looked into her eyes, huge violet eyes as innocent as a child's. He moved closer, stroking her hand. "For a moment you sounded frightened. There isn't anything to be frightened of, Eliza."

"But there is. I'm alone in the world now, an orphan . . . I don't know how I'll manage. I'm not clever like some girls. I'm not even very smart. How will I earn my living?"

"You won't have to earn a living. You'll marry and your husband will see to that."

She lowered her gaze. "Who'd want to marry me? I don't know how to cook or sew or do any of those housekeeping things. And I'm poor."

Robby tilted her face to him. "You're beautiful, Eliza, the most beautiful girl I've ever known. There isn't a fellow in the world who wouldn't want to marry you."

"And take care of me?" She sipped her drink, fluttering her lashes over the rim of the glass. "Do you think so?"

"Of course." Music was playing on a radio somewhere; he heard a throaty voice singing about love. He felt the warmth of the brandy, the heat of the fire. He looked into Eliza's eyes, those incredible eyes, and he felt engulfed, as if by flames. "Eliza," he murmured, taking her in his arms. Her perfume swirled around him. Her mouth was soft and yielding. She was naked under her sweater . . .

"The way Robby explained it," continued Jane, "he didn't even remember proposing to Eliza. He didn't remember much of anything, except that suddenly he and Eliza and Whit Palmer were on their way to Maryland."

"Well, I'm not surprised," sighed Margaret. "She set a trap, didn't she? And Robby was weak enough to crawl right in. I'll wager she was counting on that. On his weak character."

"Oh, I'm sure . . . But anyway, when Robby left here New Year's Eve, he went upstairs to tell his parents. His mother started crying, but *Mr.* Collier was furious. Boiling mad, like Pop said. He'd wanted Robby to finish college and then travel around Europe for a while . . . Learn a little bit about life before he settled down and got married. Oh, he had all sorts of plans for Robby. But all his plans went down the drain. He told Pop he'd never been as angry as he was that night."

"And that was the end of Yale?"

Jane nodded. "Mr. Collier said since Robby had a wife, he'd better have a job . . . So Robby's going to work at the radio station in Philadelphia. He's supposed to start at the bottom and work his way up."

"What difference does it make where he starts? The radio station will be his someday and everybody knows it. Meanwhile he's still the boss's son. He won't be sweeping floors."

"It would serve him right."

Margaret smoothed the coil of hair at the nape of her neck. She rose. "There's no justice in the world. Haven't you learned that yet? Look at Eliza. She did a bad thing, but instead of a punishment, she gets a reward. She gets a handsome husband, a big house—"

"An apartment," corrected Jane. "Mr. Collier is making them live in the company apartment in Philadelphia."

"I'll wager that's no hardship. And I'll wager it comes with servants."

"A housekeeper."

"A housekeeper," sniffed Margaret. "Do you see what I mean? There's no justice."

"Not in this world, anyway," said Laura, entering the kitchen. "Maybe in the next."

Jane turned. "You snuck up on us," she said, smiling at her friend.

"Well, you were so busy talking. Going on and on about the Colliers."

"I'm sorry, Laura. I guess they're still a pretty big topic of conversation."

"I've noticed," she replied with a cool smile. "The whole building seems to be talking about them."

"The whole building's on your side," declared Margaret. "Bea said so. She said there's no doubt everyone's on your side."

"Lucky me." Laura pulled out a chair and sat down. "How does Mrs. Wesley know all this? Did she take a poll?"

"I don't like your tone, missy. Whatever you think, Bea was only trying to help."

"Yes, but I don't want to be talked about. It's over, Aunt Margaret. I wish everybody would *let* it be over."

"I will when you will."

Laura frowned. "What?"

"If it's over, then you ought to stop brooding. I see the funny look you get sometimes like you're a million miles away. And I hear you pacing around at night. Back and forth, back and forth; just like an animal in a cage. If you ask me, *you're* the one who has to let it be over."

"I agree."

"You do?" Margaret was surprised; she had expected an argument, or at least a denial. She looked sharply at her niece. "What are you up to?"

"Nothing. I agree with you, that's all. And I'm going to do something about it. A few things, as a matter of fact." Laura glanced from Margaret to Jane. "I could use your help after supper. I have to clear out the closets. It's time to put together a package for Mr. Goldberg's pawnshop."

That meant Laura was ready to sort through Eliza's things and get rid of them. Jane thought it was about time. "Sure I'll help," she said. "Do you have boxes?"

"I have two suitcases. They should bring a nice price." With luck, they could bring as much as ten dollars. The beige wool coat trimmed in fox could bring another ten. The violet wool coat could bring another four or five. The alligator purse . . . She wasn't sure about the alligator purse. "Mr. Goldberg's a fair man. He'll do his best."

"Why stop with Mr. Goldberg?" asked Jane. "You can sell a lot of the other stuff to the secondhand store. You know, the one near the bakery. I'll bet you can get three dollars apiece for the dresses. Maybe even the same price for the cashmere sweaters . . . Gosh, Laura, those closets could be a gold mine!"

"I'm hoping for a hundred dollars."

"It's worth more than that."

"They *cost* more than that," replied Laura. "All those things put together cost a small fortune. But when you sell, you don't get the real value . . . I remember when Mama had to sell the silver teapot. She said she got about ten percent of what it was worth."

"That's true," agreed Margaret, taking a casserole dish out of the oven. "Oh, it was beautiful too. A Georgian silver teapot. A family heirloom . . . It had been in my family for a hundred years, maybe longer. But you have to take what you can get. That's the pity of hard times. You just have to take what you can get."

"I'll be happy to get a hundred dollars," said Laura. "It'll come in handy, because I'm going to be looking for a different job. *One* job, not three. I'd probably be earning less money with one job. I'd have to expect that."

Margaret set the casserole on the table. It was her Saturday hash and in it were the week's leftovers: sausage, chicken, macaroni, carrots, beets, a few lima beans. "You have to do what you think is right, regardless. There are only two of us now. We'll manage."

Laura thought about the bills. She'd made some progress, but it would be another year before they were all paid off. She didn't want to wait a year to change jobs; changing her job was the first step toward changing her life. "It's a risk, but I don't care."

Jane looked at the hash Margaret put on her plate. "It's good to take a risk every once in a while . . . Where are you going to start?"

"I have an appointment at the Harding Advertising Company."

Margaret's jaw dropped. "Did you say Harding? That's the place that fired your mother."

"Yes, I know." Laura glanced away. It had begun to snow, and she watched the chunky white flakes drifting past the window. "Yes," she said quietly, "that's why I think old Eli Harding will have to give me a job."

Chapter Ten

Eli Harding was not yet sixty, but for years he had been called *old* Eli Harding. Everything about him seemed to suggest age: his mournful, basset hound eyes; his manner, which was slow and deliberate; his hair, which had started graying when he was in his twenties and which was now pure white. His father had been big and robust; Eli resembled his grandfather, the lean, dapper man who had founded the Harding Advertising Company at the end of the Civil War.

Like his grandfather, Eli sometimes wore a jaunty red carnation in his lapel. It was one of his harmless eccentricities and it amused him. He didn't mind if he looked a little foolish, or if people thought he did. Unlike his grandfather, he had never taken himself too seriously.

Long ago, he had decided he was a lucky man. He loved his wife and his children and they loved him in return. He loved to play golf and he played well. He had his health. He had all the money he would ever need. And despite the ravages of the Depression, he had firm control of Harding Advertising.

The company had begun in two cramped rooms on lower Broadway. Joshua Harding, the thirty-year-old founder, had risked his savings and the proceeds of a small inheritance, but within months he'd earned his investment back. He'd earned a handsome profit also, and from then on, there'd been no stopping him. The Harding Advertising Company had prospered beyond his wildest dreams. By 1875 he'd moved the company to a lavish suite of offices in a fine new building on Fourteenth Street. By 1890 he'd moved the company to newer, more lavish offices on Twenty-third Street. In 1910, after Joshua's death, his son Aaron moved the company to the outskirts of Murray Hill.

Harding Advertising remained there through all the tumultuous years of Aaron's rule. The playboy of the family, the black sheep, he'd been a man of large appetites and little discretion, but a man with few equals in the business world. Year after year he'd produced huge profits, profits undiminished even by the uncertainties of the Great War and the first shock of Prohibition. At his death in 1922, he had been called the guiding genius of Harding Advertising—"a man who knew no limits."

Eli, taking his father's place as president, had been expected to fail. He hadn't, but he'd brought a vastly different style to the company. With his slow, methodical ways, his emphasis on the creative rather than the financial, and his great stores of common sense, he'd put his own stamp on Harding Advertising. The flamboyant Aaron was still remembered, still revered by some, but times had changed and it was felt that Eli was the right man for these times.

"We moved here in 1926," he said now. "Of course I hadn't anticipated the Depression. Back in '26, the world looked rosy. No one believed anything like this could happen."

"No, I guess not," replied Laura. She'd been ten years old in 1926. She recalled the crumbling brownstone in Yorkville; recalled her father, flushed with excitement over every new triumph at work; recalled how proud her mother had been, how happy. In those days everything *had* looked rosy. "No one can tell about the future." A picture of Madame Zarela flashed through her mind and she smiled. "At least not without a crystal ball."

"I sometimes think that's what we need in the advertising business. It's hard to know just what convinces people to buy a particular product. But we're *supposed* to know, you see. That's what we're paid for."

And paid well, thought Laura, glancing around the elegant office. It was a spacious, oak-paneled room with tufted leather chairs and sofas, and framed advertisements on the walls. The kneehole desk had the glow of old wood lovingly waxed and buffed. An oriental carpet adorned the spotless floor. "Is it guesswork, then?"

Eli pressed his fingertips together, making a tent of his hands. "Educated guesswork, perhaps. Instinct is part of it. It's been my experience that good advertising is often a matter of instinct." He paused, studying Laura. He had no idea why she had come to see him; her letter had said only that she wanted a few minutes of his time. "Are you interested in advertising?"

"I'm interested in a job, Mr. Harding. I should have told you that in my letter."

"Yes, I'm afraid you should have. There aren't any jobs here, Laura. I'm terribly sorry, but we've been cutting staff, not adding to it . . . We've lost some accounts during the past couple of years. Others have cut their own budgets to the bone. We've had no choice but to make adjustments."

"Adjustments?"

"I don't mean to sound callous. We've done everything possible to save jobs. But in certain departments there's simply not enough work. I can't help that, Laura. I assure you I've tried." Eli wondered why he felt he had to explain himself. His conscience was clear; he'd done more than most employers would have done for their employees, and surely more than his father would have done. "I've tried to be fair."

"Yes, I understand."

"These are difficult times." A cliché, he thought. Don't burden the poor girl with useless clichés. "The point is, I can't pay people to sit around and do nothing. It isn't the money. Or at any rate it isn't *only* the money. There's also a question of morale . . . It would be discouraging if part of the staff were paid to work and part of the staff were paid to do nothing. Morale would suffer. That may not seem very important, in the circumstances. But it's a problem I'm forced to consider."

Laura nodded. She was wearing one of her hand-me-down suits, a stylish charcoal wool with a fitted jacket and straight skirt. Her small, narrow-brimmed hat was tilted to the side in the current fashion. Her coat was folded over her chair. She looked confident, but her heart was racing, her fingernails digging into the palms of her hands. "I understand your problem, Mr. Harding," she replied. "And I know Mama did too. You mustn't blame yourself for . . . anything." She glanced away, but an instant later she returned her gaze to Eli. She hesitated. She'd *wanted* to make him feel guilty; that had been her plan. Now she decided she had to go through with it. "It's not your fault Mama died."

If Laura had made such a comment to Aaron, he would have laughed and then shown her the door. Eli did neither of those things. He had been troubled by Kay Bellamy's death. He hadn't blamed himself for firing her—he was a businessman after all, and he'd done what was best for his company—but still he'd had a few uneasy moments. Had Kay's firing somehow contributed to her death? He would never know. "We were all very sorry about your mother," he said, his snowy brows drawing together. "She was a fine woman."

"Thank you."

Eli waited, but Laura said nothing more. She sat silently, and her silence seemed to reproach him. He didn't doubt that she was trying to stir guilty feelings. It was a ploy, he thought, and everything considered, a clever one. "Tell me, Laura, do you believe I owe you a job because of your mother?"

"No," she replied, coloring. "No, you don't owe me anything. I want to *earn* my way. All I need is a chance."

"I'm afraid there are no chances here. There are no jobs."

"Maybe not for sketch artists like Mama. Maybe there was no job for her. But I'm a secretary, Mr. Harding. I'm a good secretary too. I have experience now. I have references . . . And nobody will work harder for you than I will. I'll work night and day, if I have to. You won't be disappointed; I promise you won't." She paused, digging in her purse for the letters of reference she'd brought. "If you'll just read them," she urged, holding out several sheets of paper, "you'll see I'm a good worker."

Eli took the letters and placed them on his desk. "This is all very well, but I can't create a job out of thin air. That's what you're asking, you know."

"It's not. There has to be a job here. There has to be something I can do, something that needs doing." Laura had leaned forward and now she was leaning anxiously across the desk, her eyes boring into Eli. "It's a big company, Mr. Harding. There *has* to be something."

He smiled. "You're very determined, aren't you? I wish that were enough . . . My dear child, you don't know the first thing about the advertising business. And business being what it is these days, we can't afford to hire inexperienced people. We can't afford mistakes."

"But I *have* experience," insisted Laura. "If you'll just read the letter, you'll see."

"You haven't any experience in advertising. You don't know—"

"I'll learn!" Laura was gripping the edge of the desk. Like a cat getting ready to pounce, her body was tensed, her back slightly arched. "I'm a fast learner. Mr. Goodfriend will vouch for that. I know he will."

"Mr. Goodfriend?"

"From the Acme Business Institute."

"Ah, yes, the Acme Business Institute." Eli's smile widened a bit. He liked this earnest, enterprising girl, but he wasn't quite sure what to do with her. The copy department was especially short on staff; Zack Reed had been begging for help. It was an interesting idea. "Creative people—copywriters, artists—can be temperamental. They can be difficult, but they're the heart and soul of this company and so I try to humor them."

"Yes?" Laura sensed he was leading up to something. Her grip tightened on the desk. "Do these creative people need a secretary?"

"Patience, Laura. I must think this through."

She eased back into her chair, watching as Eli lit his pipe. She prayed she'd convinced him to give her a job. Rashly, she promised God she'd never ask for anything else.

"You have a sister, I believe. If I remember correctly, I spoke to some Crossfield people about her a year or two ago."

"She's married now," replied Laura. "She's gone away."

Eli puffed on his pipe. "You're alone in the world, are you?"

"There's my aunt. She lives with us—with me, I mean."

"And does your aunt work?"

"No. Well, she does the cooking and cleaning at home. The chores." Laura wondered at the purpose of these questions, at the leisurely pace. Eli's pipe had gone out; he relit it. He appeared to be settling in for a nice, long chat. "My aunt doesn't have any money," continued Laura. "That's why she came to live with us."

"I see. The responsibility's on you, then. Do you mind if I ask your age?"

"Eighteen . . . Today is my eighteenth birthday," she added with a shy smile. "I was hoping it would be lucky."

"Eighteen." In some ways she's old for her age, thought Eli, in some ways she's very young. "I'd be throwing you to the lions," he said. He saw her quick frown and he laughed. "Putting you in with the copywriters would be just like throwing you to the lions."

"I can look after myself." She leaned forward again. "Really I can, Mr. Harding. I'm used to difficult people. My aunt's worse than the lions' den."

Eli's brows arched in amusement. "A terror, is she?"

"Oh yes. You could say she's been good training."

"Excellent training, for the advertising business." He put down his pipe and gazed steadily at Laura. "Very well," he said after a moment. "You'll have your chance."

"Really?" She leapt out of her chair and then fell back into it. "I don't know how to thank you, Mr. Harding. I promise I won't disappoint you."

"When do you wish to start?"

"Is next week all right? I just have to give one

week's notice to Crawford & Jones."

Eli glanced at his desk calendar. "That would be the twenty-ninth." He uncapped his pen and wrote a few lines on a note pad. "Monday the twenty-ninth," he said. He tore the top sheet from the pad and handed it across the desk to Laura. "Ten A.M. sharp."

She looked at the paper. "Zack Reed?"

"Zack is the head of the copy department. He's the man you'll have to please. If your work is satisfactory, he'll be your boss. One word of advice: when Zack yells at you—and he will—don't take it personally."

Laura smiled. "Thank you, I won't."

"The starting salary for secretaries here is $17.50 per week. Zack will explain your duties and your hours." Eli stood, ending the interview. "I wish you good luck, Laura."

"Thank you." She got to her feet, gathering her coat and purse and gloves. "Thank you very much, Mr. Harding. I'm very grateful."

He watched her walk to the door. "Laura?"

She turned, nearly dropping her purse. "Yes, Mr. Harding?"

"Happy birthday!"

"Here's the birthday girl now," said Margaret as Laura entered the kitchen. "I'm glad you're not late. We planned a little celebration. Nothing fancy, of course, but I cooked your favorite supper and Paul brought a bottle of wine."

"Nothing fancy," he said with a grin.

"Hello, Paul. I didn't know you were coming." She hadn't expected him, but she wasn't surprised to see him. Birthdays were family occasions and Margaret had herded Paul Brent into the family fold. He seemed to belong. He was a comfortable person to be around, an easy person. Laura liked the way he made himself at home. She liked the way his smile crinkled his eyes. "I'm glad you're here," she said. She meant it.

Laura couldn't have known that these visits were the happiest times of Paul's life. In large part, they were the reason he'd moved to New York City. He'd wanted to be close to the pretty, tawny-haired girl he'd loved since he was twelve years old. He'd wanted to believe that someday she would love him too. That day might be far off, he thought now, but I can wait. "This is a special birthday," he said. "I wouldn't miss it for the world . . . Do you feel any different? Turning eighteen and all?"

"I feel like a whole different person," she replied, pulling out a chair, "but not because of my birthday." Shse sat down across from Paul and smiled at him. "Because of my new job."

"What new job?" asked Margaret. "Don't tell me you got a job at Harding Advertising!"

"I start next week. I'm not sure if it had to do with Mama or not, but old Eli Harding agreed to give me a chance." Laura glanced back at Paul. "It was old Eli who fired Mama, you see. That was the day she caught cold walking home in the rain. She was never the same after that day."

Margaret picked up twin yellow potholders and opened the oven door. "It was too much for the poor woman. Being sick and out of work. Worrying about the bills all the time. It was just too much. And then when they came to take the breakfront away . . . Well, it's all in the past now."

She removed a heavy roasting pan to the counter. The beef was medium-rare: brown and crispy on the outside, pink at the center. Nestled around it were small, oven-glazed potatoes, mushroom caps, and tiny pearl onions. "I hope you're both hungry," she said as she reached for the carving knife. "Schultz the butcher did himself proud this time."

"Is it roast beef?" asked Laura, hopefully sniffing the air. "We haven't had roast beef in *years*."

"I said I cooked your favorite supper and that's what I did. It's a special occasion, isn't it? We can splurge a little on a special occasion."

Laura's mouth watered when the platter of meat and vegetables was set on the table. She'd lost her appetite after Eliza and Robby eloped, but suddenly she felt she could eat everything in sight. "It looks wonderful, Aunt Margaret. It's a wonderful surprise."

"It's a feast," said Paul, and to a man who regularly skipped lunch to save money, and whose supper was often a ten-cent hamburger, it was a bountiful feast indeed. "Is this what it's like to be rich?"

"Do you want to be rich?" asked Laura.

"No, not especially. But I wonder about it sometimes. How it would feel to be able to afford anything at all . . . I guess you'd get used to it after a while. What's that they say? It's only money?"

"Well, I want *lots* of money. And I've made up my mind I'm going to have it."

Paul grinned. "Which bank are you going to rob?"

"I don't blame you for laughing, but I've made up my mind and that's that."

"It's foolishness," declared Margaret, sitting down with a thump. "We've had enough foolishness in this house, missy. What has it brought but grief? I don't know what put such an idea in your head, but you'd better forget it. *You'll* have lots of money the day *I* take a bus ride to the moon!"

Laura smiled and said nothing. She filled her plate and soon she was scooping savory chunks of beef and potatoes and onions and mushrooms into her mouth. She took a slice of bread and slathered it with butter. Moments later she took another slice and dipped it in the gravy. She knew she was eating too fast and too much. She knew it was rude, but she couldn't seem to stop. It was as if she had never seen food before.

Her second glass of wine brought a rosy flush to her cheeks. She asked for a third glass, but Margaret snatched the bottle from the table, corked it, and hid it in the cupboard. After the dishes had been cleared away, after coffee had been poured, there was a chocolate birthday cake.

Laura counted nineteen candles—one for each of her years and one for good luck. She made her wish and blew out all the candles with a single breath.

"What did you wish?" asked Margaret.

Laura smiled again. Not too long ago her wish would have been about love, but tonight her wish was about money, lots of money. "It's a secret," she said, her eyes sparkling. "You'll know when it comes true."

"I had a nice time tonight," said Laura to Paul. They were strolling along Lexington Avenue, walking off the meal that had concluded with double portions of chocolate cake. It was a cold evening. The sky twinkled with frosty winter stars. She looked up at the sky and she smiled. "I thought it was going to be a sad birthday, but it wasn't . . . I suppose I'm really excited about my new job."

"It shows. You look . . . You look kind of shiny. As if someone poured moonlight all over you."

"Oh, that's probably the wine. I feel a little tipsy." They started across the street and Paul caught her arm. She glanced at him, thinking once more how comfortable he was to be around. He wasn't hasty or critical; he seemed to take people as he found them. She sensed she could say anything, do anything, and he would understand. "I'm glad we're friends, Paul. We are, aren't we?"

He nodded his sandy head. "Friends" wasn't exactly what he wanted to be with Laura, but it was a step up from being cousins. "Sure we are. Through thick and thin."

"It's funny . . . Well, it's not funny, but I don't really know you. I *do*, but I don't. I don't even know where you work."

"Are you asking where I work? You'll laugh."

"Laugh? No, I won't."

"Everybody does, but okay. I'm a junior executive—a very junior executive—at the Happy Child Toy Company."

"I'm smiling, not laughing," said Laura. "The Happy Child Toy Company? Is that true?"

"There was a time when I wanted to be a country lawyer. I had a picture in my mind of a small town like Greenville, only nicer. I'd have an office near the courthouse, right on the town square, and I'd smoke a pipe and I'd be the guy who fought for principles." Paul smiled at the memory. "I would have given it a try, pipe and all, but the Depression was getting worse and Dad was running out of money fast. That's when I left NYU and went back home."

"And went to work in his hardware store?"

"That was my *second* plan," replied Paul, chuckling to himself. "I forgot about being a country lawyer and decided I'd go into the hardware business instead. I'd build up Dad's store, and when he retired, I'd take it over and build it up some more. I was going to expand into farm supplies. It was a good idea, except for the Depression. That was about the time the glass factory closed. The brickyard went next . . . Main Street just died."

"Are you on your third plan now?" asked Laura.

"Now the only plan is for a steady job—which I have at the Happy Child Toy Company."

"Do you like your job?"

"I can play with the toys whenever I want," laughed

Paul. "I can also send a few dollars home each week. Dad isn't keen on taking the money, but it makes a difference. So I'm at Happy Child to stay. You couldn't blast me out of there with a cannon."

Laura was quiet for a moment, considering. The streets were almost deserted. She watched the cars streaking along the avenue; blurry, shadowy forms in the darkness. "You could go to law school at night," she suggested. "It would take more time, I guess."

"It would take forever. Anyway, it wasn't the law that interested me so much, Laura. It was the idea of being a country lawyer and what that meant. Or at least what I imagined that meant."

"You could still do it."

"No. I'm a city slicker now . . . I can see you don't believe that," he added with a grin.

Laura shook her head. She thought there would always be something of the boy in Paul, always something of the small-town boy. "You're too nice to be a city slicker."

Nice? His spirits sank. "Nice" was dull. It was bloodless; something you called your brother or your old uncle who was starting to forget things. Paul sighed. When Douglas Fairbanks swashbuckled across the screen, did anyone call *him* nice?

"What's the matter, Paul? You look far away."

He slowed his step. He stopped walking and put his hand on Laura's shoulder. "Will you have dinner with me next week? Please say yes."

"Dinner?"

"In New York City, supper means a late meal. Dinner means—"

"I know what dinner means," interrupted Laura, frowning. "I'm not sure if I know what *you* mean. Are you asking me out?"

"Please say yes."

"On a date?"

"That's right, a date. How about next Monday after work? You can tell me all about your first day at your new job."

They resumed their walk. Laura fixed her eyes on the pavement. She didn't know what to say because Paul had taken her by surprise. She hadn't thought of him as a boyfriend; she didn't dare ask if he'd thought of her as a girlfriend. "I didn't . . . expect to have any dates. Not since . . ."

"Since Robby?"

"I don't want to talk about him, Paul."

"I don't want to talk about him either. I just want to take you to dinner. It'll be fun. A celebration in honor of your new job. Nothing fancy, of course."

"You sound like Aunt Margaret."

"Do you want your life to be just you and Aunt Margaret?"

The thought startled Laura. She blinked and looked away, but an instant later she looked back at Paul. "Dinner next Monday after work," she agreed. "A celebration dinner . . . I hope that's how it turns out."

"Why wouldn't it?"

"Well, things can go wrong the first day of a new job. I want to make a good impression. I want to get off to a really good start."

Paul gazed sidelong at her. "You have big plans for this new job of yours, haven't you?"

Laura felt the wind on her face—a clean, sharp wind. She smiled. "For my job, and for the Harding Advertising Company. Yes, very big plans!"

"So you're the new girl," said Zack Reed, staring across his desk at Laura. "And you don't know a blessed thing about the advertising business. Is that right?"

"I learn quickly, Mr. Reed."

"That's what they all say."

"But I mean what I say. I *do* learn quickly."

He leaned back in his battered leather chair and laced his fingers behind his neck. He was a tall, rumpled man of forty; an excitable man with close-cut black hair and impatient gray eyes. His brow was perpetually furrowed. When he remembered to wear his glasses, they slipped down his long, thin nose.

Zack was hard on his staff, but he was liked because he was a fair man, as generous with praise as with criticism. Next to his wife and young son, his work was the most important thing in his life. He was devoted to the Harding Company and he expected the people in his department to share that devotion. Successful advertising, he believed, was a team effort, a blending of different talents. He'd been creating successful advertising for fifteen years.

"I need someone who's organized," he said suddenly, shifting around in his chair. "Someone who can keep track of details. We all scribble notes on little scraps of paper and then forget what the notes mean."

Laura ventured a smile. "Yes, I understand. That's how it was at Crawford & Jones—my last job. I can sort things out, Mr. Reed."

"Call me Zack. We don't bother with formalities here." He lit a cigarette, one of the twenty he smoked every day. Belatedly, he offered the pack to Laura. She shook her head and he tossed the pack on his desk. "Why did you leave your job? Risky move, wasn't it? In the middle of this damn Depression?"

She agreed it was risky. "But I had to take the chance," she went on. "There was no future at Crawford & Jones. There was no future at any of my jobs."

"Future?" Zack peered at Laura through a haze of

smoke. She was wearing the same charcoal suit and small, dark hat she'd worn for her interview with Eli. She'd trimmed her hair, and invested twenty cents in a new, clear red lipstick. He thought she was a very pretty girl. "I can tell you your future," he said. "You'll meet a nice young man, marry him, and raise a family."

"My nice young man ran off with my sister," she replied crisply. "That's when I decided to start relying on myself."

"Are you always so candid?"

"I . . . just want you to know how serious I am about this job. I'll work hard, and I'll learn. I promise you won't have any complaints."

"Eli said you were determined. He was right." The intercom buzzed. Zack pressed a button and picked up the telephone. "Excuse me, Laura. This won't take long."

"Sure." She relaxed a little, her eyes moving around the office. The walls were painted a bright, rosy beige, and crowded with framed advertisements. A handsome leather couch filled the far end of the room. In front of the couch was a low marble table holding several note pads and a large crystal ashtray. The carpet was the same rosy beige as the walls. Sunlight poured through the unshaded windows.

To the left of Zack's desk, she saw a typewriter sitting atop a sleek wood stand. "Do you type?" she asked when he finished his telephone call.

"With two fingers . . . I trust you can do better than that."

"Seventy-five words a minute."

Zack smoked his cigarette down to the end, depositing the crushed stub in his big brass ashtray. "I knew your mother," he said. "I liked her. She was a talented artist."

"Thank you."

"The only thing Kay lacked was ambition," continued Zack. "Her talents were wasted as a sketch artist. If she'd pushed harder, she could have moved up into layout and design."

"Instead she was fired."

"Because we had more sketch artists than we needed. Several people in that department were fired. It wasn't a surprise. Everybody knew what was coming."

Everybody but Mama, thought Laura. She put the thought out of her mind. She couldn't change the past; the future was what mattered now. Silently she promised that her own talents, whatever they were, would *not* be wasted.

She turned as the door opened and Eli Harding entered the room. "Good morning," she said, rising.

"Sit down, Laura," he said with a smile. "You make me feel quite ancient." She reclaimed her chair and he looked at Zack. "I stopped by to see if everything was all right. Are there any problems I should know about?"

"No problems," replied Zack. "I had a call from Rainbow Paint. They're happy with our suggestions. The meeting is next Wednesday at ten."

"Excellent, Zack. Excellent work . . . Is there anything else?"

He laughed. "If you're wondering about Laura, I think she'll do. We've been having a talk . . . She's young, but she's fast on her feet. Yes, I think she'll do."

Chapter Eleven

Laura stood in the outer office, surveying the two neat rows of unoccupied desks, the covered typewriters, the silent telephones. "Is this where I'll be working?"

"This is it," replied Zack's secretary, Eve Barrows. "You might as well take the desk next to mine. I'll have some company again. A few years ago, there were six secretaries for the department. Now it's just me."

"And me?"

Eve nodded. She was an attractive widow of forty-five or so, with a fringe of dark bangs and a slightly sardonic smile. Her three children were grown and living in different parts of the country; she heard from them on holidays. She had two grandchildren she'd never seen, a parakeet named Tweetie, and a friend named George who took her to movies and to bed. She was an efficient secretary. Zack had declared her indispensible. "I hope you stay a while, Laura. I need the help."

"Oh, I hope so, too. But I have a lot to learn about the advertising business."

"It's not hard." Eve bent, pulling out the desk draws. "There are your supplies," she said. "Stationery, carbon paper, typewriter ribbons." She opened the top drawer. "Pencils, rubber bands, staples. That's everything you'll need for now, but I'll get you a key to the supply room."

"Thanks." Laura sat down, spinning around in her new chair. She smiled, touching the desk blotter, the wire basket for outgoing mail, the telephone directory. "I guess I'm all set," she said.

"Not quite." Eve held out a blue folder. "That's our client list. Be sure to memorize the names. Rule One is to be extra nice and polite to our clients. If you want to be a secretary here, the client is *always* right."

"I understand." Laura glanced through the list while Eve went to answer the phone. "There are more clients than I expected," she remarked when Eve rang off.

"Don't be fooled. Some of those accounts are hanging by a thread." She took another phone call, and then pulled her chair alongside Laura's. "Did Zack tell you much about the department?"

"No, nothing."

"Okay, we'll start from the beginning. There are five copywriters left. One of them's a woman — Anne Marsh. Keep your distance; she won't be a friend." Eve looked up, pointing to a long line of doors. "That's her office at the end of the row. Anne wears hats in her office and she's jealous of other women, especially if they're young and pretty . . . Make a note of the name 'Tom Webster.' He's the senior copywriter, also the nicest person in the company."

Laura's notes covered several pages. In between telephone calls, she learned that the copy and art departments worked together as a team, but that Zack Reed had the final say in any disagreement; that Zack was considered the creative director of the company; that advertising companies were really agencies working on commission.

"Fifteen percent," explained Eve. "We buy space in newspapers and magazines. Say we buy a quarter-page in the *Times* for the Rainbow Paint Company. We bill Rainbow Paint the cost of the quarter page *plus* fifteen percent. That's our commission, our profit."

"Yes, I see. The more our clients advertise, the

more we earn."

"Right." Eve brushed at her bangs. "Of course a few of our clients advertise only in catalogs. For them, we bill fifteen percent of the printing costs. Are you with me so far?"

"Do we make up the catalogs?"

"Catalogs, ads; anything and everything a client wants." Eve dropped a thick yellow folder on Laura's desk. "You'll need to memorize these names as well. They're photographers, typesetters, engravers, printers . . . Here's a list of mailing houses. And here are our messenger services."

Laura stared at the folders overlapping her desk. She thought there must be hundreds of names. "Would it be all right if I took the lists home with me tonight? I—I'm sure I can have them memorized by tomorrow morning . . . If that's all right."

Eve laughed. "You're not being paid enough to take work home at night. Leave that to the executives."

"But what if I make a mistake? What if—"

"Stop worrying," said Eve, holding up her hand. "By the end of the week you'll know everything you have to know. I've trained most of the girls in this company, Laura. I have an instinct about these things."

"I just want to get off to a good start."

Eve was amused. Instinct told her that young Laura Bellamy wanted quite a bit more than good start.

Paul was waiting for Laura when she came out of the office building on Lexington Avenue. It was six o'clock and dark outside, but still he noticed how her face seemed to glow. "You have that shiny look again," he said. "You must have had a good day."

"Oh, it was wonderful. I was nervous in the beginning. There's *so* much to learn. My head was spinning! But one of the other secretaries is helping me. Eve— that's her name—says I'll have the hang of things by the end of the week."

Paul grinned. "Or sooner."

"No. It's probably best to take a little more time at the start. To learn things really well . . . It's sort of like . . . building a foundation, if that makes any sense."

"You always make sense, Laura. You're always a step ahead, aren't you?"

Her smile dimmed. She hadn't been a step ahead with Robby and Eliza. She'd failed to consider the possibilities, and that lapse had cost her dearly. She was determined not to repeat her mistake. "I have to think about the future. I mean, I don't want anything to go wrong."

Paul took Laura's arm as they crossed the street. "Do you have the future all figured out?" he asked.

"No, only parts of it. This job at Harding is the key. Because it could be more than a job, Paul; it could be a career."

"A career girl? Is that what you want to be?"

"I want to make money."

"Yes, I know." Paul held on to Laura's arm as they strolled up Lexington Avenue. A bright red fire engine sped past, its siren blaring, and he was reminded of the volunteer fire department in his hometown of Greenville. He sometimes missed his hometown, missed the slow, easy pace. People hadn't thought much about money in Greenville — at least not until the Depression had squeezed the town dry. "What will you do when you have all the money you want?" he asked.

"I'll feel safe." She looked at him. "Can you understand that?"

"I'm not against money, Laura. Money's important. So are other things. Love, for instance."

Love. What did love ever do but break your heart? "I know all about love," she said, her voice rueful. "You can't trust it."

"You can if it's with the right person."

She shook her head. "And how are you supposed to know who's the right person? That old expression is true—love *is* blind. When you're in love, you're blind to everything else. When you love someone you swear *he's* the right person . . . But then you find out he's a rat." You find out he's run off with your sister, she silently added. Her cheeks were burning; she felt the heat of her anger, her shame. "Let's change the subject," she said.

"The restaurant is right around this corner."

"Good."

The restaurant, in the basement of a wide brownstone building, was called Mama Stella's. It had small, cozy booths and small tables covered with red and white checked cloths. Each table had a little vase of paper flowers and an old Chianti bottle holding a white candle. The handwritten menus were presented by Mama Stella herself—a stout, gray-haired woman whose husband was the chef and whose three sons were the waiters.

"She's the boss," laughed Paul, settling back in his favorite booth. "Nobody argues with Mama."

"Do you come here a lot?"

"Once in a while. When I can't stand the thought of another hamburger, I come here."

"And when you have a date?"

He smiled. "Once in a while . . . After work I usually stop for a hamburger, and then I go for a walk, or sometimes to the movies. Then it's home to the old boardinghouse."

Laura was surprised. "I didn't know you lived in a boardinghouse."

"Sure. It's not bad, and it's cheaper than an apartment. I was lucky to find it. I have a comfortable room. My landlady gives me breakfast . . . The neighborhood's good too. I'm a few steps off Irving Place."

The waiter appeared. Paul ordered a bottle of Chianti and a plate of antipasto.

"What's that?" asked Laura when the waiter had gone.

"Appetizers. Salami and olives and peppers; a bunch of different things. You'll like it."

Laura glanced around the restaurant. There were several other couples, also seated in booths. Toward the rear, there was a counter with two large coffee machines and two large trays of pastries. The lighting was shadowy, but she thought she saw a mural of peasant women dancing in a vineyard.

The waiter brought the wine and antipasto. He opened the wine, poured it, and then left to take an order at a table across the room.

"Should we drink to the Harding Advertising Company?" asked Paul.

Laura picked up her glass and touched it to his. "The Harding Advertising Company," she said.

They drank their chianti. Paul stared thoughtfully at Laura. He seemed to be considering something, but after a moment his expression cleared. "One more toast," he said. "To Laura, the girl I love."

"Stop teasing."

"I'm not teasing."

"Paul, for goodness' sake!"

"I'm serious. I think I've always loved you—from the time I was a little boy and didn't even know what love meant, unless maybe it meant my dog Ranger. I've always had special feelings for you, Laura." He saw the astonishment in her face. She started to speak, but he held his finger to her lips. "No, let me finish," he said. "I wasn't going to tell you any of this tonight. I was going to wait . . . But I guess it's better that you know. There's another old expression about love: faint heart never won fair maiden."

"Paul—"

"It's all right, Laura. You don't have to say a word." He smiled, lightly clasping her hand. "I know you don't love me. That's all right too, because I believe love will come. Maybe not tomorrow or next week, but in time. And I have plenty of time."

There was silence. Laura was stunned, gaping at Paul. She took a sip of wine. She took a gulp, but it didn't help. She felt clumsy and awkward; she couldn't think what to say. "I'm so fond of you, Paul." She knew how lame that sounded. She blushed.

He laughed. "We're friends and you're fond of me; that's more or less what I was expecting."

"I'm sorry."

"Don't be. It's enough for now. It's a start, something to build on. Laura, I'm a practical kind of guy. I don't kid myself. I wasn't expecting you to swoon when I told you I loved you. I knew you wouldn't fall into my arms . . . But time changes things. Time is on my side."

"Your side, Paul?"

"You'll love me, in time. I believe that. I've always believed that." A smile lighted his pale blue eyes. He shrugged. "You don't have to agree or disagree. Not now. I've said what I wanted to say, and we can forget it for a while."

Forget it?

"For a while. We do have time, Laura. That's the great thing about being young." The waiter returned to take their order. Paul glanced swiftly at the menu. "Spaghetti and meatballs for two," he said. He looked at her. "Okay?"

"Oh yes, fine." She watched the waiter walk away. Her gaze moved to the table and she watched the candle flickering in the chianti bottle. "Did you tell Aunt Margaret . . . how you feel?"

"No. I didn't tell anybody. I never even said the words out loud until tonight. And I won't say them again until you're ready." He popped an olive into his mouth. "Let's just enjoy our dinner. I hope I didn't scare you out of your appetite."

Laura's appetite was fine. She sampled the antipasto, and the warm, crusty Italian bread. She devoured the bowl of spaghetti and meatballs that was set before her. Paul ordered dessert—two little paper cups of rich cream called tortoni—and she spooned up every drop. "Delicious," she declared when she'd finished. "Delicious!"

They lingered over their coffee, which was strong and black, almost bitter. They drank the last of the wine. Paul, true to his word, said nothing more about love. When the check came, he put three dollar bills and two quarters on the table. It was a lot of money, but he didn't care. He was with Laura and she was smiling; to him, that was worth all the money in the world.

Riding home on the el train, Laura began to worry that Paul would try to kiss her good night. If he did, it would change things between them; she knew it would. She fidgeted in her seat, wondering why there always had to be complications. She *was* fond of Paul, but she wasn't in love with him. She'd never be in love with him. Or with anyone else, she thought, remembering Robby.

Paul wasn't sure what Laura was thinking, but he was sure he didn't want to end the evening on a wrong note. He took her to her door and bestowed an entirely innocent kiss on her cheek. "I'm not the big bad wolf," he said, and they both laughed.

Later, alone in her room, Laura pondered the events of the evening. *I think I've always loved you.* Not so long ago, she would have given anything to hear those words from Robby. Hearing them from Paul only reminded her of how cruel life could be. Paul. What was she going to do about Paul?

Laura took out her diary and wrote down what he had said. For a moment she was tempted to leaf back through the pages to other times, other memories. She hesitated, but finally she closed the book and locked it with the little key. She didn't want to think about the past, or even about the future. She decided to think about tomorrow. Tomorrow she was going to learn what Eve Barrows called the "basics" of advertising.

"We won't be interrupted today," said Eve the next morning. "I got one of the art department secretaries to take my calls. We'll have time to go over the materials I put together for you . . . I hope you're worth the trouble, Laura."

"I'll do my best."

"Come on, we can use Zack's office. He'll be at the photographer's studio all day. They're shooting the Silktouch Soap ads. Have you ever tried Silktouch?"

"No, I don't think so. My aunt does the shopping and she buys whatever's cheapest."

"I have some samples. I'll give them to you." Eve opened the door of Zack's office. It was freezing inside and she hastily shut the windows. "He's a fresh air fiend," she explained. "He doesn't care what the temperature is. It could be below zero and he'd still be complaining there isn't enough fresh air."

Laura smiled. She turned, taking a closer look around the office. Among the ads decorating the walls, she noticed a framed quotation ascribed to Dr. Samuel Johnson: "Promise—large promise—is the soul of advertisement." She read it twice. "Does Zack agree with that?"

"Yes, because it's true. In advertising, it's all promises—buy our product and you'll be happy and healthy and rich. According to Zack, the best promise is romance—buy our product and someone will love you, marry you, take you to Paris. See what I mean? In advertising, you have to play on people's emotions."

"On their fantasies," suggested Laura with a laugh.

"Now you're getting the idea. There are a dozen different brands of soap in every grocery store. And when you come right down to it, soap is soap. A good ad is supposed to give people a reason to buy our client's brand."

"Price."

"Price is a reason," said Eve. "But people will pay a little more if they think they're getting something special. 'Always promise something special'; that's Zack's motto."

"What if there isn't anything special? What if it's not true?"

"Oh, it's never true." Eve opened a folder, removing a sample design for the new Silktouch ads. "From now on, it's going to be called Silktouch Beauty Soap. There'll be some claims in the copy about special silk oils that make the skin glow. Well, there's no such thing as silk oils! Anne Marsh made it up. And for that she got a hundred-dollar bonus from Mr. Harding, and a big pat on the back from the Silktouch people. They'd been on the verge of taking their account to another agency, but Anne saved the day. She'll get another bonus when the new ads start running. She'll probably get a raise. That's the advertising business."

"I see."

Eve sat down, spreading several large folders on the marble table. She opened the largest one. "Do you know what this is?"

Laura saw a sheet of stiff paper, almost like cardboard. Pasted to it were several lines of type and a drawing of a perfume bottle. "It's some sort of artwork," she replied.

"It's called a mechanical, or a paste-up. It's the layout of the ad—it's what we send to the engraver. The engraver makes the plate that's sent to the printer . . . I'll start from the beginning, okay?"

Laura flipped open her notebook. "Okay."

"Around here, everything begins with a meeting. First the client meets with Mr. Harding and Zack to approve the overall theme of the ads. Then Zack and one of his copywriters meet with the art department to decide the look of the ads. Then it's just a matter of procedure."

"Procedure?" asked Laura.

"A sketch artist draws the product — whatever it is — from all angles. The sketches go to layout, where the ad is designed. When the design is finished, it's sent to be photostated. When the photostat comes back, it's pasted to the mechanical." Eve smiled, brushing at her dark bangs. "Are you with me?"

"Barely," said Laura.

"Hang on, there's more."

"More?"

Eve opened another folder. "There's copy. Once the copy is approved, it's sent to the typesetter. This is what comes back," she explained, pushing the folder toward Laura. "These are type proofs and they're pasted to the mechanical as well."

Laura started a fresh page in her notebook. "Photostats and type proofs are pasted to the mechanical," she said, her eyes darting between the notebook and Eve. "Then what?"

"Then the mechanical, the layout, is finished. It goes to the engraver. The engraving plate goes to the printer."

"To the printer," repeated Laura, writing the words in her book.

"We do much more than magazine and newspaper ads," continued Eve. "We do catalogs, brochures, handbills. Sometimes we do mailings for clients. We just had fifty thousand rebate coupons printed for the Rainbow Paint Company and we're handling the mailing too. Not here, of course. We're using a mailing house. We give them the coupons and the names, and they do the rest."

Sunlight was streaming through the windows. Laura moved her notebook out of the glare. "I didn't realize there were so many different sides to the advertising business."

"There's a side we haven't even talked about yet: radio. But I think that can wait a while. Most of the work in this department is print. And you have enough to think about for now."

Laura shrugged. "I told Zack I was a fast learner. Now's the time to prove it."

"Yes, it is, as a matter of fact. This is a good week, because there's no one here to bother us. Zack and Anne are busy with the Silktouch people. Tom Webster's on vacation. Hal Russell's in Chicago. Ralph Lang is out sick. That leaves Martin Carver, and he stays in his office doing crossword puzzles."

Laura glanced up. "Really?"

"Writers love anything to do with words—word games, word puzzles. Martin claims they keep him sharp. Could be." Eve closed the folders and stacked them on the table. She stood. "I think we can use a break," she said, pointing Laura toward the door. "Has anybody shown you around?"

"No, not yet."

"Come on, I'll give you the tour."

They left the office. Laura followed Eve into a corridor, and for the first time she noticed all the other corridors branching off this one. She saw the other offices, rows of them stretching in all directions. "My goodness, the Harding Advertising Company is much bigger than I thought!"

"We have the space; we have the whole twelfth floor. But the staff's been cut to the bone. A lot of these offices are empty. A lot of desks, too."

Laura heard the clattering of typewriters. She turned her head. At the end of the corridor was an outer office similar to the one in the copy department. There were eight desks, but only three secretaries. "Yes, I see what you mean."

"Mr. Harding considered moving to a smaller space. Moving the offices. But he decided to stay put. He called everybody together—everybody who was left—and said hard times couldn't last forever. He told us things were bound to get better, and when they did, Harding Advertising would be ready." Eve smiled, glancing at her young charge. "If he's right, there may be some interesting times ahead."

"And I'll be here to see them."

"You sound very certain."

"I am." Laura looked again at the maze of intersecting corridors. She thought they were like pathways leading to the things she wanted: to money, to success, to a future that would make up for the past. A smile flashed across her face. "No matter what it takes, I'm going to have a career in advertising!"

Advertising, Laura discovered, was a billion-dollar-a-year business. The basic structure of the advertising agency had been established by the early 1860s, and the role of advertising by the first decade after the Civil War. It was a simple role: to sell mass-produced goods to masses of people. In an industrial economy, it was a necessary role.

More than $22 million had been spent on advertising in 1860, a figure that had soared to $500 million by the turn of the century. In the 1920s—with the introduction of color ads, coupons, and test markets—the advertising business had broken the billion-dollar mark.

A billion dollars. Laura could hardly believe there was that much money in the world, let alone in one industry. The Depression had hurt revenues and profits, yet the industry endured. She felt it would always endure. How else to sell dozens of different brands of soap and toothpaste and breakfast cereal? How else (as the expression went) to sell iceboxes to Eskimos?

Laura decided that she would learn all she could

about the industry. She read the books Margaret checked out of the library for her. She studied ads in magazines and newspapers. She studied the business pages. For two weeks she stayed late at the office, studying the files. When she was called into meetings to take notes, she studied the participants.

Two distinct groups faced each other at these meetings: clients and copywriters. The clients were virtually interchangeable—serious, prosperous men in dark suits and dark ties—but the copywriters were an interesting mix. There was Tom Webster, with his kindly smiles and razor-sharp mind; Laura liked Tom Webster. There was Martin Carver, with his long silences and owlish stares; she wasn't sure what to make of Martin Carver. There was Ralph Lang, hail-fellow-well-met. There was Hal Russell, so sleekly handsome he could have been a movie star. There was Anne Marsh.

Anne Marsh had worked at Harding Advertising for seven years. She was in her middle thirties, a pretty woman with wavy, chin-length brown hair and just a trace of a soft Southern accent. She was unmarried; it had been rumored that she was divorced. She favored simple but expensive suits and dresses, and small, flirty hats that she wore even in her office. She had very white, very beautiful hands.

Laura disliked Anne Marsh. She sensed that venom lay beneath the honeyed accent, that backstabbing knives fit nicely in those beautiful hands. She didn't want her for an enemy, and certainly not for a friend, but still she admired the woman. Anne was smart; Anne was quick. In the meetings where Laura sat taking notes, Anne was the one to watch.

Laura watched now as Anne settled in the chair behind her desk and glanced at the letters awaiting her signature. The desk was antique, a personal touch she'd added to the office. The carpet was a deep rose color, the same shade as the walls. On the walls were glossy copies of the ads she had supervised for her accounts: Silktouch Soap, Milady Dresses, Trushine Shampoo. Laura noticed several bottles of Trushine standing next to some artwork on a table in the corner. "Do you want me to return the layouts to the art department?"

Anne looked up. "When I want you to do something, I'll tell you. That's the way it works."

"Yes. I'm sorry."

"Sit down while I look at these letters." Anne was looking for mistakes. It was a daily ritual, though a useless one; hard as she looked, she never found anything she could complain about. Laura's efficiency irritated her — also Laura's youth and eagerness and sheer determination to prevail. Anne had always been able to recognize ambition, whether in herself or in others. She recognized it in Laura. She shouldn't have cared, but she did, and very much. For years she had been queen bee at Harding Advertising. She wanted no competition, especially from someone with tawny hair and golden skin and large, amber-flecked hazel eyes. "You don't have to wait," she said, reaching for her pen. "The letters are all right."

Laura started toward the door, stopping when the telephone rang. She hurried back to the desk and lifted the receiver. "Miss Marsh's office," she said in her best Acme Business Institute voice . . . Yes, may I ask who's calling? . . . One moment please, I'll see if she's in." Laura covered the receiver with her hand. "It's Mr. Crenshaw."

"I'll talk to him." Anne put the receiver to her ear. She smiled. "George, I'm so glad you called. I have good news for you . . . Yes, we did. Some absolutely marvelous designs. They're just darling . . . First thing in the morning, if you'd like; Zack's been keeping his schedule open . . . We'll see you then, George. I'll look forward to it . . . The research? Why yes, we have all the figures. I tell you what, George; I'll have the girl type the report tonight, and we'll bring it with us in the morning . . . Oh no, no you musn't worry about that. The girl won't mind . . ."

Laura slipped out of the office and quietly closed the door. It was five minutes to six, but her workday hadn't ended; Anne's report, with all its numbers and footnotes, would take almost an hour to type, proofread, and collate.

She gazed across the silent outer office. Eve had already straightened her desk and was about to cover the typewriters. "Not mine," said Laura. "I have another report to type."

Eve glanced at her wristwatch. "Did she do that to you again?"

Laura shrugged. *"The girl* won't mind."

Chapter Twelve

"She calls me 'the girl,' " said Laura, smiling at Paul Brent. *"The girl* will hurry downstairs and get coffee for everyone. *The girl* will be delighted to work all night. I'll tell *the girl* to go throw herself in front of a bus."

He laughed. "I hope you're exaggerating."

"I am, but not by much. Believe me, not by much."

The sudden blast of a car horn chased them back to the curb. They waited for the light to change, and then crossed the street. It was a Friday evening at the end of February. A pale sliver of moon hung in the sky. A strong wind gusted along the avenue and both Laura and Paul had to hold on to their hats.

"Maybe she's jealous," said Paul. "You couldn't blame her. You're so pretty. You must be the prettiest girl in the whole place. In the whole city, if you ask me."

Laura liked being told she was pretty, but sometimes Paul's extravagant compliments made her blush. In his eyes—and words—she was the prettiest, the smartest, the best. She was perfect. "You're going to turn my head if you keep this up. Anyway, it's not jealousy. Anne Marsh has everything."

"Is she married?"

"No." "Then she doesn't have everything. She

doesn't have a husband, a family."

"She probably doesn't want a family."

"Everybody wants a family, Laura. Don't you?"

"I don't know. Right now, all I want is dinner."

"Coming up," replied Paul as they turned the corner. They were holding hands, and he felt that was progress. At first he'd done no more than take her arm to see her across the street, but a few weeks ago he'd reached out and taken her hand. She hadn't objected.

A small victory, he thought now. Like the suitor in a Victorian courtship, he would have to be content with small victories, at least for a while. He looked at Laura and smiled. She was worth the wait. "I reserved a booth," he said as they neared Mama Stella's. "Did you tell your friends not to expect anything fancy?"

"Doris has been hearing about Mama Stella's for two months. She knows what to expect . . . She wouldn't want anything fancy, Paul. The boy she's bringing is an instructor at Columbia. I don't think he has much money."

"A mathematics instructor?"

"Naturally! I haven't met him yet, but Doris says he's very smart."

Paul opened the door and they entered the restaurant. The tiny cloakroom was in use on Friday nights, attended by one of Mama Stella's daughters-in-law; Paul and Laura checked their hats and coats. That added twenty cents to the evening's expenses but he didn't mind. He thought of these little amenities as Laura's due. It was his secret ambition to take her to the Stork Club sometime; maybe when he got a raise, he thought.

"I think I see Doris," he said, squinting in the dim light.

"We must be late."

Mama Stella appeared out of nowhere and led them to their booth. Doris glanced up, smiling and frowning at the same time. Her date, Bill Gibson, almost spilled the wine as he got hastily to his feet. "Sorry," he murmured. He looked at the new arrivals and fiddled with his tie.

"I'm Laura," she said, sliding into the booth. "And you're Bill. It's nice to meet you . . . This is Paul Brent."

The two young men shook hands and then sat down. "Did you have any trouble finding the place?" asked Paul. "Sometimes people walk right by."

"Oh no," said Doris. "We didn't do that."

"Oh no," said Bill. "We found it straight off."

Laura smiled; she thought they made a sweet couple. They were both fair, both a bit worried-looking, and both clad in suits (hers a soft pink, his a proper navy blue) that didn't quite fit. She noticed the way Bill kept taking little peeks at Doris, and the way Doris kept moving her hand closer to his. Laura decided there was more here than mathematics.

Paul was talking about Italian food, explaining the different dishes on the menu. When he finished, he put the menus aside. "I guess we've tried everything by now. We've been coming every Friday after work."

"We tried a Chinese restaurant the other night," said Bill. "It's up near Columbia. I don't know how authentic the food is, but it's not bad."

Paul poured a glass of wine for Laura, and one for himself. "I hear you're an instructor at Columbia."

"Yes, but that's just the start," said Doris, an eager sparkle in her eyes. "Bill's going to be an assistant professor next year. It won't be long before he's a full professor."

"You're too optimistic, Doris."

Laura couldn't help smiling. *Doris* optimistic?

"Nobody becomes a full professor overnight," continued Bill. "It could take years and years. But that's all right. I'm doing what I want to do. The way I see it, that's the important thing."

Doris nodded. "Bill has his master's degree and now he's studying for his doctorate. In differential calculus!"

"Whatever that is." Laura held up her hand. "Don't try to explain it. You know what a dunce I am when it comes to math. I'm hopeless."

"Don't believe her," laughed Paul. "Laura's sharp as a tack, no doubt about it."

The waiter arrived to take their order. He left and then returned a moment later with another bottle of wine—a gift from Mama Stella.

Paul refilled all their glasses. "Looks like it's going to be a festive evening," he said.

It was a wonderful evening. They stuffed themselves with Mama Stella's delicious food, with ravioli and lasagna and spicy Italian sausages. They drank wine. They talked. They laughed. They were happy, their various worries forgotten for now.

Happiness, thought Laura, was contagious. She saw the way Doris and Bill were with each other, and all at once she felt a great surge of affection for Paul. She felt warm and cozy, as if she had suddenly found refuge. Is that was love was? Refuge? It was tempting to think so.

"You should marry him," said Doris the next morning. She took a blouse from Laura's closet, looked at it, and put it back. She took out a second blouse and held it up to herself. "How about this one?"

"Yes, it's very becoming," said Laura.

Doris slipped the blouse off the hanger and folded it into a neat square. "I was serious, you know. You should marry Paul. He's so nice. And anybody can see he's crazy about you."

Laura sat down at the dressing table. She leaned forward, studying her reflection. She made a face in the mirror and then turned away. "Never mind me. What about you and Bill? You've been keeping secrets, Doris Sweeney. You and Bill are *crazy* about each other and you never said a word."

"I've only known him two weeks."

"That's no excuse."

Doris perched at the edge of the bed. She sighed. "Bill's not Irish and he's not Catholic. Can you imagine what Da will say? It's a good thing we don't have any money. If we did, he'd ship me off to Ireland. He would, Laura. That's what happened to my cousin in Ohio. My cousin Bridget. Her father didn't like the boy she was seeing. She wouldn't give him up, so she was shipped off to family in County Clare."

Laura shook her head. "This is 1934. People don't do things like that."

"Oh yes, they do. Some people do. Some *Irish*men."

"Well, that's not going to happen to you. It's your life, Doris, nobody else's. If you're in love with Bill . . . You are, aren't you?"

She colored slightly. Her fingers traced circles on the pink bedspread. "Two weeks isn't a long time . . . I have to be very sure. *Very* sure. Because I know all the trouble it's going to cause. Da will be up in arms. The whole family will be taking sides . . . You're lucky, Laura. Nobody would make a fuss if you married Paul."

"Who's getting married?" asked Jane, walking into the room. "What did I miss? I always miss the good stuff."

"Not this time," replied Laura, smiling.

Jane went to Doris and held out a necklace. "Here

are the coral beads I told you about. For Laura's gray blouse?"

"No, I'm borrowing this white blouse instead."

Jane pocketed the necklace. "Then you'll want the onyx beads, I think. We'll get them later."

"I don't know what I'd do without you and Laura to lend me things. I'd be walking around like a ragamuffin."

"You're welcome to whatever you want," said Jane.

Laura nodded. She'd sold many of Eliza's clothes, but the closets and drawers were still crammed with hand-me-downs—stylish, expensive hand-me-downs. She wouldn't have to worry about clothes for quite a while. "Whatever you want," she echoed.

"Now that that's settled," said Jane, "who's getting married?"

"Nobody. Not yet, anyway."

"I know what's going to happen." Jane paused, a smile playing at the corners of her mouth. "First you're going to marry your brilliant Bill," she said, turning to Doris. "And then you'll marry your perfect Paul," she added, turning to Laura. "And I'll be all alone."

"Poor thing."

"Yes, I'll be the One Musketeer."

"Maybe *you'll* get married first," said Laura. "Did you think of that? Doris and Bill have some problems to work out, and I don't know if *I'll* ever get married. So you could be the first . . . Don't shake your head at me. Everybody in the building knows Ted Morgan's been sending you flowers. You should be thrilled. The Morgans have pots of money."

"Oh, Ted's all right, but he's dull. Dull, dull, dull. I want excitement! Besides, Ted's nickname is Froggy. How could I marry a boy named Froggy?"

"I hope that's the worst problem you ever have," said Laura with a laugh. She glimpsed her face in

215

the mirror as she started to rise. Two months ago, her face had been pale and strained. She hadn't expected to be doing much laughing; she surely hadn't expected to be laughing and joking about marriage. It was Paul who'd made the difference, she thought. He'd helped her. Just by being there, he'd helped her.

"Do you need anything else, Doris?" she asked, moving away from the dressing table.

"No, the blouse is fine. I'll wear it with my good black skirt and Jane's onyx necklace." She frowned. "That's a nice outfit for a concert, isn't it?"

"Very nice. But I'd better go find Aunt Margaret now. She has some errands for me. If you want to wait, you can come along."

"Oh no," said Doris as they went to the door. "I have chores and I'm late getting started."

"Me too," agreed Jane. "I'm supposed to be cleaning out closets."

The girls walked into the hall. Doris and Jane said their good-byes and headed toward the front door. Laura turned and headed toward the kitchen. "Aunt Margaret?" she called.

Margaret was seated at the kitchen table, eating a cake of yeast. Her brow was furrowed. She looked weary. "Have they gone?" she asked when Laura walked into the room.

"Everbody has Saturday chores. Do you have a list for me?"

"In a minute. I want to talk to you first."

Laura didn't like the sound of that. She peered at her aunt. "What's the matter?"

"Nothing's the matter. Don't jump to conclusions."

"I'm not—"

"Sit down, Laura." Margaret took something from her pocket—a letter that had been crumpled and then smoothed out. She stared at it. "This came in the morning mail. I don't see the sense in hiding it.

You'll have to know sooner or later; it might as well be sooner."

"Know what?"

"This letter was written to both of us. It's from Eliza." The mention of Eliza brought Laura halfway out of her chair but Margaret reached across the table and grabbed her arm. "You're going to stay and listen," said Margaret. "I know it's still a sore subject; that can't be helped."

"I won't listen to a word, not a word."

"Yes, you will. Eliza's going to have a baby."

Laura heard the sharp intake of her own breath. A bright red stain spread over her cheeks as she wrenched her arm away. "A baby," she said, biting off the word. "That explains a lot."

"Don't get any funny ideas, miss. It's what we used to call a wedding night baby. There's no shame in a wedding night baby . . . Eliza did some bad things; I'm not defending her. But she didn't do what you're thinking."

"No?"

"No," replied Margaret with a firm shake of her head. "Anyhow, it's all in the past. They have their life now and you have yours. Make the best of it."

"I intend to."

"Do you want to read her letter?"

Laura's eyes flashed. "I'd rather burn it."

"Now you stop that!"

"Nothing's changed, Aunt Margaret. I haven't forgiven them. I'll never forgive them. They can have a *dozen* babies and it won't change the way I feel."

Margaret sighed. "Don't say nothing's changed, Laura. No matter what Eliza did, she's your sister and she's going to have a baby. You're going to be an aunt . . . If you'd like my advice, you ought to let bygones be bygones."

"I can't."

"You mean you won't."

Tears misted Laura's eyes. She blinked them back. "You don't understand," she said in a thin, tight voice. "This should be *my* baby. All I ever wanted was to get married and have a family. That was my dream, my only dream. But it was—it was *stolen* from me. They're thieves, both of them."

"The way you talk, you'd think Robby was your last chance to get married. You'll have plenty of chances, starting with Paul. And you'll have new dreams in place of the old. You could call it a trade."

"A fair trade?"

Margaret waved the question away. "Don't ask me what's fair. Don't expect things to be fair, Laura. Just be sensible. And let bygones be—"

"No." She pushed back her chair and stood up. "We're not going to agree on this, Aunt Margaret."

"If you'd just listen to me—"

"No," replied Laura, walking off. "I don't want to talk about it anymore. I don't want to think about it. As you said yourself, they have their life now and I have mine."

During the next few months Laura continued to learn as much as she could about the advertising business. She continued to observe, to form opinions and ideas, though prudently she kept them to herself. She was wary of overstepping her place, of risking her position, at least until the time was right. There *would* be a right time; she was certain of that. In the meanwhile, she did her job and she did it well.

She was rewarded with a modest raise. In June, six months after she'd started work at Harding Advertising, her salary was increased to twenty dollars a week. The extra money meant she could quit her Sunday job at the movie theater—the last of her part-time jobs. More importantly, it meant she was moving ahead. It was a first step and it bolstered her confidence.

Now, staring down at some sketches on her desk, Laura felt her confidence waver. She looked over at the next desk, where Eve was typing a letter. She waited until Eve finished, then asked, "Could I show you something?"

"Just a second." The letter was rolled out of the machine, proofread, and put aside. "Okay, what do you have?"

"An idea," replied Laura. "I've been thinking about the Perfume X account."

Eve's dark brows shot up, disappearing under her bangs. "*Every*body's been thinking about the Perfume X account. It's driving me crazy. Perfume X, Perfume X; that's all I hear." Perfume X was a new fragrance, a creation of the chemists at the Whitmore Company. It had been created as an inexpensive perfume, perhaps for younger women, and it had been brought to Harding Advertising to be named and then launched on the market. The copy department had submitted hundreds of names in hundreds of proposals, but all of them had been rejected. There was talk that Harding might lose the account. Eve could feel tension rising among the staff. "Everybody's so frustrated," she said. "I wish the Whitmore people would make up their minds one way or the other. Perfume X! Maybe they should just *call* it Perfume X and be done with it."

Laura glanced again at the sketches on her desk. "That's not a very romantic name. Perfume should sound romantic, don't you think?"

"That's one of the rules about perfume advertising. But when you're dealing with an impossible company like Whitmore . . . You said you had an idea?"

"Maybe I should stay out of it. I mean, it's not

really my job."

"Oh, don't let *that* stop you," replied Eve, smiling and shaking her head. "Zack is getting ideas from everywhere. Even the guys in the mailroom. So if you want to put *your* two cents in, feel free."

"Do you mean it?"

"Why not? Let me see what you have."

"I did these sketches myself," said Laura, placing them on Eve's desk. "They're pretty bad, but I thought they'd show the idea."

"Which is?"

She was about to explain, but at that moment Hal Russell came slamming out of his office. She watched as he strode quickly along the corridor, his arms filled with layouts and photo enlargements and the yellow legal pads he always used for his notes. When he reached Laura's desk, he simply opened his arms and let everything drop. "Thanks, Hal," she said. "Just what I wanted."

"I'm going to lunch now. I'll need my notes typed and ready by the time I get back. *If* I get back. There's going to be another damn Perfume X meeting this afternoon. Another one!"

Laura nodded. "The fifth meeting since Monday. I've been keeping track." She looked at the enlargements of the long-necked Perfume X bottles. She saw the mustaches Hal had drawn on them and she laughed. "I don't think the art department would approve."

"The art department can go to hell."

"They love you too," said Eve, glancing up. Hal Russell was so handsome. If only she were ten years younger . . . "I happen to have a memo from the art department. From John Ellison. He says we're ruining his photographs and each one costs—"

"I don't care what they cost," snapped Hal, striding away. "Send the bill to Whitmore Incorporated. The bastards!"

"See what I mean?" said Eve when he had gone. "This account is getting on everybody's nerves . . . But I still haven't heard your idea. Tell me."

"It can wait. Hal wants these notes." She flipped through the yellow pads. "There must be thirty pages of notes, single-spaced."

"You can spare a minute to tell me your idea. Come on, Laura. I know you don't plan to be a secretary all your life. You're after bigger things. So tell me what you've come up with."

"Well, it's . . . I was thinking that perfume ought to . . . It should sound romantic."

"You're off to a bad start," declared Eve. "If you're going to tell an idea, *tell* it. Just tell it straight out."

"Well—"

"No, Laura, start again. You've been in enough meetings with Tom and Anne and the others. You've seen how they do it. They're direct. They get to the point . . . They act as if they know what they're talking about, even if they don't."

"Yes, you're right."

"Start again."

Laura took a breath. "My idea is to call the perfume Moonlight. Each ad would be a different moonlight fantasy. For example, a boy and a girl—"

"A man and a woman," interrupted Eve.

"A man and a woman embracing in a romantic, moonlit garden, or on a moonlit terrace overlooking the city. The settings would change from month to month, but the idea would always be moonlight and romance."

"I've heard worse ideas," said Eve after a brief pause. "But your sketches are terrible. You didn't inherit your mother's talent, did you?"

"No, I can only draw stick figures."

Eve gathered the sketches together and returned

them to Laura. "Hurry over to the art department. You can catch Ronnie Woronow before he goes out to lunch. Just tell him your idea and he'll do some quick drawings. He has a crush on you, so he'll be happy to help."

Laura blinked. "A crush on me?"

"That's not important now. Hurry up or he'll be gone. You'll need the drawings in time for Zack's meeting."

Laura rose, then fell back into her chair. "I have all this typing, Eve."

"I'll get it started for you." The telephone rang and she stretched her hand to the receiver. "Go on," she said, waving her other hand in the air. "Who knows, you may be the answer to Zack's prayers!"

Zack Reed stared wearily at the layouts and proposals covering every inch of his desk. They were the latest efforts in behalf of Perfume X—and very likely the last efforts Harding Advertising would be asked to make. He had mixed emotions about that. He'd dealt with difficult clients over the years, but none as difficult as the executives at the Whitmore Company. In some ways, losing the account might be a relief.

Still, Zack had never let personal feelings interfere with business. It was his job to save the account, and no matter how he felt about the Whitmore Company, that was what he intended to do. He bent his dark head, sorting through the new layouts. A few of them were merely variations of themes that had already been proposed, but a few others offered new concepts, and these he separated from the rest. There were three he particularly liked: one of Martin's, one of Anne's—and much to his surprise—one of Laura's. He decided to include Laura in his meeting.

She brought her steno pad and a brand-new pencil. Chairs had been arranged in a semicircle around Zack's desk, but she took her usual seat at the rear. She was nervous, wondering if her proposal would be mentioned, if there would be any comments. She hoped she wouldn't have to answer questions.

Her stomach was churning. Her hands were fidgeting in her lap. She knew she was being silly but she couldn't help herself. It was like being back in high school and worrying that Miss Frobisher was going to ask her to explain the Treaty of Ghent.

One by one, the copywriters had taken their places in the semicircle: Martin Carver first, followed by Hal Russell, and lastly by Anne Marsh. "Where's Ralph?" she asked, glancing about the office.

"He caught the morning train to Pittsburg," replied Zack. "We have some problems with Burnett Tile. Nothing Ralph can't handle, though. He'll be in Pittsburg at least a week . . . And of course Tom's in Boston, so he's out of this too. *This*, I need hardly say, being Perfume X."

"What about the new proposals?" asked Hal. "Anything there?"

"I pulled three of them. We have to settle on the best two. We'll give the Whitmore people a choice of two, and we'll make a big show of the presentations. This time we're going in with guns blazing. We'll mow 'em down."

"I wish," joked Hal, and everybody laughed.

"We all feel the same way about these guys," said Zack. "But let's remember that the best revenge is to take their money. We'll do it too, if we go in with the right ideas."

Anne's skirt rose a fraction as she crossed her shapely legs. "Don't keep us in suspense, Zack. Which ideas did you choose?"

"Idea number one," he replied, holding up the first layout. "Martin has proposed the name 'Shangri-la' . . . Idea number two," he continued, holding up the second layout. "Anne has proposed the name 'Rapture' . . . And idea number three," he concluded. "Laura has proposed the name 'Moonlight.' "

"Laura who?" asked Hal.

Anne didn't need to ask; she had swung around to stare at Laura. Three pairs of eyes followed her gaze. "Aren't we lucky to have a secretary with hidden talents," she drawled. "And aspirations," she added, giving the word a nasty spin.

" 'Moonlight,' eh?" said Martin Carver. "I can see possibilities in that. It's simple, romantic. It's young." He took the layout from Zack. "It gives us a good deal of latitude, month to month. Innocent to sophisticated and everything in between . . . How do you see it, Laura?"

Her mouth was as dry as dust. Her lips seemed to be stuck together. It's no use, she thought, but suddenly she remembered something Paul had said and she knew that would be her answer. "The girl in the ad should have a shiny look, as if someone poured moonlight all over her."

It was a word picture they instantly understood. Zack smiled, visualizing the Moonlight Perfume girl in his mind's eye. Martin, smiling also, adjusted his glasses and began to scribble notes on a white index card. Hal laughed, pointed at Laura, and said, "Bravo!"

Anne was nettled, but she knew that in the long run, no damage would be done. If Harding won the perfume account, it would be given to her. All the "women's" accounts were ultimately given to her; old Eli had established the rules long ago.

Expressionless, she glanced at Laura. The upstart girl had earned a few words of praise and maybe a bonus, but what did it really mean? Anne decided she would have to think about that. In the interim, she would have to be gracious. "Shall we agree to make Moonlight one of the two presentations?"

"Absolutely," said Hal. "And I'd make Shangri-la the other one. With Shangri-la we can be a little tropical . . . A little steamy. That opens the door to some interesting possibilities. What do you think, Zack?"

He lit a cigarette and tossed pack to Martin, who passed it around. "I agree. We have two entirely different approaches here, and we can do very spirited presentations for both of them." He exhaled, leaning back in his battered leather chair. "It's settled, then. We roll the dice on Moonlight and Shangri-la."

Laura was so excited her pencil skidded across the page of her notepad. *We roll the dice on Moonlight.* My idea, she thought in pride and amazement; my idea. The meeting continued for another thirty minutes, but she couldn't concentrate. It was all she could do to sit still, Something important had just happened, and even though everybody seemed to have forgotten her presence, she was giddy with exhilaration.

"Nice work," said Zack as the meeting broke up. "Win or lose, you can expect a bonus. We like to encourage initiative."

Laura was beaming when she got back to her desk, savoring her first taste of success. She told Eve about the meeting and she left nothing out. *We roll the dice on Moonlight.* She loved saying the words.

Eve, amused, listened and smiled and was happy for the girl she had begun to regard as her protégée. She explained what would happen next. "Zack will schedule meetings with the art department. He'll assign a copywriter, probably Anne. And then Anne and Zack will handle the presentation together."

"Won't I have anything to do with it?"

Eve shook her head. "You'll need a lot more seasoning before they let you near a presentation. A lot more."

"But Moonlight was my idea."

"One idea, Laura. It could be a fluke. It could be beginner's luck. In this business, you have to prove yourself over and over again. Besides, an idea is only half the battle. The other half is finding the right way to express it . . . Don't be in such a hurry; your time will come. Zack will be keeping an eye on you now . . . Speak of the devil," sighed Eve as Zack flung open his office door and yelled for the Burnett Tile correspondence. She scooped up a file. "Coming," she called.

Laura propped her steno pad on the desk. She fed paper and carbons into the typewriter, and started to type her notes from the meeting. She was interrupted by several telephone calls; by Martin Carver, who wanted something from the files; and by Ronnie Woronow, who stood quietly at her desk until she looked up. "Oh, Ronnie," she said as she finished typing the last page of notes. "Sorry, I didn't mean to keep you standing there."

"That's all right. I was wondering how it went."

"The meeting?" Laura told him about the meeting, and again she left nothing out. She had an attentive audience. Ronnie nodded when she nodded, smiled when she smiled. She noticed what a nice smile he had, so bright and hopeful. "Now we have to wait to see what happens," she said, coming to the end of her story. "But I think Zack's going to ask you to work on the designs. I know how much he likes your work."

Modestly, Ronnie shrugged the praise away. He was twenty-five years old, a wiry fellow with pleasant features, light brown hair combed straight back, and light brown eyes. He was talented; everyone expected he would be made art director before he was thirty. Eve's observation had been correct: he had a crush on Laura. "I was thinking maybe we could . . . have dinner some night. Now that we're working together and all . . . Will you have dinner with me, Laura?"

Her lips parted in surprise. "You're very sweet to ask, Ronnie. I'm flattered. Really I am."

"But you're going to turn me down."

"You see, I have a boyfriend."

Boyfriend. The word had come so easily, as if it had been in the back of her mind all along. Laura was stunned. When had she started thinking of Paul that way? She tried to identify the specific time, the specific moment. She couldn't. She supposed it had happened slowly — not in a moment, but over the span of months. Memories swirled around her; brief, random glimpses of the past. She kept hearing Paul's voice: *I think I've always loved you.* She smiled. For the rest of the afternoon, she sat at her desk and pretended to work while she pondered life's strange twists.

Now, stepping off the elevator, Laura gazed across the nearly deserted lobby to where Paul stood. He seemed engrossed in the afternoon newspaper, but when he saw her walking toward him, he folded the paper and tucked it under his arm. She waved, quickening her step just a bit.

"What kind of day has it been?" he asked, taking Laura's hand. "Good? Bad?"

"Surprising. It was one surprise after another. It may be a while before I make sense of things."

"What things?" Paul held the door open. "What things?" he repeated as they walked outside.

"I'll start at the beginning. I told Eve about my idea for Perfume X. Moonlight?"

"Yes, I remember."

"Well, that was the beginning." Laura described Ronnie's drawings for Moonlight. She described the other drawings submitted to Zack, the other proposals. Almost verbatim, she recounted what everybody said at the meeting. "I was *so* nervous," she continued. "I didn't think I'd be able to open my mouth. But then I remembered something I'd heard *you* say."

Paul grinned. "Words of wisdom?"

"No," she replied as they reached First Avenue. "No. It was what you said about my having a shiny look. Like someone had poured moonlight all over me?"

"Yes, and I meant it, Laura."

"Well, those are the words that saved the day. If Zack really gives me a bonus, I'll treat you to dinner."

"I couldn't accept. I'm not the gigolo type."

She laughed. "Gigolo! Oh, there's more to being a gigolo than a free dinner. There are gold cigarette cases and silk robes and . . . and polo ponies."

Paul arched a sandy eyebrow. "How did you get to be such an expert on the subject? Do you have a secret life?"

"I read the newspapers. I read Cholly Knickerbocker. Rich society women are always giving gifts of polo ponies. *Strings* of polo ponies, whatever that means . . . But anyway, the important thing is I made a good impression on Zack today. It was a good start. A surprise, too; I didn't think things would go so well."

"What was the next surprise?"

"Ronnie Woronow. He asked me for a date."

Paul's hand tightened on Laura's. His eyes clouded. "What did you tell him?"

"I guess that was the third surprise . . . I told him I had a boyfriend."

"Anyone I know?"

"You may have met him once or twice," she replied with a playful smile. "My boyfriend is Paul Brent."

Thank God, he thought, as all his worries magically vanished. He spun Laura around and kissed her. "Paul Brent is the luckiest guy on earth," he said, and kissed her again. Passersby were turning to stare, but he didn't notice. Laura was the only person he saw. He had loved her for so long, and now he had her in his arms. "Marry me," he blurted.

"What!"

"Marry me, Laura," he repeated, smiling into her disbelieving eyes. "I realize I'm not the man of your dreams, but you love me a little, don't you? Just a little?"

She loved his honesty and his strength. She loved the way he refused to be daunted, the way he followed his own course. She loved the warm, snug feeling he gave her. She loved his crinkly grin. She loved, but she wasn't *in* love, and she knew it.

Paul knew it too. "Sometimes I can read your mind," he said. "I love you more than you love me. So what? You'll catch up. I guarantee you will. I'm pretty lovable, all in all."

Laura drew away. She straightened her hat and looked up at the soft June sky. She sniffed the air; rain was coming. "Should I tell you my bad points?" she asked as they resumed their walk. "I'm moody, I'm stubborn. I worry about money . . . I *think* about money, about having it. I didn't used to be ambitious, but I am now. Some people think that's not a nice thing in a girl."

"I don't care what some people think. I care about you. If you want to be President, that's fine with me. If you want to stay in the kitchen and bake cookies, that's fine also. To each her own, I always say. I don't care what you do, Laura, as long as you're happy. And as long as you marry me."

She turned her head, staring up at Paul through her dark lashes. "There are things we ought to talk about. There's Aunt Margaret; she's my responsibility now. There's—"

"There's only one thing that matters." Again he stopped walking and pulled Laura toward him. "Only one thing. It's a question. Will you marry me?"

She wanted to remember this moment, all the details of it—the color of the sky, the sound of traffic on the avenue, the scent of rain in the air. She wanted to remember the feel of Paul's arms surrounding her. She wanted to remember the sudden glad leap of her heart. When the bad times came, if they came, she would look back and remember.

"Laura?"

Gently, she touched his face. She smiled. "Yes, I'll marry you, Paul." She saw her reflection in his eyes. She nodded. "Yes," she said again. "Yes."

Chapter Thirteen

Laura and Paul were married in the last week of September. By necessity and by choice it was a simple wedding—small, intimate, and pretty. The six front pews of St. James's church were decorated with large white bows which Margaret had sewn herself. The altar was decorated with candles and masses of daisies. There were fewer than twenty guests, all wearing their best clothes and their best smiles. They glanced around eagerly as the music began.

Jane, the sole bridesmaid, walked down the aisle in a long, pale blue taffeta dress of her own creation. Following behind her was Doris, the maid of honor, also clad in blue taffeta. Both girls carried little bouquets of daisies trimmed with curly blue ribbons.

There was no one to give the bride away, and so Laura walked down the aisle alone. She wore Kay's wedding dress, an ankle-length swirl of silk and lace with a narrow waist and a fitted bodice. Her tawny hair was swept atop her head, haloed with a band of lace and tulle. She wore Kay's tiny pearl earrings, and Jane's pearl necklace. Clasped in her hands was a bouquet of daisies and orange blossoms. She looked very young, very beautiful.

Paul stood at the altar, watching his bride approach. He felt his heart swell. He gulped, for all at once there was a lump in his throat. "Laura," he murmured as she took her place beside him.

"Dearly beloved," began Reverend Fletcher.

Laura gazed steadily at Paul throughout the ceremony. When the time came to speak her vows, she spoke them in a soft, low voice. After the blessing, after the exchange of rings, she heard the words that made her both happy and sad: "I now pronounce you husband and wife."

"We did it!" said Paul.

"You may kiss the bride," said Reverend Fletcher.

It was a chaste kiss and it concluded the ceremony; arm in arm, Laura and Paul left the church. They paused on the steps while Paul's father aimed his small, boxy Kodak camera. They moved to the left; moved to the right; crouched down a little; straightened up, smiled at the camera, smiled at each other. A few minutes later, they were running through a shower of rice to the car they had hired.

"Mrs. Paul Brent," murmured Laura when they were settled in the backseat. She held out her hand, staring at her thin gold wedding ring. Her eyes moved to Paul. "I'll be a good wife. I promise. At least I'll try."

"Don't worry, everything's going to be fine." He put his arm around her shoulder, drawing her close. "It's going to be a great life, Laura. A great life."

Margaret had planned the wedding luncheon as a buffet. The kitchen table had been moved into the empty dining room, covered with a snowy white cloth, and arrayed with serving platters, silverware, napkins, and two stacks of white plates. The food was plentiful: cold ham in mustard sauce, cold chicken, string bean salad, pickled onions, homemade bread, a large wedge of cheese. There was champagne, a gift from Jane's parents. There was a wedding cake strewn with buttercream roses.

In the living room, a small table had been set aside for wedding presents. The Harding Advertising Company had sent a crystal pitcher and the Wesleys had sent a luxurious satin bedspread, but the other presents were far more modest: four hand-embroidered pillow cases from Doris, matching bedsheets from Jane, a dainty porcelain clock from Eve, and a hand-sewn quilt from Paul's parents. The newlyweds received a few gifts of cash: ten dollars from the Sam Roths, five dollars from Paul's friend Ed Taylor, ten dollars from the Happy Child Toy Company. All the gifts were appreciated, but the cash was especially welcome. It would, thought Laura, pay most of the wedding expenses.

She laughed at herself for thinking about money on her wedding day. This was a day to enjoy, to celebrate above all others. On this day she closed the doors to the past and opened the doors to the future. *It's going to be a great life.* She nodded. Yes, a great life.

She turned as Paul came up to her. He held out his hand and she saw he was holding a shiny copper penny. "A penny?" she asked.

"For your thoughts. You're a million miles away."

She smiled, linking her arm in his. "I'm right here and you're stuck with me, like it or not. You're a husband now."

"And you're my wife," he replied, kissing her. It was a real kiss, drawing cheers from some of the guests. "I'm so glad you're my wife," he said, letting her go. "I'll always be glad."

Laura felt a little breathless. She took a glass of champagne from the tray being passed by Bill Gibson, Doris's date and the volunteer bartender.

"Thanks," she said. "You're the most popular person in the room today."

"Doris thought we should make ourselves useful."

"There's nothing more useful than champagne," said Paul, taking a glass for himself.

Laura turned, surveying the crowded room. Margaret was at the piano, playing a lively version of "Here in My Arms." Eve and her date George stood behind Margaret, singing the lyrics. Doris was fluttering from place to place, emptying ashtrays. The Roths were sharing a joke with Paul's parents, and Jane was flirting with several of his friends. Jane's parents had obviously been trapped by a Beatrice Wesley monologue, but there was *Mr.* Wesley going to the rescue.

Laura smiled and sipped her champagne. She looked back at her new in-laws. They were nice people, as unassuming and down to earth as their son. Like him, they were easy to be around. She had been worried about meeting them, but her worries had soon disappeared. The Brents had arrived in the city on Monday and by Tuesday she'd started calling them Mom and Dad. She knew how lucky she was; there might be problems in her marriage, but there wouldn't be problems with her in-laws.

She glanced up at Paul, so handsome in his dark blue suit and gray silk necktie. He wasn't the husband she'd expected to have, but maybe he was the husband she'd been meant to have. She thought about that as she moved off toward her guests. She was still thinking about it an hour later, when she went to her room to change.

Laura had bought a dress for her honeymoon—a smart, caramel-colored wool jersey draped at the neck and waist. She reached out her hand, caressing the soft fabric; she couldn't remember the last time she'd had a new dress.

"Are you going to look at it or wear it?" asked Margaret, walking into the room. She bent, picking up a few stray grains of rice. "I came to see if you needed anything."

"No, I'm fine . . . Who's playing the piano?"

"That's George. You know, Eve's friend George. Oh, he's a live wire, that one."

"Yes." Laura started to undo the tiny buttons of her wedding dress. Carefully, she slipped it off. She glanced at her aunt. "There's something else on your mind. I can tell."

Margaret dipped her hand into her pocket, withdrawing two folded pieces of paper. "These are checks," she explained, "and they're made out to you. They're wedding presents."

Laura pulled the new wool jersey over her head. She smoothed the shoulders, the sleeves, the skirt. She went to her dressing table and sat down. "I don't have to ask who sent the checks. Since you've been hiding them from me, I guess I know."

"That's right, it's the Colliers. Senior and junior. Mike and Eleanor sent a hundred-dollar check, and so did Robby and Eliza."

Laura had been taking the pins out of her hair, but now her hand froze. Two hundred dollars! More than two months' salary in those two little pieces of paper!

"It's a lot of money," said Margaret, as if Laura had somehow overlooked this point. "Don't be so quick to turn up your nose."

"I never turn up my nose at money."

"Then you're two hundred dollars richer right now."

"No, I didn't say that." Laura removed the rest of the pins. She found her brush and pulled it through her hair. "Money is money, but when it comes to the Colliers, the answer is no. I won't take a penny from them. And I won't argue about it either. Send the checks back or throw them in the garbage."

"Well, if that's what you want."

"That's what I want, Aunt Margaret." She put the brush away and leaned closer to the mirror, freshening her lipstick. "So let's drop the subject."

"It's you who can't drop the subject. The subject of Robby. He's still on your mind, even though you have your own husband. A *fine* husband, too, if you'd only open your eyes."

Laura blotted her lipstick. She rose. "You don't understand. I don't care about Robby anymore. It's nothing like that, nothing. I was in love with him once, or I thought I was . . . but those feelings are gone. They died."

"Then why won't you forgive and forget?"

"No, Aunt Margaret." Laura shook her head. "No; I'm sorry, but no."

"Eliza and Robby—"

"They were the people I loved and they hurt me. They stole from me. There's nothing more to say."

"Their baby's due anytime."

"I hope it's a nice healthy baby," replied Laura, picking up her purse, "but it's nothing to do with us." She glanced about the room and then started toward the door. "Paul is waiting."

"You look very pretty. I wish your mother was here to see you."

"Yes, so do I." Tears glittered suddenly in Laura's eyes. She turned, flinging her arms around her aunt. "But we're a family all the same. The three of us: you and Paul and I. We'll be all right."

"Did your mother ever have a talk with you, Laura?"

"A talk?"

"Well, you're going off on your honeymoon, aren't you?"

She blushed. "Yes, Mama told me . . . some things." She was spared further explanation by a knock at the door. "That's Paul."

Margaret opened the door. "Your bride's all ready."

"I have to throw my bouquet. I promised . . . My bouquet! Where is it?"

"On the hall table," said Paul, smiling. "The girls are lined up . . . Aunt Margaret, you ought to get into it too. If you catch the bouquet, you might catch yourself a husband."

She sniffed at the suggestion. "A husband with one foot in the old folks' home and one foot in the grave. That's what I'd get, at my age."

She laughed, and so did the newlyweds. They walked into the hall together. Laura retrieved her bouquet from the table, stationing herself a moment later in the arched doorway of the living room. She saw five pairs of arms stretching upward. She closed her eyes and tossed the bouquet.

Eve almost caught it, but it slid off her fingertips and landed in Doris's hands. "Oh, my," said Doris.

"You're the next bride," said Paul. He turned to his own bride, lightly kissing her cheek. "Come on, we have a honeymoon to go to!"

There hadn't been any extra money for a honeymoon, and Laura hadn't wanted to take time away from work, but Paul had decided that their marriage deserved a proper start. If he couldn't give his new wife a week in Palm Beach, or even Atlantic City, he could at least give her one perfect day and night at the Plaza Hotel.

He had been tempted to throw caution to the winds and rent a suite, but in the end he'd settled for a handsome double room with a sweeping view of Central Park. The room cost fourteen dollars, slightly less than half his honeymoon budget; he thought it was worth every cent.

Laura thought it was wonderful. "So elegant," she said, looking around. The wallpaper was ivory and gold, matching the silky draperies. The carpet was a rich forest green. There were two chairs covered in a green and ivory print; the bedspread was ivory, scalloped at the edges. Above the chest of drawers was a large mirror, and opposite the chest was a slender desk supplied with a blotter, a pen stand, and a variety of hotel stationery. "Oh, Paul, I can't believe I'm really here. The *Plaza*. You're going to spoil me."

"That's what I had in mind." He turned Laura toward the windows. "How do you like the view?"

She stared down at the park, at the graceful old trees crowned with afternoon sunshine. "Oh, it's lovely, Paul. Maybe we could take a walk around the zoo."

"I have bigger plans than the zoo."

"Really?"

He snatched Laura's coat from a chair and draped it about her shoulders. "Come along, Mrs. Brent," he said, offering his arm. "I'll show you."

"Plans, eh?"

"We're going on a spree."

It began with cocktails amid the paneled splendor of the hotel's Oak Room. Paul ordered martinis, because that's what sophisticated men about town always ordered in the movies. The first icy sting of gin burned his throat. He laughed, and so did Laura. She too was thinking of the movies; she felt just like Mryna Loy in *The Thin Man*.

Twilight was gathering over the city as Paul and Laura finished their drinks and left the hotel. He led her around the corner to a long line of horse-drawn carriages. "Your chariot awaits," he said.

The driver tipped his shiny, slightly battered top hat. He helped Laura into the cab and gave Paul a lap robe. "Once around the park, sir?"

"Slowly."

"Yes, slowly," agreed Laura. "We want to see the moon come out."

The driver climbed onto his high bench and grasped the reins. The horse lifted its head and trotted briskly across the street into the park.

Laura sat back, snuggling in the crook of Paul's arm. She heard the steady clip-clop of the horse's hooves, the gentle rustling of the wind in the trees. She heard the call of a bird, and then another call, as if in reply. It was darker now. She saw shadows dancing on the grass, on the path. She smiled.

"Happy?" asked Paul, squeezing her hand.

She nodded. "Very happy." It wasn't the kind of happiness that made her feel tingly and lightheaded, but it was a deep-down kind of happiness that made her feel secure. Paul loved her and she could trust his love. She wasn't alone anymore. "Very happy," she said again.

Paul leaned forward and whispered something to the driver. Laura wanted to know what, but he wouldn't say. "It's a surprise."

"Another surprise?"

"Isn't this better than the zoo?"

Her smile widened. "Much," she admitted.

Darkness had enclosed the carriage. The sky was filled with stars, fiery diamonds strewn on black velvet. Laura and Paul looked up, looking for the moon. "There it is," he said as they were showered with silvery light. "Just in time."

The carriage had arrived at Tavern on the Green. Laura's astonished gaze jumped from the wide French doors of the restaurant, to the terrace where a band was playing, and then to the paper lanterns strung in the trees. She thought it was charming, like a country estate hidden in the middle of the city. "Paul, how beautiful!"

"Happy honeymoon, Laura."

It was past midnight when they got back to their hotel room. The windows had been opened; the bed had been turned down. Their small suitcase sat upon a rack near the closet. Laura glanced at the suitcase, thinking about her new white nightgown. She blushed and looked away. She'd had a marvelous time this evening, yet suddenly she felt awkward, ill at ease.

"Do you want anything?" asked Paul. "There's room service."

"No, I'm fine."

"Are you sure?"

"Positive."

Silence fell, an uncomfortable silence. Paul and Laura were husband and wife now, but neither of them seemed to know what was supposed to happen next. He lit a cigarette and stood smoking it, his gaze shifting around the room. She sat in one of the green and ivory chairs, absently smoothing her skirt.

"Well," he said after a while.

"Well," she said. They looked at each other. They laughed. "I guess this is pretty silly."

"Yes," agreed Paul, annoyed with himself for behaving like a timid schoolboy. He hadn't had a lot of experience but he'd had some, and certainly more than Laura; it was up to him to lead the way. "Why don't you get your things out of the suitcase," he suggested. "I'll just finish my cigarette while you change."

"Yes, all right." She went to the suitcase and snapped it open. Her nightgown and robe were folded on top. Tucked underneath was a zippered bag containing her hairbrush, her toothbrush, a tin of tooth powder, and a wrapped bar of Silktouch soap. "I won't be long," she said, walking off to the bathroom.

"There's no hurry," replied Paul. He grimaced. Had he said the wrong thing? Everything he said sounded wrong to him; everything sounded clumsy. *Why* was he acting like such a dodo?

Laura shut the bathroom door, leaning against it. "My wedding night," she murmured, but as the words sank in she felt a flurry of panic. She was married—actually married—and soon she would be lying beside her husband. Beside a stranger, she thought, because suddenly she felt as if she didn't know Paul Brent at all. Who was this man she had promised to love, honor, and cherish?

For one anxious moment she couldn't remember what he looked like, couldn't remember the sound of his voice. Get hold of yourself, she silently warned, taking little breaths until the panic eased. She had heard about wedding night jitters; she wondered if Paul was feeling them too.

Laura undressed quickly, slipping into her silken white nightgown. She brushed her teeth, scrubbed her face. She took several minutes with her hair, brushing it into soft waves. "Mrs. Paul Brent," she said to her reflection in the mirror. She took one more breath, and then opened the door.

Paul, wearing his new maroon robe, was standing near the bed. He had dimmed the lamps but there was moonlight, and in the moonlight he saw Laura walking toward him. He had dreamed this moment a thousand times; even now he wasn't sure it was real. "Laura?" he whispered.

"Here I am."

"You're so beautiful." Her gown wasn't sheer, but he could see the curves of her body straining against the fabric. His throat tightened. He reached out, drawing her into his arms. "I love you," he said hoarsely, kissing her hair, her lips. "God, I love you so much."

Laura felt his arms encircle her and she relaxed. He wasn't a stranger, he was Paul; her own dear Paul. "I love you too," she murmured as he crushed his mouth on hers. His hands slid over her shoulders, pulling at the straps of her gown. It dropped to her waist, and now his hands were stroking and fondling her breasts. Her body began to stir. "Paul . . ."

He pushed her down on the bed and gently removed her gown. He gazed at her nakedness, throwing off his robe. His breath was quick, his mouth moving hungrily from her lips to her throat to her swelling breasts. His hands were everywhere, feverish hands driven by the passion of a thousand dreams, a thousand fantasies. His body pressed closer, lost in passion now, utterly lost.

Laura's arms were wound around Paul, her fingers digging into his back. She felt as if she were being carried off on the crest of a great tall wave. She clung to Paul, moving against him, pulling him closer, closer. There was a brief instant of pain, and then the wave engulfed her; sweeping her under, sweeping her away.

They sank into an exhausted sleep. Laura lay on her side, her face almost covered by a spill of tousled hair. She was dreaming, chasing odd, disconnected images from one shadowy place to another. She saw trees glowing with lights that took on the shape of owls. She saw old Eli Harding in a top hat, driving a hansom cab. She saw Myrna Loy holding a martini glass, and Anne Marsh running after a sleek black cat. The cat belonged to the fortune-teller Madame Zarela. When Laura awoke the next morning, she glanced around as if expecting Madame Zarela to suddenly appear.

It was Paul she saw — a smiling Paul already showered and shaved; wearing his robe over his shirt and trousers. She pushed the hair out of her eyes, raising herself on her elbow. "Now you know how I look in the morning. I must be a sight!"

"You're beautiful." He crouched down beside the bed and gently tucked the blanket around Laura. "Morning, noon, or night, you're beautiful."

"Love is blind," she replied, falling back on the pillows. "Good thing, too." She clasped Paul's hand. "You were an early bird today, weren't you?"

"It's after eleven."

"Eleven!"

"I didn't have the heart to wake you. I started to, but you were sleeping so peacefully."

"Eleven o'clock," said Laura. "I *never* sleep that late."

He kissed her. "It's all right to pamper yourself a little. Especially on your honeymoon." He kissed her again, and then stood up. "I'm going out for a minute; there's something I want to get. If you hear a knock on the door, it's room service with our breakfast. Are you hungry?"

"Starving."

Paul traded his robe for his suit jacket. He slid his tie under his collar, knotting it as he went to the door. "You won't run away?"

She smiled. "You're stuck with me. Reverend

Fletcher said so. Til death do us part, remember?"

He rushed over and kissed Laura one more time. "You're terrific," he exclaimed, rushing out of the room.

She watched him go, glad once again that she'd married him. She was happy—not deliriously happy, the way brides were in books—but happy nonetheless. She was content, and it was a nice feeling. A very nice feeling, she thought, swinging her legs to the floor.

She wrapped herself in a blanket and walked off to the bathroom. Paul's shaving things were scattered on a glass shelf above the sink. She stared at them. She turned, staring at her reflection in the mirror. Did she look different now that she was a woman? Would anybody notice? No, probably not.

There was a whooshing sound as Laura ran her bath. She dropped the blanket and stepped into the tub, splashing about in the warm, soapy water. Ten minutes later, bathed and dressed and brushed, she went to answer the knock at the door.

A young room service waiter wheeled in a cart laden with food: scrambled eggs, pancakes, bacon, sausage, popovers, jam, coffee and pastries. Deftly, he arranged the dishes on a table by the windows, drawing the two green and ivory chairs alongside. Laura sat down, marveling at the sight of the huge breakfast.

Paul returned in time to sign the check. After the waiter had gone, he sat across from Laura and held out a bouquet of violets. He called it a honeymoon bouquet, and to her it was a cherished keepsake to add to the others—to the matchbook from the Oak Room, the leaves from Central Park, the tiny cake of soap stamped with the Plaza name, the pretty ashtray from Tavern on the Green. Our whirlwind honeymoon, she thought as she heaped Paul's plate with eggs and bacon. Our wonderful, extravagant, whirlwind honeymoon.

They checked out of the hotel at one o'clock. After paying the bill, Paul had exactly seventeen cents in his pocket. "Enough for the crosstown bus," he remarked with a laugh, "and seven cents left over!"

"Let's walk home." Laura paused on the steps of the Plaza, shading her eyes in the brilliant afternoon light. It was Sunday. There were strollers on the avenue, well-dressed men and women enjoying the autumn weather. There was a big red kite soaring in the sky above Central Park. She heard the clip-clop of hooves and she turned to see a hansom cab rounding the corner. "It's so lovely here," she said. "It's just like a picture postcard."

"We'll come back again. We can come for dinner sometime."

"On a special occasion."

Paul grinned, taking his wife's arm. "We're bound to have a few of those sooner or later."

"Sooner or later," she agreed. She looked up; the red kite was snagged in the branches of a tree. "Come on, let's go home."

Laura and Paul went home to the Lexington Avenue apartment. Margaret had moved the last of Kay's things out of the master bedroom, and then moved Laura's things into it. There was more than enough space, even when Paul added his few possessions: his clothes and books and photographs, and his vast collection of tin soldiers. He added a chess set too, and during long winter evenings he set up the board in front of the fireplace and taught Laura how to play.

From the start it was a cozy kind of marriage. To

everyone's surprise, Margaret stayed out of the way, giving the young couple all the privacy they wanted. They had the run of the living room, where they listened to the radio and played Monopoly with their friends. They had the bedroom, where they played chess; where they read their favorite books; where they made love. Once a month they went out to dinner—to Mama Stella's or to Wo Fat's Chow Mein Palace. Every Sunday they took a long walk, or sometimes a ride on the Staten Island ferry. Every Sunday night they went to the movies, holding hands through the double feature and the newsreel.

There were special occasions in the first year of Paul and Laura's marriage—or at least milestone occasions. The Colliers' baby was born, a beautiful boy who was christened John Bellamy but called JB. Margaret celebrated her fiftieth birthday. The initial ads for Moonlight Perfume appeared and Laura got a five-dollar raise. Jane became engaged, then broke the engagement a month later. Doris, resisting her parents as well as her cousins in Ohio, married Bill Gibson and moved to his bachelor flat near Columbia.

The year seemed to pass very quickly and that troubled Laura, because she felt she wasn't getting anywhere. There were two things she wanted desperately—a child and a promotion at work. Of course she knew she couldn't have both; if she had a child, she would have to leave Harding Advertising, and if she were given a promotion, she might be less anxious to have a child. It was a quandary, but still she couldn't help wanting, *wishing*.

She was at the hospital when Doris's baby was born. One look at the tiny pink bundle and something twisted in her heart. After almost two years of marriage and several visits to Dr. Weston, she was no closer to having a child of her own.

She was no closer to a promotion either. Zack had given her some small jobs beyond her regular duties, but they were just the routine, boring jobs no one else wanted to do—writing the copy for the spring and fall editions of the Speed-Grow seed catalogs; writing and producing the annual sales letter for Burnett Tile. He hadn't given her anything that required imagination or style, anything that might make the client notice her work. He urged her to be patient, and his advice was echoed by Eve. Laura tried, yet she couldn't shake the feeling that time was passing too quickly, passing her by.

"A failure at twenty!" laughed Jane, after listening to Laura's tale of woe. "Shocking!"

"Don't forget I'll be twenty-one next month."

"Oh, well, that's different. Twenty-one? Yes, you should at *least* be vice president of the company by now. At the ripe old age of twenty-one—"

"All right, all right," said Laura, smiling. "I get the point. Everybody thinks I'm in too much of a hurry." She leaned back in her chair, glancing around at Doris's little kitchen. It was a bright, cheery room. She had helped to hang the starched white curtains; Paul had helped Bill paint the walls a lustrous shade of yellow. Pots and pans were stacked on shelves beside the ancient stove. The open cupboards were lined with red oilcloth and packed with dishes and canned goods and small jars of spices from the Hungarian delicatessen in Yorkville. Laura had tasted a bit of paprika in Doris's Irish stew. "You're very quiet," she said as Doris finished scraping the dinner dishes. "I'd like to hear your opinion."

Doris put the dishes in the sink, sprinkled soap flakes over them, and ran the water. She dried her hands on her apron and turned, shaking her blonde curls. "I don't know. You're getting experience, Laura. You're learning. Maybe that's all you can expect for now." She frowned. "I mean, you really are sort of young to have an executive job, aren't you?"

"I'm young in *years* but not in other ways. With all the things that happened, I had to grow up pretty fast . . . Besides, it isn't as if I expect Zack to make me a full-fledged copywriter in charge of accounts. I'd be happy to be a junior copywriter. Eve told me there were a lot of junior copywriters at Harding, before the Depression. Anne Marsh was a junior copywriter once. So was Hal Russell." Laura sipped her coffee. "It's a stepping-stone job," she continued. "It could mean some extra money, too."

"Oh, you must be rolling in money," teased Jane. "You have three salaries coming into your house."

Laura stared at Jane over the rim of her cup. "Three?"

"You and Paul. And Margaret's giving piano lessons; that's like earning a salary."

"At fifteen cents a lesson, it's not much of a salary. Her only pupils are Beatrice Wesley's grandchildren, and the Sylvester kids from around the corner."

"The Sylvester *hooligans*."

"Aunt Margaret has them tamed. All she has to do is look at them and they're little ladies and gentlemen."

"More coffee?" asked Doris, carrying the percolator to the table. "It's still hot."

"I'll have more," said Jane. She sat back, turning her head to Laura. "Okay," she went on, "maybe not three salaries. But two, anyway. Yours and Paul's."

Laura glanced off toward the living room, where Paul and Bill and Jane's date Ted were arguing about last week's Giants game. Her eyes seemed to flicker, to cloud. She sighed. "Did you know Paul's had only one raise in all the time he's worked at Happy Child?"

"The Depression," said Doris.

"Yes, the Depression. But a month ago there was an ad in the paper for an assistant product manager at Willoughby Toys. I wanted Paul to talk to them. Just talk, for goodness' sake; there's no harm in talking. He laughed and said it wouldn't be right. That was the end of the conversation . . . Paul won't ask his boss for a raise and he won't look for another job. Won't even *talk* about another job. So there we are."

"Where?" asked Jane, adding sugar to her coffee. "Are you mad at him?"

"No, not mad. How could anyone ever be mad at Paul? But I wish he were more ambitious."

"Like you?"

Laura shrugged. "I want to get ahead. Paul's happy to stay where he is. I'm not going to push him . . . It would be a waste of time to try," she added with a laugh. "Paul is Paul." A good husband and a good man, she thought, staring into her coffee cup. But a man who's not the least bit interested in success. "I can't complain, because we agree on most things."

"I know," said Jane. "I keep waiting to hear about a nice, juicy fight."

"We hardly ever argue, much less fight. I guess money is the only sore subject. To this day, Paul won't let me help with the rent or the grocery bills. No matter what I say, the answer is always no. He gets a funny look on his face and reminds me that he's not the gigolo type."

"Well, he's not."

"I never said he was, Jane. But I'm his wife and

I'm earning the same money he is; it's silly not to let me help. Especially since he sends a check to his parents every month. By the time he gets through with all the monthly checks, he doesn't have a penny left for himself. That's wrong."

"It's what he wants."

Doris had been listening closely to Laura and Jane. Now she leaned forward, ready to add her views. "I grew up listening to arguments about money," she said. "It was awful. I'll bet money is what people argue about most. Those arguments just go on and on. They do a lot of damage, and nobody ever wins. You have to be careful, Laura."

"I know. I've been lucky—Paul doesn't mind my working, or even my plans to work up to a better job. That's very lucky."

"Paul understands you," said Doris. She turned suddenly, wondering if she'd heard the baby. "I'd better go have a look at Alice. Sometimes she's a little fussy."

"Can I help?" asked Laura.

"Oh no, you'll start playing with her and then I'll never get her back to sleep."

Doris rushed away, the long sleeves of her sweater flapping around her wrists. Jane watched, exhaling a great sigh. "She's still wearing clothes from those stupid cousins in Ohio. You'd think they'd know her size by now."

"I'm sure they know; they just don't care. And Doris has no choice. She has no money for clothes. Bill's devoted to his work, but assistant professors don't earn much." Laura drained her cup and carried it to the sink. "Things will improve once he has his doctorate. Doris should have her degree by then, also. They'll be all right."

"I suppose."

Laura studied Jane's profile. "You're wearing a

different face powder. It's very becoming."

"Thanks. A different lipstick, too. Both by Jobina Cosmetics, in case you had any doubt. I love her cosmetics. I'd wear them even if I didn't work there."

"Tell me about her."

Jane glanced up. "Her? Jobina Grant, do you mean."

"Yes, Jobina Grant."

"Why?"

"Curiosity," replied Laura.

Jane shifted around in her chair. "Come on, what's the *real* reason? It's more than curiosity. You're up to something. You are; I know that look."

"And I thought I was being so subtle . . . Okay, the truth is I'd like to arrange a meeting with Jobina Grant. There's one sure way for me to move up at Harding—that's to bring in a new account. If I could bring the Jobina Inc. account to Zack, he'd have to take me seriously."

"God, Laura, you're aiming high. Jobina Inc. is big business."

"That's what makes it such a valuable account. Tell me about Jobina Grant."

Jane shrugged. "She's gorgeous, about forty or forty-one. She built the company from nothing, she and her partner Emile Lanteau. He's a funny little Frenchman, very chirpy. A genius in the lab."

"But Jobina runs the company."

"She runs it exactly the way she did when they were just starting out. The old-timers say everything's the same. *Bigger,* but the same."

Laura nodded. "Yes, I'm counting on that."

"I don't think she ever meant to be in business. There's an interesting story about it."

"I know. According to the story, Jobina's husband was caught embezzling from some trust accounts at his law firm. He couldn't repay the money, and so he killed himself."

"Shot himself," said Jane, holding an imaginary gun to her temple. "Bang."

"Then Jobina got a job working behind the toiletries counter at a pharmacy. She met Emile there and they went into business together. Now it's fifteen years later and they're rich as Croesus."

"How do you know all that?"

Laura laughed. "Surprised? I did a lot of research on Jobina Inc. I read everything I could find . . . She's the key, Jane. A man isn't likely to give me a chance, but a woman might. Particularly a woman who built a company from nothing."

"How long have you been thinking about this?"

"A few months. Long enough to do the research and study the Jobina ads. They're good, but they could be better. Ronnie Woronow and I have been working on some ideas."

"Ideas?" asked Paul, sticking his head in the door. "What dangerous ideas are you two girls cooking up now?"

"I was talking about the Jobina Inc. account."

"Oh, I see."

"I'm going to be the company spy!" said Jane with a gleeful smile.

Laura shook her head. "I don't want you to spy . . . But I *could* use a color chart. You know, all the Jobina Inc. colors?"

"Sure. I can sneak one out of the lab. Anything else while I'm there?"

"Just the color chart. And please don't make it sound so illegal."

"Why not? That's the best part."

"If I can get a word in," said Paul, "it's starting to snow and I think—"

"Snow!" cried Jane. "Damn, I'm wearing brand-new shoes!" She rose, walking quickly to the door. "Maybe Doris can lend me some boots . . . She'd better, or Ted will have to carry me on his back!"

"You have crazy friends," laughed Paul when Jane had gone. "Crazy." He drew Laura into his arms and held her for a moment, stroking her hair. "Did you have a nice time tonight?"

"A lovely time."

"From the little I heard, I guess you're ready to go see the famous Jobina."

"If I can get an appointment. She's a busy woman. She's important."

"You're important."

Laura touched Paul's cheek. She smiled. "Am I?"

"You're the most important thing in my life."

That ought to be enough, she thought to herself, but it's not. Dear God, it's not.

Chapter Fourteen

It was a sparkling February morning in 1937 when Laura arrived at the headquarters of Jobina Inc. From the outside, the building looked like all the others in the neighborhood—drab, graceless, a huge old factory building scarred by time and city soot. But that was the outside; inside, everything was bright and clean and splashed with color. The scent of flowers seemed to drift through the corridors; the scent of roses, thought Laura, sniffing the air. Glancing around, she saw one wall covered with sketches of butterflies, the company symbol.

Four silk butterflies as large as kites adorned the pale mauve walls of Jobina Grant's outer office. Laura gazed at them, studying the hues: the intense pinks and fuchsias and scarlets.

"May I help you?"

Startled, Laura wheeled around. "Oh, I'm sorry," she said to the pretty young secretary seated behind the fan-shaped desk. "I was looking at the butterflies."

"Yes, everybody does that."

"My name is Laura Brent. I have an appointment to see Mrs. Grant."

"Have a seat. I'll tell her you're here."

Laura put down her oversized leather portfolio. She took off her coat and draped it on one of the silken couches. Again her eyes traveled to the butterflies; their colors matched the most popular lipsticks in the Jobina line.

"If you'll just come with me," said the secretary, rising from her desk. "Mrs. Grant will see you now."

Laura had spent months preparing for today, but that fact did nothing to calm her nerves. She reached for her portfolio and nearly knocked over a lamp. "Sorry," she mumbled, righting it.

"This way, please."

Laura got a firm grip on her portfolio and followed the young woman across the room. At the door, she took a deep, steadying breath. Here goes, she thought.

The door opened, revealing a large, elegant office decorated in shades of ivory, with strong accents of green and blue and yellow. "Thank you," said Laura, walking inside. The door closed quietly behind her. She took another breath.

"Good morning, Mrs. Brent. I'm Jobina Grant. Please sit down."

"Thank you." Laura sat in a chair at the corner of the desk. "I appreciate your seeing me."

"Jane Walder put in a good word for you. We're all very fond of Jane . . . But as I explained, I have no plans to hire an advertising agency. We have quite a fine advertising department of our own, and I'm entirely satisfied." A sudden smile lighted her face. It was a beautiful face, the porcelain skin and wide amber eyes framed by gleaming chestnut hair. She was beautifully, expensively dressed. "Before you comment on our ads, I ought to warn you that many of the ideas are mine. I sketch my ideas and send them up to advertising."

Laura could almost hear Eve's voice urging her to be direct and to the point. "They're good ads, Mrs.

Grant," she replied. "But they could be better. They could be stronger . . . Mrs. Grant, I'd like you to understand that I'm not here to suggest we replace your advertising department. The Harding approach is always to work with the client's own staff, if they have a staff. Some clients don't. They don't want the expense."

"An advertising agency doesn't save expense. It adds fifteen percent to the budget. The fifteen percent commission."

"Yes," agreed Laura. This was one of the points she had heard discussed in numerous presentations, and one she had gone over with Eve. She started to relax. "But if an advertising agency is used the right way," she continued, "you can expect your total budget to decrease and your profits to *in*crease."

"Oh?" said Jobina Grant, arching a chestnut brow. "Do you offer a guarantee?"

"Speaking for the agency, no. Speaking for myself . . . yes. Because I've been studying the figures."

"Figures?"

"In the old days, advertising agencies just designed the ads and placed them in newspapers or magazines. But now we can do so much more." Laura leaned forward, warming to her subject. "Do you know the term 'market research'?"

Jobina Grant shrugged. "You're talking about statistics."

"Yes. Detailed statistics to tell you everything about the women who buy your cosmetics. Statistics to tell you their likes and dislikes. It's very exciting, Mrs. Grant. That information can help to focus your advertising. Certain publications are wrong for your product; you should drop them. Certain publications are exactly right and you need to start using them. Of course the ads have to be right also."

Laura blushed. "I'm sorry if I seem to be lecturing. Sometimes I get carried away."

"You seem to be trying to tell me my business."

She thought about this. "In a way," she replied carefully, "that's what a good advertising agency should do. Maybe not *tell*, but interpret."

A look of surprise flickered in Jobina Grant's eyes. She was silent, not at all sure what to think of the eager young woman who sat across from her. She had agreed to see Laura as a favor to a company secretary, but now she realized that her interest had been piqued. "Go on," she said. "I'm listening."

"I brought some things to show you, if I may." There was a brisk nod. Laura stood, lifting her portfolio onto the chair. "I have some layouts and some charts and a display; they're kind of bulky."

"Yes. Perhaps we ought to use the conference table."

Laura carried the portfolio to the polished oak table in the rear of the office. She put it down, struggling with the zipper. She blushed again, but finally she slid the zipper open and withdrew the display that Ronnie Woronow had put together. It was a series of twenty small panels affixed to a long strip of pasteboard; she set it on the table and stepped back.

"But those are our ads," said Jobina Grant, scanning the panels. "You don't need to show me our own ads, Mrs. Brent."

"Please call me Laura."

"Laura, then. I'm quite familiar with our ads."

"Yes, these are your ads for January, as many as we could find. But did you ever look at them all together like this? Did you ever study them as a group?"

"Should I have?"

Laura moved her hand to the display. "They're good ads, Mrs. Grant, but you'd never know they were all for the same company. There are twenty ads here and each one has a different style. Even the butterfly is different in each ad."

"There's nothing wrong with a little variety. It keeps our ads from getting stale."

"Too much variety . . ." Laura's voice trailed away. All at once she felt foolish giving advice to such a rich, successful businesswoman. All at once she felt she was in over her head. Anxiously, she glanced off toward the door. She could gather up her things right now and walk through that door, or she could stay and finish what she had started. She gulped and decided to stay. "Too much variety weakens your ads," she continued quietly. "The butterfly is an example. It's a wonderful symbol for your company, but it's useless if people don't recognize it. Sometimes people just glance at an ad. You have only a fraction of a second to get their attention."

"We try to have some fun with the butterfly, you see."

"Oh, you can put lots of different butterflies in your ads, but the butterfly in your logo must always look the same."

"Must?"

Laura nodded. "Why confuse your customers, Mrs. Grant?"

She smiled slightly. "An excellent question. Perhaps you would like to explain what else I've been doing wrong."

"Not 'wrong,'" replied Laura hastily. "But I do have something else to show you, if you don't mind."

"Not at all."

"Well, it's these two ads." She pointed to an area of the display, drawing a circle with her fingertip. "They're for the same lipstick, but one ad seems to be designed for society women, and the other one for young working women."

"That's exactly how the ads were designed. Our typical customers are young working women and young housewives—women who may be a little starry-eyed about high society. That's why we occasionally try to give our ads a high-society gloss." Jobina leaned closer to the display. She frowned. "Looking at it now, I'm not certain we accomplished our goal."

"There's a better way. If you want a society ad, you can get a society woman to endorse your cosmetics. You pay a fee and it's done . . . But instead of a society woman, it should be an actress. A movie actress." Laura paused, taking a layout from her portfolio. "Something like this," she said. "The idea is glamour. I've looked at the research, Mrs. Grant. These days, young women would rather be in the movies than in the Social Register."

"You're very thorough."

She smiled. "I'm after your account . . . Harding Advertising can give you a strong, focused advertising campaign that's backed up by the latest market research. We'd like to make a full presentation, including suggestions for radio."

"Radio? Not one of those terrible serials?"

"The more terrible they are, the more popular they are."

Jobina laughed. She turned, fixing her amber eyes on the display. A moment passed. After another moment, she sighed and shook her head. "I'm afraid I'm beginning to see what you mean. These ads look a bit strange, side by side. They look a bit haphazard. I never noticed that before . . . You may be right: we can do better."

"I think you'll like the ideas we've been working on at Harding. We have several interesting approaches, Mrs. Grant."

"Perhaps." She glanced up. "Tell me, Laura, how would you describe your own approach to this company's products? Can you tell me in a word what it is?"

"Well, maybe three words. Colors, because the Jobina colors are extraordinary. Glamour, because cosmetics should make a woman feel glamorous . . . And I think the third word would be 'youth,' because most of your customers are young . . . and the others are hoping the right cosmetics will erase a year or two. The trick is to design a campaign that appeals to younger women, but that doesn't exclude older women."

"Not an easy trick."

"It can be done. Eli Harding says a good advertising agency thrives on challenges."

"How long have you been with Harding?"

"Three years," replied Laura. "I fit the definition of your typical customer, Mrs. Grant. That gives me an advantage. Another advantage is my aunt Margaret. She's an older woman and very particular about what she buys. So I can look at your products from two points of view, hers and mine."

"Yes. Yes, I see." Jobina's expression was thoughtful, her gaze measuring Laura. "Come and sit down," she said finally, returning to her desk. She glanced at her watch, and then at her appointment calendar. She pressed a switch on the intercom. "I'm going to need another ten minutes," she said to her secretary. "Tell Emile I'm running late; and when Mr. Claymore calls, ask him to change our meeting to eleven-thirty." She switched off the intercom, settling into her chair. A smile edged her mouth as her gaze moved back to Laura. "All right, let's talk."

Laura was flushed with excitement when she emerged from the Jobina Inc. building. The first hurdle had been overcome; one down, she thought, one more to go. She walked quickly to the curb, her big portfolio banging against her leg. For a moment she stared out at the sea of trucks and cars. She could walk three blocks to the subway, or she could treat herself to a cab. Smiling, she thrust her hand in the air. "Taxi!" she called.

All the way uptown, she rehearsed what she would say to Zack. He would be surprised by her visit to Jobina Grant, by the charts and layouts in her portfolio. He would be surprised, yes, but would he be angry? She shrugged. When he learned the results of her visit, he'd be delighted. Nobody ever quarreled with success.

Laura was climbing out of the cab when she noticed a panhandler standing on the corner. She dropped a dime in his tin cup, then went back and put in fifteen cents more. It was an impulsive gesture—she wanted to be generous today, to share her good luck. That was what Paul would have done. The Depression had started to ease, there were fewer people begging coins and scavenging in garbage cans, but still Paul budgeted fifty cents a week for what he called "sidewalk charities." She smiled again, thinking about him. He had predicted that her meeting would be a triumph.

Eve hadn't been so certain. Now, as Laura came into view, she stopped typing and jumped to her feet. *"Well?"* she asked eagerly. "What happened?"

Two new secretaries had been added to the office. Laura saw them glance up from their typewriters. "Good morning," she said. "I guess I'm late."

"What happened?" repeated Eve, though in a quieter voice.

"Well, there's nothing definite yet."

"But?"

"But I think we did it!" She crossed her fingers. "I *hope* we did. Maybe I shouldn't speak too soon."

"Maybe you should speak to Zack and let him know what's going on. He's in his office . . . Here, I'll take your coat . . . And your hat . . . Okay, you're all set. Don't beat around the bush, Laura. Just tell him straight out."

"I will." She picked up her portfolio and turned toward Zack's office. "I will."

His door was open, but she knocked anyway. "Do you have a minute, Zack?"

"Come in . . . Have you seen the layouts for Portman's Gin? Slick, very slick." He nodded, holding one of the layouts to the light streaming through the windows. "Look at the way the ice cubes glitter. Look at the clarity of the gin. Doesn't it make you thirsty for a martini?"

She laughed. "Not on an empty stomach . . . But it's a good ad."

"A damn good ad." He put the layout back on his desk and sat down. "Whose portfolio is that?"

"Ronnie Woronow's. I borrowed it to take some things to a meeting. I should have told you about the meeting in advance, Zack."

"What meeting? What have you been doing?"

Don't beat around the bush. "The truth is, I've been working on a special project. Ronnie's been helping me. The project is the Jobina Inc. account and we have—"

262

"Jobina Inc.? The cosmetics company? You're wasting your time, Laura. All their advertising is done in-house. The Grant woman won't even talk to ad agencies."

"She talked to me. I saw her this morning. I've just come from there."

Zack's gray eyes fastened on Laura. "Come from Jobina Inc.? You had a meeting with Jobina Inc.? *You?*"

"Yes, that's right."

"The hell it is! You'd better start explaining! If you've been arranging meetings with clients . . ." He shook his head. "How the *hell* did you get a meeting with Jobina Grant?"

"Well, I have a friend who works there."

"That's it? A friend who works there?"

"Yes."

"And through your friend, you took it upon yourself to set up a meeting. A meeting! What were you thinking of, Laura? You're a secretary, for Christ sake. Secretaries do not — repeat, *do not* — meet with clients."

"I knew that's what you'd say. That's why I didn't tell you. It was a chance to prove myself."

"It was a damned stupid thing to do. I could fire you right here and now. I *should* fire you. I should put us both out of our misery."

Laura paled a little, but her gaze remained steady. "Zack, I don't think you understand. If you'll just let me finish . . . The meeting went very well. It was a success. Mrs. Grant agreed to a full presentation, and I'm almost positive we'll wind up with the account."

"What!"

"It's true."

Amazement was stamped on Zack's face. "I seem

to have underestimated your powers of persuasion."

"It was more than persuasion." Laura unzipped the portfolio. "These are Ronnie's layouts," she explained, placing them on the desk. "And then we decided to do charts, too. We used the latest figures from the research department . . . We spent months on all this, Zack. Not company time; we used our lunch hours, our weekends. It was a lot of work. By now I'm an expert on Jobina Inc. I went into the meeting prepared for anything."

"I want to hear more about your meeting. I'd better get Anne in here; she'll have some—"

"No, don't," said Laura as he reached his hand toward the intercom. "Anne is the other reason I didn't tell you about the meeting in advance. She would have taken over, Zack. It would have been my project but *her* account. I've worked too hard for that to happen."

He sat back in his old leather chair and lit a cigarette. "Are you telling me whom to assign to accounts? The last time I looked, those decisions were entirely mine."

She reddened. "Sorry. I'm so keyed up about this. I've worked hard and I think I deserve a chance. I won't get it if you bring Anne in . . . Zack, this really *is* my project."

"A project, is all it is, so far. If we land the account—and that's a *big* if—what do you expect out of it? I certainly couldn't put you in charge. You're too young and inexperienced."

"I don't expect to be in charge, but I want to be part of the team. Martin Carver could supervise the account; Martin, Ronnie, and I would make a great team."

"Why Martin?" asked Zack, dragging on his cigarette. "What's so special about Martin?"

"He's quick. I've watched him in meetings. You only have to say a few words about a product and he starts filling his index cards with ideas . . . I've watched and I've learned."

Zack laughed. "Obviously." For three years, she'd been like a sponge soaking up all the fine points of the advertising business, all the tricks. She'd stayed on the sidelines, watching how things were done, listening to how things were said. She hadn't hidden her ambition, but she'd been smart enough not to make an issue of it. She'd just waited till the time was right and then gone after an account she could make her own. Jobina Inc. Quite a prize, and maybe the first of many. "You're very bright and determined, Laura, but we're going to do this by the book. I want a memo summarizing your meeting with Jobina Grant. I want a separate memo outlining your ideas for the presentation."

"We don't have much time, Zack. Mrs. Grant set the presentation for next week."

"That's plenty of time, if you're as ready as you think you are."

"I am, but I need Ronnie for the art and Martin for the finishing touches. For the polish."

"Oh, he'll love that. Third billing on the marquee." Zack stubbed out his cigarette. "I'm not promising anything until I see your memos. That's the way all projects begin around here, as you well know. That's the book and we're doing this by the book."

"You'll have the memos before lunch."

He looked at his watch. "Chop, chop, Laura."

"Yes," She stood, turning toward the door. "I'll start right now. If you're done with me."

"Is there anything else I should know?" She shook her head and he smiled. "Then I'm done with you."

265

Laura was halfway out the door when she stopped, looking at Zack over her shoulder. "We're going to get the account," she said, smiling back at him. "I can feel it."

"I don't believe in women's intuition."

"Wait and see—we're going to get the account!"

Despite Laura's confident prediction, she left nothing to chance. For the next six days she worked virtually around the clock, arriving early at the office each morning, leaving late each night, taking work home. There never seemed to be enough time. She wrote a blizzard of memos for Zack. She had endless meetings with Ronnie and Martin. She saw dozens of models and searched dozens of shops for precisely the right shade of scarlet silk in which to drape them. She dashed from the photographer to the typesetter to the printer, and then began the race all over again the following day.

Martin Carver had been assigned to supervise the presentation, but everyone, including Martin, considered his assignment a technicality. The presentation, the whole project, very clearly belonged to Laura. With all the zeal of the beginner, she fussed over the tiniest details: the shadow on a model's hand, the placement of a comma in a block of copy. She worried about the copy and she revised it several times. The headline that was finally emblazoned across the presentation was not Martin's but Laura's—a big, splashy headline, a happy command to PAINT THE TOWN SCARLET.

It took Jobina Grant and her advertising manager less than fifteen minutes to approve the presentation. They listened to Laura's introductory remarks, examined the sample ads, asked a few questions, made a few changes, discussed the schedule, and then went on their way. For Jobina, it was simply another meeting, one of the twenty or so she had every month. For Laura, it was a turning point. The successful presentation earned her a promotion to assistant copywriter, a small office of her own, and a raise. She would be getting forty dollars a week now, ten dollars more than Paul.

"I'm married to a tycoon," he laughed when he heard her news later that evening. "I'm proud of you, sweetheart. You did it. Didn't I say you would? Cream always rises to the top."

"Am I the cream?"

"Grade A."

Laura smiled. Paul was still her biggest booster—ardent, uncritical, unwavering. She knew she had neglected him during the past few months. She'd been so caught up in her layouts and graphs; she'd been so tired when she crawled into bed after yet another fourteen-hour workday. She hadn't been much of a wife recently, but Paul had never once complained. "You're wonderful," she said suddenly, tears springing to her eyes. "You're the best husband in the world."

He left his chair and went to sit beside Laura on the couch. "What did I do to deserve such compliments?" he asked.

"Nothing. Everything. You've been so good to me, Paul."

"Good to you? That's a funny thing to say. As if you were a lapdog waiting for a pat on the head . . . You're no lapdog," he added with a grin.

"That's just it, sometimes I wish I were. I might be a better wife. I'd be here to greet you when you got home from work. I'd have your pipe and slippers—"

"But I don't smoke a pipe."

"Well, you know what I mean . . . I feel guilty sometimes. I don't even cook your meals or darn your socks; Aunt Margaret does all those things for you. It doesn't seem right."

"It's the right way for us, Laura. Every marriage is different. I guess I could put my foot down and tell you to quit your job. Some of the guys think that's what I should do, but I don't agree. You wouldn't be happy, and if you weren't happy, *I* wouldn't be happy. So what would I gain?" Paul took his handkerchief from his pocket and dried her eyes. "What's really bothering you? I want the truth."

"I told you: I feel guilty sometimes. I feel like I'm not . . . doing my part. And it's probably going to get worse, now that I have this job. Have you thought about that, Paul?"

"Sure I have. I try to keep a step ahead."

"Well?"

He shrugged. "Well, I know this job is only a stepping stone to the next job. You don't want to be an assistant anything. You want to be the boss."

"Not the boss, exactly. I just want my own accounts. I want the title, the responsibility, and the money . . . There I go talking about money again. Sorry."

It was a sensitive subject between them. From the beginning, Paul had maintained that his earnings belonged to both of them, but that Laura's earnings belonged to her alone. On that one point he couldn't be budged. Laura had decided to have a telephone installed and he let her pay the monthly bill because a telephone wasn't a "necessity" like rent and food and electricity—bills which he insisted upon paying himself. As far as he was concerned, there were extras and there were necessities, and it was a husband's duty to provide the latter. "I don't mind talking about money," he said now. "But every time you get a raise, we get into an argument."

"No, we don't. It's impossible to argue with you. It's one-sided. You won't argue back."

"Not about money."

"We have nothing else to argue about."

"Then we're lucky." Paul wrapped his arms around Laura. He kissed her. "Aren't we?"

"*I* am. But how lucky do you feel every first of the month when you have to pay so many bills? If you'd only let me help."

"Not a chance." He shook his head, smiling into her eyes. "I can support my wife."

"I know you can, Paul."

"You're going to get a lot of raises, but they won't change how I feel . . . I just hope they won't change how *you* feel. About me."

"Oh, Paul, of course not! What a thing to say!"

"For richer or poorer; that's what Reverend Fletcher said. I'm going to hold you to it."

"Stop being so silly. You don't have to *hold* me to anything. I love you. You know I love you . . . There's a little extra money now, that's all. If you don't want it, I'll put it in the bank. We'll have a nice nest egg . . . It might come in handy someday."

Paul was quiet, staring thoughtfully at the flames leaping and dancing in the fireplace. "It might," he agreed after a few moments. "Especially if we happen to add a fledgling to our nest. A little girl fledgling who looks just like you? Or a little boy fledgling I can take to baseball games?"

Laura's eyes flickered. She let go of Paul's hand and stood up, walking over to the windows. "I just don't know what's wrong. Dr. Weston keeps insisting there's *nothing* wrong, but I don't know." She parted the draperies, staring out at the shadowy night. She felt a chill and she closed the draperies. She turned. "Dr. Weston always says the same thing: 'Stop worrying and relax.' It's not easy, is it? Not for either of us. I want children too, Paul."

But maybe a little less now that she'd won her promotion. He rolled the thought around in his mind, then chased it away. "The doc is right. We're young; we have lots of time." He grinned, wiggling his sandy brows. "Meanwhile, we have all the fun of trying and trying again."

She laughed. "Yes, there's that." She took the evening newspaper from atop the mantel, folded it open to the sports pages, and carried it to Paul. "Enjoy yourself. I'll be in the kitchen, helping Aunt Margaret with dinner."

"Okay, sweetheart."

Laura switched on the radio before she left the room. A Glenn Miller song was playing and she hummed the melody as she walked through the hall to the kitchen. "Aunt Margaret," she said, pausing in the doorway, "what smells so good? I'd swear it was roast beef."

"That's what it is. Paul said we had to have a celebration dinner tonight. On account of your big promotion."

"He was pretty sure I'd get it, wasn't he?"

"Of course he was," replied Margaret, taking milk and butter from the icebox. "To hear him talk, they'll be making you president of the company any day now." She added the milk and butter to a bowl of steaming potatoes, mashing them with a wooden spoon. "According to him, you won't be a junior copywriter for long. You're moving up, up, up."

"Which sounds better—junior copywriter or assistant copywriter?"

"What difference does it make?"

Laura ducked her head. "Well," she answered slowly, "I'm thinking about having some business cards printed."

"Business cards! You really *are* moving up in the world, aren't you? A career girl. Well, there's nothing wrong with that . . . Of course it was a different story in my day. Back then, when a girl got married she stayed home and looked after her husband. But times change. It was the war, you know. The war changed everything . . . And the Depression."

"Times aren't as bad as they were, Aunt Margaret. Business is starting to improve. Zack says the worst is over."

"Thanks to Mr. Roosevelt . . . Here, finish these potatoes while I make the gravy."

Laura took the spoon from her aunt. "The point is, there's more opportunity now. I'd hate to miss out. That's why I have to work even harder. I have to take advantage of every opportunity that comes along."

Margaret removed the roast beef to a serving platter. She stirred the drippings in the pan and then stirred in a spoonful of flour. "Are you doing this just for the money?"

"Money's important."

"Is that what I asked you? Any fool knows money's important, but that doesn't answer my question.

"At first, I guess it was just for the money." Laura whipped the spoon through the potatoes, beating them into smooth peaks and valleys. "There's more to it now. I like working, Aunt Margaret. I like the advertising business."

"So everything turned out fine after all."

"What do you mean?"

Margaret shrugged her bony shoulders. "Maybe this isn't the life you'd planned for yourself, but it's a good life. You should be grateful."

"I am."

"You should be willing to forgive and for—"

"Oh, I see," interrupted Laura. "I see where the conversation is going. Did you have a letter from Eliza today? Whenever you get one of her letters, you start urging me to 'forgive and forget.'"

"She's going to have another baby."

Laura's fingers tightened around the spoon. "I don't care."

"You've never even seen her little boy, *your* nephew. JB's almost two and a half, and you've never set eyes on him. Your own nephew! But with a second baby coming, you have the chance to put things right."

Laura threw down the spoon. She took the potatoes to the table, and then went back for the white china gravy boat. "Dinner's ready; I'll get Paul."

"Did you hear what I said?"

"Yes, and I'm not interested."

Margaret planted her hands on her hips. "What am I going to do with you, Laura Brent? Such a stubborn girl, I've never seen the like!"

"I'll get Paul."

A frown darkened Laura's brow as she walked quickly away. She was angry at herself, because once again she found herself envying Eliza. She couldn't help it. She thought about Eliza's growing family and she felt bereft. She felt a kind of ache, a yearning for the child she wanted but hadn't been able to have. Was there something wrong with her? Despite Dr. Weston's assurances, she was beginning to wonder if she'd *ever* have a child.

She was quiet at dinner that night, offering little to the conversation. Her mood was pensive, almost wistful . . . and it lasted for months. During the day she had work to distract her, but at other times she couldn't stop thinking about babies. If she saw a woman walking a baby carriage, she stopped and peered inside. If she went to a department store, she made a detour to the baby department. If she saw a picture of a baby in an ad, she paused to study the tiny face. "I'm obsessed," she said to Paul, trying to make a joke of it.

But her "obsession" disappeared as suddenly and mysteriously as it had come. In April, after two months of pondering and worrying and imagining, she turned her full attention to the Jobina Inc. account. The first of the PAINT THE TOWN SCARLET ads were ready, or nearly so. There were final touches she wanted to add; a final coat of polish to give the ads sparkle and shine. There were last-minute meetings with the client, and with Zack, who had to approve the finished layouts. There were last-minute jitters, soothed only when the ads appeared and were immediately acclaimed.

Laura, awash in work, in praise, had stopped thinking about babies. She declared herself cured, released from the strange mood that had held her captive. "I'm back to normal," she assured Dr. Weston during her June visit to his office. He listened and smiled and ran more tests; four days later, he told her she was pregnant.

Chapter Fifteen

"He said the rabbit died." Laura smiled, remembering her conversation with Dr. Weston. "I'm sorry for the rabbit, but I'm so happy for myself."

"And for Paul," added Jane.

"Paul's *thrilled*. He's walking five feet off the ground. His parents are thrilled. Aunt Margaret's thrilled. It's just a wonderful time for us, Jane. I'm very lucky." Laura took a sip of water, glancing around the crowded Schrafft's. Every table was filled, every space at the long counter. There was a pleasant hum of voices, and in the background the clink of glassware and crockery. Young Irish waitresses scurried about, smiling politely as they recorded lunch orders. "I like Schrafft's, don't you?"

"It's boring."

"Well, it's not the Stork Club."

"You can say that again." Jane lit a cigarette and began to cough. She waved the smoke away. "I'm hopeless," she lamented, flipping her cigarette into the ashtray. "One or two puffs and I practically choke to death."

"Why do you keep trying?"

"Because I want that slinky, sophisticated look. I've seen it in the movies. You have too; you know what I mean. The sexy women always smoke cigarettes."

"Cigarettes make your fingers turn yellow," said Laura, thinking of Zack's nicotine-stained right hand.

"A small price to pay."

Their waitress appeared, a scrubbed, wholesome girl with coppery hair tucked under a white cap. "Would you be ready to order?" she inquired in a soft brogue.

Laura nodded. "Chicken salad on toast and iced tea, please."

"Me too," sighed Jane, handing over the menu. "Chicken salad," she said when the waitress had gone. "Boring, boring, boring."

"What's the matter with you today?"

"Oh, it's not just today. It's *every* day. Every day I do the same boring things . . . Do you remember when we were working Saturdays at that awful insurance company? We promised ourselves we'd have exciting jobs and do exciting things."

"You promised, Jane. All I wanted was a paycheck."

"But you're the one with the exciting job, or at least as exciting as any of us is going to get . . . I have a *nice* job, I suppose, but so dull. And time is passing."

Laura stared at her friend for a moment, considering. "Did Doris tell you her news?"

"Doris is going to have another baby; I know. Doris is going to have a baby and you're going to have a baby and the whole world is going to have a baby. Swell."

"Don't be angry, but maybe it's time for you to have—"

"A baby?" squealed Jane. The women at the next table turned to look at her. She bent closer to Laura. "A baby?" she whispered.

275

"A husband! First things first."

"Well, now that you mention it . . ."

"Yes?"

Jane reached for her pack of Old Gold cigarettes, then pushed it away. "I've nearly made up my mind to marry Ted," she asserted. "I know you've heard that before, but this time . . . This time it's probably true. I haven't met anyone else I like as much, not anyone else who's offering a wedding ring. And I'm *so* bored with my job. I've been thinking I ought to get married and start a new life."

"You like Ted; you've never said if you love him."

"Sort of."

The waitress brought their sandwiches and tea. Laura squeezed a wedge of lemon into hers. "Sort of? What does that mean?"

"I'm not crazy about him the way Doris and Bill are crazy about each other, or the way Paul is crazy about you. I like him, I respect him, and I sort of love him. It's just not a grand passion, that's all. I could wait for a grand passion to come along, but what if it never does?" Jane munched on her sandwich. "I think I ought to take the plunge with Ted," she concluded, dabbing her napkin to her mouth. "What do you think?"

"This is too important for advice. You shouldn't listen to anybody but yourself."

Jane shrugged. "I might listen to you because you understand what I'm talking about. You and Paul don't—"

"I love Paul. And not *sort of.*"

"Gosh, Laura, I know you do. I never doubted it . . . I'm talking about something different—that *extra* edge of excitement that makes a woman all breathless and fluttery. *You* know what I mean."

Yes, she knew. She loved Paul and it was a happy

marriage, but she'd never felt the extra edge that quickened the blood. It was the one thing missing from her marriage, the only thing. "Life isn't like the movies, Jane. Or like books. We can't all be Cathy and Heathcliff."

"Would we want to be?"

Laura smiled. "No, maybe not. Maybe we should just count our blessings."

"Speaking of blessings, what are you hoping for—a boy or a girl?"

"When I think about the baby, I see a little girl. A cuddly, pink little girl."

"Have you thought about your job, Laura?"

She nodded, cutting her sandwich into quarters. "I'm going to keep the baby a secret for a while. There's no reason for Zack and the others to know, not yet anyway." She laughed. "Of course in a few months I won't be able to keep it a secret, but by then I plan to be indispensable. So indispensable that Zack will let me work from home. One thing's certain; I'm not going to hand the Jobina Inc. account to Anne Marsh. It's mine."

"And after the baby is born?"

"Well, Aunt Margaret says I can't have everything: a husband and a baby and a job." Laura took a bite of her sandwich, washing it down with a gulp of iced tea. "A husband and a job, yes, but not a husband and a *baby* and a job."

"Obviously, you don't agree."

"I don't know. Maybe I *can't* have everything, but I can try. Oh yes, I can try!"

"You're just in time," said Eve when Laura returned from lunch. "Zack moved up the Primm's Furniture Polish meeting. He's getting ready to start. Here, I typed your notes."

"Thanks, Eve." Laura dropped her purse and gloves on the desk, and took off her hat. "What about Martin?"

"I gave him copies of everything. You're all set."

"Good." She glanced over the notes. "What kind of mood is Zack in?"

"I've seen worse, but you'd better not keep him waiting. He's edgy about this account. There's talk it'll probably go to the Maitland Agency, and you know how he feels about Maitland."

"They're not going to beat us out, not this time. Harding is strong again. We're back in the game."

"Tell that to Zack."

"I'm on my way."

Laura hurried through the outer office, cheered by the clattering typewriters and jangling telephones—proof of Harding's renewed strength. She knew she'd played a part in it; the Jobina Inc. account had brought both increased revenues and increased prominence. It was only one account, but it was showy and it had made a difference. Remember that, she urged herself as she walked into Zack's office. Remember, you've earned your place here.

"Come in," said Zack, waving her to a chair. "We have a lot of business, so let's get to it. First on the agenda: Primm Furniture Polish."

Laura took the chair next to Martin. On Martin's left sat Ralph Lang, at thirty the youngest of the senior copywriters. He was a glad-hander, a backslapper; Laura thought he was a crackerjack salesman. Beside Ralph sat Ronnie Woronow. Beside Ronnie sat Anne Marsh, chic as always in a suit of navy silk and a matching hat. It occurred to Laura that she had never seen the top of Anne's head. She smiled.

"Something funny?" asked Zack.

"Sorry."

"This is Primm's Furniture Polish," continued Zack, holding up a small, flat metal can colored a muddy brown. "Ugly. And that's why we redesigned it to look like this." He held up a slightly larger can colored a bright yellow and blue. "Our presentation is going to recommend that all their packaging be redesigned. The colors used in the packaging will be the colors used in the ads. In other words, a coordinated campaign. Questions? Comments?"

"Market research tells us the brighter colors could mean a thirty percent rise in sales." Ronnie looked from face to face. "At minimum. But they don't have to be those colors. We could use reds, oranges—"

"No," said Zack. "The colors are set. Let's move on." He lit a cigarette and tossed the pack to Ralph. "Stanley Primm has expressed some interest in a Primm's Furniture Polish girl."

"He would," said Ralph, exhaling a curl of smoke. "He's a dirty old man. The thing is, you have to give a client what he wants."

"Maybe that was true in the old days," said Laura. "But now, with research, and with marketing studies, we can tell a client what he actually needs."

"There are clients who don't care to hear about market research," drawled Anne. "Primm Furniture Polish is a family business, and Stanley Primm is the head of the family. He prefers to trust his instincts."

"It doesn't sound like instincts to me," replied Laura, meeting Anne's cool gaze. "If Ralph is correct, Mr. Primm's main instinct is for pretty girls."

"I don't see what's wrong with that," countered Anne. "If you knew the advertising business better, you'd know pretty girls sell products."

"Certain products, yes." Laura paused, wondering if she should go on with this. Anne was glaring at her now, and things could only get worse. Well, what if they did? In for a penny, in for a pound. "You're talking about men's products, not—"

"Don't tell me what I'm talking about."

"I didn't mean—"

"I haven't the slightest interest in what you mean."

"Ladies!" said Zack. "The subject is Primm's Furniture Polish. Laura, is there some point you're trying to make? And if there is, would you please get to it."

"*Women* buy furniture polish, Zack. Housewives. That's my point. Pretty girls aren't going to sell furniture polish to housewives."

"She's right," said Martin. "We've been worried about pleasing old man Primm, when we ought to be worried about pleasing his customers. It's Laura's idea to put a housewifey kind of woman in the Primm ads." Martin adjusted his horn-rimmed glasses and glanced at his white index cards. "Another idea is to forget about models entirely—the young pretty ones, the housewifey ones, all of them—and just aim for prestige . . . 'Primm's Olde English Furniture Polish.' It has a nice ring to it; that's a bonus if we want to sell them on radio spots."

"Primm's Olde English Furniture Polish," repeated Zack. "And a radio announcer who sounds like Leslie Howard. No, like Ronald Colman . . . I'd have to see copy, Martin. It's an idea all right, but it could be difficult to sustain."

Anne shifted slightly in her chair. "Especially since Primm's was founded in New Jersey," she said, looking at Laura. "There's nothing English about it, you see."

Laura's eyes flashed. "There's no 'silk oil' in Silktouch Soap either."

"That campaign made millions for Silktouch," snapped Anne.

"And we're trying to make millions for Primm," snapped Laura in reply.

"Ladies, please," said Zack, thumping his fist on the desk. "The subject is *still* Primm's Furniture Polish, and at this rate we'll be here all day. Damn it, let's stick to the point!"

Laura settled back, glad that she had found her voice at last. This was the first time she'd responded in kind to Anne Marsh, and if necessary she would do so again. Even if they had to be here all day. Even if they had to be here all summer.

It was a brutal summer. Day after day, a fat, fiery yellow sun blazed over the city, sending temperatures into the nineties. Storms came nearly every night; lightning split the sky, thunder crashed, and rain poured down, rain that cleansed but didn't cool. Day and night the air was thick, a sultry prison impossible to escape. There was no breeze, no relief; there was only the relentless heat.

Toward the end of summer, on a stifling Saturday in late August, Jane married her longtime beau, Ted Morgan. She was a pretty bride, demure in a ruffled white gown of organdy and silk. She carried an old-fashioned bouquet of freesia, and the same flowers were woven into the lacy wreath she wore atop her upswept red hair. For luck, she wore the strand of pearls that Laura, and then Doris, had worn at their weddings.

She was a nervous bride, though not as nervous

as the groom, who stumbled through his vows and twice dropped the ring before putting it on Jane's finger. There was an audible sigh of relief in the church when the "I dos" were finally spoken, and the couple pronounced husband and wife.

The bridesmaids, Laura and Doris—both four months pregnant, both wilting with heat—looked at each other and smiled. "I was afraid Ted was going to faint," whispered Doris during the recessional. "He was so pale."

"Pale green," whispered Laura. "I know the feeling." She hadn't suffered any morning sickness, but the torrid heat and humidity often made her queasy. The moment she left the church, she reached into her bouquet for the soda crackers she had hidden there. "Want one?" she asked Doris.

"Thanks."

They nibbled on the crackers as a photographer snapped the wedding party. There was a shower of rice, and then the newlyweds were sprinting toward the waiting limousine. Tears glistened in Laura's eyes. The last of the Three Musketeers was married.

For several days after the wedding, Laura found herself caught in a mood she could describe only as nostalgic. Her thoughts, and even her dreams, were filled with random recollections from her childhood: two small girls jumping rope in the schoolyard; a doll with glossy black hair; a snowman wearing a raggedy wool cap; hopscotch squares chalked on the sidewalk; a report card with three As and two Bs, the best report card she'd ever had. Laura found the report card in her old keepsake box. It made her cry. For those several days, almost everything made her cry.

Margaret said not to worry; expectant mothers

had their moods and their tears. They were supposed to; it was nature's way. But once again, Laura's mood disappeared as suddenly and mysteriously as it had come. She stopped crying, she returned her keepsake box to the closet, and she returned her thoughts to the present. "Whatever it was," she told a much-relieved Paul, "I'm over it now." He took her to Mama Stella's to celebrate.

There was another celebration a few days later when Harding Advertising was awarded the Primm Furniture Polish account. Laura knew she would be assigned to work on it with Martin, and that fit right into her plans. Looking at the calender, and at her expanding waistline, she reckoned she had two months to make an impression — to make herself "indispensable."

"You can't put Laura on the Primm account," said Anne Marsh to Zack. She rubbed her hands together. It was a chilly September morning, but all the windows in the office were wide open. "One of these days you're going to get pneumonia."

He looked up from his desk, frowning. "What's this about Laura?"

"You can't put her on the Primm account."

"Why not?"

Anne moved a chair away from the draft and settled into it. "Men are fascinating creatures. They look but they don't see."

"I don't like cryptic remarks so early in the morning." Zack lit a cigarette, staring at her through a cloud of gray smoke the color of his eyes. "Let's start over. Why can't I put Laura on the account?"

"Because she's going to have a baby."

"A baby? Ridiculous! She's too serious about her

work to give it up for a baby. Right now, anyway. It might be a different story in the future."

"I know what I'm talking about, Zack."

"How do you know? Has she told you?"

"She hasn't told anybody. But there isn't a woman in this office who doesn't know."

"Well, Laura's gained some weight. I *did* notice that, unseeing though I may be." He stubbed out his cigarette, grinding it into the ashtray. "A baby just when we're beginning the Primm campaign. Damn! Damn, damn, damn!"

"I want the account, Zack."

"No. It was Martin's concept that won the account, his and Laura's. If you're right about Laura, she'll have to quit, but the account stays with Martin."

"He's already juggling too many accounts. I could do a better job."

"I've made my decision, Anne. If things change, you'll be the first to know. You always are."

She smiled. "I do try to keep my eyes open."

"A baby," he said, leaving his chair. "Of all the damn times to have a baby!"

Anne's smile widened as she rose to her feet. "Why, Zack, you look positively ferocious. I'm afraid I've ruined your morning."

He brushed past her, opening the door. "Laura!" he shouted.

The secretaries in the outer office were used to his bluster. They glanced up, but an instant later they went back to sorting the mail.

"Laura!" he shouted again. A door opened at the far end of the corridor. "Get in here," he called. "Right now!" He returned to his desk, standing behind it. "You can go," he said to Anne. "I'll handle this."

She wondered if he would, wondered if Laura wouldn't somehow manage to get the better of him. Laura, for all her youth and relative inexperience, was a clever girl. "I hope you don't let her talk you into anything."

"Like what?"

The question seemed to catch her by surprise. "I'm not sure, exactly. But you know how she is."

"Zack," said Laura, rushing into the office, "I'm . . . Oh, hello Anne."

"I was just leaving."

Laura watched her go. "Is something wrong?" she asked when the door closed. "The Burnett report is almost finished, if that's the problem."

"It isn't." He stared at her for a moment, his gray eyes sweeping from her head to her shoes. "Sit down, Laura. I'm going to ask you a direct question and I want a direct answer."

"Certainly."

"Are you . . ." He paused, seeking a phrase that was direct but not indelicate. "Are you expecting a child?"

There was a brief silence. Laura's gaze skidded away, then came back slowly to Zack. "Yes," she replied. "In January."

"I see."

"You're angry because I didn't tell you—"

"You're damned right I'm angry, Laura! You put me in a terrible position with the Primm people. They never liked the idea of having a woman on their account. They had to be sold and you sold them, but now they'll have to be *un*sold. You make us look like fools."

"I can still work on the account. I *can*," she insisted, "I have it all figured out."

"Ridiculous! Preg . . . Women in your condition

have no place in business. It simply isn't done, Laura. My God, can you imagine what people would say? Eli would be mortified. And our clients! Well, we'd lose our clients, that's all. We'd be finished."

She couldn't help smiling at the idea of one little baby wreaking such havoc. "Zack, our clients won't have to see me. They won't even have to know I'm pregnant. Tell them I'm out with a broken leg; tell them anything you want. Meanwhile I can work from home."

He rubbed his finger across his chin. He frowned. "From home?"

"Why not? Martin and Ronnie and I can have our meetings there instead of here. In between meetings we can keep in touch by telephone. And if we need to send work back and forth, we can use messengers . . . It's a different way of doing things, but it's not impossible."

Zack lit a cigarette. "You've given this some thought."

"A lot. I wanted to be ready . . . The point is, I can still do the work. I'm not *sick,* I'm just going to have a baby." She shrugged, tiny amber lights dancing in her eyes. "Your wife would understand."

"I understand too, Laura. I'm getting tired of women telling me I'm deaf, dumb, and blind. I'm perfectly capable of understanding the situation."

"Sorry."

"But you've overlooked a few things. Client meetings, for example."

"First of all, how often do we *have* client meetings? Once a month?"

"In theory, we're available for meetings round the clock. At the client's pleasure."

Laura nodded. "Yes, I know."

"Well? What's your solution?"

"I have more leeway with Jobina Inc. because Mrs. Grant's been in my situation herself. I can go to those meetings without upsetting anybody. At least for the next couple of months."

"You have *no* leeway with Stanley Primm."

"Martin won't mind handling the Primm meetings alone. He handles most of his meetings alone, Zack. And besides, the campaign's all set. Everything's approved—everything from the store displays to the Christmas ads. It's just a matter of finishing touches."

Zack had smoked his cigarette down to a yellowish stub. He tossed it in the ashtray, and then sank into his battered old chair. He was quiet, thinking that Laura had a gift for presenting any argument in simple, reasonable terms. She was persuasive, effortlessly persuasive. What had Anne said? "Don't let her talk you into anything."

"Zack?"

He laughed. "I was thinking about some advice someone gave me. Good advice, but I probably won't take it . . . Or then again, maybe I will. I'm not sure about this scheme of yours, Laura. Even if I were, you must see it doesn't solve the problem. Not the long-range problem. This working at home might be all right for a few months, but not permanently."

"No, I didn't mean it to be permanent."

"Didn't you? Are you planning to abandon your child once it's born?"

Laura's head snapped up. "Zack, what an awful thing to say! Of course I don't plan to abandon my child!"

"I didn't mean it literally. But how are you going

to manage both a job and a child? I have a right to know if we can depend on you, Laura. Business is business."

"I'll find a way to manage. I may have to work part-time for a while. I may have to take work home with me at night. I'll do whatever needs to be done. And you can depend on me because I need this job. I need the money." That was true. Much as Laura enjoyed her work, money was still the main factor. Paul hadn't received the raise he had been expecting, and his salary stretched only so far. The old bills had been paid, but now there would be new bills: the doctor, the hospital, furniture for the nursery. Yes, she thought to herself, I need the money. "But that doesn't mean I plan to abandon my child," she added in a frosty voice.

"All right, all right, I apologize. I shouldn't have said that." He sighed, slumping in his chair. "Sometimes you wear me down, Laura. You wear me out."

"Sorry."

"You're not at all sorry. But never mind." He reached for his cigarettes. "I'll agree to let you work from home for a few months. I'll even make up some story for the Primm people. Just remember there are no promises. If anything goes wrong . . . If problems arise, or there's any sort of trouble—"

"There won't be, Zack. I'll see to it."

"Yes," he said, striking a match. "I expect you will."

It took Laura only a few days to turn the empty dining room into an office. She bought almost everything she needed at the secondhand store: a desk and chairs, a lamp, a card table, a cabinet for her files, a set of shelves for the supplies Zack provided. She dug into her savings to buy a new typewriter—a stately black Underwood. She had another telephone installed; a month later, she added an extra line.

She tried to keep regular office hours, starting her day as soon as Paul left, breaking for a hot meal at noon, and then working until six. Eve came to help with the monthly sales reports for Burnett Tile; Ronnie and Martin came for meetings at least once a week; messengers came and went all the time. She was busy, busier than she had expected to be, but somehow everything got done.

Margaret tried to stay out of the way. She did her cleaning in the evenings and switched her piano students to Saturdays, finishing at one o'clock so she could do her errands. She stayed in the kitchen when meetings were going on in the dining room. She was careful not to use the phone during Laura's working hours, not to play the radio too loud.

She was the soul of cooperation, but in return she insisted on watching over Laura, making sure her niece got proper food and rest. A stick-to-the-ribs breakfast, a hot lunch, cocoa instead of coffee, plenty of fresh fruits and vegetables; those were Margaret's rules and she stuck to them. As December neared, and Laura began to tire more easily, another rule was added to the list: an afternoon nap.

By Christmas, Laura was feeling fat and uncomfortable. She couldn't bend, couldn't get out of a chair without help, couldn't stop bumping into things. Her back ached; her ankles swelled. Her face was as round as a muffin. She sighed whenever she glimpsed her puffy self in the mirror. She was happy to be pregnant, but why did it have to go on so long?

Laura began her official vacation from Harding Advertising right after New Year's Day of 1938. She had three weeks until the baby was due, and she used that time to finish preparing the nursery. One Sunday she went with Paul to Orchard Street, the chaotic pushcart market on the Lower East Side. There, for a fraction of the uptown price, they bought tiny shirts and sleeper suits and a box of four dozen diapers. They bought flannel blankets, and pillows to fit the bassinet. They bought a dozen baby bottles, a teething ring, and a cuddly brown teddy bear. Just before they left, Laura spotted a large Raggedy Ann doll and she bought that too.

The doll sat cradled in her arm during the subway ride home. Paul, all but surrounded by boxes and shopping bags, gazed at Laura and smiled. "I wish I had a camera," he said, shifting one of the shopping bags aside. "You and that doll would make quite a picture. It would make a great ad."

"An ad for what?"

"Motherhood."

Motherhood. Laura had found herself thinking a lot about her own mother in the last few weeks. Had her mother once felt what she was feeling now? The surges of happiness? The moments of uncertainty? The love? She drew the doll closer as tears started in her eyes. "Mama," she whispered.

"What's the matter?"

"I wish Mama were here. She's been on my mind lately."

"That's natural at a time like this."

"Yes, I guess so." She took the handkerchief Paul offered and dried her eyes. "Don't worry, I'm not getting all weepy again. I just happened to think about Mama. I'm fine now . . . *Fat,*" she added, looking at her bloated stomach, "but fine."

"It won't be much longer, sweetheart. Only another week."

"Only?"

"A slip of the tongue," laughed Paul. The subway train was approaching the station. There was the usual screeching and hissing of brakes, the usual clang of metal as the cars lurched to a stop. The shopping bag's fell over. One of the boxes slid off his lap, but he caught it before it hit the floor. "No harm done," he said, rising carefully to his feet. He held out his hand, pulling Laura up. "You okay?"

"Let me take a couple of shopping bags."

"No, I told you they're too heavy." He gathered the boxes and bags, taking a step toward the doors. Another passenger stepped back to let him pass. "Thanks. Come on, Laura."

Together, they struggled onto the platform and headed for the stairs. Laura was reaching for the handrail when she felt the first sudden, sharp pain. She gasped.

"Laura?"

The second pain was sharper, stronger than the first. She grabbed the rail, looking around at Paul. "I think it's the baby."

Chapter Sixteen

Laura stirred, awakening slowly from the oblivion that had engulfed her. She heard sounds — muffled footsteps, muffled voices. She tried to raise her head, but the effort took all her strength and she fell back against the pillows.

"Feeling a little weak? Or are you still groggy?"

She blinked and Dr. Weston's face swam into view. Groggy? Yes, it was as if her head were stuffed with cotton wool. She frowned at the unfamiliar surroundings. She was about to ask where she was, but then she remembered the subway station, the sudden pain, the taxi ride to the hospital. "My baby!" she cried, her eyes imploring Dr. Weston.

"A healthy girl; six pounds, two ounces. The nurse will bring her in a few minutes."

Laura smiled. "A girl. I knew it would be a girl . . . Where's Paul? Has he seen her?"

"He most certainly has. Judging by his big grin, I'd say he liked what he saw. He'll be along in a few minutes also, Laura." Dr. Weston pressed his fingers to her wrist, checking her pulse. He nodded. "You're right as rain, my dear. Even after thirteen hours of labor and our best knockout drops . . . We put you out, you know. Or don't you remember that?"

She remembered the pain, sharp claws of pain raking her body, splitting her body in two. She remembered Dr. Weston telling her to bear down. She remembered someone wiping her streaming brow. That's when the really terrible pain had come, the worst pain of all. "I'm sorry I screamed at you, Dr. Weston."

He laughed. "Women have been screaming at me for years. I'm quite used to it."

"Can't I see my baby now? And Paul? I want to see Paul."

"I'll send him in," said the doctor, going to the door. "Just lie back and relax. Don't try to get out of bed, Laura. If you need anything, ring for the nurse. Promise?"

"Promise."

"Good girl."

He left the room and Laura raised herself slightly on the pillows. She ran her hand through her hair, smoothing the tangles. A week ago she had packed a small suitcase for her hospital stay, but there hadn't been time to collect it. She didn't have any of her things here, not even a comb.

Laura was still fussing with her hair when Paul appeared in the doorway. He was rumpled and unshaven, but his smile stretched from ear to ear. "She's beautiful!" he exulted, rushing over to take his wife in his arms. "She's the most beautiful baby in the whole place! Wait'll you see her, Laura. She looks just like you!"

"And she's all right?"

"She's *perfect*. Just like her mother . . . How do you feel, sweetheart? Are you tired?"

"A little. But Dr. Weston says I'm fine." Laura stroked Paul's stubbly cheek. "You've been here all night, haven't you?"

"Where else would I be? There were three other guys in the waiting room. We paced around, played some gin, paced around some more. I smoked a whole pack of cigarettes . . . It was a long night."

She smiled. "What time is it now?"

"Almost seven. Aunt Margaret was here for a while last night. She was going to come this morning, but they won't let anybody up until visiting hours start. So she'll be here later. Jane too."

"Did you call Doris?"

"That's the other news," replied Paul with a grin. "Doris had her baby this morning also. A boy. According to Bill, she practically had it in the taxicab. You should have heard him! The poor guy was a nervous wreck."

"A boy? They wanted a boy, you know."

"James William Gibson; that's his name."

The door opened and Laura looked up, hoping to see her baby. Instead she saw a huge basket of flowers. Paul took the basket from the nurse and read the card. " 'Congratulations to Mommy and Daddy. Love, Jane and Ted.' How did they find a florist at this hour? It isn't even daylight."

"Oh, you can find anything in New York. Especially if money's no object."

Paul placed the basket on the bureau opposite Laura's bed. He culled a single red rose and gave it to her. "Don't start worrying about money again. We'll manage. I can pay the hospital bill in installments."

Laura had enough money in her savings to pay the bill in full and that's what she wanted to do. It scared her to think of being in debt; it reminded her too much of the past. The hospital wasn't going to repossess the baby, but still she wouldn't feel secure until the bill was paid.

She hadn't been able to make Paul understand. Money remained the one sore subject between them, the one friction in their marriage. Deep down, she knew that was never going to change. "We don't have to talk about it now. We're both tired."

"We don't have to talk about it at all. I'll take care of the bill my own way. I'm the daddy here. Daddies pay the bills."

Laura was debating an answer when the door opened again. She looked up, her heart leaping as she glimpsed a tiny pink bundle. "My baby . . . Oh, let me have her."

Gently, the nurse lowered the baby into Laura's waiting arms. "We must be careful to support baby's head," she warned. "Yes, that's right. We musn't be nervous, Mrs. Brent."

"She's so little."

"She won't break, I assure you."

Laura gazed at her daughter. She saw a fluff of platinum hair, a wide, wrinkled brow, drowsy blue eyes, fat pink cheeks, a tiny mouth, a tiny dimpled chin. She saw a miracle. "My baby," she said, nearly overcome by the love she felt. "My darling baby."

"What are we going to call her?" asked Paul. "I don't have the list of names."

"I remember them," said Laura. She and Paul had been trading names back and forth for a month, but there were only a few they'd both liked: Elizabeth, Sarah, Molly. She gazed again at her daughter. She smiled. "Let's call her Molly."

"Hi, Molly," said Paul, touching the baby's downy cheek.

"Molly Katherine," amended Laura. "Mama would have liked that. Molly Katherine Brent."

Laura and Molly Katherine went home ten days later. Laura's old room—used for storage during the past few years—had been made into the nursery. Margaret had scrubbed every inch of it with a hard brush and strong yellow soap. Paul had sanded the floor, hung the shelves, and painted the walls a light, rosy pink. He'd moved in the furniture: a chest of drawers, a changing table, a crib, a rocking chair, a white wicker bassinet. He'd found a large Raggedy Andy doll to match the Raggedy Ann, and he sat them both on their own little bench in the corner.

Laura took a leave of absence from Harding Advertising after Molly was born, and she spent most of that time in the nursery. She stayed there even when the baby was asleep—whispering lullabies to her, watching her for hours on end. She was filled with wonder at the sight of the tiny girl, at the day-to-day changes she was certain she saw. She gazed into the bassinet and felt such love she thought her heart would burst.

She was supposed to return to Harding Advertising in March, but she couldn't bear the idea of being away from Molly. She delayed for another three months, until finally an exasperated Zack gave her an ultimatum: "Come back to work now or you're fired." There was no doubt he meant what he said, and she knew there was no recourse. Zack had been patient; he'd been more than fair. She couldn't expect him to go on bending the rules for her. Quietly, she scheduled her return for the first Monday in June.

"Because I don't want to lose my job, Paul," she said on the morning of that first Monday. "We've been over it a hundred times. I thought everything was settled."

"I thought you'd change your mind at the last minute. Like you did before. You decided you couldn't leave Molly. Remember?"

"I remember." Laura finished applying her lipstick and blotted it with a tissue. She rose from the dressing table, smoothing the skirt of her new black linen suit. "I remember," she said again. "I was able to talk Zack into giving me another three months. But that was then and this is now. I can't stall any longer."

Paul shrugged, a faint smile playing about his mouth. "I thought you wanted to be with Molly."

"Of course I want to be with her. But I need . . . I want my job, too."

"You said 'need.' You're talking about money, aren't you?"

She glanced at the clock on the mantel. "It's ten past eight. You're going to be late for work."

"Answer my question, Laura. Is it the money?"

"Not just the money, no. You know I enjoy my work . . . But is it so bad to want to get caught up with the bills? To want some money in the bank?" She sighed. Nothing would come of this conversation; nothing ever did, not when the subject was money. He wanted her to stop caring about money, to stop worrying about it. He wanted her to leave money matters to him. She had tried, but she couldn't. If it was true that she worried too much, it was also true that he didn't worry enough. "It scares me to be in debt, Paul. It brings back too many memories. If you're expecting me to change . . ."

He shook his head. He didn't want her to change; he didn't even want her to stop working. But he wanted her to trust him to take care of his family. He felt it was that simple: trust. "Laura, we're young. Things are a little tight now, with the baby and all, but they'll get better."

"I know they will."

"Do you?"

"I just want to help, Paul. Why should you carry the whole burden? It's not fair."

"Sounds fair to me. It's all part of marriage. So what if we have to struggle for a while? We'll get through it. My job isn't flashy but it's steady and that's more important. Ten years from now I'll be a vice president . . . Remember the story of the tortoise and the hare? Well, I'm the tortoise. Just give me a chance to win my race."

Ten years? Had he said ten years? It might as well be a lifetime. She turned, glancing at the clock. "You're going to have a race to the subway if you don't hurry."

Paul snatched up his briefcase. He went to Laura, tilting her face to him. "Come on, a kiss for the tortoise."

"For the tortoise I love."

They kissed, and then his arm fell away. "Off I go," he said. "See you tonight."

"Tonight."

Laura took a breath. She listened to Paul's footsteps in the hall; a moment later she heard the front door slam. She sighed again, gathering her purse and gloves, snatching her own briefcase from beneath a pile of newspapers. After another glance at the clock, she left the bedroom and went to the nursery.

Margaret was standing on a stepladder, hanging summer curtains. Molly, who had outgrown her bassinet, was peering through the slats of her crib. She smiled when Laura appeared, offering all the squeals and squeaks and gurgles in her vocabulary.

Laura laughed. "Somebody's very talkative this morning."

"She's probably hungry."

"Hungry! She had breakfast only an hour ago." Laura reached into the crib and picked up Molly. "You're not hungry, are you? No, of course you're not." There were more squeals and gurgles. "I agree completely," said Laura as Molly grabbed her nose.

Margaret descended the stepladder. "Did you have words with Paul?" she asked.

"Words?"

"I heard the door slam. It's hard to tell when he's upset, but sometimes he lets the door slam."

"We were talking about money. That's never a good conversation." Laura kissed Molly's pink cheek. She gazed at her—at the platinum hair that was beginning to curl, at the dark blue eyes that seemed to twinkle, at the sweet smile. "Mommy has to go out, darling."

"Did you tell him you paid off the hospital bill?" asked Margaret.

"No. I'm hoping he's forgotten that bill by now." Laura kissed Molly's brow and put her back in the crib. "He paid almost half of it, you know, but he hasn't been keeping track of the balance. Out of sight, out of mind; at least I hope so."

"A man likes to feel he's the head of the house."

"I'm not trying to take that away from him, Aunt Margaret. All I did was pay off a bill, a bill nearly five months old." She looked down at her daughter and smiled. "Now Molly is really ours... And now I have to leave her. It's so hard."

"She'll be fine. We're going to the park after lunch."

"She'll miss me."

"Well, that's life, isn't it? Life is full of disappointments. Best to learn the lesson early." Margaret turned. She gazed across the nursery at Molly and all at once the sharp planes and angles of her face seemed to soften. She hadn't been anxious to have a squalling baby in the house, but her feelings had changed the first time she'd held Molly in her arms. She'd started to think of the child as her granddaughter, thus completing the family she had been denied when Wilbur Hobart ran off with the minister's wife. "There's no reason to be worried," she said, glancing suddenly at Laura. "I'll take good care of Molly. A lot better care than those nannies I see in the park. They're so busy gossiping to each other, they wouldn't notice if the sky fell in."

"Let's hope it doesn't." Laura picked up her purse

and gloves and briefcase, and went to the door. She paused for a moment, blowing a kiss to Molly. She felt tears sting her eyes. " 'Bye," she called, walking quickly from the room.

She hurried through the hall, trying to channel her thoughts to Harding Advertising and the client meeting that had been scheduled for this morning. Think about the meeting, she told herself, slipping out of the apartment. Think about anything but Molly.

She rang for the elevator, shifted her purse to her other hand, and rang again. "Come *on*," she muttered under her breath. She was about to ring a third time when the doors slid open.

"Morning, Mrs. Brent," said the elevator operator.

"Morning, Fred," she replied, rushing into the car. Only then did she see the handsome little boy and the beautiful woman who was obviously his mother. She froze. "My God!"

A smile touched Eliza's rosebud mouth. "Hello, Laura . . . How nice you look."

Laura was too astonished to speak. Somewhere in the back of her mind she had always known that she was bound to run into her sister sooner or later. Eliza came to New York every month, came here to this building because the elder Colliers still lived here. It was inevitable, thought Laura. In the elevator, in the lobby, in the street; it was inevitable that she would cross paths with Eliza.

She didn't know what to say, nor even what she wanted to say. The anger had burned itself out long ago, but not the hurt. She had been betrayed by her sister and that was something she couldn't forgive. "Hello," she murmured cooly, turning her back on Eliza.

The elevator reached the lobby and Fred opened the doors. Laura hurried out, her high heels clicking on the marble floor. She nodded good morning to the doorman, streaking past him to the street. She dropped her purse; when she bent to retrieve it, she dropped a glove.

Eliza picked it up. "Here you are."

"Thanks. I have to go now."

"Laura—"

"There's nothing to say. Absolutely nothing."

"Perhaps not, but wouldn't you like to meet your nephew? His name is John Bellamy; we call him JB."

"Yes, I know." Reluctantly, she lowered her gaze to the little boy. He was very handsome, with Eliza's spun gold hair and Robby's jade green eyes. She couldn't help smiling at his earnest expression. "Hello, JB." She bent slightly, catching his small hand in hers. "I'm your aunt Laura."

"Hello, Aunt Laura. Do you have a dog?"

"A dog? No, I don't. I have a baby, though."

"Oh," he sighed, losing interest. "We have a baby too."

"My son Michael," explained Eliza. "He's eight months old. But I'm afraid JB would much rather have a dog. That's all he talks about." She looked down at her child, fluttering her long lashes. "Maybe for your birthday," she said. She looked back at Laura. "He'll be four in a few months. I suppose that's old enough."

"It's getting late. I have to go now."

"We'll be here another day or two. Could I stop by and see Molly?"

"No." Her harsh tone seemed to startle JB. She reached out her hand again, ruffling his hair. "No," she said in a softer voice, "that wouldn't be a good idea."

"You're still being silly about things, Laura. Molly is my niece and I'd like to see her. She ought to know the rest of her family."

"Family! Oh, you're a fine one to talk about family!" Laura glanced off, trying to compose herself. It was a lovely June morning—sunny, breezy, warm but not hot. People were hurrying along the avenue, some to the bus stop, others to the subway station. All the shops and stores were open. The newsstand was doing a brisk business. She studied these sights and then returned her gaze to Eliza. "I'm going to be late for work," she said, edging toward the curb. "Good-bye, JB. I hope you get your dog."

He grinned. "A *big* dog."

Eliza's beautiful violet eyes moved from her son to her sister. "If you weren't so stubborn, you'd admit everything's turned out for the best."

Laura reached the curb and held up her hand, waving for a taxi. She had planned to take the subway, but now she just wanted to escape as fast as she could. When a taxi stopped, she wrenched the door open and jumped inside.

"Did you hear what I said?" called Eliza. "It was all for the best."

"Remind me to thank you," she snapped, slamming the door. "Just drive," she said and the cab sped away. For the second time this morning she felt tears sting her eyes. She pulled out her handkerchief, dabbing at her tears. It *was* all for the best, she silently conceded, but that didn't excuse anything. Even now, years later, she could still feel the hurt.

She settled back in her seat and gave the driver the address of her office. The day had started so badly; she hoped it wasn't an omen of things to come.

All four men rose when Laura entered the conference room. She took her assigned place at the long, polished table and folded her hands atop her notebook. "Good morning, gentlemen," she said.

"Good morning," they chorused.

At the head of the conference table sat old Eli Harding, a dapper figure in a chalk-stripe suit and red silk pocket handkerchief. His presence at the meeting underscored its importance: the Bystrum Pharmaceutical account could be worth millions.

At Eli's left sat Zack, and next to Zack sat Martin Carver, paired as usual with Laura. Sitting in solitary splendor at the other side of the table was Claude Gower, executive vice president of BPC, as it was called. Brisk, bespectacled, middle-aged, Claude Gower was a grandson of BPC's founder, and a shrewd businessman in his own right. "There's no need for small talk," he said now, smiling pleasantly. "We all know why we're here. BPC makes thirteen different products for sale over the counter, but our new cold and cough syrup is the subject I've come to discuss."

Eli nodded his snow-white head. "How many presentations have you seen, Claude?"

"Too many."

"This will be the last. It's quite good . . . Zack, we're ready to begin."

"Just one moment," said Claude Gower. "This is no reflection on you, Zack, but personally I prefer to go straight to the horse's mouth."

"I beg your pardon?"

"I prefer to hear ideas from the people who thought them up. Are the ideas in the presentation yours?"

Zack and Eli glanced at each other. "Advertising is a collaborative effort," said Eli.

"A team effort," said Zack.

"I prefer an individual point of view. Perhaps you'll humor me."

Eli smiled. "Here at Harding, we believe the client is always right. Therefore I will turn the meeting over to the creators of the presentation, Martin and

Laura."

She started at the sound of her name. It was true that she had provided the idea for the presentation, but Martin had done all the work. While she'd been at home, looking after her baby, he'd been writing copy and choosing models and supervising layouts. He'd brought her idea to life, and she felt he deserved the credit. "It's Martin's presentation," she said.

"And Martin's idea?" asked Claude Gower.

"Laura's idea." Martin shuffled his white index cards and passed them to her. "Laura's idea from the start."

"Then I will hear from Laura. Go ahead, young woman. I'm waiting."

Again, Zack and Eli glanced at each other. They had the same misgivings: If Laura faltered, a million-dollar account could be lost.

She shared their misgivings. This was her first client meeting in eight months; she was rusty, out of practice. She was less informed about this account than she should have been. And unlike Jobina Inc., this was by no means a "woman's" account. She had faith in her idea, but would she be able to convince Claude Gower?

Laura cleared her throat. She took a sip of water, glancing through the white index cards. "I'm not sure where to begin, Mr. Gower," she said, lifting her eyes to him. "I guess I ought to warn you there aren't any tricks or gimmicks in our presentation. We wanted to create a symbol for your new product . . . a symbol that would inspire confidence, that would be soothing."

"Soothing?"

She shrugged. "We live in a modern world, but our research shows there's a lot of nostalgia for the past. For old-fashioned ways. Years ago, people didn't go to the doctor when they had a cold or a cough. There were home remedies. Everybody had a grandmother or a mother or an aunt with a special remedy of her own."

"BPC was founded on home remedies," said Claude Gower. "The company's very first product was a spring tonic that my great-grandmother swore by. But this is 1938. As you say, it's a modern world. We have to keep up with the times."

"Yes and no," replied Laura. She glanced again at the index cards, separating one from the rest. "May I ask you a question, Mr. Gower?" He nodded and she continued. "If you were sick in bed . . . Oh, nothing serious, you understand. Let's just say you were sick in bed with a cold, a cold that made you feel miserable and cranky. Would you rather be tended by a doctor, or by a loving member of your family? Maybe a kindly old aunt."

"What Laura means—" began Zack.

"I'm quite able to follow what Laura means," interrupted Claude Gower. He looked back at her, his eyes glittering behind the polished lenses of his glasses. "When the question is phrased that way, there's only one answer. Of course I would prefer the kindly aunt. But what if the question were phrased to describe a modern, efficient doctor versus a doddering old woman? The answer would be entirely different. The deck can be stacked either way, as you know."

"It can, Mr. Gower, but we'd like to stack it in your favor."

"I'm listening."

"According to our research, people believe home remedies are as useful for colds as anything a doctor might prescribe. A number of people believe home remedies are *more* useful . . . So no matter how you phrase the question, most people would still choose the kindly aunt, doddering or not."

"I have the research right here," said Eli, thumbing slowly through a leather folder stamped with his initials. "I know it's here somewhere . . . Ah yes, here's the report. We've all studied it, Claude. I assure you Laura is on very solid ground."

"Then let's get to it, shall we? I assume you have a kindly old aunt all ready for me."

Eli nodded at Laura and she left her chair. She went to an easel that had been placed a few feet away from Claude Gower. "Her name is Aunt Martha," she explained, uncovering the first layout. "And here she is at her nephew's bedside, pouring a spoonful of Aunt Martha's Cold & Cough Remedy."

"Aunt Martha's, eh? I don't know what our salesmen will have to say about that. They wanted a product name with some punch to it."

"We've test-marketed the name," said Martin. "It tests well, Mr. Gower."

"Each of these layouts," continued Laura, "shows Aunt Martha in a different situation, but each carries the same tag line: 'No cold is safe when Aunt Martha's around.' We plan to use that line in the radio spots too. It'll be spoken by Aunt Martha herself. By one of them, anyway."

"One of them? How many are there?"

"Five, maybe six."

"Regionals!" boomed Zack. "Each region of the country is going to hear a different Aunt Martha. In the South, she'll have a Southern drawl. In New England, a Yankee twang. We have five regions all told. We're toying with the idea of a sixth—a slightly comic Aunt Martha who speaks Brooklynese."

"Ye gods!"

"Claude, this regional approach is exactly why your salesmen are going to *love* Aunt Martha. She'll be like one of the family. She'll be a symbol of trust.

You know the power of radio as well as I do. A couple of weeks on the air, and Aunt Martha's will be outselling every other product you make."

"I don't know. This is obviously going to be an expensive campaign. I don't know if I want to gamble that much money on nostalgia."

Laura shook her head. "There's more to it than that, Mr. Gower. It has to do with cycles, with good times and bad. During the boom years of the 1920s, the idea of family wasn't so important. But when the Depression came, family was more important than ever."

"The Depression is over, young woman. Despite a few residual problems, the Depression is certainly over."

"Yes, but now there's talk of war in Europe."

Claude Gower, who had three sons of draft age, didn't want to think about war in Europe. He pushed back his chair and went to examine the layouts. "I must agree with you, Laura," he said after several moments. "Aunt Martha is a soothing figure, quite appealing. She might appeal especially to children and that would be a great asset. Our salesmen would like that."

"Your salesmen will *love* Aunt Martha," insisted Zack. "The possibilities are endless."

Claude Gower removed his glasses, rubbing the bridge of his nose. He replaced his glasses, looked again at the layouts, and then turned to Laura. "I've heard you were responsible for the Jobina ads. Excellent work; some of the best I've seen . . . But Jobina is small potatoes compared to BPC. We're worldwide. We're on the Stock Exchange. We have two former Vice Presidents on our board of directors . . . The point is, your work on this account could make or break you."

"Yes, Mr. Gower, I know."

"And do you still say the Aunt Martha approach is the correct one?"

"The winning one, Mr. Gower. Yes, I do."

A smile shadowed his mouth. "Is there an Aunt Martha to look after your colds and coughs?"

"No," she laughed, relaxing for the first time that morning. "But there's an Aunt Margaret. My mother used to say no cold was safe when Aunt Margaret was around."

"You've put your family to good use."

"She's a clever girl," said Eli. "Instinctive, you know."

"Oh?" Claude Gower glanced again at Laura. "What does your instinct tell you now?"

"That you're going to buy this campaign."

"Why?"

"Because Aunt Martha is going to make a lot of money for BPC."

Laura sounded so certain; there didn't seem to be any doubt in her mind. She's paid to be certain, he thought, and yet he believed her. All at once he saw the Aunt Martha campaign the way she saw it and he was persuaded. "Very well," he said, resuming his place at the conference table. "We have a deal."

Those were the words she had wanted to hear. She smiled at Martin, at Zack and Eli, bestowing her most brilliant smile on Claude Gower. "You won't be sorry," she promised.

"I'm never sorry. I cut my losses and move on." He turned, shifting his gaze to Eli. "Laura and Martin will handle the account together; I don't want a whole crowd of people. Zack, you can keep an eye on things."

"Right."

"And see to it that Laura has a proper title and salary. I can't have some little assistant representing BPC. That's not the way we do business."

"Right," said Zack again.

Claude Gower took a fountain pen from his inside jacket pocket. "Now let's hear what kindly old Aunt Martha is going to cost."

"We have the figures here," said Eli.

Eli, Zack, and Claude bent their heads over the projected budget. Laura, looking a bit dazed, sat down. Martin winked at her but didn't notice. She sat perfectly still, staring into space.

A proper title and salary; the words ran through her mind like a song. She would get another raise now, probably a big one. She could almost see her new business cards: *Laura Brent, Account Executive.* "Oh my," she murmured. "Oh my."

Laura remained in a daze long after the meeting ended, but when the fog cleared, she went directly to Martin's office. "Do you have a minute?" she asked, poking her head in the door.

"Take two, they're small."

That was as close as he'd ever come to making a joke. She smiled. "I see you're in a good mood."

"Why not? We were a hit today."

"That's what I wanted to talk to you about." She sat in the sleek leather chair beside Martin's desk. The chair matched the couch, but he'd made no further attempt at decorating his office. The white walls were unadorned, the windows uncurtained. A narrow bookcase in the corner was empty save for several dictionaries and a thesaurus. The desk was neat as a pin, graced with only one personal touch—a small photograph of his wife. I wanted to apologize," continued Laura. "I was in such a state when the meeting ended, I didn't even thank you. It was your work, Martin. We got the account because of your work. It was all your doing."

"No, not all. You said the magic words: Aunt Martha."

"That wasn't hard. I was thinking of my aunt and how she is when somebody's sick."

"That's a talent you have. To be able to associate A with B and come up with C is a talent. Especially in the ad game. I can't do it; I have to wait for an idea, for something to set me off." He leaned back in his chair, put his feet up on the desk, and lit a cigarette. "I don't give a damn about credit. I'm in this for the money, and that's why I like our arrangement. You keep coming up with the ideas and I'll keep giving them the polish that makes them special . . . We're a great team, Laura. We're the Rodgers and Hart of advertising."

She laughed. She knew very little about Martin Carver and that seemed to be the way he wanted it. He had no close friends at the agency, no buddies. He and his wife appeared at the annual Christmas party, but they never invited agency people to their apartment in Murray Hill. They never mixed business with pleasure.

Martin was about forty-six now, still a man of long silences and owlish stares. Still a man of crossword puzzles, thought Laura to herself as she spied the puzzle book peeking from beneath a file folder. "I like our arrangement too," she said. "I just want it to be fairer. It's wrong for me to—to take over in meetings."

"Wrong? It's the secret of our success . . . You have a knack for making clients believe what you're saying. That's your other big talent and that's the one that'll take you to the top someday." Martin puffed on his cigarette. "Do you want to talk about what's fair? We're both going to get raises, but my salary is already much larger than yours and my raise will be larger as well. My bonuses on this account will be larger than yours. I have no complaints."

"No, I guess not."

"I've always wondered about something, though . . . A few years back, when you had to choose someone to work with . . . why me? Eve must have steered you toward Tom; he's everybody's favorite. And Hal looks like he stepped out of an Arrow shirt ad. So why me?"

"Oh, that's easy; you have the quickest mind."

"Thanks."

She smiled. "Or maybe I sensed we'd be a good team."

"A *great* team, Laura. That's what we are, a great team."

In the weeks and months that followed, they were the most sought-after team at Harding Advertising. The BPC account brought them considerable prestige; the first series of Aunt Martha ads brought them considerable success. Laura was given the sunny office next to Martin's, an expense allowance, and a raise that more than doubled her salary. She had the title she had fantasized about, and the recognition. She wasn't *the girl* anymore, not even to Anne Marsh.

Success, Laura discovered, was contagious. During the next year, new accounts flowed to Harding Advertising and each success led inexorably to another. The agency expanded its staff and its offices, occupying both the tenth and eleventh floors. All the conference rooms and outer offices were redecorated with oak paneling and handsome, thick carpets. The reception desks bloomed with bouquets of fresh flowers delivered twice a week. The scent of roses lingered in the air; Laura said it was the scent of money.

For a while she felt as if money were raining on her. There were raises; there were bonuses; there were expense allowances that bought lovely free lunches and taxi rides even in nice weather. She couldn't quite believe it was happening and she couldn't talk about it with Paul, who was increasingly troubled by the difference in their incomes. She knew his salary would never catch up to hers and that made her feel guilty, as if she were doing something wrong.

She felt guilty about Molly, too. She rose at six every weekday morning so she could spend a few hours with her daughter before leaving for work. After work, she tried to get home in time for the child's dinner and bath. In the summer months, she tried to juggle her business lunches so she could occasionally meet Molly and Margaret in the park. No matter the season, every Sunday belonged to Molly and that was an unbreakable rule.

Laura did the best she could, but still she missed some important moments in Molly's life. She was at home when seven-month-old Molly first used elbows and knees to crawl across the nursery floor, but she was at work when thirteen-month-old Molly hoisted herself up and took her first step. She heard Molly's first word, which was "cookie," but not Molly's first sentence. She was on a day trip to Philadelphia when Molly fell and needed five stitches. Hearing about the accident hours later, Laura burst into tears.

There were times when she came close to quitting her job, and yet there were other times when she couldn't imagine doing such a thing. She groped her way through a maze of mixed emotions, trying to find a balance for Molly, for Paul, for herself. Every day was different. Some days were hard.

On the first day of September in 1939, Hitler's armies invaded Poland. Laura heard the news just as she was coming out of a meeting. *War*, she thought, suddenly frightened for her family. She wanted to run home and hold Molly in her arms, wanted to wrap her arms around Paul and keep him near. But as much as she wanted to leave, she knew she couldn't. She had a report to dictate for Claude Gower, and then a meeting with Zack. There were letters awaiting her signature, telephone calls to be returned. Business is business, Zack would have said, and he would have been right.

Two days later, Great Britain and France declared war on Germany. America declared itself neutral, but Laura took no comfort in that. America wouldn't remain neutral, not with a madman like Hitler on the loose; the whole world would be swept into war. She didn't know when, but she knew it would happen and she knew all their lives would be changed.

Chapter Seventeen

Laura and Paul gave a small champagne party to welcome the new decade of the Forties. Only a few years before, all the talk would have been about the Depression, but now all the talk was about war. What would Hitler do next? What did Hitler want? What would Roosevelt do? The conversation made Laura edgy. She listened as long as she could, and then retreated into the kitchen, fussing with a tray of cheese puffs.

She didn't want to think about war, didn't want to hear the talk, the rumors. As months passed, she grew adept at avoiding the subject, especially with Paul. Paul would enlist if war came; she couldn't bear to think about it.

Against all evidence, she tried to convince herself that Hitler would simply stop. He would call off his quest, whatever it was; he would call back his armies. Maybe he would be ousted by a coup. Or maybe he would be assassinated. She pretended these things were possible, but in her heart she knew none of these things would happen. She had only to look at him in the newsreels to know that he would never stop, never.

All pretense ended as 1940 wore on. Germany invaded Norway, overran Denmark, Luxembourg, Belgium, and the Netherlands, and presided at the fall of France. In summer, the Battle of Britain began, and night after night bombs rained from the sky over British cities. The new Prime Minister, Winston Churchill, stirred his nation and much of the world with a speech vowing "blood, toil, tears, and sweat." The speech was broadcast many times on American radio. Whenever Laura heard it, or even thought about it, she cried.

Laura and Paul celebrated another New Year's Eve, but she couldn't shake the feeling that this might be their last celebration for a long time. It was a feeling of dread, as if she were waiting for something awful yet inevitable to happen. The waiting ended on a clear, sunny December afternoon.

On December 7, 1941, Japanese planes bombed American naval bases at Pearl Harbor. The first news bulletins coming out of Hawaii were sketchy, but by early evening everyone knew the full scope of the disaster.

Paul and Laura had been at a puppet show with Molly and had missed the early reports. Returning home, they'd heard about the attack from the elevator operator. They'd heard something about "Japs" and Pearl Harbor, but they hadn't understood a word of it until Margaret had settled them in front of the radio.

"Listen to this," she said, turning up the volume.

"But—"

"Just listen." Margaret bent down, helping Molly out of her coat and unzipping her leggings. "Your dinner's in the oven," she said to the child. "Are you hungry?"

"Yes." Molly was almost four, a pretty little girl with pale blond hair, Laura's tawny skin, and huge blue eyes. She was always hungry. "Is it chicken?" she asked.

"It's Sunday, isn't it? Chicken and dumplings every Sunday, missy."

"We'll all eat together," said Laura.

"No, we won't. I'll give Molly her dinner. You two just listen to the radio."

They listened, horrified by what they heard. Amid reports of bombs blackening the sky, of a harbor in flames, of screams and sirens and chaos, there were reports of the casualties. By nighttime it was known that the battleships *Arizona, California, Oklahoma,* and *Utah* had been sunk. Three other battleships had been badly damaged, as had several destroyers and a minelayer. In all, nineteen ships had been sunk or damaged. Three thousand Americans had been killed.

Laura was as silent as a statue, and as white. Her fingernails dug into the palms of her clenched hands. Her mouth was a tense line. "My God," she murmured. "My God, how terrible."

Paul had been stunned but now he was angry. "The bastards," he said, glaring at the radio. He thought about the thousands of dead and wounded, about the poor sailors who had been trapped on board when their ships had gone down in flames. He shook his head, hardly able to believe it. "Those bastards will be sorry. Wait till *our* planes get over there. They'll be sorry, all right."

"We're in the war now, aren't we?"

"You bet we are! And we're in it to win."

Laura left the room to check on Molly, but she came back a few minutes later. She and Paul stayed close to the radio for the rest of the evening, weighing every bit of news from Hawaii and Washington. Margaret brought a plate of chicken sandwiches and pot of coffee, and then marched away.

"Don't you want to hear—"

"No," she replied without breaking stride, "I've heard enough. The last war was supposed to *be* the last war. That's what they said back in 1918, but now we're at it again . . . I've heard enough."

Paul and Laura exchanged glances. They continued listening to the broadcasts, but at eleven o'clock she rose from her chair and switched off the radio. "The reporters are just repeating themselves," she said. "There's no new information. I guess we'll know more tomorrow."

Paul rose too. He clasped her hand, offering a weary smile. "President Roosevelt will probably declare war tomorrow. An official declaration, with Congress and all that."

She shrugged. "It was official the moment the first bomb hit our ships . . . It's strange, though. All this time I've been wondering if the Germans might attack. I never thought about the Japanese. In a way, we'll be fighting two wars now. One in Europe and one in the Pacific."

"We'll win them both, Laura. It may take a while, but we'll win."

They carried the dishes into the kitchen. Laura washed them and set them in the rack on the drainboard. Paul gave her a towel and she dried her hands. Paul's arm went around her shoulder as they walked into the hall. "I'm scared," she said. "Are you?"

"Right now I'm angry, damned angry."

They crossed the hall and tiptoed into Molly's room. She was curled up in her bed, her pale hair spread out on the pillow, her hand tucked under her chin. Laura bent, straightening the covers. "Sweet dreams, she whispered.

Paul gazed at Molly, his anger rising at the thought that war might touch her in some way, might hurt her. In the glow of the hall light he could see the outlines of all the toys he'd brought from his office — the dolls and the games and the golden carousel with tiny plumed horses. Laura worried about spoiling

Molly, but he couldn't resist the child's squeals of excitement when a new toy was set before her. Next to Laura, Molly was his greatest weakness.

They tiptoed out of the room, leaving the door open just a crack. "Sometimes I wish I were her age again," said Laura. "A little girl without a care in the world."

"You're tired."

"I guess so."

Paul followed Laura into their bedroom. She kicked off her shoes. He shed his jacket, unknotted his tie. "My boss has a son in the Navy," he said quietly. "I hope the poor guy wasn't at Pearl Harbor."

Laura sighed. Until today she'd never heard of Pearl Harbor, but now it was an instant synonym for death and destruction, for war. Everything had happened so fast.

She looked at Paul, thinking that he might soon be gone, gone to some dangerous, faraway place. She went to him, covering his face with kisses.

"Laura—"

"Don't talk," she murmured, unbuttoning his shirt. "Not now."

There was something urgent in their lovemaking that night, something frenzied, as if they were using their bodies to keep the world away. They thrashed about the bed, racing toward a fiery collision of pleasure. The darkness seemed to break into a million pieces. The air seemed to rush. A sharp cry ended in a sigh.

Later, she pulled the blankets to her chin and stared up at the ceiling. "You don't have to enlist, you know. You could wait to be called."

"I didn't say anything about enlisting."

"You didn't have to. I could see what you were thinking." She turned her head, looking at the red-gold tip of Paul's cigarette. "I understand how you feel," she went on, "but there's no hurry. The war isn't going to end next week. You'll have plenty of time to do your part."

"That's exactly it, Laura. I have to do my part." He drew on his cigarette, exhaling a stream of gray smoke. "If that means fighting for my country, then I'm ready to fight."

"I'm just asking you to wait a while, Paul. You don't have to be first in line at the recruiting office."

He reached over to the night table and stubbed out his cigarette. "Don't worry," he said, slipping his arm around Laura's shoulder, "I won't be first."

"You won't be last either," she replied, snuggling close to him. "I know how you are."

"Then you know I have to do this."

There was a long silence; a long, reluctant sigh. "Yes. Yes, I know."

In the spring of 1942, Paul enlisted in the Navy and was assigned to Officer's Training School. Ninety days later he was a lieutenant j.g. on leave in New York before heading to the Pacific, to the war.

It was a week's leave; not much time, but he and Laura were determined to make the most of it. She took the week off from work so she could be with him, and for the next seven days and nights they were rarely apart.

They spent the days with Molly—at the zoo, at Coney Island, at the Planetarium—but they kept the nights for themselves. Hand in hand they strolled around the city, seeing it as if for the first time. They went to smoky jazz clubs in Greenwich Village, to gaudy penny arcades in Times Square. They gazed out at the city from the top of the Empire State Building and the top of a double-decker bus. They went dancing at a Yorkville beer garden. Stopping at a tiny park on Sutton Place, they watched dawn break over the river. On Paul's next-to-last night in

New York, they relived part of their honeymoon—drinking martinis at the Oak Room of the Plaza, and then taking a hansom cab to the Tavern on the Green.

He had planned a surprise for his last night in the city: a small party at the Stork Club. Jane and her husband Ted were known there, and they helped with the reservations. It would be a party of six: Jane and Ted, Doris and Bill, Laura and Paul. He wanted champagne, perhaps not the best in the house, but certainly not the worst. He wanted white orchids for the ladies.

Laura was the only one of the ladies who knew nothing about Paul's surprise. When the taxi came to a halt outside the Stork Club, she looked at him and shook her head. "We'll never get in," she declared. "You have to be famous. Or at least rich."

"Let's see, shall we?"

She didn't want Paul to be embarrassed. If she could just get to a telephone, she could call somebody. Ted? Eli? Eli would surely be able to get them into the Stork Club, even on short notice. She glanced around. There was a telephone booth near the corner. "I was thinking—"

"Never mind what you were thinking," laughed Paul. He paid the driver and took Laura's arm. "Just come with me."

She looked at him again. He was so handsome in his crisp new uniform, so proud. He was past thirty, but his grin was still boyish and the twinkle had returned to his eyes. "Promise you won't be upset if we don't get in."

"Oh, we'll get in. You worry too much, sweetheart."

Without another word, he steered her through the door. The moment she stepped inside she heard the music, the voices, the laughter, the tinkle of glass. Every seat at the bar was taken. A dozen or so people waited behind a velvet rope. "Paul," she began, but he was already giving his name to the captain.

To her utter amazement, the rope came down and an instant later they were being led into the main room. A rumba was playing; she would always remember that. She would remember gazing at the crowded dance floor, at the women in wonderful summer gowns and the men in dinner clothes and officer's uniforms. She would remember gazing at the crowded tables. Was that really Walter Winchell? Was that really Joan Crawford? Was that really Barbara Hutton?

"Paul," she said, raising her voice to be heard over the music, "did you see . . ." She didn't finish, because just then she spied her friends sitting in a banquette on the far side of the room. "Oh, Paul," she laughed, looking up at him over her shoulder, "you tricked me!"

"And it wasn't easy."

"I love you."

The music was louder now; he didn't hear her. "What?"

She shrugged. She would have to tell him later.

It was a marvelous night, one of the best they'd ever had. They danced and drank champagne and gawked at celebrities and danced some more. Jane's husband, Ted, regaled the table with a couple of very funny, very risqué jokes. Doris's husband Bill made everybody laugh with a few atrocious puns. Paul brought tears to everybody's eyes with a sentimental toast to old friends. "The Six Musketeers," murmured Laura, raising her glass.

The original musketeers—Laura, Doris, and Jane—went off to the ladies' lounge to repair their makeup. They were all wearing long, bare-shouldered dresses in light summer colors. Laura's dress was ivory, Jane's petal pink. Doris's dress was lilac, and although she'd chosen it herself, it was a size too big. They all wore the white orchids Paul had ordered; Laura's was pinned to her small evening purse.

They walked into the lounge as two older women were leaving. "Oh, it's nice," said Doris, glancing from the couch to the cushioned benches to the wide mirrors set above slender dressing tables. Everything seemed very pink, but she thought maybe that was the effect of the champagne. "Look at the carpet," she added with a puzzled frown. "It's better than I have at home."

"You also have three kids at home," replied Jane, sitting down at one of the tables. "Not to mention the dog, who's *always* shedding."

"Myron's a wonderful dog," insisted Doris, coming to the defense of her shaggy friend. "He can't help it if he sheds . . . You can't help having dandruff, can you?"

"Dandruff?" cried Jane, leaning closer to the mirror. "Where?"

Laura laughed. She sat next to Jane, taking a lipstick out of her purse. It was a Jobina Inc. lipstick, one of the new shades. "Did you know we lost the Jobina account? Did I mention that?"

"Yes. But that's the advertising business, isn't it? You're always losing accounts and getting accounts. Losing and getting, getting and losing. I wonder how you keep it all straight."

"You must have been disappointed," suggested Doris.

"Yes, I was. But Jane is right; that's the advertising business. The same day we lost Jobina Inc., we got the Elegance Lingerie account. It all works out." She freshened her lipstick, blotting it with a tissue. "Jobina was never comfortable having an ad agency, and she said the meetings took too much time. I guess time is more of a problem now that she's married again."

"She married an Army general," said Jane to Doris. "Isn't that exciting?"

"Is he bossy?"

"All I know is he's *gorgeous*. I envy her."

Laura capped the lipstick and dropped it in her purse. She studied her face in the mirror; a little shiny, she thought. She pulled out her compact. "Envy? If you ask me, we all did very well in the husband department." She glanced up, and for the first time she noticed the uniformed attendant sitting quietly at the side of the room. She thought about the conversations the woman must hear every night — the silly ones, the sad ones. She wondered how this conversation would be described, "We got the right husbands, Jane."

Jane supposed that was true, more or less. Doris loved Bill. He was one of the youngest full professors at Columbia and she was proud of him. She was happy with their life — with his career, with the modest tutoring service she operated out of her kitchen, with their children, and even with their dog, Myron. Doris certainly had the right husband.

And Laura? Yes, Laura too, in a boring sort of way. It wasn't a great love affair for Laura, but she did love Paul and he was still crazy about her. They were both crazy about Molly — that was another bond between them. Maybe it wasn't a storybook marriage but it was a *good* marriage; they were happy.

That leaves you, thought Jane, staring at her reflection in the mirror. Is Ted the right husband for you? She had to admit he'd done the right things. He'd joined a law firm and buckled down to work. He'd surprised her with a charming little apartment in Beekman Place. He'd been so sweet after her miscarriage. It wasn't that she didn't appreciate all those things, it was that somehow they weren't enough. She liked Ted better than any man she'd ever known, but there was no spark, no excitement. Sometimes she felt as if she were still waiting for her life to begin.

"Jane?" Laura's brows knitted together. "Jane, for goodness' sake, what's the matter with you? You're a million miles away."

She shook her head, trying to clear it. "I'm sorry. I was thinking about Ted."

The door swung open and four women spilled into the lounge. They were youngish women, beautifully gowned and coiffed, laughing at some private joke.

"What about Ted?" asked Laura, looking back at Jane.

Tears sprang suddenly to her eyes. "He's enlisted also," she replied. "The Army. I wasn't supposed to say anything yet, but what the hell." She took the tissue Laura offered and blew her nose. "I don't want him to go." She didn't want him to go, she didn't want him to stay; she really didn't know what she wanted. "I hate this damn war."

"I don't want to talk about the war tonight. It's Paul's last night, Jane. In the morning he . . . he'll be gone."

"I hate good-byes too."

Laura nodded. "We all hate good-byes."

Paul refused to let Laura see him off. He had spent a couple of days with his parents after Officers' Training School and those good-byes had been hard enough; he couldn't face a long, drawn out scene with Laura.

She understood. While he finished dressing, she finished packing his kit bag. She had promised herself she wouldn't cry. There was so little time left; she wanted Paul to remember smiles, not tears.

"I guess I'm all set," he said now, buttoning the

jacket of his uniform. "How do I look? Like a Navy man?"

"Navy all the way. You look so handsome, I don't know if I should let you out of my sight."

"It's safe," he replied, grinning. "I'm going to get into a cab and go straight to the airfield. No detours."

"I could ride along with you, Paul."

"No, sweetheart, I want you to stay here. It's better for you to stay here."

"All right, if that's what you want."

"How about a kiss?"

Laura flew into his arms. She pressed close to him, lifting her gaze to his pale blue eyes. "I love you," she said.

"I love you, sweetheart. I'll write as soon as we get to San Francisco."

"Promise me you'll be careful. Don't be a hero . . . Promise you'll take care of yourself."

Paul smiled, stroking Laura's cheek. "I will if you will. Do we have a bargain?"

"I'll be fine."

"That's my girl." He let her go, snatching his bag and his hat from the bed. "Come on," he said, walking to the door, "there's time for one more peek at Molly."

They walked into the silent hall. Margaret had already said her good-byes, but now she poked her head out of the kitchen. "Don't you volunteer for anything, Paul Brent," she cautioned, wagging her finger at him. "Just do your part and be done with it."

"That's my plan, Aunt Margaret," he replied, amused. "Give the Japs a good trouncing, and then home I come."

Laura opened the door to Molly's room. They went inside, passing a whole menagerie of toy animals on the way to the child's bed. The first rays of morning light streamed through the curtains, falling on her golden hair. She was still asleep, snuggled next to a fuzzy yellow duck.

"Don't wake her," Paul said catching Laura's arm. "I told her yesterday that Daddy had to go away." He bent over, gently kissing Molly's cheek. She stirred, but didn't waken. He watched her for another moment or two, as if he were committing the picture to memory. "Time to go," he said, swallowing. "I'll write to you, Laura."

They kissed, and then suddenly Paul was striding away. "Remember, you're my girl," he called softly. "My one and only."

"Oh, I'll remember . . . I'll remember," she whispered as the door closed.

Laura went to the window and parted the curtains. She saw a lone bus lumbering along the avenue. She saw a few cars, a few taxis. Mr. Pilker's newsstand was open; a man walking a large brown dog stopped to buy a *Times*. Laura kept watching, and soon Paul emerged from the building. The doorman put his whistle to his lips, rushing to the curb. A taxi pulled up. Paul was halfway inside when he turned, his eyes searching the row of windows on the tenth floor. She opened the window and waved. "Good-bye, Paul," she murmured as tears rolled down her her cheeks. "I love you."

With Paul gone, Laura divided her life into three parts: Molly, work, and the war effort. Molly was a pleasure, a happy little girl who loved bedtime stories and chocolate cookies, who refused to wear anything green, who often dissolved into fits of giggles. Molly was the joy of Laura's life.

Work was her distraction. It kept her busy, kept her from brooding; sometimes she felt it kept her sane. Each day brought different challenges and she relished them. Harding Advertising continued to expand and she continued at the center of things, landing new accounts, rejuvenating old ones. BPC was her largest account: eight separate products and all of them represented by kindly old Aunt Martha.

The Aunt Martha campaigns earned Laura another raise early in 1943. It put her a bit ahead of Anne Marsh, and far ahead of the other female copywriters at Harding. The presence of other female copywriters was due in large measure to the war. In advertising, as in a host of professions, women had taken the place of men who had gone off to fight.

There didn't seem to be any job women couldn't do. They operated cranes, ran lathes, cut dies, read blueprints, serviced airplanes, maintained roads. They were mechanics, drill press operators, lumberjacks, stevedores, blacksmiths. They drove taxis and trucks and tractors. They did whatever needed to be done, and Rosie the Riveter became their symbol — a symbol of confidence, of the American spirit.

Laura never doubted that America and the Allies would win the war. She immersed herself in the war effort, giving time and money to the USO, organizing a bond drive at Harding Advertising, setting up a collection area for packages going to servicemen overseas. Margaret and Beatrice Wesley were co-chairwomen of the neighborhood scrap drive; Laura helped with that, adding a clothing drive to the agenda.

She looked forward to Paul's letters, though sometimes weeks passed without word, sometimes letters came in bunches. She knew he was the communications officer on a minesweeper somewhere in the South Pacific. She knew he admired the ship's crew, and especially the captain. "We're all pulling together," he wrote in one of his letters. "Captain Hiller is a great guy, a sly old sea dog who keeps us sharp. There are a lot of ships out here and we're all looking sharp . . . Don't ever lose faith, Laura. We're getting the job done."

Paul's letters were always optimistic, and they eased her mind. Like everyone else, she mourned American defeats in the Pacific and cheered the victories—major victories at the Coral Sea, Midway, Guadalcanal. In the Battle of the Bismark Sea, an entire convoy of twenty-two Japanese ships was sunk by American bombers, and more than fifty Japanese planes were shot down.

The agonizing struggle continued in the Pacific and in Europe. Rome had been spared for four years, but in July, some 500 Allied planes bombed the city's strategic network of railroads and freight yards. Allied troops swept across the Mediterranean to Sicily, and then to the Italian mainland itself. In September, Italy surrendered unconditionally to the Allies, though German troops fought on. That same month, the Allies scored another victory in the landings at Salerno.

Laura tried not to think about the price of victory, about the young men who were dying in numbers and ways too terrible to comprehend. The lucky ones would return, but many of them would return crippled or blind or sick in heart and soul. That's what war was—any war, every war. It was an appalling price, but she knew it was also the price of freedom.

We're getting the job done. Thank God, she thought, pondering the alternatives. Thank God.

"Aunt Jane would like to hear your prayers too," said Laura to six-year-old Molly. "Are you ready, sweetheart?"

The child nodded. Clad in a pink flannel nightgown and little pink slippers, she knelt beside her bed and folded her hands together. "Now I lay me down to sleep, I pray the Lord my soul to keep. If I should die before I wake, I pray the Lord my soul to take. God bless Mommy and Daddy, Aunt Margaret, Aunt Jane, Aunt Doris, Alice and Jimmy and Grace, Myron, Fluffy, Miss Richter, all the soldiers, and President Roosevelt . . . And please let me have a pony. Amen." She shook off her slippers and climbed into bed, settling her golden head on the pillows. "I always forget some God-blesses, Mommy."

"You did very well."

"Yes," agreed Jane, who had never viewed this bedtime ritual before. "You blessed everybody but the man in the moon."

"Who's the man in the moon?"

"No one you know," answered Laura. It was a cool October evening; she bent over and tucked the blankets around Molly. "Sweet dreams," she said, kissing her daughter's cheek.

"G'night, Mommy. G'night, Aunt Jane."

"Good night, pumpkin."

They turned out the lights and left the room. "Did you notice how big she's getting?" asked Laura. "I mailed some new snapshots to Paul. I hope he got them . . . Molly's changed so much in two years."

"I see she's still a good Democrat."

"What?"

'God bless President Roosevelt?'

"That's the way we all end our prayers in this house."

"Who's Fluffy?"

"A white rabbit," explained Laura as they returned to the living room. "The first-graders at Molly's school help take care of him. Miss Richter is Molly's teacher."

Jane sat down on the couch and reached across the table for her cigarettes. "How is she liking school so far?"

"It's only the second month, but so far so good." Laura freshened Jane's drink, adding a splash of water to her own. "If you're ready to eat, I'll heat up the stew."

"Margaret's special beef stew?"

"Well, there may be more vegetables than beef. We're running a little short of ration coupons this month. Somehow we got the sugar coupons confused with the meat coupons. I'll never know how we did that."

Jane put down her cigarette and opened her purse, fishing around in it. "Here," she said, tossing out several coupon books. "Meat, canned goods, sugar."

"I can't—"

"Sure you can. I keep all my coffee and gasoline coupons, but I don't need the others. I don't eat at home very much now that Ted's gone."

"I know. Whenever I telephone you, I get the maid."

Jane shrugged. "Mondays and Tuesdays I'm at the USO."

What about the rest of the week? wondered Laura. She sipped her scotch, staring thoughtfully at Jane. Something was different, something more than the sophisticated new hairstyle, the expensive new green suit. "Is Ted's unit still in France?"

"Yes, but I don't know where . . . I hadn't heard from him in a month, and then yesterday I got six letters all at once. The same thing happens with my letters to him." She gulped her drink. "They're hard to write."

"Why?"

"I don't know; they just are."

A frown crossed Laura's brow. "What's bothering you? I can tell you're not yourself tonight. What is it?"

Jane held out her glass for a refill. "Do you mind?"

"Help yourself," said Laura, pointing to the cocktail shaker.

Jane emptied the contents into her glass. She sat

back. "I seem to be developing a taste for Manhattans."

"Don't change the subject. I asked what was bothering you."

She took another gulp of her drink. "If you really want to know, I met somebody."

"Met somebody?"

"Do I have to draw you a picture?"

Laura's frown deepened. "I guess so. What are you talking about?"

"A man. I met a man."

"Jane!"

"It's all right; nothing's happened." Not yet, anyway, she thought. Her cigarette had burned out. She picked up the pack, then threw it down. She shifted her position slightly, her gaze darting around the room before coming to rest on Laura. "We've been seeing each other for dinner, the theater—things like that. It's all perfectly innocent . . . You could call it a—a flirtation. A perfectly innocent flirtation."

"Which you haven't mentioned in your letters to Ted."

"No, of course not."

"Then it's not so innocent, is it?"

"But he's marvelous, Laura. The most exciting man. He's a director, a *Hollywood* director. You've seen lots of his pictures. *Afternoon Romance* was his. You know, that comedy with Jean Arthur? Charley's so talented . . . And the brightest man I've ever met."

"Why isn't this paragon overseas, fighting for his country?"

"Not everyone is overseas, Laura. Bill isn't. He's still at Columbia."

"Bill is working on some secret project for the government and you know it. He goes down to Washington three times a week. He goes to some kind of lab there . . . But Bill isn't the subject. You're trying to change the subject again."

Jane drained her glass. She looked at the empty cocktail shaker, looked away. "Charley's a little over the age," she said after a moment. "He's forty-five."

"My God, Jane, you're not only seeing another man, you're seeing someone who's practically old enough to be your father!"

"He is not!"

"You're twenty-eight; he's forty-five . . . Should we get Bill to do the math for you?" Laura rose. She went to the couch and sank down beside her old friend. "Jane, it's wrong," she said quietly. "You can't do this to Ted; you can't do this to yourself. It's wrong, that's all. Just plain wrong."

"But nothing's happened."

"Something will, if you don't stop right now. I think you know that, Jane. Look at the ashtray; it's spilling over with cigarette butts. And there's hardly a drop left in the cocktail shaker. It's not like you."

"So I'm jittery. Everybody's jittery in wartime."

"Yes, but this is different."

Jane clenched her hands in her lap. "I feel so damn guilty. I start thinking about Ted . . . I mean, there he is risking his life in a war, and I'm going out on the town with Charley. I feel like such a rat."

"You're not a rat. There's not a single rat bone in your body. But you're being awfully foolish, Jane, and you have to stop. Stop now, before it's too late."

"I don't know if I can."

Laura sighed. She was about to speak when she heard a noise at the front door. She looked up. "Aunt Margaret?" she called. "Is that you?"

They heard quick, light footsteps, and then Margaret appeared in the doorway. "Of course it's me. Were you expecting someone else?"

"No."

Margaret glanced sternly at Laura's half-finished drink, at the empty cocktail shaker. "Having a party, are you?"

"Just relaxing a little, Aunt Margaret."

"I suppose you left the dinner dishes in the sink. I have to do everything, don't I?"

"Well, we haven't actually . . . had dinner yet."

"What! Do you mean you two have been sitting around here drinking all night? Aren't you ashamed of yourselves? Acting like a couple of Bowery bums! In my day—"

"Please, Aunt Margaret," interrupted Laura, rolling her eyes heavenward, "that's enough."

"It's my fault," said Jane. "I kept Laura talking."

"I don't care whose fault it is. Get into the kitchen, both of you. Get some food into your stomachs. There's a big bowl of stew in the icebox. There are eggs. Take your choice."

Laura and Jane glanced at each other. They rose.

"And clean up that mess," added Margaret, waving her hand at the glasses, the brimming ashtray. She turned sharply as the doorbell rang. "I'll get it," she said, bustling away. "Though I can't imagine who'd be calling at this time of night."

"This time of night?" said Jane when Margaret had gone. "It isn't even nine o'clock."

"Pay no attention. She's always in a state when she comes home from her scrap drive meetings." Laura smiled. "I think the power goes to her head." Laura's smile faded moments later as Margaret reappeared. She frowned, for all at once her aunt looked pale and unsteady. "What's the matter?"

"Sit down."

"But you just told us to—"

"Never mind what I told you. Sit down."

"All right," sighed Laura, "I'm sitting down. Now what's the matter?"

Margaret brought her hand from behind her back. "This just came for you," she said, holding out a telegram.

Laura felt a terrible chill. She took a breath and

then ripped open the envelope. The words leapt at her: "We regret to inform you that Lieutenant Paul Brent was killed in action during . . ."

Killed in action. The telegram fluttered to the floor. A scream pierced the silence. *Killed in action.*

"Laura?"

She was staring blindly into space, shaking her head back and forth. Tears were splashing her face. *Killed in action.*

Chapter Eighteen

She couldn't stop crying.

Margaret and Jane forced some brandy down her throat and put her to bed. Jane rushed upstairs to get Dr. Cobb, who administered a strong sedative. It should have calmed her, but it had no effect at all. Hour after hour, her tears continued to flow. Dr. Cobb left the apartment, came back, left again. Margaret was in and out of the bedroom—bringing cups of tea which nobody drank, straightening blankets, plumping pillows. Jane telephoned Doris and a few other people, and then stationed herself at her friend's bedside. She said all the right things, the things that were supposed to be said at a time like this, but it was no use. Laura gazed off into the distance and cried; she couldn't stop.

Jane decided to stay the night. "I don't know what good it'll do," she said to Margaret, "but I'll feel better if I'm here."

"There's an extra bed in Molly's room. Or I can fix up the sofa for you."

"The sofa will be fine. Thanks." It was past midnight. Jane stood, massaging the tight muscles at the back of her neck. She walked away, taking a deep breath as she turned and retraced her steps to the bed. "Laura, you have to talk to me. You have to tell me if you want anything . . . Is there anything I can do?"

She shook her head. Jane gave her another tissue — the last one in the box. "No, there's nothing," she sniffled, pressing the tissue to her red, swollen eyes. "Nothing."

"I wish you could sleep for a while. Maybe I ought to get Dr. Cobb back here."

Laura shook her head again. "No," she said amid a rush of fresh tears. "I . . . I just want to be alone."

"Alone?" Jane looked doubtful. "I'm not sure that's a good idea. Dr. Cobb said you had to cry yourself out, but he didn't say you should do it alone."

"I'm all right."

"Oh yes, I can see that. You're in great shape, if you don't float away." Jane turned to the night table, dipping a cloth into a bowl of cool water. Gently, she wiped Laura's tear-stained face. "I don't suppose I could interest you in a small meal? A scrambled egg? A piece of toast . . . No, I didn't think so." She opened the new box of tissues Margaret had brought. "Here, you'll need these . . . I'll leave you alone for now, Laura, but I'll be in the living room. I'll try to keep Margaret occupied."

Laura nodded. When the door clicked shut, she pushed the blanket aside and struggled out of bed. The room started to spin; she had to grab onto the bedpost. After a moment she took a cautious step and then another, slowly crossing the room to Paul's closet. She pulled his old tweed jacket from the hanger and slipped into it. "Paul," she murmured, rubbing her cheek against the nubby fabric. "Paul."

Her tears had stopped at last. She put out her hand to steady herself as she returned to the bed. She sat at the edge, hugging her arms around her waist. After a few moments, she crawled under the covers and leaned her head back. Safe in Paul's jacket, she slept.

"You have to tell Molly," said Margaret three days later. "I know it's hard, but you have to do it." She bent, plucking Laura's robe from a chair, gathering up the tissues strewn around the wastebasket. A breakfast tray sat untouched atop the mantel. Stacks of unread newspapers covered the bureau. "And you have to stop living in this one room. You can't shut yourself in here forever . . . Are you listening to me?"

"Yes, I'm listening. Molly's too young; she won't understand."

"All she has to understand is that her father's not coming home. That's the truth and that's what you have to tell her. It's wrong to lie to children."

"Tomorrow. I'll tell her tomorrow."

"Today," insisted Margaret. "What's the point in waiting? It won't be any easier tomorrow." She flung open the windows and the room filled with cold air. "That's better," she said. "It's been too cozy here."

Cozy? Maybe so, thought Laura. She'd spent the last couple of days going through her diary and her keepsake box — reliving her years with Paul. Ten years. Not enough time; not nearly enough. "I was lost in my memories," she explained, a pale, sad smile edging her mouth. "You're right, Aunt Margaret, there's something cozy about memories. Something soothing."

"You can't live on them, Laura."

"I know."

"You have to start pulling yourself together, and there's no time like the present. Get out of that bed and go talk to Molly. You'll feel better once it's done."

"I don't know what to say."

"The truth. Just say the truth."

Laura sighed, slowly swinging her legs over the side of the bed. She stood, reaching for her robe as she walked off to the bathroom. Bright morning sunlight was streaming through the uncurtained window; she blinked and turned away. She washed her face, rinsed her mouth, dragged a comb through her hair. She tried not to look at her reflection in the mirror because she knew what she'd see—puffy eyes, sunken cheeks, sorrow.

"Stop dawdling," called Margaret.

"Stop nagging," replied Laura. She came out of the bathroom, glancing wearily at her aunt. "I'm doing the best I can."

"And you'll keep on doing your best, too. It's a hard life, missy. We all have to do our best."

Laura didn't want to hear any more. She slid her feet into her slippers and walked into the hall. She thought she ought to plan what to say to Molly, but her mind went blank. She paused halfway between her room and Molly's. After a moment she shrugged and continued on her way. I'll find the words, she told herself, praying that was true.

Molly was happily engaged in what had become a Sunday morning rite: dressing her dolls for church. She was allowed to take only one doll to Sunday school at St. James's, but still she insisted upon dressing them all. Now seven dolls were arrayed across her bed, each waiting its turn.

"Hello, Mommy," she said, looking up as Laura entered the room. "We're not ready yet. It's Susie's fault. She doesn't like her green dress. We *always* argue about it."

Laura smiled. "I want to talk to you, sweetheart. Do you think you could finish dressing your dolls later?"

Molly's narrow shoulders jerked up and down. "I don't know. There's so many."

"I really have to talk to you. And you really have

to listen. Okay?"

"Okay." She tossed her golden head. "But don't sit *there*, Mommy; you'll squash Elizabeth."

"Sorry." Laura went to the other end of the bed, perching at the side. She reached out and took Molly on her lap. "It's about Daddy. You know why Daddy had to go away."

"To fight the bad men."

"Yes. Daddy was very brave." *Was*. Laura's arms tightened around her daughter. "He went away because that was the right thing to do, but all the while he wanted to come home to us. He loved us so much."

Molly had begun to fidget. Her gaze skipped back to her dolls, and she wondered which dress Susie should wear today.

I'm making a mess of this, thought Laura. She didn't know what to do. Molly had been only four when Paul left; that was two years ago, and two years was a third of Molly's life. "Sweetheart, do you remember your daddy?"

"Sometimes." Sometimes there was a stirring of memory when she looked at his picture, or when Laura read from his letters. It was a faint stirring — pleasant, but always quickly forgotten. "That's Daddy," she said, pointing to the photograph on her bureau. "He brought me toys."

"He certainly did. A whole roomful of toys . . . Molly, what I want to tell you is that Daddy won't be coming home. He . . . he died. Do you know what that means?"

"Ellen Burke's turtle died. She told me." Molly stopped squirming and jumped off Laura's lap. "He was a nice turtle."

"Daddy was nice. Don't you remember how he used to make you laugh?"

Molly shrugged. "Where is he, Mommy?"

Laura didn't know how to reply. Molly was indeed

too young to understand about war, about a fierce naval battle in Leyte Gulf, about bodies lost at sea. What could she say that the child would understand? "Daddy is in heaven, sweetheart."

"With the angels?"

Tears burned Laura's eyes. "Yes, with the angels," she agreed, her voice breaking. "With God."

"Ellen's turtle is in heaven. Maybe Daddy will see him."

Laura went to Molly, kneeling down to take the little girl in her arms. "I love you," she murmured.

"I love you, Mommy. Can I dress Susie now?"

"Yes, of course." Laura dried her eyes. She watched as Molly squinted in concentration, holding up one doll dress and then another. Life goes on, she thought. Turtles die, men die, but life goes on.

Laura returned to work a week later. She was thinner, still a bit pale, but she was rested and that helped, because she returned to find her desk covered with messages and memos and reports. There were layouts to be approved, ad schedules to be revised. There were new budget figures for BPC, new proposals for Morning Dew Shampoo. There were several thick folders from the research department. There were condolence letters, and those she put to one side.

It was a daunting accumulation, but not unwelcome. She could lose herself in work, in the demands and distractions of Harding Advertising. Work kept her going from one day to the next, and each day she felt a little stronger, a little more able to cope. Time softened the sharp edges of her grief. Paul was dead; with time came acceptance.

War still raged in Europe and the Pacific. Iwo Jima, Okinawa, the Bulge, Remagen—in all these places men were fighting and dying. Hitler's armies launched their last major offensive at the Bulge, breaking through Allied defenses in the Ardennes. American forces were surrounded and bad weather hampered Allied air operation, but within days reinforcements reached the besieged Americans, and the weather lifted. German armored columns were destroyed; lost ground was retaken. After a month of fierce fighting, after five years of war and misery and death, Hitler was beaten.

President Roosevelt didn't live to witness the formal surrender. He had rallied America during the Depression, during the worst days of the war, and America wept at his death. A month later the nation wept again when the new President, Harry Truman, announced the unconditional surrender of Germany.

Laura was at Mark Ralston's photography studio when the news flashed over the radio. A darkroom assistant turned up the volume on the Philco and they all gathered around: the assistant, Mark, his stylist, two lingerie-clad models, Eve. Laura stood a short distance away, her eyes glittering with tears. "Come on, Mark," she said, "let's break out the scotch. This is a celebration!"

V-E Day was celebrated all across the country, in towns and cities and tiny rural villages. In New York, huge crowds thronged Times Square, shouting and cheering. Strangers embraced strangers, laughing and crying at the same time. Children sat atop their parents' shoulders, waving flags and tossing confetti. Church bells rang, a message of hope to a war-weary people.

There was another celebration three months later, a celebration more joyous than the first, for it marked the unconditional surrender of Japan. General MacArthur, accepting the surrender aboard the battleship *Missouri*, offered the hope that "peace be now restored to the world, and that God will preserve it always."

When the celebrations ended, people looked around and realized that much of the world lay in ruins. Cities had been bombed into smoldering rubble. Once fertile land had been blackened and scarred. Refugee camps overflowed with desperate men and women who had lost everything. Orphanages overflowed with frightened, sad-eyed children who had lost everything that mattered most.

These were the truths of war, and perhaps the worst truth of this war was the revelation of Hitler's death camps. Ten million men, women, and children had been exterminated by the Nazis, six million of them Jews for whom the Final Solution had been devised. In newsreels and news magazines, a stunned world saw pictures of the survivors—skeletal figures who had been starved and beaten and tortured, who had seen their loved ones marched into Nazi gas chambers. It was a testimony to the human spirit that there had been any survivors at all.

"It was the most devastating thing I've ever seen in my life," said Jane's husband, Ted. He had been discharged from the Army a month ago and now he sat in Laura's living room, recounting his experiences to Doris and Bill. "My unit was part of General Campbell's division. Toward the end, we were sent to liberate Dachau. We'd all heard stories about the concentration camps, rumors. But God knows we weren't prepared for what we saw. The survivors had been starved down to skin and bones. They'd been tortured. 'All the tortures of hell'; that's what our padre said."

Jane finished her drink. "General Campbell is Jobina Grant's husband," she explained, breaking the silence. "An odd coincidence, isn't it?"

Ted lifted his dark head and looked at Jane. "That's hardly the point of the story," he said. He looked at the empty glass she held in her hand and his eyes flickered. "Or are you tired of my stories by now?"

"They're depressing."

"And you'd rather be entertained. Of course you would; we all would. Why let reality interfere with good times?"

"Jane," said Laura, rising from her chair, "come and help me in the kitchen. You can fix the salad while I check on my roast."

"I'll come too," offered Doris. "We'll leave the men to their war talk."

Jane stopped to refill her glass, sipping the cocktail as she followed Doris and Laura through the hall into the kitchen. "Do you really want me to make the salad?" she asked.

"Sure."

Jane took a swallow of her drink and then went to the icebox, removing lettuce, tomatoes, green onions, and radishes. She dumped it all on the counter, drawing the old wooden salad bowl closer. "You noticed that Ted and I aren't exactly getting alone," she said, tearing the lettuce into pieces. "There's a certain tension in the air."

"Yes, I noticed," replied Laura as Doris nodded. "He seems upset about something. Something other than concentration camps."

"He's obsessed with those damn camps . . . But yes, there's something else. He found out that I'd been seeing Charley Swanson. I didn't deny it. I couldn't; our names had been in Winchell's column. I just explained—tried to—that it was innocent."

Laura closed the oven door and straightened up. "But it wasn't innocent."

"It was in the beginning," insisted Jane. "A flirtation, that's all it was at first. That's all I meant it to be." She paused, bowing her head over the counter. "But then things changed. I couldn't seem to help myself. I just couldn't."

"Thank God it's all in the past," said Doris hastily. "Ted's back home now and your friend is back in Hollywood. It's all over. A lot of people lost their way in the war, Jane. You're not the only one."

"A wartime fling? Is that what you think?"

"Whatever it was, it's over. Now you can put things right with Ted."

"I'm not so sure," replied Jane. She finished chopping the onions. She threw down the knife and wiped her hands. A moment later she went to the table and reclaimed her drink. "Charley's going to shoot his next picture in New York," she explained. "Or at least some of it. He arrives in three weeks."

"Then you plan to see him again?" asked Laura.

"I don't know."

"Oh, you mustn't," said Doris, her small face crumpling in concern. "What about Ted? What about your marriage?"

"I don't know."

"You know, all right," said Laura. "You just don't want to say so. And for the record, I think you're doing a pretty rotten thing to Ted."

"When did you and Ted become such pals?"

"He was Paul's friend."

Jane nodded. All their husbands had been friends from the start. Paul was gone now, but Ted and Bill were still close. "Yes," she said, "and you're right to stick up for him. It *is* a rotten thing."

"If you know that—" began Doris.

"Of course I know that," interrupted Jane. "Why do you suppose I always have a glass in my hand these days? It's guilt . . . Because I also know all Charley has to do is call and I'll go running."

"But why?"

"You wouldn't understand, Doris. It's not mathematical. Quick—what's 68,937 multiplied by 893?"

"Are you saying you love him?"

"She doesn't love him," sighed Laura. "It's not love, it's the excitement . . . Isn't it?" she asked, draping her arm about Jane's shoulder. "It's exciting to be pursued by a famous Hollywood director. To hobnob with movie stars. To imagine yourself in one of those Beverly Hills mansions. Maybe lounging around the pool with Clark Gable?"

"Good choice," said Jane.

"You're risking your marriage for a fantasy."

"Sometimes I'm so confused I'm not sure *what* I'm doing."

"I'm sure." Laura dropped her arm and walked back to the stove. "We've known each other a long time, Jane—almost fifteen years. And all that time you've been looking for excitement."

"The spice of life." Jane drank the last of her cocktail and put the glass down. "Everybody's looking for *some*thing, Laura. What about you?"

"At the moment, I'd settle for a perfectly done roast—medium rare."

"Answer my question: what extra something do you want out of life?"

"Money."

"Money's what you need. I'm asking what you *want*."

"Money," said Laura again, peering at her roast. "The more the merrier."

"We're trying to hold the line on prices," said Claude Gower, "but inflation is hurting BPC as much as it's hurting every other company. Inflation always follows war. We knew that; we knew what was coming. I expect we'll hold the line through the rest of this year. After that, it's anybody's guess. We may have to raise prices by ten to twelve percent."

"Ouch," said Zack. "Ten to twelve percent at the wholesale level, and then retailers will add increases of their own."

Claude nodded. "I'm afraid so. Laura, I'd like your thinking as to how we should handle this with the public. We don't want to appear to be taking advantage. We're not that kind of company."

"Aunt Martha will handle it. We'll just have to find the right approach. Fortunately, we have time. Everything will be ready when and if you raise prices. In the meanwhile, we'll work up some projections on what effect price increases might have." Claude nodded again. His hair was completely gray now. Behind the polished lenses of his glasses, she saw something quiet and sad in his eyes, something put there by the death of his youngest, most beloved son at Anzio. In a way, she felt it was a bond between them: he had lost his son; she had lost her husband. "I hope increases won't be necessary," she continued. "We have an excellent position in the market."

"Yes, but I must also consider profits. BPC has stockholders, Laura. I spend a great deal of time trying to balance the wishes of my family against the best interests of the stockholders." He glanced around the conference room, his gaze settling briefly upon a collection of small, narrow bronze plaques affixed to the wall. He looked back at Laura, smiling slightly. "Aunt Martha's made my job somewhat easier," he said. "The family likes her, and the stockholders like the profits . . . That's why I've decided to accept your proposal to consolidate the entire BPC account. Starting in January of '47, Aunt Martha can take all sixteen products under her wing. We'll make the announcement — probably next month."

All sixteen products. The entire BPC account. Laura had to squeeze her hands together to keep from jumping out of her chair. She felt her heart thumping; she felt a smile spreading across her face, growing wider and wider. This was what she had been working for; she savored the moment, basking in it as if it were an especially dazzling sun. "You won't regret your decision," she said when she was able to speak. "The best is yet to come."

"I hope that's true. It's an enormous responsibility, Laura. I hope you're up to it. You and Martin . . . if he ever gets back from Boston."

Laura had already apologized for Martin's absence and now she apologized again. "I'm sorry he's not here," she said. "He'll kick himself for missing the good news, but there really was a client emergency. Martin had to catch the first train out this morning."

"In future, I'll expect you both to be available for meetings. BPC is your largest client. It would be a serious error to take us for granted."

"I promise you that won't happen," said Zack, responding quickly to Claude's warning. "Laura and Martin's schedules will be cleared to accommodate BPC. Of course they'll be given whatever staff they need. BPC is top of the list, Claude. We're ready to pull out all the stops."

"I'm glad we understand each other."

"We're all on the same side. We all want what's best for BPC."

"Indeed." Claude slipped a folder into his briefcase and snapped it shut. He rose. Zack and Laura rose also, starting toward the door. "Laura, I'd like a word with you, if you don't mind."

"Certainly."

"You needn't stay, Zack."

He knew he had been dismissed. If there were any loose ends, he would have to leave them to Laura. "I'll see you next week, then," he said, exiting the room.

"What can I do for you, Claude?" asked Laura.

"You can give me a straight answer. I've heard you got an offer to go to Leland Advertising. A handsome offer, by all accounts. Are you considering it?"

"No."

"Would you care to elaborate?"

She smiled. "I'm happy here. That could change, but right now I'm exactly where I want to be."

"You would be earning more money at Leland, or so I understood."

Her smile widened. "I started here as a secretary. My salary was $17.50 a week and I was glad to have it. That was back in 1934." She paused. Her smile vanished so suddenly it was as if a light had been switched off. "Desperate times," she continued after a moment. "Eli didn't want to hire me, but he did. I'll always be grateful. Always. You might say Harding Advertising saved my life."

"I might also say you've repaid the favor. You've helped breathe new life into the Harding Company."

Laura glanced up, shaking her head. "Certain favors are never repaid, Claude. Besides, gratitude isn't my only reason for staying. Far from it. I'm earning fifteen thousand a year now. Fifteen thousand! Back in 1934, I didn't know there was that much money in the world."

"Leland's offer was better."

"Only temporarily. Now that we're getting the whole BPC account, Eli will top the Leland offer. Eli is very generous with his people . . . We all get other offers, you know. Zack gets lots of offers, but he stays because Eli is a good man to work for. He's generous with money and with his support. He gives us the freedom to try new things."

"All right, you've convinced me. I had to be certain there were no changes on the horizon. We value continuity at BPC."

Laura shrugged. "Well, people do leave us occasionally. One of our art directors just went over to McClennan. One of our copywriters is going to Fields & Yost. And most of the women who were here during the war are gone now . . . But Zack and Martin and I are staying put. We're the old-timers, along with Anne Marsh." Laura knew that Anne Marsh was waiting for Eli to retire. According to the grapevine, Anne had a group of investors ready to buy Harding Advertising. It was a troubling prospect, one which Laura chose not to share with Claude Gower. "We're a good team, Zack and Martin and I."

"Quite good."

"I warn you—now that we have all your advertising in the U.S., we're going to go after your overseas account."

"Harding doesn't have an overseas office."

"Not yet."

He laughed. "Yes, I see what you mean." He picked up his briefcase and turned away. He was almost at the door when his gaze moved back to the narrow bronze plaques studding the paneled wall. He went to take a closer look. "Is this a memorial?" he asked.

"Yes. It was Eli's idea." Laura came around the side of the conference table and stood next to Claude. "These are the names of Harding employees killed in the First World War," she explained, gesturing toward a row of plaques on the left. "And these are the men who died in World War II."

He adjusted his glasses, staring at all the carefully inscribed names and battle sites. So many young lives lost, he thought, thinking of his own son. "War," he said, biting off the word. "What madness."

Laura nodded, gazing at the names. There was Ralph Lang; cheerful, backslapping Ralph Lang killed at St. Lo. There was the office boy Billy Simms, a day past his eighteenth birthday when he died at Normandy. There was Carl Hoeffler from the accounting department; Mike O'Brien from the mail room; Ken Tabler from research—all marines, all killed at Iwo Jima.

The names seemed to run together, and for a split

second she imagined she saw Paul's name spiraling across the others. She felt her throat tighten. She had to look away.

"My wife says it helps to cry," remarked Claude.

A soft smile touched Laura's mouth. "It took a long time," she replied, "but I'm all cried out."

Chapter Nineteen

Laura peered through the window of the taxicab. She saw a deserted street bordered at one end by what appeared to be an abandoned factory building, and on the other by a series of faded storefronts. She frowned. "Are you sure this is the right address?"

The driver shrugged, tugging his cap lower on his forehead. "24 Boyne Place, Brooklyn," he said. "It's the only 24 Boyne Place we got, lady."

"What do you think?" whispered Doris.

Laura looked at the slip of paper in her hand. "I guess this is where we're supposed to be. Leave it to Jane to bring us to the wilds of Brooklyn."

"She must have a reason."

"A weird reason." Laura smiled, shaking her head. Today was Jane's thirtieth birthday and they'd let her decide how she wanted to celebrate it. They'd hoped she would choose a fancy restaurant; instead she had chosen Boyne Place. "You know Jane."

"The meter's running, lady," said the driver. "You getting out or what?"

"Yes, but would you wait for us? We'll be going back to Manhattan."

"I'd like to help you, lady, but my shift was over twenty minutes ago. I got to get this cab to the garage."

"Could you wait just a little while?"

"Jeez, lady, I can't." He glanced at the meter. "That's

$6.10," he said, shutting it off.

Laura reached into her purse. She took seven dollars from her wallet and handed them to the driver. "We'll probably be stranded here," she muttered, climbing out of the taxi.

Doris followed, nearly tripping on the curb. "Maybe Jane has her car."

"That's even worse. Jane is a menace behind the wheel."

The two women watched as the cab drove away. It was a freezing December afternoon. Doris pulled up the collar of her coat and squinted into the shadows. "Oh, my goodness, I know why she brought us here! Look!"

Laura turned. "I don't see anything."

"Look!"

She took a step forward, her gaze scanning the storefronts. In one of the dingy plate glass windows she saw a vase of paper flowers and a large paper cutout of a hand. She lifted her eyes to the sign. "It's the fortune-teller!" she laughed. "It's Madame Zarela, the fortune-teller! How in the world did Jane track her down after all this time? It's been ten years."

"Thirteen."

"What?"

"Thirteen years," said Doris. "We went to see her the day you and Jane graduated from the Acme Business Institute. I remember."

"Yes, so do I. But thirteen is an unlucky number, isn't it?"

Doris ducked her chin into the big collar of her coat. "There's no such thing."

"No? Well, let's see what Madame Zarela has to say about that."

There was a black cat curled in a corner of the window. "Look," said Doris, pulling at Laura's sleeve.

"God, you don't suppose it's the *same* cat?"

"This is getting spooky. Maybe we shouldn't have

come."

"It's too late to think about that now. We're here."

A bell tinkled above the door as they walked inside. Jane beamed when she saw them. "Happy birthday to me," she cried, jumping up from her chair. "I've already had my reading and the future is rosy!"

"I'm glad to hear it," said Laura. "That almost makes the trip worthwhile." Steam heat was hissing in the storefront parlor. She drew off her gloves and unbuttoned her coat. "Interesting neighborhood."

"I knew you'd like it."

Jane went back to her chair. She seemed to lose her balance for an instant, putting out her hand to steady herself. Laura and Doris glanced at each other; Jane wasn't drunk but she was tipsy. "Who's going next?" asked Doris.

"You go ahead," replied Laura. "I'm sure you'll have the nicest fortune of all of us."

"Not nicer than mine," disagreed Jane. "I'm going to be terribly happy."

Laura wondered if there was something a little desperate in Jane's enthusiasm, something a little forced. Jane and Ted had been separated for the past three months. It was an amicable separation—at least as far as anyone knew—but Laura knew it must be painful nonetheless. The Charley Swanson episode had ended, though too late to heal the wounds.

She sat down beside Jane in one of the mismatched chairs hugging the wall. Out of the corner of her eye, she saw the cat washing its paw. She watched for a moment. She decided it was probably the same cat.

"We will begin," said Madame Zarela, taking Doris's hands.

Laura glanced around, looking more closely at the fortune-teller. There was a streak of gray in her mane of black hair, but otherwise the woman had changed very little. Her olive skin seemed to be unlined. Wide gold hoops dangled from her ears, and a colorful shawl was draped about her shoulders. Her manner was precisely as Laura remembered it—quiet, a bit solemn, all knowing.

"Isn't this fun?" asked Jane, poking Laura's arm. "One of my better ideas, I believe."

"I feel as if we've stepped back in time."

"You can say that again. Doris is getting another boring fortune, just like years ago."

Laura didn't think it was so boring. Madame Zarela "saw" a fourth child in Doris's future, a trip to faraway places, and a business success. "It's a lovely fortune, Jane, if it comes true. Doris wants another child. And Bill wants to take her on a second honeymoon. On a trip, maybe even to Europe. What's boring about that?"

"Well . . . ordinary, then. Kids and second honeymoons." She shrugged. "It lacks imagination, wouldn't you say?"

"No, I think it's lovely."

Jane lit a cigarette, coughing as she always did with the first puff of smoke. "Your turn, Laura," she urged when Doris left Madame Zarela's table. "And remember I'm expecting big things from your palm."

Laura took a seat at the table and held out her hands, palms up. "You read my fortune a long time ago," she said. "That was back in Yorkville."

"I have been many places," replied Madame Zarela. She lowered her dark gaze, sliding her hands under Laura's. "You have a strong lifeline," she began. "You will live to old age. Maybe eighty years . . . There is work in your life. Business. You are very determined in business." She nodded, her eyes sweeping from one hand to the other. "Yes, there is money here also. Business and money; they are together."

"Is she going to be rich?" called Jane.

"It is not for you to ask the question," said Madame Zarela.

Déjà vu, thought Laura. All this has happened before. She smiled. "*Am* I going to be rich?"

"There is money here, if you . . . Business and money are together, if you follow what you believe. If others don't stand in your way. They will try, but this you must not allow . . . There has been tragedy. A man, a man with light hair." Madame Zarela paused, and again her eyes swept left and right. "There is another man—"

"Now we're getting to the good stuff," remarked Jane, leaning forward in her chair.

"There is a man with light hair," continued the fortune-teller, "but there is another man, a different man. He has dark hair. He is also determined in business."

"A competitor," suggested Laura.

"This is not clear. The man is not clear. I see him in the shadows, stepping out of the shadows. A dark-haired man. Perhaps you will marry him."

Laura's head snapped up. Marry him? "No," she said.

Madame Zarela frowned. "There is something between you. You and the dark-haired man."

"He's your *lover*," insisted Jane. "I knew you wouldn't let me down."

"You are going on a trip," said Madame Zarela. "A vacation, maybe. The man will be there." She paused once more, studying Laura's palm. "A dark-haired man stepping out of the shadows. Maybe he will be your husband."

Laura couldn't help smiling. The only vacation in her plans was a week with Molly at Lake Placid. There would be skating and sledding and snowball fights, but no mysterious men stepping out of the shadows. That was just as well, she thought. She didn't want any entanglements, much less any serious entanglements. The first man in her life had betrayed her, the second had died. Twice her heart had been broken and twice was enough.

Kilroy was here. The phrase had been popular during the war, a slogan scribbled by American GIs on streets and walls and fences overseas. Now Doris saw it chalked on the side of the abandoned factory building. "Kilroy again," she laughed.

Laura nodded. "I hope he's still here and I hope he has a taxi with him."

"Didn't you hear me?" asked Jane. "We don't need a taxi; my car is right across the street." She stretched out her arm, waving in the direction of the cream-colored De Soto. "It's right there."

"It's not hard to spot, since it's the *only* car there."

"Then why are you making such a fuss about taxis?"

"Because I don't like to drive with you, Jane. I don't like the way you swerve in and out of traffic. It makes me nervous . . . And besides, I don't trust that old car."

"It's not old." It was a 1941 model, a gift from Ted that had been delivered two weeks before Pearl Harbor. He'd had it custom-painted, and even the interior had been done in the lighter colors Jane preferred. She was happy with her car; sometimes she got behind the wheel and drove around for hours. "My De Soto runs like a dream."

"Oh? Do you remember when it stalled in the middle of Lexington Avenue? During rush hour? Horns were honking and people were yelling. Remember how angry the cop was?"

"I thought he was going to arrest us," said Doris.

Jane shook her head. "That was during the war. It was hard to get parts then. But now the car's in perfect condition. I'm telling you, it runs like a dream."

"What if it decides to stall again? We'd be stranded in this godforsaken place."

Doris frowned. "We're already stranded. Aren't we?"

"Maybe we should walk a few blocks," sighed Laura. "Maybe we'll spot a cab."

"Not around here," said Jane. "Down that way are a couple of stores and some old wooden row houses," she explained, stretching out her arm again. "If you go the other way, you'll get run over, because that's the Boyne intersection. Trucks and cars zoom past as if they were in a race. The traffic light's broken."

"Naturally." Laura smiled. "All right, we'll be your passengers. But first you'd better breathe more of this cold air."

"Why?"

"To undo the cocktails you had at lunch."

"I had a whisky sour. Is that such a big deal?"

"*A* whisky sour. One?"

"Okay, two. A girl's entitled to celebrate her birthday, isn't she?"

"You looked a little unsteady in there," said Doris, glancing back at Madame Zarela's. "We noticed."

"I guess the second drink went to my head, but it's worn off by now . . . It *has*," she insisted, laughing. "Do you want me to walk a straight line?"

A sudden wind gusted along the street. They all held on to their hats, hunching their shoulders as they went to the car. Jane opened the door. "Who wants to sit up front?" she asked.

"I'll sit up front," replied Doris. "Your cigarette smoke makes Laura sneeze."

They climbed into the De Soto, settling into their seats. Jane started the engine. "Smooth as silk," she said. "I told you so."

"Let's get going," said Laura. "It'll be dark soon."

Jane glanced in the rearview mirror then pulled away from the curb. "Where are we having dinner?"

"How about the French place," suggested Doris. "They have all those wonderful desserts."

"Yes, but the service is so slow. I promised Molly I'd be home early."

"You could bring her one of their chocolate tarts."

"That's a good idea . . . Okay, the French place."

Laura took off her hat and leaned her head back. It was a Saturday, but she'd been up since six and she was tired. She closed her eyes, thinking about the latest Aunt Martha campaign for BPC. She had decided that Aunt Martha needed a new look, something slightly more modern and youthful; now she had to convince Claude Gower. Martin would help, and Ronnie. She would have to ask Ronnie to do some sketches.

It was warm in the car. Laura started to drowse, but a squeal of laughter pulled her from the brink of sleep. She rubbed her eyes. She yawned. "What's so funny?"

"I've been hearing the latest adventures of Myron the dog," said Jane. "You know, I'm thinking about getting a dog for myself. Something small and . . ." Her voice trailed away. Her hands tightened on the wheel. *"Damn,"* she cried. "I took the wrong turn."

Laura looked out the window. She blinked. All at once the De Soto seemed to be lost in a sea of traffic. "Where are we? Where did all these cars come from?"

"This is part of the intersection. Traffic moving north and east spills over onto this road. We'll have to stay on it for a while."

"Why are you going so fast?"

"I don't have any choice."

Laura saw that they were caught in the flow of traffic. They couldn't pull ahead, couldn't drop back; if they slowed down, they would surely be hit from behind. "Where does this road take us?"

"I don't know."

"Swell."

Doris turned, looking at Jane. Jane's hands were tensed on the wheel. Her whole body was tensed, and yet she was smiling. "You're enjoying this," said Doris.

Jane cast a quick glance at the speedometer—holding steady at 70 mph. This part of the road was straight, but there was bound to be a turn somewhere along the line. She thought about making a sharp turn

358

at seventy miles an hour, at eighty miles an hour. Her heart was pounding with excitement. Her eyes were glittering. She knew what she was going to do: at the first turn, she would shoot past the car up front, cut between the cars on the right, and veer into the side road. Exhilaration swept over her. She was in a race and she was going to win.

"Jane?"

"Hmm?"

Doris noticed how intently Jane was watching the road. "Never mind."

The afternoon had lengthened into evening. Laura stared out the window, her gaze following the play of headlights on the shadowy road. She yawned again. Her eyes were starting to close, but just then the De Soto accelerated, breaking out of the traffic flow to streak past the car ahead. "Dammit, Jane," she cried as she was thrown forward. "What are you doing?"

Jane laughed. "Hold on."

"Mother of God," murmured Doris, her head pressed to her heart.

There was a deafening blast of horns, a screech of brakes. *"Jane,"* shouted Laura as the De Soto swerved sharply right, cutting through traffic. Everything was a blur—cars, lights, signs, everything. We're going to die, she thought, clutching the edge of her seat. Dear God, what will happen to Molly?

"Here we go," called Jane, her voice rising above the din. "Hold on to your hats!"

With a final burst of speed, the De Soto shot straight across the intersection, skidding past the flood of onrushing traffic, skidding off the road. Jane's hands leapt upward on the wheel, twisting it to the left, then to the right, then to the left again. Her hands relaxed as she brought the car under control and drove into a quiet side street.

It was several moments before anyone spoke. Doris was chalk white, her little chin quivering. Laura was furious. "How could you?" she demanded. "How could you do a crazy, stupid thing like that?"

"I'm sorry," said Jane.

"*Sorry?*" Laura paused, trying to calm herself. She fell back against the seat and took a deep breath. "God, Jane! What got into you?"

It had been an impulse, an unexpected and entirely irresistible impulse. Danger had been part of the lure. Those few dangerous minutes had been the most exciting of her life. "Whatever it was, it's over now." She looked at the speedometer: 50 mph. "All over. I'm sorry I scared you, Laura. You too, Doris; I'm very sorry."

Doris took a handkerchief from her purse and touched it to her mouth. "I hope this is the way back to Manhattan," she said in a shaky voice.

Laura turned to the window, squinting at the traffic sign posted near the corner. "Jane," she cried as she glimpsed the arrow, "We're on a one-way street and we're going the *wrong* way."

"What?"

"Pull over! We're going the wrong way!"

Her warning came too late. They saw the blue sedan careen around the corner. They saw headlights bearing down on them, hurtling closer and closer. Jane tried to pull away but there was no time. She screamed.

They were all screaming. Laura heard the desperate squeal of brakes as the sedan tried to stop. She threw her arms up in front of her face, and at that instant the sedan smashed head-on into the De Soto. There was a tremendous crash of metal. Both cars were spun around, colliding again under a shower of glass. There was a single shuddering cry, and then there was silence.

Laura wondered at the profound silence as she

struggled back to consciousness. The silence of the grave, she thought, wondering if she was dead.

Her eyes fluttered open, searching the darkness. She was lying on the floor of the De Soto, her body wedged in the space between the front and rear seats. She tried to move, but her shoulder was caught in a tangle of webbing and wire springs. Anxiously, she stretched out her hand, feeling around. A jagged shard of glass sliced into her thumb. The pain was sharp, quick. She jerked her hand away, staring at the long ribbon of blood. "I'm not dead," she murmured, startled by the sound of her own voice. She was confused, trying to remember something just beyond the reach of memory. Something terrible had happened, but what?

It came to her in bits and pieces. The De Soto . . . Jane . . . the intersection . . . Doris . . . the one-way street . . . the headlights . . . the crash. *The crash.* "Oh, my God," she murmured. "Oh, my God." She wrenched her shoulder out of the webbing and pulled herself to her knees. "Doris?" she called. "Jane?"

There was no answer. The left side of her face was throbbing; her shoulder ached. She swallowed, and then drew a breath. "Doris?" she called again. "Jane?" She pulled herself higher, looking into the front seat. "Oh God," she cried. "Oh God, *no.*"

Jane was slumped over the wheel, face down. She was very still. Doris was lying half off, half on the seat. She, too, was very still. She was covered with blood.

"Oh God." For a moment Laura thought she was going to pass out. She shook her head, trying to chase the darkness away. She took another breath, another and another. She knew she had to get to her friends; somehow she had to help them.

She couldn't open the door. She pulled on the handle, she pounded on it, but to no avail. She stuck her arm through the shattered window, trying to open the door from the outside, but again to no avail. Tears were coursing down her cheeks. She was sobbing. In one sudden, frantic move, she threw herself at the front seat and crawled over the top.

There was no room for her in the front seat, and so she dropped to the floor, crouching amid mounds of broken glass and twisted pieces of metal. "Doris," she cried, "wake up!" She knew she was supposed to feel for a pulse, but Doris's big coat kept getting in the way of her nervous fingers. "Doris . . . Doris, for god's sake, wake up!"

There was only silence. She reached out to Jane, but at her touch, Jane fell over to the side. "Oh God," sobbed Laura. "Oh, my God."

She looked at Jane's white, still face. She looked at Doris, almost unrecognizable for the blood splashed across her profile. Laura realized that her own blood was dripping on Doris. She pulled her hand back, pulling a handkerchief from her pocket and wrapping it around the wound.

"You have to get help," she told herself between sobs. "You have to be calm . . . and you have to get help."

She reached for the door, praying it would open. It did. She crawled out, her eyes darting wildly about. She didn't see any people, any houses. On one side of the narrow street was an auto supply shop, but it was closed, as was the delicatessen next door. On the other side of the street was a vacant lot. "Be calm," she told herself again, thinking that she would have to find a telephone booth. She had taken a few steps when she realized that she would need change. She reached into the car, grabbed Doris's purse, and stumbled off into the night.

The blue sedan had been hurled backward by the force of the second crash. Laura saw it. She stopped, looking warily through the smashed windshield. She saw the driver and she moved nearer. She saw his head lolling on his shoulder, saw the blood-soaked jacket.

She saw the piece of glass sticking out of his throat. She screamed, stumbling away.

She wondered if she was dreaming all this, if it was some horrible, unspeakable nightmare. But the blood was real. She looked down, and in the light from the street lamp she frowned at the splotches of blood on her coat, on her torn stockings, on her shoes. It was real.

She started running, counting the blocks as she went. Four blocks later, she dashed into a phone booth and tossed Doris's purse on the shelf. She riffled through it, looking for a nickel or a dime. "Come on, come on," she murmured. With shaking hands, she turned the purse upside down and dumped out the contents. She found a quarter and dropped it in the slot.

She dialed the operator, tapping her fingers while she waited. "Help us," she cried, when finally the operator came on the line. "An ambulance, we need an ambulance . . . There's been a terrible accident. *Help us.*"

Doris limped slowly, painfully out of the De Soto. She was dazed; her mind was just clear enough to know she had to find Laura, had to find help. She took a step, but that was all she could manage. She sank down on the curb, crying and shivering in her big coat.

She thought she heard her name. A voice seemed to be coming from a great distance, and it seemed to be calling her name. She tried to turn around but she didn't have the strength. She dropped her head into her hands. Blood seeped through her fingers; she felt the wet, sticky mess. She didn't understand. Why was there so much blood?

"Doris?"

The voice was closer. Laura's voice, she thought,

lifting her head.

"Doris, is that you?" Laura ran to the huddled figure sitting on the curb. "Oh, Doris, thank God you're alive!"

"Jane is dead."

"No, don't say that."

"She is. She's dead." Doris raised stricken eyes to Laura. *"Jane is dead."*

"The ambulance is on the way. Everything will be all right."

"No. It's too late."

Doris was still shivering, rocking back and forth. Laura tore off her coat and draped it around her friend. She knelt down, trying to wipe some of the blood away. She didn't see any cuts, but when she looked again she saw that Doris's right ear had been split nearly in half. Blood poured from the wound, and from another, smaller wound beneath her nose. Laura found one of Doris's gloves, folding it into a makeshift bandage. "Take this," she said, "you can use it to help stop the bleeding."

"Is the ambulance here?"

"Soon."

Laura rose. It was a freezing night, and she hugged her arms around herself as she walked a few steps back to the De Soto. "Jane?" she called, moving unsteadily toward the driver's side of the car. She was about to open the door when she heard the high-pitched wail of a siren. "Thank God!" she cried. "Thank God!"

Two ambulances and a police car arrived within seconds of each other. The young hospital intern went first to the smashed blue sedan, but he emerged only a few moments later and shook his head no.. He saw Doris sitting on the curb and he went to her next. Working quickly, he checked the pupils of her eyes, checked her breathing, checked for broken bones. When he finished, he dusted a white powder on her wounds and applied two huge bandages. "You'll have to go to the hospital for x-rays," he said quietly. "There may be concussion."

"Jane is dead," she murmured in reply.

The intern assumed that Jane was the other driver; almost certainly dead, he thought. He threw his bag into the De Soto and climbed in after it. He raised his flashlight. Strange, there wasn't a mark on her.

Laura saw the pale gleam of the flashlight. She started forward, but a policeman stopped her. "Sorry, miss. You'll have to wait here till the doc is finished."

It wasn't a long wait. The flashlight switched off and the intern climbed out of the De Soto. He walked slowly to Laura; this was the part of his job he hated most.

She saw the expression on his face and she knew what he was going to say. "Dear God," she murmured as tears glittered in her eyes. "Jane."

"I'm very sorry. I think your friend probably died instantly. There wasn't any pain, if that helps."

"I guess it helps a little," she sniffled.

"I'd better have a look at you now. You have some nasty bruises. And those lacerations ought to be treated."

"Is Doris all right?"

He glanced over at the small figure still huddled on the curb. He nodded. "I'm sure she'll be fine. I'm taking her to the hospital for tests . . . I'd really better have a look at you now."

Laura shook her head and turned away, walking back to Doris. "I'll go to the hospital with you," she said. "You'll be fine."

"What are they doing to Jane?"

"What?" Laura looked up. She saw two orderlies removing Jane's body onto a stretcher. She saw them draw a blanket over her face. "They're taking her to . . . to the morgue."

Doris had risen and now she clung to Laura's arm. "This is so awful. How can Jane be dead?"

Laura had no answer. She stood with Doris, tears rolling down both their faces as the stretcher was placed in the ambulance. All at once they looked at each other, struck by the same idea. "Doctor," called Laura, "we're going to ride in the ambulance with Jane."

"I'm sorry, but you can't do—"

"Yes, we can."

"But—"

"We're going with her." Doris and Laura made their halting way to the ambulance. "You have to let us go with her," said Laura to the young intern. "We used to be the Three Musketeers."

"It was a nice funeral," said Margaret, settling into the chair beside Laura's hospital bed. "A very nice funeral." Afternoon sun was streaming through the windows. She turned her chair slightly and glanced around. The room was meant for two patients, but the second bed was still unoccupied. There were lots of flowers, lots of cards. A huge bottle of Chanel N° 5 — a gift from Ronnie Woronow — sat atop the bureau. "There were about eighty people. That fellow from Hollywood was there too. At least Bea said he was. I wouldn't know a Hollywood director if I fell over him."

"Where's Molly?"

"At school. You told me to take her to school after the funeral and that's what I did."

"How was she? Upset? I don't know if I did the right thing, letting her go to the services."

"Of course you did the right thing. Molly's not a baby anymore. And she's not upset. She's sad about Jane, but there's nothing wrong with that. You can't protect her from all the sadness in the world. She has to learn what the world is like."

Laura tossed restlessly beneath the covers. "I should have been at the funeral."

"It's not your fault you couldn't go. The doctor said you had to stay here a couple of more days and the doctor knows best." Margaret shrugged. "It's too late to do anything for Jane, so you might as well do what's best for yourself."

"I'm fine."

"Fine? With a sprained shoulder, a black eye, and an infected hand? Not to mention that you were suffering from exposure. If the doctor hadn't kept you here, you'd have pneumonia by now. And all because Jane was larking around."

"I don't want to talk about it, Aunt Margaret." Laura sat up, impatiently smoothing the blanket. "I'm all talked out." She'd had to describe the accident many times — to police, to Jane's husband Ted, to Doris's husband Bill, to Margaret, to a second team of police who'd arrived at the hospital just as Doris was being taken into surgery. There had been so many questions, often the same questions asked over and over again until she'd wanted to scream. She hadn't been able to explain Jane's reckless behavior, not even to herself. Whatever the reason, a terrible price had been paid. "Have you seen Doris today?"

"Not yet." Margaret looked at her watch. "Her sisters are probably up there now; I'll go up a little later . . . I saw the doctor, though, and you can put your mind at ease. He said Doris will have some bad scars around the ear, but otherwise she'll be good as new. She'll be released next week."

"When will I be released?"

"Two more days," replied Margaret, holding up two fingers. "You'll be home by the weekend. Two more days won't hurt you."

"I miss Molly."

"Yes, and she misses you, but first things first." Margaret's pale blue eyes fastened on Laura. "Besides missing Molly and worrying about Doris, what kind of mood are you in?"

"What?"

"Are you in a good mood? A bad mood? I can't tell."

She's up to something, thought Laura, studying her aunt. Margaret was past sixty, but she looked much the way she had always looked. Her face was still a collection of sharp planes and angles; she was still thin, still bustling with energy. There was more gray in her blond hair now, but she hadn't changed the style in forty years. Wilbur Hobart would have had no trouble recognizing his former fiancée.

"What are you staring at, missy? What's the matter with you?"

"I know you're ready to spring something on me. Something I probably won't like."

"You won't if you're going to be stubborn, but if you'd keep an open mind on the subject—"

"Stop right there," interrupted Laura. "Whenever you talk about keeping an open mind, you're really talking about Eliza. Did you have her come from Philadelphia to pay a sick call? I'm not interested."

"Eliza came to New York for the funeral, and now she's come to see you."

"I'm not interested."

Margaret rose. "Stubborn as a mule," she sighed, walking to the door. "You must have inherited that from your mother's side of the family." She opened the door, waving Eliza into the room. "I'm going upstairs to see poor Doris," she explained to her black-clad niece. "I wish you luck with this one!"

"Will I need luck?" asked Eliza, gliding to the bed. "I hope not."

Laura glanced up. Eliza was perhaps a few pounds heavier, but she was as beautiful as ever. And as beautifully dressed: the chic black suit was a Dior. "Thank you for the flowers," said Laura. "It was nice of you to come, but I want you to leave."

"I just got here."

"We have nothing to say to one another. There's no

reason for you to be here."

"You were very nearly killed, Laura. Isn't that a reason?"

"No." She reached back, rearranging the pillows. "It's a bit late for sisterly concern."

"I met Molly after the funeral. She's a lovely girl. So pretty."

"Yes." Laura's expression softened, but only for a moment. "I want you to leave," she said, meeting Eliza's violet gaze. "Can't you see there's no point in this?"

"I see you haven't changed. I thought you might have, after the accident. After an experience like that, I thought you might have a different view of things. I was wrong." Eliza turned and glided to the door. She paused there, looking back at her sister. "It's a shame, Laura. Life can end so suddenly. We never know, do we?"

Eliza disappeared into the hall. Laura collapsed against the pillows, exhaling a great breath. She hadn't needed Eliza to remind her of how suddenly life could be snatched away. She would never forget the last terrifying moments in the De Soto, the desperate screams. She had believed she was going to die—she *could* have died, and then what would have happened to Molly?

The question haunted her. If she were to die—next week or next month or next year—Molly would be an orphan. There was Margaret, but Margaret was getting old. There were Paul's parents, but they were also getting old. There were Eliza and Robby, but she couldn't bear to think of them raising her little girl.

Laura sat up straighter, reaching to the night stand for her yellow notepad. She tapped her pencil on the pad, thinking of the things she had to do. She had to make out a will naming Doris and Bill Gibson as Molly's guardians. She had to buy more insurance. She had to start putting money into a trust for Molly's future.

She thought about the future and a faint smile touched her lips. The future was bound to be better than the past—the world was peaceful; the economy was surging ahead; the scent of money was in the air again. Her smile grew wider as she drew a giant dollar sign on her pad. The future was going to bring her a lot of money. Madame Zarela had said so.

Chapter Twenty

Eli Harding was seated at the head of the conference table, Zack on his right, Laura on his left. He smiled at her and then glanced around at all the faces turned in his direction. He counted fourteen people in the room, fourteen uneasy people. He had called this meeting, and the rumor was that he planned to announce his retirement. "I won't keep you in suspense," he began. "I have some announcements, perhaps not the ones you were expecting."

His hands shook slightly as he opened a file folder. He started to thumb through it, stopped, put on his glasses, and started again. After another moment or two, he found the page he wanted. "Each decade has its own challenges," he continued. "In the Thirties there was the Depression; in the Forties there was the war. Now it's 1950 and I believe this decade will be one of extraordinary progress. I've seen the beginning of it with the introduction of television. I don't know how much I'll see—I'm an old man after all—but I know this agency must progress in new directions."

Eli paused to have a sip of water. Anne Marsh watched, shifting about in her chair. She thought: That's Eli all over; he promises not to keep us in suspense, then he rambles on and on and on. Will he *ever* get to the point?

"We must find new markets," he declared. "And that is why I have decided to open an overseas division of Harding Advertising. Zack is going to London next week to get the ball rolling."

Zack was the only one who had known in advance about Eli's announcement. He saw all the surprised faces and he laughed. "Not what you were expecting, eh?"

"No," replied Laura. "We had no idea."

"There's more. Eli?"

"Indeed. The second part of the announcement is that Laura will serve as creative director while Zack is away. She'll have complete authority. The last word, so to speak."

He glanced around the table again. Laura had obviously been startled by the turn of events; he saw both surprise and elation in the hazel depths of her eyes. Anne Marsh had been startled also; she was wearing a tight, chilly smile. Everyone else appeared to be pleased. He nodded, looking down at his folder. For an instant he couldn't make any sense of his notes—it was as if his mind had flickered off. Yes, I'm an old man, he thought to himself. "I . . . have another announcement."

Fourteen pairs of eyes shifted back in his direction. He smiled, enjoying all the attention. "As most of you know, we never made a fuss about titles here at Harding. I favored a rather informal structure, and as a matter of fact I still do. Too much structure interferes with creativity . . . But we've grown quite large since the war, and *some* structure is essential. And so we come to the matter of titles."

Laura glanced quickly at Martin; he shrugged. She looked at Zack. "Titles?" she whispered.

"This is the first I've heard about it."

Eli lifted a silver pitcher and refilled his water glass. He took a long sip and put the glass down. "I see many new faces at this table. I know we'll all benefit from the fresh perspectives and ideas you bring with you. At the same time, I know the value of experience. Zack and Martin and Anne and Laura are the lifeblood of Harding Advertising. They're our veterans, the last of the group that worked so hard to keep the agency afloat during the Depression."

"I'm sure we all appreciate the compliment," said Anne Marsh. "Thank you, Eli."

He rearranged his glasses on his nose and continued. "I'm happy to announce the promotion of Martin and Anne to vice president; the promotion of Laura to vice president and associate creative director; the promotion of Zack to senior vice president and creative director." He removed his glasses, folding them into their leather case. "Congratulations," he added with a smile.

One of the young copywriters started to applaud. The others joined in, and all at once tears sprang to Laura's eyes. She had been stunned by the announcement. Vice president. Vice president *and* associate creative director. Was she dreaming?

She repeated the question to Martin, who laughed and wrote something on a white index card. She took the card, frowning at it. "$5000 a year more?"

'That's the raise that'll come with the promotion. The minimum raise. You may do even better . . . This may be your decade, Laura. I have a feeling you're going places."

She laughed, blinking tears away. Impulsively, she leaned over to Eli and kissed his cheek. "I don't know how to thank you. I'm . . . I'm so grateful."

"Nothing to be grateful about. You earned it. We've all come such a long way." Such a very long way, he thought, suddenly feeling his years. He wasn't ready to retire, to let go, but he was ready to step back. Zack and Laura would be given far more responsibility and far more authority. Soon enough they would be running the show.

"If there's nothing else," said Anne Marsh, rising, "I have work to do."

Eli heard the angry edge in her voice. Well, he couldn't blame her, not really. She had been promoted to vice president, but Laura had been promoted a notch higher than that. He wondered if perhaps he had been unfair. He shook his head; business was business. "There's nothing else," he replied.

Anne left the room without another word. The meeting broke up, each of the younger employees stopping on their way out to congratulate Zack and Laura and Martin. There were many smiles, many kind words. Laughter rose in a kind of arc; a nice sound, thought Eli.

It was a glittering February day, and he decided he would walk to his club for lunch. An ice-cold martini, or maybe two. Some good conversation. And then the Dover sole. He wouldn't have to rush; he had vice presidents now.

Laura decided she could afford to redecorate her apartment. She studied color swatches and wandered through furniture stores and clipped pictures from magazines. She talked to decorators. One of them suggested French Provincial; another suggested the paler woods and simpler lines of Scandanavian Modern, a style just beginning to emerge. She listened to all the suggestions, but in the end she made her own choices.

Cream, apricot, bottle-green; those were the colors she wanted. She chose a comfortably elegant

English country look: chintz sofas and chairs, a few antique pieces here and there, a good though faded antique carpet, bowls of fresh flowers, a bit of clutter. She'd always liked a bit of clutter.

Work began in August, and for the next five months the apartment was in chaos. There was an unending parade of workmen—painters, paperhangers, carpenters. The floors had to be sanded and stained and polished. The window moldings had to be scraped. The fireplace hearth had to be retiled. Deliveries arrived at all hours, and never when they were expected. Twice, the wrong furniture was delivered and had to be taken back. After a wait of three months, the new curtains finally arrived and were too long; they had to be returned also.

Laura was determined to have the apartment ready in time for Molly's birthday party, and she succeeded. The very last deliveries—a side table and two footstools—arrived at noon that Saturday; an hour later, the party guests began streaming through the door. There were fifty guests in all, most of them Molly's friends from school. This year there were almost equal numbers of boys and girls—proof, if proof was needed, that Molly was growing up.

She was thirteen, a pretty girl with huge blue eyes beneath a fringe of golden bangs. She was tall for her age, and a little self-conscious about it. Sometimes she felt clumsy, as if she were all arms and legs. "Stork legs"—that's what Tommy Spenser called her. He was always teasing, but she tried not to mind too much; she knew boys only teased girls they liked.

Tommy was the reason she'd spent hours getting ready for her party. She'd wanted to look just right, wanted to show him that she was as grown up as he was, even though he was fourteen. She'd lost her campaign to wear lipstick, but she was wearing her first pair of nylon stockings and her first pair of heels. Laura had helped her practice walking in them until she felt confident. Her mother had really been okay about things, Molly thought; most things anyway.

Things such as dancing; Laura had agreed to roll back the new living room carpet for dancing. And things such as food; she had agreed to serve the party food Molly requested: hot dogs on buns, French fries, potato chips, Cokes. Laura knew it was a menu of Tommy Spenser's favorite foods, and so she'd overruled Margaret, who'd wanted to serve sandwiches and punch. She'd ordered a hundred hot dogs from Mr. Schultz's butcher shop, but after considering the appetites of teenage boys, she ordered a hundred more.

Now Laura carried a large platter of hot dogs and buns into the dining room. The table had been covered with an oil cloth, and over it, a cloth of starched white linen. There were stacks of paper plates, stacks of paper napkins, and half a dozen kitchen towels for wiping up spills. She smiled when she saw the coasters Margaret had set out; teenagers using coasters?

She put the platter down and went to the kitchen for another, putting it beside the first. A large bowl of French fries was already on the table. There were bowls of potato chips, bottles of ketchup and mustard and relish. Cokes were cooling in a big tub of ice. "That's everything," she murmured to herself, sliding open the dining room doors.

The music seemed to rush at her, music mixed with laughter and the quickness of young voices. She took a step back, smiling at the scene. Some of Molly's friends were dancing, some were clustered around the new television set, some were digging into bowls of peanuts and pretzels, but they all looked like they were having a good time. "Food," she called, shouting to be heard. "In the dining room," she added with a wide sweep of her arm. "First come, first served!"

It wasn't exactly a stampede, but at least a dozen boys charged past her, racing to the table. She watched them loading their plates and she was glad she'd ordered the extra hot dogs.

"Mother?"

Not too long ago she had been Mommy; now she was Mother. She turned, reaching her hand to Molly's cheek. "Are you enjoying your party, darling?"

"Oh yes, but . . . but you don't have to help anymore. I mean, I can help with the food and stuff. You don't have to."

"You'd like me to make myself scarce. Is that it?"

A smile crept along the edges of Molly's mouth. She nodded and her bangs flopped up and down. "For a while," she said.

"All right, I'll be in the kitchen."

"Aunt Margaret too?"

"I'll keep her with me. There's lots more food, by the way." Laura glanced at the young people crowded around the table. "You're going to need it."

Molly hurried off, throwing a bright smile over her shoulder as she slipped into the crowd. She managed to slip in next to Tommy, and now she was helping him fill his plate.

Laura started toward the kitchen, pausing on the threshold to glance back at her daughter. Suddenly she felt as if Molly's childhood were passing before her eyes. She saw the curious infant who'd loved to stare out between the slats of her crib, the giggly four-year-old who'd loved bedtime stories, the determined six-year-old who'd dressed all her dolls for church. She saw Molly at ten, excited about her riding lessons in Central Park, and at twelve, excited about her first dance. She saw Molly now, bewitched by her first crush. Laura watched a moment longer, then turned and went into the kitchen.

"What's the matter?" asked Margaret, looking up from the stove.

"My little girl's not a little girl anymore. Soon she'll be grown and gone."

"It's about time you finally figured that out." Margaret gave the frying pan a quick shake and returned it to the burner. "Keep an eye on these potatoes," she said to Eileen, the young Irishwoman Laura had hired to help with the chores. "They're almost done."

"Aye, mum, I will."

Margaret wiped her hands on her apron. "Molly will be grown and gone," she said, sitting down at the table, "and you'll be all alone. That's what I've been trying to tell you. Of course you never listen to me."

"I won't be alone. Not with you and Eileen around. And him," she laughed, pointing to the cat sitting atop the breadbox. He was the other new addition to the household, a small black and white cat named Oreo. "I'll be fine."

"Oh yes, that's a fine life for you. Fine companion too—an old woman, a young Irisher, and a cat."

"I do have friends, Aunt Margaret."

"Friends aren't enough. You ought to have a man in your life. Someone like Ronnie Woronow. He's a nice, dependable kind of fella, even if he is divorced. I'm not saying I approve of divorce, mind you, but there are always two sides to the story . . . The important thing is you should be going out and having a good time."

Laura had had several dates recently, dinner and theater dates with men she'd met through business. She'd enjoyed herself, but she'd declined to see any of the men more than twice. She was afraid of getting into something complicated or involved, something that might entangle her emotions, and that was why she kept Ronnie at a safe distance. She was fond of him, but that was all.

"Did you hear what I said?" asked Margaret.

"Yes. I wish you'd stop fussing. I'm perfectly happy."

"Are you?"

Laura watched the cat leap off the breadbox and streak across the floor. That's the way to live, she thought to herself—come and go as you please, no apologies and no explanations.

"Are you really happy?" persisted Margaret. "Sometimes I wonder."

Sometimes Laura wondered also. She had a charming daughter, good friends, a good job, money in the bank, and a newly redecorated apartment. She should be happy, yet she wasn't. Something was missing. Not love, she decided, because she was through with love. But something.

Oreo jumped up on the counter and meowed at her. She bent over, looking into his unblinking green eyes. "Life's a puzzle, isn't it?" she said. "A puzzle."

"What's taking so long?" asked Claude Gower, checking his watch. "I'll never understand the television business."

Laura went to the front of the sponsor's booth and stared down at the chaotic studio. People were rushing around, stepping over cables and trying not to bump into the television cameras. Furniture was being moved on to the set. A huge bank of lights was flashing on and off. A disembodied voice shouted orders, but no one was paying attention. It was 5 P.M.; the dress rehearsal of tonight's play had been scheduled to start at three.

She sighed and turned away. "I'm sorry, Claude. They don't seem even close to starting."

"But they go on the *air* in a few hours. Do they know what time it is?"

"Don't worry. It's always bedlam before a show. You mustn't take it too seriously."

"This is our premier show, Laura. I take it very seriously indeed. I want everything to be right."

She nodded. This was BCP's first venture into television—a weekly drama series called "Bystrum Presents." It had been her idea, and in some ways an uphill battle. Like many of Harding's clients, Claude was still more comfortable with radio. "I promise you everything will be fine," she said. "I did warn you about rehearsals, you know. Once the show actually begins, you'll feel much better."

"*If* it actually begins."

"Eve," said Laura, turning toward the back of the booth, "why don't you go down to the set and see if there are any last-minute problems? Talk to Jerry Falk . . . And tell him the sponsor's here."

"Does anyone care?" asked Claude when Eve had gone. "Does anyone care about the sponsor?"

"The network cares. There'll be a bunch of network executives here later to watch the show with you. To make sure you're happy." Laura sat down, her gaze moving idly about. The front of the booth was glassed-in. To the left was a portable bar and a tiny refrigerator; to the right were several telephones. There were six rows of seats—comfortable seats, the kind usually found in the theaters. The carpet was dark green; the color of money, she thought. "That's why these booths have all the amenities. *Two* television sets," she laughed. "One for each eye!"

"Big, ugly boxes. That's all they are."

"Television is going to change the world, Claude."

"Change it? How?"

"I'm not sure, but I know it's going to be a powerful influence. Much more powerful than radio."

Claude checked his watch again. He took a cigar case from his jacket pocket. "Do you mind, Laura?"

"No, go ahead." She looked down at her yellow pad, scanning her notes. "While we have the time, can we talk about the new Aunt Martha campaigns for England and France?"

"I'm willing to approve the preliminary layouts. But not the budget. It's too high."

"Well, it's a saturation budget. Zack and I feel that we should cover all the bases with this new campaign. Pull out all the stops."

Claude drew on his cigar. "I don't know. I don't like to get psychological about things, but I think people overseas resent splashy American-style ad campaigns. Especially now. They're still recovering from the war over there. It's an entirely different perspective. Though apparently not for Zack. How long has he been in London anyway?"

"Off and on, about two years." Zack had first gone to London in the spring of 1950. He'd returned in autumn, and then gone back again in 1951 and early in 1952. He was in London now, and Laura knew this stay would be permanent. He was running Harding Advertising Ltd.; he was happy. "The announcement won't be made until next month, but Zack's decided to stay in London. He's moving his family there, bag and baggage."

"I see."

"He's very excited about it."

"I suppose he plans to Americanize the British ad business."

Laura smiled. "Well, you know Zack."

"Yes, I do. I'm convinced he's a superb adman, but I'm *not* convinced his American-style approaches will work overseas." Claude studied the glowing tip of his cigar. After a moment his gaze fastened on Laura. "I want you to go to London. Take a good look at the situation. If you still agree with Zack, I'll reconsider the budget . . . I assume you can clear the time."

"For London? I certainly can." She had been longing to get away. She felt she needed a change of scenery, a break from the pressures of her life in New York. Last year she had almost asked Eli to put her in charge of the London office. She'd been sorely tempted, but she abandoned the idea when she thought about uprooting Molly and Margaret. A business trip — perhaps two or three weeks — wouldn't uproot anybody, wouldn't upset anybody. A business trip to London; she would clear the time or die trying. "I don't have my calendar with me, Claude, but I'm sure I can go in October."

"Work out the details and let me know."

"Yes, I will. I'll talk to Eli as soon as I get back to the office. Martin can take over for me while I'm gone. There won't be any problem." She laughed and her eyes twinkled. "I won't allow any problems! I've never been to Europe, you know. This is my big chance."

Laura wanted to be sure nothing would happen to delay her trip. She tried to plan ahead, to anticipate the small and large troubles that might arise. She checked her files; she double-checked production schedules; she went to so many meetings she lost count. With only a week left before her departure, she had begun working almost around the clock, tying up all the loose ends she could find.

One of the loose ends was a public service ad the agency had volunteered to create for the Red Cross. The ad was to be an appeal for blood donations—an appeal made more urgent by the Korean War. Laura understood the urgency. She'd been struggling with the ad for days, but to no avail. "Something's wrong with my brain," she sighed, tossing some sketches on her desk. "I just can't figure out the way to do this. I can't get a handle on it."

"There's time," replied Ronnie Woronow.

"Not much. If we don't get it done by tonight, I'll have to work all weekend. I wanted the weekend for myself . . . There are a million things to do before my trip."

"Give the ad to someone else, Laura. Or leave it for Martin; he'll be back on Monday."

She shook her head. "I said I'd do it and I will. God knows it's not complicated. It *shouldn't* be complicated. Blood and soldiers; that's the idea, isn't it? Not very complicated." She picked up one of the sketches and threw it down again. "God, I hate war! Why does there always have to be another war?"

"I'm beginning to see the problem here." Ronnie smiled. He'd just recently celebrated his forty-third birthday and he looked a bit younger than that. His light brown hair was still combed straight back, though he wore it a little shorter now. His light brown eyes were exceedingly gentle. After a marriage, three children, and a divorce, he still had a crush on Laura.

He left his chair and went to stand behind her. "The problem is you're thinking of this as an ad about war. It's not. It's about saving lives, soldiers' lives."

"Their lives wouldn't *need* saving if it weren't for the war." She thought of it as the war of the hills. There was Porkchop Hill and Christmas Hill and Dagmar, the latter named after a curvaceous American television personality. There were hills named simply by number, endless hills that were taken and then lost and then retaken in bloody battles. "Two years of bloody battles," she said, "and no end in sight."

"That's why the Red Cross needs help."

"I know, Ronnie. But every time I think about our soldiers dying over there . . ." Laura paused, glancing once more at the sketches. "These are all wrong. We ought to have a drawing of soldiers — not a recruitment poster kind of drawing, though. Something realistic."

"A drawing of soldiers in combat, but looking the way they really look: tired, muddy, angry, scared. Wondering if this is going to be their last moment on earth."

"Right," agreed Laura, making notes on her yellow pad. "And the copy will read 'Give blood . . . Do it for Our Soldiers in —'" She frowned. "No," she said, crossing out the words. "The copy will read 'Give blood . . . Do it for Our Boys in Korea.'"

"Bingo! That's the ad."

Laura swept the rejected sketches into her wastebasket. "Let's print up some posters, too."

"Fine. I'll put Craig Mayer on the art. He's our man for gritty reality. This is perfect for him." Ronnie tore Laura's notes from the pad and tucked them in his pocket. "How about dinner to seal the deal?"

"I'd love to, but —"

His sudden laugh interrupted her reply. "I'm going to start cataloging your excuses," he said. "Why don't you just tell me to go peddle my papers?"

She blushed. "It's not like that, Ronnie. It's . . . Well, we work together and that complicates matters. Besides, I sometimes get the feeling you're thinking romance while I'm thinking friendship." Her blush deepened. She looked away, then looked back at him. "Maybe I'm presuming, but that's how it seemed to me."

"A guy can hope, can't he?"

"You're too nice to waste your time that way. You're too eligible."

"I'm old enough to decide how to spend my time, Laura. Now how about dinner? I promise I won't give you an engagement ring."

She laughed. "Okay, but a quick dinner. I want to get home to Molly. With her busy schedule, I won't see much of her over the weekend. And then I'll be gone for three weeks."

"Aren't you taking her to London?"

"No, I can't keep her out of school that long." Laura smiled. "Which is a lucky thing, since she's hoping a certain Peter Dennison will ask her to the Halloween dance."

"Young love."

"Very young love." She gathered her files together and stacked them atop her desk. "Eve's going with me, so at least I'll have someone to talk to on the plane." She looked at her watch. "It's nearly seven, Ronnie."

"Yes, I'll just get my coat."

He left the office. She rose and went to the closet, taking her purse from a shelf. She pulled out her compact and powdered her nose. When she turned, she saw Anne Marsh standing in the doorway. "I guess we're all working late tonight."

"I guess," drawled Anne. She was wearing an exquisitely cut gold suit and matching cape. Her hat was a small gold pillbox; her black leather gloves were clasped in her beautiful hands. "Zack won't like you meddling in his work. He won't like it one little bit."

"I have no plans to meddle. That's not why I'm going to London." Laura applied a new coat of lipstick, blotted it, and dropped the plastic case into her purse. "Meddling is more your style than mine," she added with a tart smile.

"Is that what you think?"

"That's what I know . . . I've never forgotten that you went to Zack to tell him I was pregnant. Trying to get me fired, even though I was no threat to you." Laura shook her head. "There was enough work for both of us, Anne. There were enough clients to go around. But you still tried to get me fired. And kept trying, in your own quiet, sneaky way. I never understood why."

"I didn't need any little Miss Nobody girls around here. That's what you were, a little Miss Nobody. An upstart . . . I was the star of Harding Advertising until you came along. The brightest star. I'd *own* Harding by now if you hadn't got your hooks into Eli. As far as he's concerned, you're some kind of advertising wizard. Well, as far as I'm concerned, underneath the expensive clothes you're still Miss Nobody."

Laura raised a tawny brow. "I'm also the creative director of this agency. Technically, that makes me your boss."

"Not for long."

"Oh?"

Anne smiled. "We all know Eli's going to retire next year. The word's out. He'll be selling the agency and I'll be buying. And when I do, you'll be the first to go. Maybe you ought to go now, while the offers are still coming in."

"There won't be any shortage of offers," replied Laura. "Because if I go, I'll take BPC with me. BPC and half a dozen other clients. Not to mention half the staff." She put on her coat, slowly buttoning the buttons as she regarded Anne Marsh. "I'll be in London for a few weeks, perhaps longer. You'll have plenty of time to maneuver. But when I get back, I may just do some maneuvering of my own. I'd keep that in mind if I were you." She saw Anne's indignant expression and she laughed. "You're right, Eli *is* retiring next year. Everything *is* going to change . . . But here's a piece of free advice—be careful what you wish for."

Chapter Twenty-one

"Welcome to London," said Zack, coming around the side of his desk to greet Laura. "You look marvelous. I thought you'd be tired after the long flight."

"I slept most of the way," she explained with a sheepish smile. "I was a little nervous about flying and so I took a tranquilizer. The next thing I knew, the pilot was telling us to fasten our seat belts. Poor Eve tried to wake me but it was no use."

"How is she?"

"Fine. She'll be here later. Right now she's at the hotel, getting all the luggage straightened out. We have a ton of luggage." Laura settled herself in the chair Zack offered. She smoothed the skirt of her red wool dress, her gaze moving across the office. It was a fairly large office, and bright with morning sun. The furnishings were simple: a leather couch, a small glass table, several chairs, some bookshelves, a bookcase, a handsome oak cabinet. Layouts were arranged in stacks atop a square oak table at the other side of the room. There were more layouts on Zack's desk; just behind the desk were two windows, wide open on this brisk October Monday. "I see you haven't changed," she said. "Still a fresh air fiend. And the colder the better."

"That's one of the things I like about England.

There's really no central heating to speak of." He sat down and lit a cigarette, tossing the match into an ashtray. "I know Claude's concerned about the budget. Do you want to go over it now, or do you want to wait?"

"First I want to get the feel of things over here. Claude's not concerned about the budget per se; he just has a few doubts about our approach. He thinks it's too American, too much of a hard-sell."

"Our hard sell approach has worked brilliantly for BPC."

Laura nodded. "Yes. But he's not convinced that the same approach will work here. BPC's advertising in Britain has always been rather restrained."

"It's your job to convince him."

"After I convince myself. He may have a point, Zack. I don't know, and that's why I want to get the feel of things. I want to see the way products are sold in this country."

"Methods don't change much from country to country. We've just added some zip, that's all. In advertising, it's better to overstate than understate." Zack dragged on his cigarette, exhaling a wavy stream of gray smoke. "Why the sudden jitters, Laura? If Claude wants to keep doing British-style ads, why didn't he stay with his British agency? Ashton is small but damned good. It was Nick Ashton who dreamed up Captain Birley, the guy who's in all the Birley's Gin ads." Zack laughed. "Half the women in England are in love with Captain Birley, my wife included . . . So why did Claude leave Ashton? I assumed it was because he wanted less restraint and more rock 'em, sock 'em."

A smile traced Laura's mouth. "He's just a little nervous, Zack. He was nervous about the new look we gave Aunt Martha, and now he's nervous about introducing it in Europe. We'll have to reassure him before we can start rocking and socking."

Zack stubbed out his cigarette. "Yes, I suppose you're right. What do you need from me? I can show you some of our campaigns for other accounts—biscuits, cereal, toffee, crisps; take your choice."

"I'll be glad to look at them all, but not today."

"Well, whenever you're ready. I've had an office set aside for you . . . Are you going back to your hotel for a nap?"

"A nap! Do you think I'd waste my first day in London on a *nap?* No, I'm going to roam around for a while. I have a guidebook in my purse. I want to see everything. And I might as well get started," she added, rising to her feet. She gathered her things together and smiled at Zack. "If I get lost, I'll ask a bobby for help."

Zack left his desk again, walking with Laura to the door. His hand went to the knob, then fell away. "Good Lord, I almost forgot! We planned a small party for you this evening. A cocktail party; or a drinks party, as they say here. I wanted to give you time to get settled, but Helen said you ought to begin meeting people . . . You don't have any other plans, do you?"

"No, of course not. You and Helen are the only people I know in London."

"You'll know thirty more, after tonight. Come about six o'clock. Six, six-thirty."

"Can I bring Eve? She doesn't know anyone here either."

"Yes, bring her along. We're in Kensington. Do you have the address?" Laura nodded. "Good," he said, opening the door. "I'll walk you to the lift."

She smiled. "The lift? If you mean the elevator, I

can find my way. See you tonight, Zack. Sixish."

She said good-bye to his secretary, and then walked past a row of offices and into the corridor. A tiny white light blinked above one of the elevators. The doors opened and she stepped inside. She took her guidebook out of her purse, staring at the photograph of Big Ben on the cover. Quickly, she flipped through the pages, her smile growing wider as she wondered where to go first. Buckingham Palace, she decided. Maybe she would see the Queen.

A taxi took Laura to the gates of stately Buckingham Palace. She saw the flag, the Royal Standard flying from the masthead, and she knew that meant the Queen was in residence. Her eyes scanned the deep, handsome balconies, the scores of windows. There was no sign of the young Queen Elizabeth, nor of anyone else, but still Laura felt a surge of excitement. Even at this distance, she was closer to royalty than she had ever expected to get.

It was a splendid autumn day. Laura glanced up at the vast, cloudless blue sky and she started walking. She went to St. James's Park, one of five royal parks in the center of London. She saw ducks gliding on the lake; she saw willow trees and fountains and winding paths. She came upon a romantic footbridge, and for an instant she felt an odd yearning—a yearning to be dreamily, crazily in love. She laughed at herself and walked on.

Somehow Laura found her way to Piccadilly Circus, to the churning crowds and converging traffic and huge advertising signs that reminded her of Times Square. She wandered around, happily soaking up the atmosphere. She nearly wandered into the path of a red double-decker bus, but she heard the horn and she jumped back, no harm done.

She kept walking, changing direction at random. She strolled along Bond Street, gazing into the elegant shop windows. She found a pretty tearoom and went inside, ordering buttered scones and a pot of India tea. Afterward, she checked the map in her guidebook and strolled to Baker Street—the Baker Street of Sherlock Holmes and Dr. Watson and Professor Moriarty. She smiled. She was having a wonderful time.

The sky had begun to darken when she looked at her watch. Five o'clock; where had the day gone? She hailed a taxi, but there was rush-hour traffic in London also, and twenty minutes passed before she reached her hotel. She still hadn't quite figured out English money, and once again she offered a palmful of shillings, asking the driver to take what was right, plus a tip for himself. The transaction concluded, she raced into the hotel and upstairs to her room.

She allotted fifteen minutes to bathe, dress, put on her makeup, and do her hair. She rushed, but she took twice that long. It was six o'clock when she hurried down the hall to Eve's room. "We're late," she gasped as the door opened. "It's my fault."

"Take it easy," laughed Eve. "Zack's house isn't too far from here. We were leaving the office at the same time and we shared a cab. I just dropped him off a little while ago, Laura. It's not far."

"Oh, good. I hate being the last to arrive."

Eve ducked back inside her room to get her purse and coat, then stepped into the hall. "You look smashing. That's a British way of saying you look great. I learned it from Zack's secretary."

Laura was wearing a slender black silk cocktail dress, and a matching black silk coat lined in ivory satin. Pearls glowed at her ears and at her throat. Her tawny hair had been brushed into a French twist, à la Grace Kelly. "Do I really look all right?"

"Sexy, in a ladylike sort of way. Maybe you'll meet a lord."

A small romantic adventure with a lord, thought Laura to herself—an interlude. She laughed, dismissing the idea as quickly as it had come. "I never meet anybody interesting at parties."

"Maybe this will be your lucky night."

A maid in starched black and a lace cap opened the door of Zack's Kensington house. She smiled politely, stepping aside to let Eve and Laura enter. "Please follow me," she said, leading them through the reception hall to a graceful staircase. "This way."

Laura heard the sound of voices as she started up the stairs. She heard a stream of well-bred laughter and she glanced at Eve. "The party's already begun."

"We're not late. It's exactly six-thirty."

They reached the landing and turned right, walking through the wide double doors of the drawing room. Zack's wife, Helen, an attractive, exuberant woman of fifty, broke off her conversation and hurried over to greet them. "Laura," she said, holding out her hands, "it's terrific to see you. Welcome to London. And you too, Eve. Goodness gracious, it's been years!"

"The Christmas party three years ago."

"That's right. You still have your amazing memory. Mine gets worse every day."

"So does mine," said Laura.

Helen laughed. "Oh, I doubt it. My dear, I wish I could be your age again. If I were your age and had your looks . . ." She shrugged good-naturedly, taking Laura's arm. "Come, I'll introduce you to everyone."

"Eve?"

"You go ahead. I want a drink before I start mingling."

There were about two dozen people in the elegant gold and green drawing room, almost all of them British, and many of them in their thirties and forties. They were a prosperous-looking group, and friendlier than Laura had expected. A few of the women were in advertising; a few were wives; a few were cheerfully idle and cheerfully rich. Among the men, there were editors, brokers, solicitors, advertising directors, a Scotland Yard superintendent, and a Sir Peter Wembly, a baronet.

Laura chatted with them all; after her second drink, she flirted a little with both Sir Peter and Superintendent Steed. It was fun and it was exciting, as if she were a character in a movie; as if she were the star.

She began to feel a bit giddy and she slipped into the hall to clear her head. Voices drifted out of the drawing room. She listened for a moment, and then crossed the hall to the library. The door was open; a light was burning. She went inside. "How wonderful," she murmured softly, glancing around.

Bookcases covered three of the walls from floor to ceiling. Framed pen and ink sketches of Victorian London were arrayed on the other wall, directly above a glowing antique library table. There was a leather sofa, a knitted afghan folded over the arm. Near the marble fireplace were two cozy wing chairs.

Laura turned, peering into a shadowy alcove at the far side of the room. She jumped when a man stepped out of the shadows, a handsome man with dark chestnut hair and china blue eyes. She stared at him and her heart fluttered. She stood very still, recalling Madame Zarela's prediction about a dark-haired man. A dark-haired man stepping out of the shadows. "Oh my," she said.

"Did I startle you? Sorry." He was tall and lean, with a quick, suggestive smile. Almost nothing in life surprised him and almost everything amused him. He was known, affectionately, as a lady-killer. "I'm Nick Ashton. And you must be Laura Brent . . . Otherwise known as Aunt Martha."

"Are you otherwise known as Captain Birley?"

"Ah, so you've heard about the captain, have you? One of my better ideas." His gaze moved over Laura and the blue of his eyes seemed to deepen. "You're not what I expected, you know. I thought you'd be rather fierce."

"Fierce?"

"I was all ready to do battle with you . . . But now I'll have to send you flowers instead."

A smile played at Laura's mouth. Her heart fluttered again, like a leaf caught in the wind. "Why would you send me flowers?"

"Because you're beautiful. Because you're smart. Because I intend to sweep you off your feet."

"You're too sure of yourself, Mr. Ashton."

"Nick."

"Nick, then. You're too sure of yourself."

"I trust my instincts."

"Are they ever wrong?"

His shoulders lifted slightly in a shrug. "I'm not wrong about you," he replied with a quick and dazzling smile. "At least I don't want to be. I think we'll do very well together."

Something in his smile, in the tone of his voice, made her blush. She tried to look away but she couldn't. Her heart was beating faster; her thoughts were skipping and sliding about, making no sense at all. A moment passed, another and another, and still he held her gaze. He. Nick Ashton. A dark-haired man stepping out of the shadows.

"I'd give quite a lot to know what you're thinking, Laura. Will you tell me?"

"Certainly not."

"In that case, have dinner with me. Let me ply you with wine and lamb chops."

Laura had no chance to answer, because Helen Reed had appeared suddenly in the doorway. "Oh, here you are," said Helen. "I couldn't imagine where you'd gone. Of course I should have known. Nick always makes off with the prettiest girl at every party."

"I haven't made off quite yet. Laura's still deciding about my dinner invitation."

Helen looked from Nick to Laura. "Sir Peter's going to ask you to dinner also."

"Really?" She smiled. "How nice."

Nick's dark brows rose a fraction. "Wembley? He'll bore you to death. He's a perfectly decent chap and all that, but he grows mushrooms at his place in Norfolk and he likes to *talk* about mushrooms. I warn you, Laura, your ears will be crumbling with boredom and he'll be only halfway through the life and times of fungi."

"Is that true, Helen?"

She laughed, shaking her head. "I ought to be impartial, but it's true you'll have more fun with Nick. Anyway, it's up to you. I'd better get back to my other guests . . . Behave yourself, Nicky," she added, sailing out of the room.

Laura turned, gazing into his eyes. "Do you need to be told to behave yourself?"

"Reminded, perhaps. But not often. I'm misunderstood, you see."

"Poor thing."

Another smile flashed across his face. "Yes, that's it exactly; I'm just a poor misunderstood lad trying to make my way in the world. Now what about dinner?"

A little voice was telling her to run while there was still time; to run as far and as fast as her legs would take her. Sensible advice, she thought, though all at once she had no interest in sensible advice.

"Dinner?" asked Nick again.

"Yes," she replied. "Why not?"

"Here's my car," said Nick, taking Laura around the side of a sporty red MG. He bent, opening the door. "In you go . . . Comfortable?"

"Yes, fine."

"Good." He closed the door and retraced his steps, folding himself into the driver's seat. He turned the key in the ignition and the car glided smoothly away from the curb. "What have you seen of London?"

"I only arrived this morning, Nick."

He liked the way she said his name, liked the sound of it on her lips. "Yes, I know, but what have you seen?"

"Well, Buckingham Palace," she began. She told him about her day, recounting her adventures. She kept taking little peeks at him, studying his handsome profile; she noticed how easily he smiled.

The night was clear, drenched in moonlight. Laura leaned her head back, savoring the cool, fresh breeze. Wisps of hair blew about her face. Her eyes seemed to glow. "It's only been one day, but so far it's been marvelous."

"We'll do the grand tour tomorrow."

"We will? *We?*"

"Yes, of course. You'll want to see the Tower of London; we'll start there, I think. And then—"

"Don't you work?"

Nick laughed. "Very hard. And all the harder, since you stole BPC away from us." He glanced at Laura. "It's all right, I forgive you," he said, returning his eyes to the road. "Life does have its little ups and downs."

She looked at him again, at his profile, at his strong hands gripping the wheel. "I'm going to ask a rude question: why aren't you married?"

"I was married a long time ago. My wife was killed in the Blitz."

"Oh, Nick, I'm so sorry."

"It was long ago." Twelve years, and for the first two of those years he had been nearly consumed by grief. He had carried his grief with him when he'd gone off to fight in the war. He'd been a fearless soldier, a dangerous soldier, because for a while he'd wanted to die himself. "We'd been married only a few months, Lucy and I. She was twenty-four. I was a few years older . . . She was visiting her aunt the night it happened. A bomb leveled the house."

"I'm sorry. It must have been awful for you."

Nick shifted gears and the MG picked up speed. "For you as well. Zack told me your husband was killed in the war."

"Yes, in the Pacific."

They glanced at one another, though they said

nothing. They had both lost people they'd loved and they had both grieved, but years had passed and now there were only memories — happy memories just a little blurry with time.

Laura looked up at the sky glittering with stars. After a moment she turned her head to Nick. "You didn't remarry."

"Perhaps I've been waiting for the right girl, as they say. Perhaps I've been waiting for you."

She laughed. "Oh, that would be a very long wait."

He turned the car into Piccadilly Circus. "The hub of the British Empire," he said, smiling. "It's more interesting at night."

She looked around at the crowds, the swirling traffic, the huge signs ablaze with light. "It's like Times Square, only not so . . . seedy. Times Square is sort of disreputable."

"I'm taking you somewhere disreputable. Or at least semidisreputable. Tomorrow we'll be very proper and go to Claridge's, but tonight we're going to a favorite restaurant of mine in Soho . . . Where are you staying, Laura? I don't think anyone said."

"The Connaught."

"Ah, I'm in the presence of another rich American."

"An American, yes, but on an expense account."

"Same thing, isn't it?" He glanced sidelong at Laura, his eyes dancing with amusement. "During the war and just after, there was a kind of saying about Americans: overpaid, oversexed, and over here. The Yanks always seemed to have money in their pockets. And chocolate bars," he added with a laugh. "Most of us hadn't seen chocolate in years. Or real eggs. Or oranges. I suppose there was a sense of Americans having everything so easy."

"Not everything, and not all Americans."

"No." He shifted gears again, steering the MG away from Piccadilly. "Here we are," he said several moments later. "Welcome to Soho."

Laura's first impression was of busy streets crowded with exotic shops and restaurants. She saw a window display of Chinese incense, another of Indian spices. She saw a Greek delicatessen, an Egyptian tobacco shop, a restaurant named Little Shanghai, and across the street, a restaurant named Little Algiers. "Very colorful," she said, smiling at Nick. "There's something for everyone, isn't there?"

"If one knows where to look." He drove a couple more blocks and then pulled smoothly into a parking space. "Are you hungry?"

"Starved."

He took her to Bistro Loup, a small, charming restaurant shining with candlelight. The decor was simple—a scrubbed wood floor, pale walls, blue and white cloths covering the tables, baskets of paper flowers, and bunches of candles in fluted white cups. The menu was written on a chalkboard at the rear of the room.

She studied the menu while Nick went to have a word with the restaurant's owner. There were delectable aromas coming from the kitchen; she tried to match them to the five or six dishes listed on the board. "What smells so good?" she asked when Nick returned.

"Well, of course there's your perfume." He sniffed the air. "And there's also chicken poached in wine."

"I'm going to have lots of that."

The owner, Marcel, took their coats and then led them to Nick's usual corner table. A bottle of wine arrived; it was opened, tasted, and poured. "Shall we have a toast?" asked Nick when both Marcel and the waiter had gone. "What do you think? A toast to us?"

"Us? Is there an us?"

"There could be." He lifted his glass, touching it to hers. "Let's drink to the possibilities."

Laura sipped her wine, staring at Nick over the rim of her glass. She watched a smile curl around his handsome mouth and her heart thumped. I'm acting like a silly schoolgirl, she thought, but she knew she couldn't help herself. There was something mesmerizing about this man.

The waiter took their order and withdrew to the kitchen. Nick leaned toward Laura. "It's time," he said solemnly.

Her eyes widened. "Time for what?"

"Time for what's known as 'getting acquainted.'" He laughed. "You know—the conversation about where we were at school and where do we live now and do we like our work?"

"Oh yes, *that* conversation. You first, Nick . . . I've been thinking you're a little young to have your own ad agency."

"It was my uncle's agency, as a matter of fact. There wasn't much to it in those days—it was really quite small and boring. But my uncle died shortly after I left Oxford, and I decided to have a go."

"Just like that?"

"Well, I had a job in the City. In finance. I'd been there a couple of months, long enough to know I was in the wrong line. I wasn't sure what to do about it, really. Then my uncle died and I decided to have a go at the advertising business. I borrowed a few thousand quid and plunged ahead."

"Obviously you have no regrets."

"No, not now," he replied. "Although there were some thin years at the start. We were swimming in debt. I can remember wondering what I'd got myself into. But we worked bloody hard and we took insane risks, and now we're fine." He lifted his glass, his eyes twinkling at Laura. "We're not Harding Advertising, but we're very good at what we do."

"Yes, Zack said you were good."

"A fact which makes it more annoying when you Americans come over here and steal all our clients."

She shrugged, mirroring his smile. "That's business."

"It is indeed. And turnabout is fair play. That's why I'm going to be opening offices on your side of the Atlantic." Nick drank off his wine and poured a little more. "The British are coming," he laughed. "We plan to make a better job of it this time."

Surprise was stamped on Laura's face. "You're opening an agency in New York? Zack didn't say a word about that."

"He doesn't know. There have been rumors, of course, but no official announcements. It's all right, though; I'm making the announcement next week . . . I expect we'll do well in New York. The Ashton Group may even give Harding Advertising a run for its money."

Business was the last thing on Laura's mind. She was thinking about Nick; if he had offices in New York, he would have to spend time in New York, and suddenly she realized she was glad. Too glad, she fretted, and once again she heard a little voice warning her to escape while there was still time.

"I won't be easy to get rid of," said Nick, as if reading her thoughts. "Assuming you wished to get rid of me." He brushed a wisp of hair from her brow. His hand lingered for an instant, and his expression seemed to change. He loved women, all women, but he felt drawn to Laura in a way he hadn't been drawn to any of the others. When he had first glimpsed her, he had imagined a lively evening, perhaps a lively week. Now he was imagining more than that, and he wasn't sure why. "Tell me about Laura Brent."

"Oh no, you haven't finished yet. There's your family."

"Ah, yes, my family. Dad was a barrister—that would be roughly like a trial attorney in the States."

"Yes, I know," said Laura. "I read Agatha Christie."

"As do I. As do we all . . . Anyway, Dad has retired himself to Kent and a rather large garden. My mother died years ago, but he has all the widowed ladies of the village fussing over him. He's having a grand time. Then there's my brother John; he's in publishing. He has a pretty wife and nice children and everybody is terribly fond of John. Last is my brother Nigel; he followed Dad into the law. He's stuffy; he has a stuffy wife and stuffy children. Nobody likes Nigel." He smiled. "That's the lot," he said with a shrug of a well-tailored shoulder. "Now it's your turn."

She was temporarily spared her turn when Marcel came to the table. "It is done, monsieur," he said, bowing slightly. "Just as you ask."

"That's very clever of you. Thank you very much."

He bowed again and left the table.

Laura watched, frowning. "What was that all about? It sounded sinister."

Nick laughed. "Nothing of the sort. It's a surprise, actually. Something I thought you would like."

"A surprise for me?"

"Patience, old chap."

The waiter brought their first course, a thick onion soup bubbling with cheese and bits of crusty bread. Laura's mouth was watering. She thrust her spoon into the bowl. "Delicious," she said.

"Yes, but I still want to hear about Laura Brent."

"I don't know where to start."

She started with her mother's death and the mountain of bills that had been left behind. She went quickly through all the jobs she'd had, smiling when she recalled Eli's reluctance to hire her. She recalled her very first idea: the name "Moonlight" for the Perfume X account. Almost twenty years had passed since then. Twenty years; it hardly seemed possible.

The waiter took away their soup dishes and returned with the entrées: chicken in wine for Laura, steak au poivre for Nick. He cut into it, spearing a piece of beef with his fork. "Tell me about your daughter," he said.

Laura's face lit up. "Oh, Molly's wonderful. She had these funny quirks when she was little. She wouldn't wear certain colors, and for a while she wouldn't eat foods that began with certain letters of the alphabet. She stuck to her guns, too. Molly was a sweet child, but so stubborn . . . She's still sweet, still stubborn, and now she has a crush on a different boy every month."

"How old is Molly?"

"Sixteen in a few months. Sweet sixteen." Laura popped a bite of chicken into her mouth. "I promised to bring back some cashmere sweaters."

"When you smile that way, you look sixteen yourself." He wanted to kiss her, to take her in his arms and kiss her. He picked up his glass, glancing swiftly around the crowded restaurant. "Tell me about your first love," he said after a swallow of wine. "Your very first love. Was it the happiest time of your life? A magical time?"

"It didn't last." Laura hadn't thought about Robby in years, but she thought about him now. There was no anger left, no bitterness; there was a kind of nostalgia—for youth as much as for first love. "His name was Robby Collier," she said. "He ran off with my sister, eloped. I always blamed my sister more than I blamed Robby. I felt betrayed."

"Tell me."

"Oh, Nick, it all happened a thousand years ago. You couldn't be interested."

"But I am. You're a fascinating creature, Laura. Part of you is a woman of the world, and part of you is a young girl—eager and wide-eyed. The contrasts are intriguing. They make a fellow want to know more and more. *I* want to know everything."

During dinner she told him about Robby and Eliza, about the rage she had felt at their betrayal, about the ache that had settled in her heart and stayed such a long time. She'd never discussed these feelings before, but now the words tumbled easily from her lips. It was because of Nick, she thought. He knew when to draw her out, when to keep silent. He was a good listener, and good at reading between the lines.

Over coffee and brandy, she told him about Margaret—going on seventy and still going strong. She told him about Doris and Jane, and about the car crash that had taken Jane's life. She talked and talked, hardly pausing for breath, and it was as if she were exorcising all the ghosts of her past.

Laura didn't notice the other diners paying their bills and leaving the restaurant. She didn't notice the waiters sitting down to their own meal. When she happened to glance at her watch, she was amazed to see that it was after midnight. "My goodness, Nick," she said, blushing, "you should have stopped me. I didn't mean to go on and on like that. I'm sorry."

He smiled. "I'm not. I really do want to know everything about you."

"I've been talking for hours. There's nothing more to know."

"There'll always be more, Laura. We've only just begun." He motioned for the check and it was brought instantly by Marcel. "Excellent meal," said Nick to the beaming owner. He dropped a five-pound note on the table, put a ten-pound note into Marcel's hand, then helped Laura out of her chair. "What would you say," he began as they gathered their coats, "if I asked you to my flat for a nightcap?"

Her heart thumped again. She wanted to say yes, but this time she listened to the little voice. "It's late, Nick. I ought to get back to the hotel. I have a busy day tomorrow."

"You're spending tomorrow with me."

"But—"

"With me," he said, opening the door.

The street was quieter now, emptier. They climbed into the MG and drove off. Laura knew that Zack would be expecting her at the office tomorrow; she wondered what she would tell him. The truth, she finally decided; she would call him first thing in the morning and tell him the truth, that she was spending the day with Nick. Spending the day with Nick? When she had so much work to do? Yes, and it didn't matter what anybody thought. There was more to life than work—a lot more.

"What are you smiling at?" asked Nick, momentarily taking his eyes from the road. "Come on, the truth."

"You," she replied. "I'm smiling at you."

He turned the car into Carlos Place, gliding to a stop outside the Connaught. "Tomorrow," he said, taking her hand in his. "I'll come round to fetch you at ten."

"Yes, tomorrow."

Nick wasn't a man for public displays but he leaned over suddenly and pulled Laura into his arms, crushing his mouth on hers. "I've been wanting to do that all night," he said when finally he let her go. "That and a few other things."

She had to catch her breath, had to calm her racing heart. "Nick," she murmured. "I . . . I'd better go." He started to get out of the car but she stopped him. "No, don't bother. I'll be fine . . . I'll see you tomorrow at ten."

"Good night, Laura."

"Good night."

She left the car and hurried into the hotel. She paused, looking over her shoulder as the MG drove away. After a moment she went into the small, wood-paneled lobby. To the right was the reception desk; to the left was the desk of the hall porter, a dignified man wearing a dark blue tailcoat. He rose and gave Laura her room key. "Thank you," she said, lowering her voice to suit the late hour. "Do you know if there were any messages?"

"There was a delivery, madam." He smiled; whatever the delivery was, he seemed to approve. "You will find it in your room."

"Thank you. Good night."

"Good night, madam."

She turned and entered the waiting elevator. She wondered about the delivery as she rode upstairs; something from Zack, she thought, though the instant she walked into her room she realized it must be from Nick. She smiled. Sitting atop the antique secretary was the largest bouquet of roses she had ever seen; yellow roses; dozens and dozens of yellow roses.

Laura ran across the room and snatched up the card. "Welcome to my world," it said. "Yours, Nick."

Chapter Twenty-two

"I've never seen so many roses," exclaimed Laura the next morning, climbing back into the MG. "It was a wonderful surprise, Nick. I don't know how you managed it, with the flower shops already closed for the day, but I'm awfully glad you did."

"Marcel can manage anything. With Marcel, and an account at Harrods, I believe I could conquer the world." He smiled, looking at Laura. "You're ravishing this morning, Mrs. Brent. I'm in awe."

"I was a little worried about wearing green. A green suit and a red car . . . I didn't want to look like a Christmas tree."

Nick turned the key in the ignition. "You look absolutely radiant," he said as the car shot away from Carlos Place.

"I *feel* radiant. I ought to feel guilty for taking off from work, but I don't." She laughed. Larking around, Margaret would have called it, but she didn't care. She'd slept better than she had in years, she'd eaten a huge breakfast, and she'd indulged herself with a long, luxurious bubble bath. All the while she'd known that Nick would be waiting for her—handsome, dashing Nick Ashton. She'd gazed at the masses of yellow roses and felt a tug at her heart.

Now she tied a scarf around her head and looked up, watching as puffy white clouds scudded across the sky, uncovering wide patches of blue. "Is the weather always so beautiful here? Where's all the rain I heard about?"

"Do you like rain, then?"

"I like the sound of it. I used to listen to the rain and think of romantic, faraway places. I was a dreamer, once upon a time."

Nick shook his head. "You've tried to bury that part of yourself, the dreamer part. But it's still very much alive."

"Is it? How do you know?"

"The way I know most things—by instinct. We have that in common, don't we?"

A smile traced Laura's mouth. "I wonder if we have anything in common."

Nick glanced sidelong at her, his dark brows arching in amusement. "I wonder if you wonder."

She laughed. A car horn beeped and she looked around, surprised to see all the traffic. It wasn't as bad as New York traffic, but it was heavier than she'd expected. "Where are we going?"

"To the Tower." His blue eyes scanned the long line of cars in front of the MG. "If we ever get out of this muddle," he added, shifting gears as he made a sharp, sudden turn. "Not to worry, Laura. I'm quite good at this."

"And modest, too."

"Eternally modest," he agreed, his eyes twinkling. "Do you know the legend of the Tower? Was it in your guidebook?"

"If it was, I missed it."

"There are ravens at the Tower, you see. According to legend, the end of the British Empire will come when the ravens desert the Tower."

"It must be such fun to live in England," said Laura, "what with all your legends and ghost stories."

"We'll have a look at the ravens first, and then I'll see what I can do about finding you a ghost."

Laura nodded. She thought that was a good idea.

She saw the ravens strutting on Tower Green—where two of the wives of Henry VIII had been beheaded. She saw the Tower guards, the Beefeaters in their scarlet tunics and white ruffs and black hats. Inside the Tower she saw the magnificent Crown Jewels—bedazzling rubies and emeralds and the world's largest diamonds.

After the Tower they went to St. Paul's Cathedral, then to Fleet Street, home of the city's newspapers. Laura had her first pub lunch—a slice of shepherd's pie and a half pint of ale. She found herself wishing the day would never end.

Nick had no trouble reading her thoughts because they were his own. Suddenly the world seemed brand-new to him. He felt like a schoolboy again, a schoolboy on the brink of discovery, on the brink of love.

Love. It was a word he'd used sparingly since Lucy's death. There had been many women in his life since then but no serious involvements, and that was the way he'd wanted it. He'd had his fun, he'd played by the rules, and no one had been hurt. Now, out of the blue, he realized the rules had changed; he thought he was falling in love.

He bought Laura a present at their next stop—a small Victorian music box he found on a shelf at The Old Curiosity Shop. She carried it with her all afternoon—to Dickens House, to the British Museum, to high tea at Brown's Hotel.

It was past five when Nick brought Laura back to the Connaught. She watched the MG drive off and then rushed upstairs, running her bath while she debated what to wear this evening. The black velvet sheath, she decided, taking it from the closet. Nick would like it.

She bathed and dressed and fixed her hair. She was brushing mascara on her lashes when she heard a knock at the door. "Come in," she called, glancing up. "Oh, Eve . . . I . . . My goodness, I forgot all about you." Laura frowned. She had promised to telephone the office after lunch but the promise had completely slipped her mind. She hadn't even thought about the office today. "I'm sorry, Eve. I was having such a good time, I just forgot."

"We were a little worried, Zack and I. It's not like you to disappear without a word." She regarded Laura for a moment. She smiled. "I guess you had your reasons, though. What's his name?"

Laura blushed. "His name?"

Eve walked over to the antique secretary and pointed to the huge bouquet of yellow roses. "Who's the guy? Zack thought you might have gone to Norfolk with Sir Peter Somebody-or-other. Then he decided you were probably with Nick Ashton."

"Yes, he was right."

Eve sat down in one of the two armchairs. She was nearing sixty-five and she'd already announced her intention to retire next year. She was thinking about marrying her longtime beau, George Clooney; maybe they would take a cruise to the Caribbean. "They say Nick's Ashton's a real charmer, a lady-killer."

Laura finished applying her mascara and picked up her lipstick. "Who says that? Zack?"

"Well, you can't blame him for being concerned. You're kind of an innocent in the dating game."

She laughed. "I'm almost thirty-eight years old, Eve. I can take care of myself." She hoped she could. It was hard for her to think clearly when she was with Nick, hard to think of anything but him. "I had such a lovely time today."

"It shows. You're glowing."

Laura capped her lipstick and dropped it in her purse. She rose. "How do I look?" she asked, twirling around.

"Sexy. Are you seeing Nick again tonight?"

She nodded. "Theater and a late supper afterward. Doesn't that sound wonderful?"

"It sounds like you won't be in the office tomorrow. Don't worry; I'll start setting up the files. And I already have one of the girls putting sales figures together."

"I don't know what I'd do without you, Eve, I really don't. But I'll be in the office tomorrow; ten sharp.

"You're entitled to some time for yourself, you know . . . Look, Laura, it's none of my business, but if Nick Ashton can make you forget work, he must be something special."

"He is. But I still have to do my job. Besides, Claude will start calling any day now and I'd better be there to talk to him. This *is* a business trip, Eve."

"If I were you, I'd mix business with pleasure. A good man is hard to find."

Laura laughed. "I'll be in the office tomorrow."

"I'm sorry to hear it," replied Eve, rising from her chair. "How many chances do we get at romance?"

Romance. The word made her heart beat a little faster, made her feel breathless and giddy. "Nick's waiting," she said, smiling as she hurried to the door.

He took her to the Ritz for cocktails, and then to a sprightly West End comedy called *Feathers*. She laughed and applauded, but ten minutes after the play ended she couldn't remember anything about it. She was distracted by Nick, intoxicated by him. When she gazed into his eyes she could scarcely remember her own name.

He understood how she felt because he felt the same way. When he looked at Laura, when he touched her hand, it was as if they were the only two people in the restaurant, maybe the only two people in the world. Each passing moment seemed to draw him closer to her. Irresistibly closer, he thought; a moth to the flame.

They took a taxi back to the Connaught and neither of them spoke during the first half of the ride. They knew they had reached a crossroads. They didn't want to part, to say good night and go their separate ways, yet they sensed that anything else would change their lives forever. A fling, an affair, wouldn't be enough—not for them. They would want more from each other, so much more.

Nick helped Laura out of the taxi but he held on to her hand, unwilling to let her go. "My flat's only a few minutes away," he said, his gaze intent. "Come home with me."

She stared at him. Her thoughts were jumbled, sliding and spinning in all directions. *Come home with me.* "I can't," she murmured after a moment. "Nick, everything's happening too fast. It scares me."

"Do I scare you?"

"Oh yes. Oh yes, you most of all." She pulled her hand free, taking small backward steps toward the hotel entrance. "I don't want to be in love with anybody again. I don't." She gave her head a tiny shake. "I don't."

Laura took one last look at Nick, and then turned, fleeing into the hotel. She went directly to the elevator, trying to sort through her thoughts as she rode upstairs. A frown gathered on her brow. She wished she'd gone with Nick, wished she could have put all the old fears aside and rushed to his arms. You're a coward, she told herself. A coward and a fool.

The scent of roses greeted her when she entered her room. She walked to the secretary, bending her head over the yellow blooms. Wearily, she straightened up, kicking off her shoes. It was 1 A.M., but only 8 P.M. in New York. She sat at the edge of the bed and reached for the telephone, placing a call to New York.

Molly wanted to know if she had seen the Queen, and if she had bought any cashmere sweaters yet. Margaret delivered another warning about drinking "foreign" water. The sound of their voices cheered Laura, but only for a little while. Her thoughts kept slipping back to Nick Ashton. She needed to talk about him, and so she placed a call to Doris. "I met the most wonderful man," she explained to her startled friend, "and I don't know what to do."

She couldn't sit still. She paced back and forth during her call to Doris; when the call ended, she paced around the room. She thought a bath might help but she couldn't seem to get the water to a comfortable temperature. She twisted the faucets, surprised to see that her hands were shaking.

The latest Agatha Christie mystery was waiting on Laura's night table. She buttoned her robe and picked up the book, but after a few minutes she put it down. She was too restless to read; she started pacing again. She couldn't stop thinking about Nick. *Come home with me.*

She felt flushed. She touched her forehead to see

if she had a fever. No, she thought, probably not. She opened the window, closed it a bit. She went to the closet for her briefcase, then changed her mind and left the briefcase where it was. There were postcards to write, dozens of them. She fished around in her purse until she found her pen, but she didn't want to write postcards either. She returned to the window and stared outside. *Come home with me.*"

When the telephone rang at 2 A.M, she lunged for the receiver. "Nick?" she cried.

"I can be there in fifteen minutes," he said.

"Yes, fifteen minutes. I'll be downstairs."

Laura was downstairs in ten. Dressed, combed, lipsticked, she was standing at the curb when Nick pulled up in the MG. "Did you read my mind?" she asked as he opened the door.

"Something like that." He slid behind the wheel and put the car in gear. "I tried to sleep but I kept thinking about you. I had a feeling you must be thinking about me too."

"I was."

A smile streaked across his handsome face. "All's well that ends well, Laura. We're going home."

Home was a duplex in Chelsea, once known for its artists and Bohemian ways, but now a prosperous, casually stylish area of shops and restaurants and charming old townhouses. "Here we are," said Nick, unlocking a bright red door. "Be it ever so humble and all that."

A single lamp burned in the living room. Laura glanced around, her eyes moving over the polished woods, the brass fire screens, the tall bookcases, the Vlaminck lithographs on the walls. Magazines and newspapers were scattered on a table. A crumpled

Players cigarette packet floated in a half-empty teacup. "It's just what I expected," she said, smiling. "Even the little bits of clutter. It's perfect."

"Needs a woman's touch, I expect." Nick took Laura's coat and tossed it on a chair. "Would you like a drink?"

"No."

"Good."

He drew Laura into his arms. He kissed her, a long fiery kiss that made her gasp. There was a roaring in her ears, in her heart. Little lights seemed to dance before her eyes. "Nick," she whispered, melting against him.

She clung to his hand as they climbed the stairs to the bedroom. He kissed her again and a thrill rushed up her spine. She wasn't scared anymore. She was in Nick's arms and that was where she wanted to be.

They undressed each other, strewing their clothes across the floor. They sank onto the bed, Nick's hands moving slowly, very slowly over Laura's body. His fingers stroked and caressed and teased; his mouth moved over her breasts. "Nick," she murmured softly, her arms tightening around him, pulling him closer. "My darling," he said.

Their bodies arched and swayed, locked in a white-hot blaze of passion. Time had stopped; there was nothing but this moment, this truth, this pleasure so intense it was a kind of madness. "Nick," she whispered as her body trembled. She felt as if she were soaring through air; soaring, leaping, spinning; falling off the edge of the world.

Afterward, Laura snuggled in the crook of Nick's arm. She smiled, savoring the memory of the love they'd shared. She used to think love like that happened only in books, but now it had happened to her. Amazing.

When she peeked at Nick, she saw that he was awake too. "Hello," she murmured.

He turned his head and kissed her bare shoulder. "Do you believe in magic?" he asked.

"I didn't," she said, snuggling closer. "But I do now."

They slept. For Laura it was a sleep filled with dreams, with flickering images of roses and ravens and a shiny red MG. She saw Nick sitting behind the wheel of the MG, holding out his hand to her. She started rushing toward him, but in the next instant the dream faded and her eyes blinked open.

The other side of the bed was empty. She looked around, squinting in the first pale rays of morning light. She heard the sound of running water. "Nick," she murmured, reaching down for his discarded shirt. She slipped into the shirt, easing quietly out of bed.

The bathroom door was open. Nick, in dressing gown and bare feet, was lathering his face. Laura watched as he dipped a gleaming razor into the basin, flicked excess water from the blade, and then dragged it across his jaw. There was a scratchy rhythm to his strokes: long, short, short, long. He moved the razor a little to the left and made fresh tracks in the snowy lather, tracks exactly like the others: long, short, short, long. She smiled. "Good morning," she said.

"Morning, darling." He pulled a towel from the rack, patting his face as he went to Laura. He kissed her; after a moment he stepped back, his hands resting lightly on her shoulders, his eyes twinkling. "You're very beautiful this morning. Blooming like a flower."

"A yellow rose?"

"I'm falling in love with you, you know."

She nodded. "Yes, I know."

"And you with me."

"Yes, I know that too."

"And just what do you intend to do about it, old chap?"

She laughed, fluttering her lashes. "Do about it?"

"What are your intentions?"

"They're strictly dishonorable."

"I see." He wiped a bit of lather off her nose. "We shall have to talk about that. Oh yes, a very long talk." He kissed her again, and again he stepped back. "Of course it may be difficult to keep my mind on conversation. You're such a distracting female, Laura. We may never leave here today."

"We're going to our offices today."

"Do you mean you're deserting me for Harding Advertising?"

"I'm afraid so," she said, whirling out of his reach. "My nights are yours, but my days belong to Zack."

Zack couldn't help noticing the change in Laura. She was utterly radiant, her step so light she seemed to float an inch above the ground. Her voice was eager, almost breathless; her eyes glittered. At odd moments she smiled to herself, as if she had suddenly remembered something wonderful.

Zack knew that she was seeing Nick Ashton; by the end of her second week in London, everybody knew. There was talk that he had finally met his match, that he had been tamed. Laura heard the talk and laughed it off. She and Nick were just good friends, she insisted, and she was just here to work.

In the beginning it was hard for her to concentrate on work. Again and again she had to pull her wandering mind back to the layouts on her desk, back to the budget figures and the market research and the cables from New York. She had to force herself to concentrate, especially on the budget, which had been calculated in pounds sterling. "Twelve pennies to a shilling," she prompted herself every morning, "twenty shillings to a pound. A pound equals two dollars and eighty cents."

After a while she learned to think in pounds instead of dollars, and only then did she understand the budget figures she had been staring at for a week. Once she understood them, she started picking them apart. Ten days into November, she had a budget she felt Claude Gower would approve. A few days and a few corrections later, she had a campaign she was certain he would approve. "But I'd like us to be in agreement," she said to Zack, "before I send anything to New York. Claude will feel better about things if he knows we agree."

Zack shrugged. "Claude couldn't care less whether we agree or not," he replied, lighting a cigarette. "BPC has always been your account, Laura. It'll be yours till Claude's dying day. That's why he sent you here to look over my shoulder. You're the only one he really trusts with Aunt Martha."

"He didn't send me here to look over your shoulder. Come on, Zack, we've been all through this." She moved her chair a little to the left, out of the draft from his open window. It was a cold day. Eve, sitting off to the side, was wearing a sweater. The art director, Tony Steele, had buttoned his jacket and thrust his hands into his trouser pockets. "Claude wanted another opinion," continued Laura. "It's nothing personal."

"Not another opinion, *your* opinion . . . But all right, let's see what you've done to our budget. Let's have the bad news."

She rose, passing a folder across the desk to

Zack. "No bad news; I cut less than twenty thousand pounds. I did move a few things around, though."

"Such as?"

Laura bent over the desk and turned a page. "For starters, I moved a quarter of the store display budget back into the ad budget. I don't think we can expect to put counter displays and posters in every single store. In America, yes, but not here . . . I also moved some of the newspaper budget into magazines. I'd rather we didn't bombard people with full-page ads in the daily papers. Smaller ads will do just as well for us. I'm trying to scale everything down just a bit, Zack."

He looked at the figures and then looked at Tony Steele, who nodded. "Well," said Zack, "I suppose we can live with that. What else?"

Laura passed a second folder across the desk and gave a duplicate to the art director. "The other budget changes are minor; technical changes. But—"

"Yes," interrupted Zack, "I knew there'd be a 'but.'"

She laughed. "Nothing to do with the budget. It's Aunt Martha . . . The redesigned Aunt Martha is perfect for America, but not so perfect for the overseas market. I've been studying the market since I've been here, and I'm convinced we need to do some tinkering."

"Yes," said Tony Steele, a fair-haired man in his thirties, "that's been my feeling too. Aunt Martha's looking rather sleek, isn't she?"

"Sleek!" scoffed Zack. "Aunt Martha is many things, but sleek isn't one of them."

"Think about it," said Laura. "We made her slimmer, trimmer. We gave her a new dress, a new apron, and a June Allyson pageboy. She looks at least ten years younger, Zack. And that's on top of the ten years she lost the first time we redesigned her. She looks somewhere in her forties now. I'd like to add a few years for this campaign. Let's make her fiftyish, and a little more—a little more homey. Just a little softer around the edges."

"Fluffier," said Tony. "Like fluffy wool."

Laura's brows drew together. "Yes . . . Yes, I think I see what you mean. Could you do some sketches?"

"Straight away. But can we agree that we're going to keep her American look? It's quite a nice look; I wouldn't want to change that part of it."

Zack crushed the stub of his cigarette in the ashtray. "There's no reason to change it," he said. "We're selling an American product and Aunt Martha is an American."

Laura nodded. "Yes, that part is fine."

"I'll start on the sketches, then," said Tony, glancing at his watch. "I should have something to show you early this afternoon. Say two o'clock?"

"Better make it three," said Eve, looking up from her notebook. "Laura has a two o'clock at the photographer's."

"Done," agreed Tony, striding to the door.

"Well, that's that." Laura returned to her chair and sat down, lifting her gaze to Zack. "We should be able to put the new sketches and a draft budget on a plane tonight. As soon as Claude approves the changes, you can get things moving. Do we have a kickoff date?"

"In time for holiday colds and flus, I hope. Holiday aches and pains."

"Fine. Eve, you might as well type up the budget. We'll need six copies for New York."

She rose. "Anything else? Do you want a conference call for this afternoon?"

"We'll wait until tomorrow." Eve snapped her notebook shut and left the office. Laura glanced again at Zack. She smiled. "Cheer up. You'll be rid of me any day now."

"I don't want to be rid off you; I just want to run my own shop . . . And speaking of running one's own shop, what's the latest on old Eli? Is he retiring or isn't he?"

"He is, right after the first of the year. There have been all sorts of rumors—Anne Marsh still expects to buy the agency. But I think Eli's going to surprise everybody."

"I have a brand-new two-year contract, you know."

"Yes, I know," said Laura. "So have I. So has Martin. Eli's obviously anxious to keep his top people in place . . . He's been playing his cards close to the vest, but he did tell me there won't be any major personnel changes after he retires. I think that means he's not going to sell—not to Anne or anybody else. Someone will be brought in as president and we'll go on as usual. Eli can sit back and enjoy the profits."

"If he sold, he could sit back and enjoy a small fortune."

Laura nodded. "Anne's associates are prepared to pay a small fortune, and they're not alone. But Eli's already a rich man. At this stage of his life, there are more important things than money. Family, for example. Harding Advertising has been the family business for almost a hundred years."

Zack shuffled some papers on his desk. "The family's come to the end of the line," he said. "Eli's children never had the faintest interest in the agency. They all have their own lives, their own careers."

"Yes, but you're forgetting about the grandchildren. Two of them will be graduating from college in the spring. I hear they've been taking courses in marketing and promotion."

"Oh?"

"I may be wrong, but I think Eli's hoping his grandsons will carry on the family business."

Zack smiled. "You know, I hope they do too. I'd hate to see the end of Harding Advertising; or worse, see it swallowed up by some other agency. There's always been something special about Harding . . . I suppose that's why I've stayed all these years, why we've all stayed. Look at you."

"I love Harding. I can't imagine working anywhere else. Even if Eli does decide to sell, I'll be the last person out the door. They'll have to *drag* me out." Laura rubbed her cold hands together. "It's sad talking about endings."

"Nothing's ended yet."

She shrugged; it was only a matter of time. Eli's retirement would mark the end of an era, would inevitably change her life—though in what ways she wasn't quite sure.

Laura's thoughts skipped past Eli to the other change in her life: Nick Ashton. Her eyes softened. A smile drifted across her face. Somehow she'd known all along that Nick wasn't an end but a beginning.

"I'm going back to New York on Monday." Laura said the words quickly, getting them out before she lost her courage. "I have a reservation on the noon plane."

"Monday!" Nick's dark head snapped up. "Do you mean *tomorrow?*"

"Yes. BPC approved everything a few days ago— the budget, the campaign . . . Now it's time to go home." She lowered her eyes to the path, a wide path bordered by yew trees in the little village of Hurlybone. The rain had stopped. A pale, gauzy sun crept between the clouds. "I put off telling you as long as I could," she continued quietly. "I-I knew it wouldn't be easy."

"Stay another week, Laura. Surely you can take a holiday."

"I could, but there's Molly. I promised her I'd be home for Thanksgiving. She has the week off from school and I want to spend some of that time with her. I've missed her, Nick. Letters and phone calls are fine, but I want to *see* her."

"Of course you do, and it's really very simple, isn't it? Bring Molly to London." He stopped in the middle of the path, turning Laura to him. "She'll have her holiday here, with us."

"I thought about that but it wouldn't work. I'd have to bring both Molly and Aunt Margaret, and it's just too complicated. Besides, Molly doesn't know there *is* an us. I wouldn't want to spring anything on her."

"I'm rather good with children, Laura."

"Molly isn't a child. She isn't grown up, but she isn't a child. I guess she's kind of an in-between."

"In that case, I'm rather good with in-betweens."

She laughed. "You're irresistible, but I still have to go back to New York . . . I wish there were two of me, Nick; one to go home to Molly and one to stay here with you."

He buttoned the top button of Laura's jacket, catching her hand as they resumed their walk. She bent suddenly, picking up a small bluish pebble. He frowned as she dropped it into her pocket. "What on earth do you do with all those odd bits you've been collecting? I've been watching you for weeks, you know. You keep sneaking things into your pockets."

"They're my keepsakes. I told you about my keepsake box." She looked up at him, smiling. "It'll comfort me till you come to New York . . . You are coming soon, aren't you?"

"The end of January. It seems like such a bloody long time."

Laura felt a rush of tears. "Let's not talk about it, Nick. This is our last day; let's not spoil it."

He gathered her into his arms and kissed her. "I love you," he said when he let her go. "You know that, don't you?"

"Yes," she sniffled. "Oh, Nick, I love you too." The idea was still new to her, still tinged with wonder. She'd never loved anyone the way she loved him—mind and body, heart and soul. It was as if she had been awakened from the deepest sleep, awakened by his smile, his touch, his kiss. By magic, she thought.

She took the handkerchief he offered and dabbed at her tears. "We ought to get back to the cottage. Your father said not to be late for lunch."

"He'll forgive us. Or you, at any rate. He's quite taken with you, darling."

Laura shaded her eyes, staring into the distance. "There he is," she said, glimpsing a tall, gray-haired man trailed by two shaggy terriers. "And there are the dogs."

"Cornelius and Alfie. Dad usually has them out for a run before lunch. That's one of the pleasures of living in the country."

"It's so beautiful here, Nick."

"Come, I'll show you the pond." He clasped her hand again, leading her onto a narrower path bordered by box hedges and great clusters of shrubbery. "This way," he said, a smile tugging at his mouth. "We keep it hidden."

Beyond an old stone wall, beyond a carpet of autumn wildflowers and a screen of coppery beech trees, she saw the pond—smooth and clear and shimmering with gauzy light. "Oh, Nick, how lovely." There was something timeless about the setting, something dreamlike. She wouldn't have been surprised to see King Arthur pop out from behind a tree, the wizard, Merlin hovering at his side. "How can you bear to leave such a beautiful place?"

"I've come to an amazing conclusion—I can bear anything as long as we're together."

A lump swelled in Laura's throat. "If you keep talking that way, I'm going to dissolve in tears."

Nick wandered a few steps to a stone bench entwined with leaves and the last wild roses of the season. He plucked one of the blossoms and brought it to her.

"Another keepsake," she murmured, touching the yellow rose to her cheek.

"Will you marry me, Laura?"

Her breath caught. Her heart flurried. "Marry you?" She had expected the question, though not so soon, not nearly so soon. She felt a thrill race along her spine; she felt a little weak. She wanted to say yes, wanted to shout it, yet something was holding her back. "Nick . . ."

He gazed into her eyes, watching as she struggled with her doubts. "I promise we'll live happily after."

"Will we?" She sighed. It had taken her twenty years to build the life she wanted, a life she trusted and understood; a safe life. Marriage, she thought; it would be like starting all over again. "Nick, I—"

"Marry me, darling."

She bent her head and a curtain of tawny hair slid across her cheek. "No, I can't," she murmured. "I love you, Nick. I do love you . . . But I can't."

He drew back her hair, tipped up her chin. "That's the wrong answer."

"I'm a coward. It scares me to think of turning everything upside down and starting a new life. But even if I did, it wouldn't work. What kind of marriage would we have with you in London and me in New York?"

"Planes fly across the Atlantic every day, Laura. I expect I'll be spending a good deal of time in New York. And you can easily schedule time in London." He paused, draping his hands on her shoulders. "We'll live in both places and let the airlines sort out the details."

"It's not that simple."

"I didn't say it was simple. Nothing about love is simple, is it? But there are ways to get round the problems."

"I'm pretty set in my ways, Nick."

"I'll *un*set you, then; shall I?"

Laura smiled. She glanced off, watching a coppery leaf twirl in the breeze and tumble into the pond. "How long would it be before you asked me to quit my job?"

"Oh, I see. But aren't you jumping to conclusions?"

"I don't know. Am I?"

Nick laughed. "All right, I confess. I thought about it—your job, your career. I had a few qualms, I suppose, but when I thought it through, I saw there was no cause for worry. Quite the opposite, in fact. We're going to be competitors, and that's a rather stimulating idea. Adds a dash of spice." He smiled, kissing the top of her head. "I won't ask you to quit. Promise."

"You're wonderful."

"Wonderful enough to marry?"

"Nick, I . . . I can't. It's not just my work, it's everything. Everything would change. I'm not ready for that." She couldn't tell what he was thinking. His gaze was steady, though his eyes seemed a darker shade of blue. A frown had come and gone and now his expression was unreadable. "I didn't expect to fall in love," she continued. "I need time. I love you, Nick; you know I love you . . . But I can't marry you."

"That's still the wrong answer."

"It's the only answer I have."

"For now, perhaps. I'll keep on asking until I get the answer I want." He smiled again, wrapping his arms around Laura. "You're such a complicated female, and stubborn into the bargain. But marry me you will."

"Nick—"

"We'll resume this conversation in New York."

"But—"

"New York," he repeated firmly, kissing her before she could say another word.

Chapter Twenty-three

"And then what happened?" asked Doris, perching at the edge of her chair. "Tell me the rest."

"Well, then we went inside and ate lunch with Nick's father. A very charming man." Laura glanced around at the suitcases lined up like soldiers along a wall of her bedroom. She had been back from London for two days but she hadn't yet unpacked. It was, she thought, as if she didn't want her trip to be over. "I can't seem to get organized," she sighed, waving a hand in the direction of her luggage. "I have a million things to do, but I can't get started. My mind keeps wandering."

"That's because you're in love. I'm so happy for you, Laura. It's so romantic. A dark, handsome stranger . . ." Doris's voice trailed off. Her brow wrinkled. "Isn't that what the fortune-teller predicted? Madame Zarela? Didn't she say there was a dark-haired man in your future?"

"A dark-haired man stepping out of the shadows." Laura smiled. "That's exactly the way it was, too. I've been trying to remember if she predicted what the outcome would be. I don't think she did."

"We could find her," suggested Doris, "but the outcome is up to you. Don't you want to marry him?"

"I love him. I want to be with him. God knows

I'm always thinking about him." Laura sat at her dressing table, reaching for the photo of Nick she had propped against the sea shell lamp. She held the snapshot to the light. "I wish he were here. I miss him."

"Aren't those good reasons to marry him?"

Laura shrugged. She replaced the photo, staring at it for another moment before turning to look at Doris. "Marriage changes things, and that scares me. I'm used to my life just as it is. I know what to expect from one day to the next. You have no idea how safe that makes me feel."

"Oh, I understand." Doris nodded, her chin disappearing into the big collar of her sweater. She thought back to the years right after Kay Bellamy's death, years of such uncertainty for Laura. There had been so many debts, so many worries—and then Robby had run off with Eliza. Laura had found a measure of happiness with Paul, and then he had been killed in the war. "You're afraid of being hurt again," continued Doris. "You think if you only give part of yourself, you can't be hurt too badly . . . But if you only give part of yourself, you'll lose him."

Laura looked sharply at her friend. "I'm trying to be sensible. Nick and I haven't known each other very long. We had a few weeks together, that's all."

"How long does it take to fall in love? To know this is the man you want to spend your life with?"

An instant, thought Laura. There had come an instant when she'd gazed at Nick and seen her future. It had been a strange feeling—wonderful and terrible at the same time. She'd laughed about it afterward, but the memory was still clear in her mind. "Falling in love was so easy for you," she said now. "You met Bill and that was that. No doubts, no questions; you were sure from the start. Of course you were the right age."

Doris blinked. "The right age?"

"Well, I'm a little *past* the age for secret smiles and girlish blushes. In a year and two months I'll be forty. Forty!"

"Yes, I've been thinking about my own fortieth birthday. But that's not old, Laura. It's not. Bill and I are happier than we've ever been." He was chairman of the mathematics department now; she had given up her tutoring service and was busy with all the faculty clubs. Her eldest child was at Barnard, her youngest almost ready for kindergarten. There was a new summer cottage at the shore, a "practically new" Oldsmobile, and a special bank account that would one day provide a trip to Europe. "We're happier than we were twenty years ago. We took everything for granted then, but now we know better." Doris ducked her head, looking at Laura through her pale lashes. "It's *because* we're older that everything means so much more." She frowned. "I'm not saying this very well."

"Yes, you are, and I suppose you're right . . . But marriage is still a scary idea to me." She turned as the black and white cat Oreo strolled into the room and leapt up on the bed. He washed a snowy paw, and then stretched out for a nap. "Not a bad life," said Laura, smiling.

"His or yours?"

"Both. You mustn't worry, Doris; I'm fine. I just need some time to think about all this."

"No," replied Doris softly. "You need to trust your heart."

The sudden silence was broken by Margaret, who strode into the room and clapped her hands together. "Off the bed, Oreo! Off the bed, you lazy cat!" He looked up, staring impassively at her. After a moment he leapt to the floor and padded away, tail and head held high. "Now for you two," she said, shifting her gaze. "Are you going to stay in here gabbing all day, or are you going to help me get dinner started? You're in here, Molly's at the library— am I supposed to do everything?"

"You're supposed to let Eileen do the cooking," said Laura. "That's her job."

"Eileen! Does Eileen know how to make pot roast?"

"Yes."

"Not like mine," declared Margaret with a triumphant smile. "So finish your talk and give me a hand in the kitchen."

"We'll be right there."

She nodded, walking briskly to the door. "And when are you going to unpack your suitcases?" she asked on her way out. "No good comes of putting things off."

Laura sighed. She moved her chair back and stood up, brushing past the suitcases as she went to some shopping bags clustered in the corner. "I almost forgot."

"Forgot?"

"Presents," she laughed, holding up a bulging shopping bag from Harrods and another from Burberry. "I brought you in here to get your presents . . . You're frowning again, Doris. What's the matter?"

"Oh, I was just thinking about what Margaret said, that no good comes of putting things off."

"You're thinking about Nick."

"If you wait too long, you might lose him."

Laura's smile faded. Her mouth seemed to tense. "Come on," she said, thrusting out her chin, "let's look at your presents."

"Are you going to marry Nick Ashton?" Molly bent her head to the bouquet of yellow roses sitting atop her mother's dressing table. A different bouquet had arrived every week since her mother's return from London. She'd counted six so far, including this old-fashioned nosegay trimmed with lace. She smiled; she thought it was very romantic. "Mom? Did you hear me? I asked if—"

"Yes, I heard you." Laura slipped a pale silk stole out of her closet and shut the door. "As I recall, I told you I wasn't going to marry anybody."

"Not *any*body, Mom, Nick Ashton. The *dreamy* one."

Laura laughed. Ever since Molly had seen Nick's picture he'd been known as "the dreamy one." Both Molly and Margaret seemed pleased there was a man in her life, even a man thousands of miles away. They'd both asked a lot of questions—only some of which she'd answered. "Here's the stole," Laura said now. "It will be perfect with your dress. And what else did you want? Oh yes, my pearls. I'll just get them."

"And the earrings?"

"Yes, all right." Laura took her jewerly case from a drawer and carried it to the dressing table. She frowned as her glance fell upon a small ormolu clock. "Look at the time, Molly. My goodness, we'd better hurry. We *can't* be late for Eli's retirement dinner."

"I'm almost ready."

"Yes, I can see that," replied Laura, pursing her lips in a smile. "I like your outfit: bathrobe, fuzzy slippers, and pincurls."

"Well, it won't take me long to get dressed and brush out my hair. I don't have to fuss or anything. No one's going to see me; my friends, I mean."

Laura watched Molly rummaging through the jewelry case—holding up a double strand of pearls, putting it down, choosing a single strand instead. "When you were little, you used to love to play with my jewelry. Your favorite was a bracelet of shiny crystal beads. Do you remember?"

"Gosh, Mom, I don't know. I guess I did a lot of goofy things when I was young."

"Yes " agreed Laura, suppressing a smile, "when you were young." Molly was sixteen now, and feeling very grown up. She was allowed to wear lipstick, allowed to stay out till eleven o'clock on Fridays and Saturdays, allowed to go steady. It was an exciting time in her life; Laura wanted her to enjoy every moment. "Did you find what you were looking for, darling?"

"This necklace and these earrings. Okay?"

"Fine. Now scoot. I have to get ready too."

Molly left the room. Laura slipped off her robe and took her new dress from the hanger. She stepped into it, reaching around to do up the zipper.

"Do you need help?" asked Margaret, throwing open the door. "You don't want to tear that dress. It cost the earth."

"Yes, but it was worth it." It was a long-sleeved black chiffon with a narrow waist and a full, swirly skirt. The neckline was a deep V, and at its base she wore the diamond clip that had been left to her by Jane. She wore pearl and diamond earrings—a parting gift from Nick—and a slender gold bracelet she had bought for herself.

She took a step forward, pirouetting in front of

the mirror. "Well? What do you think, Aunt Margaret?"

"It's a shame your Nick isn't here to see you. And on your big night too."

"He's not *my* Nick." Laura glanced up. "What do you mean my big night?"

Margaret shrugged. "Everybody knows Eli's going to make you president of the company."

"It may be the shortest presidency in history. If the agency is sold, there's no telling what will happen. And *no*body knows if the agency is going to be sold."

"Never mind all that. It's still a big night for you, and I say it's a shame Nick Ashton isn't here."

"He'll be here in two weeks." Laura had been counting the days, marking them off on her calendar. She wasn't sure what the outcome of his visit would be, wasn't sure if her family would like him, if he would like her family, but she put those worries aside. For now, all that really mattered was that he would be here, and soon. "Two weeks," she murmured, as if to herself.

Margaret smiled at Laura's starry-eyed expression. Laura had gone too many years without love but that was the past, and the past was a closed chapter. A new chapter had begun in London; maybe a whole new book, she thought, enjoying her small flight of fancy. "You have to admit everything turned out for the best," she said. "I'm not one to look back, but if you ask me, things turned out exactly the way they were meant to."

Laura was quiet, an uncertain smile flickering about her mouth. "Yes," she replied after a moment, "you may be right." She dabbed perfume on her throat, her wrists. "Do you want some?" she asked. She glanced at her aunt, and then glanced again.

"Why, Aunt Margaret, what have you done to yourself?"

"I've been waiting for you to notice, missy. I went to the beauty parlor! I had 'the works'; that's what the girl called it. I had a manicure," she explained, holding out ten pink-tipped fingers. "I had a facial. I even had a color rinse. That's why my hair looks silver instead of gray. And naturally I bought a new dress."

"You look marvelous, just marvelous."

"Well, it was extravagant. But we never had a president in the family before . . . Your mother would be proud of you. I want you to know that, Laura; your mother would be proud."

"You're going to make me cry," she said, quickly hugging her aunt. "Don't forget your part in all of this. If you hadn't been here—"

"Oh, I know my part. If I hadn't been here, you wouldn't be president of Harding Advertising or anything else. I'll take the credit due me. Why not?"

Laura laughed. "Yes, why not?"

Molly had come to the door. She stood there, folding the silk stole over her arm. "I'm ready," she said. "Do I look all right?"

Laura turned, startled by the sight of Molly in her first formal. It was a bare-shouldered dress of pale blue taffeta—almost the color of her eyes. Her golden hair was curled softly around her face. Her lips were tinted pink, and just a touch of rouge tinted her porcelain skin. "Darling, you're beautiful," said Laura. "Breathtaking."

"Oh, Mom."

"It's true." She gazed at Molly and her thoughts drifted back through the years. There had been sorrows in her life, but beyond the sorrows were the joys. All at once she saw how lucky she had been—a happy marriage, a happy career, a beautiful daughter, and now there was Nick. Her smile grew wider; things really had turned out for the best. "Shall we go?" she said, linking arms with Molly and Margaret. "It's a perfect night for the Rainbow Room."

The Rainbow Room soared sixty-five stories above the city. With its wraparound views, its revolving dance floor, its shimmering crystal chandelier, it was probably the most romantic room in New York. Laura had always thought it was like something out of a movie; maybe a Fred Astaire—Ginger Rogers musical, or maybe something with gorgeous Cary Grant.

She heard music playing now as she stepped off the elevator ahead of Molly and Margaret. "We're in time for cocktails," she said. "Let's check our coats, and then we can go inside."

Margaret glanced about. She seemed a bit anxious, but an instant later she smiled. "Give me your coat."

"What?"

She tugged Laura's coat off and threw it over her arm. "I'll see to this while you see to Eliza."

"Eliza!"

"You're almost forty years old; it's time you put things right with your sister. There she is.'" Margaret patted Molly's shoulder, shooing her in the direction of the checkroom. "Unfinished business," she said to the bewildered girl. "We'll leave them to their unfinished business."

Laura spun around. She saw Eliza sitting calmly in a small gilt chair at the other end of the foyer.

"What are you doing here?"

"This is a big night for you, Laura. I wanted to be here."

"It's a private party."

"I have a ticket," replied Eliza with a faint smile. "Aunt Margaret made the arrangements."

"I see." Laura turned her head as the elevator doors opened and a dozen people spilled out. She recognized some of them and she waved. "I ought to be going inside now, Eliza. It was nice of you to come, but I ought to find my table."

"Can't we talk a moment?"

"I don't know." She glanced toward the entrance of the Rainbow Room. Music was still playing; she saw waiters carrying trays of drinks. "I ought to go in."

"Please."

She shrugged, taking a few tentative steps. "There really isn't anything to talk about, you know. It's been too many years."

"Yes, the years go so quickly. JB's a senior at Yale, and Mike will be going to Penn in the fall. Mike's the athlete in the family—football."

"There's a girl too, isn't there?"

"Ellie. She's nearly thirteen."

Laura took another few steps. She looked warily at the empty chair next to Eliza. She hesitated, moving the chair a short distance away before she sat down. "I don't know what you want from me," she said as a frown deepened on her brow. "We haven't been sisters for a long time. There's no going back to what we used to be . . . We can't be sisters, we can't be friends. I—I don't know what you want."

Eliza blinked her eyes slowly, like a cat. "We can stop being enemies. The years *do* go quickly, Laura.

Our children are almost grown; one of these days we'll have grandchildren. Isn't it time to end this feud?"

The elevator came again, delivering another thirty or so people. Laura watched them for a moment and then shifted her gaze to Eliza. Eliza was a little heavier now, perhaps a size 8 instead of a size 6. She was still beautiful, still exquisitely dressed. Looking at her, it was hard to believe that twenty years had passed. Twenty years, thought Laura. My God, twenty years. "Why do you care if there's a feud or not? What difference can it make to you?"

"I'm not sure," replied Eliza with a shrug. "I'm not sentimental, as you know . . . But regardless of what we haven't been lately, we *are* sisters. As much as I could love anyone, I loved my sister. I still do, I suppose."

"How could you betray someone you loved? That was what hurt so badly. That was the part I couldn't forgive. Robby broke my heart, but what you did was worse."

Eliza lit a cigarette, watching a ring of blue smoke float away. "You were my sister and I loved you, but I loved myself more."

It was a simple, unapologetic statement of fact. It was, thought Laura, vintage Eliza. She couldn't help laughing. "I hardly know what to say."

"I did what was best for me. As things turned out, I did what was best for you, too."

"Oh?"

"It's true, isn't it?"

A happy marriage, a happy career, a beautiful daughter, and now there was Nick. "Yes," said Laura. "Yes, it's true."

"Then perhaps we can be friends after all."

Laura smiled. "Well, we're older and wiser now.

Maybe that's a place to start." She turned her head as another group of people departed the elevator. "I'd better go inside," she said, rising. "Eli will be wondering where I am."

Eliza put out her cigarette and rose also. "I think Aunt Margaret has us sitting at the table next to yours."

"Us? Is Robby here?"

"Yes . . . Oh, there he is, standing by the door."

Laura had always wondered how she would feel seeing Robby again. Would she be angry? Would she be nervous? Would there be a sudden leap of her heart? Would there be some small, lingering regret for what might have been? Slowly, she looked up. She saw him, and to her surprise she felt nothing but a vague nostalgia for her own youth. She smiled as she walked toward him, remembering what it was like to be seventeen and in love.

"Hello, Robby," she said, holding out her hand. "It's good to see you after all these years."

"You look wonderful, Laura."

"Thanks, so do you." His hair was thinner, his waist thicker, but otherwise he was much as she remembered him—a handsome man with an aristocratic profile and an easy smile. "It was nice of you to come."

"We're delighted to be here. Eliza always said you'd be running Harding someday. You deserve a lot of credit, Laura. Congratulations."

"Thank you."

Robby wondered if there shouldn't be something special to say, especially after all these years. He searched his mind, but he couldn't think of anything. He'd loved Laura once, he was sure of that, yet he hadn't loved her enough to try and understand her. Life with Laura would have been complicated; life with Eliza was smooth as silk. He and Eliza were alike—he was sure of that, too. A matched set, as Jane Walder had remarked so long ago.

He smiled now. With a flourish, he brought Laura's hand to his lips. "I'm glad you got what you wanted."

She smiled back at him. "I guess we all got what we wanted. Strange, isn't it?"

Candlelit tables encircled the dance floor. A microphone had been placed at the head table, where Eli sat with his family and friends. He'd had mixed emotions about stepping down from the company begun by his grandfather, but he'd never doubted it was the right decision. He was an old man and recently he had started to feel his age. There had been memory lapses, lapses in concentration. The arthritis in his hip seemed worse, and of course there was that annoying ringing in his ear. He was approaching eighty; it was time to step down.

Once the decision had been made, he'd felt as if a weight had been taken from his shoulders. It had occurred to him that his retirement could be anything he wanted it to be. Golf was no longer practical, but he could enjoy his books, his billiard table, his clubs, his opera tickets, his houses in Old Westbury and Palm Beach. He could enjoy an extra martini at lunch, an extra hour with his grandchildren, or with anyone at all. For the first time in seventy years his days would be his own, and that thought was immensely pleasing.

He looked pleased as he gazed around the Art Deco splendor of the Rainbow Room. Every seat at every table was filled, and he kept lifting his hand in a jaunty wave at the friends and clients he recognized. He saw Laura coming to his table. His smile grew broader. "Well, my dear," he said, clasping her hand, "this is it."

"Any second thoughts?"

"None. I'm quite ready to bid farewell to the troops."

She laughed. "That's what I was wondering about, Eli. Do you want to make your speech now or do you want to wait until after dinner?"

"Oh, not a speech; just a few words. And I think I'll do it now. Might as well put all the rumors to rest and let people enjoy their meal."

"Fine," said Laura. "I'll tell the waiters not to serve the shrimp cocktail till you've finished."

"Shrimp cocktail? Ah, yes, shrimp cocktail." Eli waited while Laura went off to speak to the maître d', and then while she returned to her own table. He kissed his wife's cheek, gathered his notes, and rose from his chair. He reached out, adjusting the microphone. He tapped it, and the orchestra stopped playing. "My friends," he began as everyone looked up, "I'm happy to welcome you to our little party tonight. It *is* a party, and so my remarks will be mercifully brief. "

Eli glanced at his notes. "This evening marks the end of my advertising career," he went on, "but not the end of Harding Advertising. There have been a great many rumors; we've all heard them. Well, I won't keep you in suspense any longer. Harding Advertising is not for sale." He heard the sudden murmur of voices and he paused. He glanced quickly at Anne Marsh's table. She was glaring at him; he glanced away, looking again at his notes. "The agency will continue," he declared when the room quieted, "although with one important change. As of tomorrow, Laura Brent will be the new president and managing partner. As of tomorrow, the agency will be known as Harding & Brent."

There were twelve people at Laura's table, twelve voices congratulating her, but she didn't hear a word they said. She sat absolutely still, her body, her face frozen in surprise. *Partner? Harding & Brent?*

The murmuring in the room had grown louder. Eli tapped the microphone once more and the voices subsided. "This should teach you to disregard rumors," he said with a wry smile. He listened to the ripples of laughter, shifting his gaze back to Anne Marsh. She had already risen; trailed by her escort and two other men, she stalked off toward the door. Eli looked down at his notes. He had meant to have a word with Anne; he would send her a note instead, and perhaps a check in appreciation of her many years at the agency.

Eli's wife was tugging at his sleeve, a signal to him to get on with it. He looked up. "In conclusion, I will simply say that I have the utmost confidence in Laura, and indeed in all the men and women who comprise Harding Advertising . . . It's always sad to say good-bye, but perhaps not so sad when one believes, as I do, that the best years are still to come. Thank you."

He smiled, savoring the applause for a few moments before he held up his hand. "You're very kind, but I think I must share this with Laura." He turned toward her table. "Laura, do come and say a few words."

She didn't seem to hear. Doris shook her arm. "Laura, he wants you to say something . . . Laura?"

"Mom," sighed Molly.

"Lights, camera, action," laughed Zack. "You're on, kid."

"Yes. Yes, all right." Laura left her chair and joined Eli at the microphone. "I'm just stunned," she said to him. "I had no idea. A partnership!"

"You earned it, my dear. And more . . . Now say your piece and we can all have our shrimp cocktail."

Laura gazed around at the sea of upturned faces. She took a breath. "Twenty years ago, in the middle of the Depression, Eli Harding gave me a job. It was a secretarial job, it paid seventeen dollars and fifty cents a week, and it saved my life. I will be forever grateful.

"Eli assigned me to Zack Reed," she continued, looking in Zack's direction. "I know he wanted to fire me a couple of times but he didn't. He let me make mistakes, let me take chances. He let me learn. Thank you, Zack." Laura's gaze moved to another man at her table. "For years, Martin Carver has been bringing my ideas to life; giving them the extra spin, the gloss that makes them special. Thank you, Martin." Her gaze moved past him. She smiled. "There are lots of Harding clients here tonight, but to Claude Gower of BPC, thank you for being so kind to Aunt Martha."

Laughter swept through the room. Laura paused, her gaze moving to her now-retired secretary. "Twenty years ago," she went on, "I didn't know the first thing about advertising. Eve Barrows was there to help, and she's been helping me ever since. Thank you, Eve." Laura paused again, dabbing at her eyes. "People have always been the key to Harding Advertising—good people, talented people. Because of them, I know Eli is right: the best years are still to come. Thank you very much."

Thunderous applause followed Laura as she stepped away from the microphone. She had started back to her table when she happened to glance toward the door. She looked and then looked again; standing in the doorway, arms folded across his chest, was Nick Ashton. She blinked. Nick? Was it really Nick? She saw him touch his fingers to his brow in a crisp salute. Even at a distance, she saw the dazzling flash of his smile. "Nick," she murmured, hurrying past a long row of tables.

There were voices calling congratulations to her, there were hands reaching out, but she never took her eyes from the man in the doorway. "Nick," she cried, rushing into his arms. "Why didn't you tell me you were coming? Oh, Nick, is it really you?"

"It is. Are you surprised? Good, that was the plan."

"Plan?"

"Your Aunt Margaret rang Eve, who rang me in London. When I heard about tonight, I booked a flight to New York. I flew over with Zack and Helen, as a matter of fact; the three of us singing your praises . . . Congratulations, darling—president and managing partner all in one shot."

"And you're here. That makes everything perfect."

The orchestra was playing "Thou Swell." Nick tightened his arms around Laura and spun her onto the dance floor. "Did you miss me?" he asked. "Were you lost without me?"

"Utterly lost," she said, smiling up at him. "I've been counting the days until I saw you again. I've been *wishing* for you."

"Some wishes are meant to come true."

"Yes, I'm beginning to believe that."

The orchestra segued into " 'S Wonderful," and Nick and Laura glided across the floor. From the corner of her eye she glimpsed a quick swirl of yellow. She turned, watching in delight as busboys carried large bouquets of yellow roses to each table.

"Oh, Nick, how lovely! How did you manage it?"

"I have my ways."

"You're marvelous. I'm going to steal one of the flowers for a keepsake."

"A flower, yes. But I don't want to be a keepsake, darling. I want to be your flesh-and-blood husband. Marry me, Laura."

Her heart was fluttering and thumping. It wouldn't be an easy marriage; there would be problems, all sorts of problems and snags. There would be conflicts, and compromises that pleased no one. There would be these things, but there would also be Nick. Her lips parted, closed, parted again. "I . . . I'll think about it."

"Well, that's an improvement over your last answer but it's still not good enough. Marry me, Laura."

Her breath caught. All at once she felt dizzy, drunk with music and candlelight and the scent of roses, drunk with love. She gazed into the mesmerizing blue of his eyes, and moment by moment her doubts fled. Again, she saw her future. "Yes," she murmured.

A smile streaked across his face. "Yes . . . you'll marry me?"

"Yes, I'll marry you," she laughed. "Yes, yes, yes."

Because some wishes are meant to come true.

STAY IN-THE-KNOW WITH PINNACLE'S CONTEMPORARY FICTION

STOLEN MOMENTS (17-095, $4.50)
by Penelope Karageorge
Cosmos Inc. was the place to be. The limitless expense accounts and round-the-world junkets were more than perks. They were a way of life—until Black Thursday. Cosmos' employees, who jockeyed for power, money, and sex, found that life was indeed a game of winners and losers.

DUET (17-130, $4.95)
by Kitty Burns Florey
Even as they took other lovers and lived separate lives, Anna and Will were drawn together time and again, their destinies mingling in a duet of wistful hopes and bittersweet dreams. Unable to move ahead, Anna surrendered at last to the obsession that held her with chains more binding than love, more lasting than desire.

SWITCHBACK (17-136, $3.95)
by Robin Stevenson and Tom Bade
Dorothea was in a movie, starring Vernon Dunbar, the love of her life. She was sure that she had never made that film. Only her granddaughter, Elizabeth, could help prove this fact to her. But Elizabeth could only do this if she could travel back in time.

ENTANGLED (17-059, $4.50)
by Nelle McFather
Three women caught in a tangle of lies and betrayal. And one man held the key to their deepest secrets that could destroy their marriages, their careers, and their lives.

THE LION'S SHARE (17-138, $4.50)
by Julia Kent
Phillip Hudson, the founder of Hawaii's billion-dollar Hudson Corporation, had been a legendary powerhouse in his lifetime. But his power did not end with his sudden death, as his heirs discovered at the reading of his will. Three beautiful women were candidates for Hudson's inheritance, but only one would inherit The Lion's Share.

THE LAST INHERITOR (17-064, $3.95)
by Genevieve Lyons
The magnificent saga of Dan Casey, who rose from the Dublin slums to become the lord and master of the majestic Slievelea. Never seeking love nor asking for it, the strikingly handsome Casey charmed his way into the lives of four unforgettable women who sacrificed everything to make his dreams a reality.

Available wherever paperbacks are sold, or order direct from the Publisher. Send cover price plus 50¢ per copy for mailing and handling to Pinnacle Books, Dept.17-539, 475 Park Avenue South, New York, N.Y. 10016. Residents of New York, New Jersey and Pennsylvania must include sales tax. DO NOT SEND CASH.